Reviews of *Changing Tides* posted on Amazon

This is the second book in K.D. Mason's Jack Beale Mystery series. However, you need not read the first book to appreciate the second. Similar in style to Robert B. Parker's Spenser novels, Mason's main character Jack lives in Rye Harbor, New Hampshire and most of the events take place in or around the New Hampshire seacoast. However, in this novel, a good part of the story takes place in the turquoise waters of Belize. The story was gripping and wondered while reading the adventure, whether or not Mason pushed Jack and his love interest Max, to the breaking point. Would the two lovers ever be able to be together again or would this mystery and the fiendish Daniel tear them apart.
Chris Obert – 5 stars

* * *

I have placed KD Mason as my favorite author, all of his books are great. He knows how to keep you intrigued enough that you can't put the book down. Being that the heart of the story is in New Hampshire makes it all the more special. Highly recommend everyone to read all of the books. GREAT JOB.
Cat Vaillancourt, NH – 5 stars

* * *

Very delightful and well written from a first time author! Run, don't walk, to grab this book for your summer read, especially if you are familar with the New England coast!
Susan J Brett – 5 stars

* * *

My wife reports that after reading Mason's first Jack Beale novel, she eagerly awaited *Changing Tides*. Her expectations were high, and she was not disappointed. She devoured the book while sitting on the beach during a winter vacation from the New Hampshire winter. Put it on your summer reading list. Like *Harbor Ice*, it is a page turner and a fun read. I read *Harbor Ice* on the same trip and will now read *Changing Tides*. Y
don't need to be in order to attach quicl
David McGrath – 5 stars

Other Titles by K.D. Mason

HARBOR ICE

DANGEROUS SHOALS

KILLER RUN

EVIL INTENTIONS

UNEXPECTED CATCH

BLACK SCHOONER

Dedicated to Paul Steele

* * *

THANK YOU'S

Special thanks go out to my many friends who have patiently given their time and opinions when asked. The following deserve special heartfelt thank yous:

Nancy, just for being my wife.

John, for his knowledge of the waters surrounding Newport, Rhode Island.

Nigel, for his knowledge of the running scene in Newport.

All my many friends in Belize, especially everyone at TMM Yacht Charters.

And lastly, a special thanks to my longtime friend Paula, Bartender Extraordinaire. Without her help, counsel and encouragement none of this would have been possible.

Thank you.
K.D. Mason

CHAPTER 1

Crang. Crang. Crang. Crang. The sound of his footsteps pounding on the aluminum ramp shattered the quiet of the early morning as he ran down to the floats to which his boat was tied. His heart was pounding and the voice in his head kept saying, "It can't be. You'll see." But he would see, and that voice would be wrong.

* * *

JACK BEALE STARTED HIS DAY STANDING in the parking lot of Ben's Place looking out over Rye Harbor. It was around 7 A.M. and the sun had been up for almost two hours. To the east, on the jetties that created the entrance to the harbor, he could see the early fishermen casting their lines and settling in for a day of patient waiting. He turned his gaze back across the harbor to the north where he could see the main road as it crossed over the creek that led out into the salt marsh. The endless stream of summer traffic had not yet begun in earnest. Only the early morning runners, power walkers, and roller bladers could be seen crossing the bridge along with an occasional car.

The sky was that perfect shade of blue that you only see in the early morning of a summer's day, unbroken by clouds not yet formed. The water, a mirror with two of each boat, connected at the waterline, waiting for the first hint of breeze to appear that would break the glass. The last remains of the evening's coolness lingered as the sun's warmth was beginning to be felt. This was the mid-July Monday morning that greeted Jack.

Jack was early into his second half century although you would never know it save for a few gray hairs at the temples. He ran to stay in shape, had an easygoing disposition, and spent as much time as possible working on or sailing his boat. For as long as he had lived in Rye Harbor, he only has a few really close friends, the closest being Tom, the town's detective, although he seemed to be on good terms with just about everyone.

It was more than twenty-five years ago that he had sailed into Rye Harbor on his now vintage sloop, *Irrepressible*, after experiencing a life-changing loss. He had been sailing around the Caribbean with the love of his life, Marie, when a stray bullet from a street-side shooting killed her while they were in Martinique.

Jack was devastated and the only person that he could think to call had been Tom, who responded like the true friend he was. No questions asked, he flew to Martinique and stayed with Jack, eventually convincing him to return with him to Rye Harbor.

While Jack had been sailing the Caribbean with Marie, Courtney, and her sister, Kara, had just inherited Ben's Place and began to change the longtime watering hole into a real showplace that catered to both tourists and locals throughout the year, but it was during the summer when the real money came in. With their spacious outdoor deck, live reggae, and drinks flowing freely, it was always a full house.

The quaint cottage that Ben had lived in was remodeled, then Kara married and moved away, leaving Courtney on her own. Tom knew that she wanted to repair the old barn out in back of the cottage and he thought that Jack would be perfect for the job. He was. The barn was rebuilt, Jack moved into the apartment that was created upstairs while the lower floor became a shop. It didn't hurt that he was also an experienced bartender so he was able to help out at Ben's as well. Courtney became his second closest friend after Tom.

His other close friends were Dave, his running buddy, and Patti, a waitress at Ben's and aspiring photographer who was dating Dave and happened to be Max's best friend. And Max. Max was the bartender at Ben's and she and Jack had been friends ever since she came to work at

Ben's in the mid-eighties. It took his dramatic rescue of her from a ruthless killer after the murder of her aunt last year for Jack to finally admit the obvious: he was in love with Max and had been for some time.

A private man, Jack masked his past in an openness of the present. Few people knew anything specific about his past and that suited him just fine. By all appearances he was quite well off, source unknown. He was always busy helping someone, doing something, and his lack of a job—in the sense of a nine to fiver—had led to much speculation among the locals about his lifestyle.

Standing there, overlooking the harbor, he was mesmerized by the peace and calmness that the start of the day always brought. The chaos of crowds on the previous day and night were distant memories against the promise of the new day. His eyes scanned the harbor, noting which boats were still on their moorings and which were out. Finally, his eyes returned to the pier that began in the corner of the parking lot and extended out toward the commercial wharf.

At the end of the pier, tied to the floats, was in his opinion, the most beautiful boat in the harbor. She was named *Irrepressible,* and she was his. Her bow rose up from the water in a gentle curve that projected a sense of graceful strength and power. The soft curve of her sheer as her deck sloped back toward the stern was like the sensuous curve of the back of a beautiful woman lying in the sun. Her single mast was just the right proportion, not one of those tall, bendy racing spars that was all the rage nor was it too squat like you see on many cruising boats. *Irrepressible* spoke to him. Freedom, adventure, security, comfort, the happiest and the saddest days of his life were all rolled up into that beautiful hole in the water.

The tide had turned and was beginning to ebb. The current of water flowing from the marsh had begun to deposit a mat of sea grass and other floating marsh debris between the bow of his boat and the float. Normally, he wouldn't have even taken notice except that there was something else bobbing in that pinched space. It appeared larger than the expected collection of discarded coffee cups, small pieces of driftwood and scraps of line and other reminders of man's existence that had washed out of the marsh. "What the hell is that?" he thought as he stared. What ever it was, he had decided that it was large enough that it should be cleared away before it could either damage his boat or any others should it break free and drift out into the harbor.

As he walked the length of the pier, his view of it was blocked and he began considering different possibilities of what it could be. By the time he reached the end of the pier, he had had decided that it was probably a large piece of rigid foam, like the kind that would be under a float or raft.

He stopped before heading down the ramp and saw it clearly for the first time. It wasn't foam. It wasn't anything that should have been there.

"Oh, shit," he said under his breath as he froze. His heartbeat grew louder. It pounded in his ears as he stood looking down on the lifeless form bobbing among the collection of flotsam caught in that narrow space between his boat and the float. Amid the sea grass, a paper cup from the local donut shop, a scrap of cloth and a paper plate, there was a body.

He didn't remember running down the ramp as he stood at the edge of the float looking down on the body. The man was face down, wearing khaki cargo shorts and a striped tee shirt. A sandal remained on one foot. There was a tattoo of a snake on his arm and bits of sea grass clung to his hair. He was either well tanned or he was a very light skinned black man; Jack couldn't be sure which.

The tide was flowing out from the marsh with increasing force, simultaneously pushing the body into that small wedge of space between the float and the bow of his boat while at the same time trying to force it free. Jack didn't move for what felt like an eternity. He just stood there, under that perfect blue sky, feeling unable to look away as the body rose and pulsed with the rhythm of the rushing tide.

The cry of first one gull followed by a chorus of cries from the rest, brought him back to the present. He stepped back, not taking his eyes off of the body and reached for his cell phone.

CHAPTER 2

HIS FIRST CALL WAS TO THE police station to report his discovery. Tom, his close friend and the local detective, was not in yet although he was expected soon. Jack filled the answering officer in on what he had found and was told to wait there and not touch anything. That was fine with him, so he climbed on board his boat to sit and wait, all the while keeping an eye on the body. It was one of those sights that you didn't want to see but it was hard to look away.

He placed a second call, this time to Max. He knew that he would be waking her up this early in the day, but if he didn't call her with this piece of news, he knew that she would never forgive him. The phone rang several times before Max answered. He could tell that she had been deep asleep. She sounded groggy, not at all awake, her voice had that sexy, smoky quality to it that is only possible when just awakened. "Hello?" There was a bit of a soft moan to it. "This had better be good, Jack Beale."

How did she know? he wondered as he responded with a too cheerful and enthusiastic, "Good morning, Sunshine."

"This had better be good or I will kill you when I get my hands on you."

Jack continued in his teasing way, "Max, I'm down on the boat, the sun is out, the sky is blue and the birdies are chirping, it is a glorious morning and there is a body floating next to the boat."

There was silence on the other end of the line and then Max's voice returned, this time much clearer and fully awake, that sexy, just barely awake timbre gone. "Did you just say that there is a body floating next to the boat? You better not be messing with me, Jack."

"Yeah, there really is a body floating next to the boat. I've called the police and they are on the way; I thought that you'd like to know. You know how you always complain if I don't tell you things first."

Before she could say anything else, Jack saw the body beginning to come unwedged from its place between the boat and float. "Max, I gotta go," he said as he closed his phone and jumped off of the boat. He got to the end of the float just as the corpse was beginning to float away and he was just able to grab a foot. At that moment, he saw the cruiser speeding over the bridge and he heard the sirens of the rescue team in the distance. All this activity had caught the attention of the few people across the way at the commercial wharf and a crowd began to form. The current was tugging on the body so Jack had to lie down on the float and hook his feet over the other side to avoid being pulled off. He did not want to go swimming with a corpse, and besides, the water was just too damned cold.

It felt like an eternity before anyone got down to where he was. The first to arrive was the patrolman who had answered the call. He just stood there looking at Jack, lying on his belly, holding onto the swimming corpse. Then in his by-the-book cop voice he said, "What seems to be the trouble here?" Jack could only look over his shoulder in disbelief and thought to himself, *You dumb shit, I'm lying here holding onto a dead body by its foot as the current tries to take it away and you have to ask me what's going on. Fuckin' idiot.* What he said was, "Officer, give me a hand, grab one of those lines on the boat so we can tie him off. It's getting really hard to hold on."

By the time they got a rope around the corpse and pulled him in, the fire department's rescue team arrived, followed by Tom, then Max, Patti with her camera, and then the rest of the town—or so it seemed. Jack moved out of the way as the rescue team pulled the corpse out of the water and up onto the float.

The yellow tape began to go up to keep the crowd away from the area, but not before Max and Patti joined Jack on *Irrepressible.* Coffee seemed in order, so Jack went below and started some water heating; instant would have to do. By the time the coffee was ready, Tom had joined them on the boat. Jack brought four cups up. If it weren't for the fact that there was a waterlogged corpse lying on the float, it would have been the perfect morning to just sit with coffee in hand watching the harbor wake up.

"Thanks. Tell me what happened," said Tom as he took his cup from Jack.

Jack took a sip then glanced over to where the corpse was lying on the float like some big fish and said, "All I did was come down to the harbor early to watch the sunrise and to enjoy the early morning quiet. It's really beautiful down here early in the morning,"

At that, both Max and Patti rolled their eyes. Neither one of them could grasp the concept that the day began much before 10 A.M. Jack went on, "I was up in the parking lot just looking over the harbor thinking about what I would do today. It looked like it might be good for a sail. I noticed that some junk from the marsh had washed into the gap between the bow of my boat and the float. There was something large in with all the grass and garbage, I couldn't tell what it was, but whatever it was, I thought that it was large enough that if it could either damage *Irrepressible* or someone else's boat if it escaped out into the harbor. So I walked down to see what it was. It turned out to be him." He looked over toward the corpse, now covered with a blanket. "When I got close enough to see it more clearly, I saw that it was a body, so I called the police. By then, the tide was really beginning to run out hard and it, he, began to swim away, so I grabbed his foot."

Max and Patty in two-part harmony sang out "Gross. You touched it. That's disgusting." Max then added, "I hope you washed your hands before making the coffee."

Jack shot her a look and continued. "That's when Officer what's-his-name showed up. He helped me get a rope around the body since it was getting hard to hold on to and we pulled him in. As soon as we had him tied off, everyone else showed up and here we are."

"Do you recognize him?"

"Don't know. I've only seen him face down in the water."

"Come with me and see if you recognize him." Tom said. Jack followed Tom off the boat, coffee in hand and went over to the body that the rescue team was preparing to carry up to the parking lot. Max peeked out from behind the dodger on the boat, not really wanting to get up close and personal with a corpse. Patti, on the other hand, grabbed her camera and followed.

Although Patti worked at Ben's to pay the rent, she was an absolutely terrific photographer. She had the artist's gift of a great eye and could really get to the core of a subject. Tom saw her following them as they approached the body and he knew that it would be useless to try and keep her away. He also knew that her photos might be more revealing than the ones taken by the police photographer. He remembered the pictures she shot last winter when she found the body in the ice, and how they had helped the investigation.

Tom pulled the corner of the blanket away from the body's head, revealing a very calm and peaceful face staring up at them. Jack looked closely at him. His skin was the color of light coffee, and there was a band of faint freckles across his nose. His eyes were blue and his short cut hair was tightly curled against his head. Jack thought he looked Haitian or Jamaican. Whatever his heritage, he was (or had been) a handsome man. Jack continued to stare at him, thinking, remembering. Finally Jack said to Tom, "I know him."

"You do?"

"He's been at Ben's a few times this summer on Sundays. He was there yesterday, but I feel like I know him from somewhere else. I'm just not sure where."

Jack continued to stare at the body while the shutter on Patti's camera clicked away rhythmically. Tom turned to Patti and asked if she recognized him. She stopped shooting and looked carefully at the lifeless face staring up at her. She had been so busy taking her pictures, only seeing the corpse as an artistic composition, that she hadn't really looked at it. Now she did, and in a hushed whisper she said, "I know him, too. I waited on him at the reggae party yesterday. He was drinking Captain and Cokes. He wasn't there with anyone in particular, although he was working the crowd. I did see him talking with the band during one of their breaks. It was odd though, they seemed to know each other and at a glance seemed to be friends, but there was something about the body language that said otherwise. It was so busy that I really didn't notice him again."

"Thanks, Patti," said Tom as he pulled the blanket back up, covering the face again. Tom signaled the rescue squad that he was finished with the body and he, Jack, and Patti returned to the boat. Max had watched the whole scene and was now full of questions.

CHAPTER 3

IN THE NEARLY TWO HOURS SINCE Jack had found the corpse, the tide continued to drop and the ramp leading up to the pier was getting pretty steep. As Tom took preliminary statements, Jack watched the rescue team struggle to lug the body up the increasingly steep incline, hoping that they didn't drop it.

The tide was nearly low enough that the float that *Irrepressible* was tied to would soon be grounded on the edge of the stone-covered flat. Over time, the natural rush of the outgoing tide had created a bank covered with cobblestones that was exposed each day at low tide. This made for a convenient place for the local fishermen to beach their boats whenever they needed to work on the bottoms. Jack had driven down onto the flat many times himself when bringing large or awkward things down to the boat. He always felt that the less distance you had to carry something, the better. Now he wondered why the rescue people didn't just wait for the tide to drop a little more, drive down onto the flat, load up and leave. It would have been much easier and it's not like their cargo needed immediate medical attention.

He must have had a funny look on his face because all of a sudden he heard Max's voice. "Jack . . . Jack are you all right?"

As he turned, he saw that all three of them were staring at him. "Yes, I'm fine. I was just thinking about how much easier it would have been for them to have waited a little and driven the ambulance down onto the flat to pick up the body rather than wrestle it up the ramp. Say, I'm hungry. Anyone for breakfast at Paula's?"

"Not me," said Tom.

In unison, Max and Patti said, "Yes, I'm starved."

"Okay if we leave?" Jack asked Tom.

Tom put on his serious cop face and said in his television cop voice, "Alright. But stay available and don't leave town." This brought giggles from Max and Patti and a grin from Jack.

"Yes, officer," said the girls, feigning seriousness as they hopped off the boat and began climbing up the ramp.

Tom waited while Jack finished locking up the boat. As they stepped onto the float, he said, "Jack, stop by the station later, I'd like to talk to you some more."

"Sure. No problem."

The body had been carted off and most of the crowd had dispersed by the time Jack and Tom reached the parking lot.

"Don't forget," said Tom as he turned and headed for his cruiser.

"I'll be over as soon as I can get away," said Jack.

Jack looked around for the girls and saw them about to go into Ben's with some of the early crew. "Hey!" he shouted.

"We'll be right back," they shouted back then disappeared into the building.

As Jack walked toward his truck, he was glad that the few onlookers that remained were all tourists so he didn't have to stop and chat. Besides, everyone would be at Paula's and he'd get grilled there.

CHAPTER 4

BY THE TIME MAX AND PATTI came out, Jack was waiting for them in front of Ben's. He had the radio on and was listening to Johnny Cash singing one of his classic hits. It seemed like a country kind of a morning, so Jack had his radio set to the local country station, much to the dismay of his passengers. Most mornings, Jack would listen to the local "shock jock" who was more funny than shocking, but that show was over for the day. The rest of the day, depending on his mood, Jack would listen to National Public Radio, Oldies, Country or Sports talk. Max and Patti groaned their dismay at his choice of music as they climbed into the truck, but Jack just sat there, tapping the steering wheel, lost in his thoughts.

The drive to Paula's only took five minutes and his passengers survived Johnny Cash. Since the parking lot was full, Jack had to park down the street a ways. Max and Patti were out of the truck before Jack had even turned off the engine. "See you inside," Max called back as they deserted him. He grinned.

There was still a pretty good crowd at Paula's and knowing how fast news traveled down by the harbor, he knew what this morning's topic of conversation would be. He took a deep breath, got out of the truck and went in. The girls had already taken seats at the counter and were saving one for him. Beverly waved hello as she went about filling and refilling coffees and otherwise working her magic.

Beverly had worked at Paula's for as long as anyone could remember. She could wait on a full house, hold several conversations, never let a cup go dry and make everyone feel like they were her only customers. She would be a great country song, Jack thought. John and Fred, two of the local fishermen, were there and nodded hello. Leo, Ralph and Paulie shouted out their hellos. Those three had opinions about everything and were not afraid to voice them. As he sat down, Beverly filled his cup.

Paulie was the first to approach Jack. "Jack, is it true that you found a body floating down by your boat this morning?"

Ralph chimed in, "I heard that it was some black guy from Jamaica."

Leo, not to be left out added, "I heard that he had drugs in his pockets and that he had been shot." Paulie, Ralph and Leo were nice enough guys, just not always on the same page as the rest of the world, so Jack could only grin and try to humor them because he knew that to try anything else would be an exercise in futility. Besides, it was a good story. Before he finished telling them the story in as simple a way as possible, Max interrupted, "Jack, we've ordered, what do you want to eat?" He told Max what he wanted and quickly finished the story, and the guys, while not the sharpest tacks in the box, did get the hint, thanked Jack for filling them in, wished him a good breakfast, and left.

Beverly came by with a fresh pot of coffee, topped up their cups and then returned minutes later with their food. They all had the same breakfast, the No. 1, two eggs over easy with hash browns, toast and either bacon or sausage. Jack had sausage and the girls, bacon. It was a classic breakfast and Jack marveled as the girls began wolfing it down. This getting up early and body finding business sure did help the appetite. As they ate, Max and Patti discussed the events of the morning. Jack's thoughts were of yesterday.

CHAPTER 5

JACK HELPED OUT AT BEN'S ON Sundays, the busiest day of the week during the summer. A reggae band played out on the deck and the place was filled to capacity. Sometimes he would check I.D.'s at the door or provide backup for the bartenders or just help the girls out on the deck by picking up empties in an attempt to maintain some order. It was hard work, but there was a kind of challenge to it that Jack didn't mind.

Yesterday had been the perfect day with bright sun, a clear blue sky dotted with a few white puffy clouds, and just a hint of a breeze. It had been hot. The girls had been hot. The guys had been hot. The music was hot. The grill was scorching and the dancing hotter still. The staff had been pumped by the promise of a kick-ass afternoon while the lunch crowd filled the deck as soon as the doors were opened.

Jack's thoughts drifted. It was not unlike running a marathon. You had prepared well, your training was complete and it was time. The gun would go off and instantly you were racing, fast because of the excitement, but not too fast because it would be a long afternoon.

After the initial rush and all the tables were filled, everyone settled into a rhythm. Greet your table, check for drinks, place orders, serve drinks, answer tourist questions, serve lunch, offer another drink, clear the table, sell dessert, get the check and say good-bye.

Get into the rhythm, breathe easy, feel your legs, don't go too fast. Find your pace and relax. Relax. Breathe. Remember to drink early and often, keep focused.

The band arrived to set up, as did the regulars, who staked out their regular tables, waiting for the lunch crowd to leave so they could settle in for the afternoon. Just as in running, pace was everything. The day would be long, so those first drinks were only sipped.

At the first 10K, you know how the day will go. The legs feel good. Shoulders are relaxed. You aren't running, you're flowing like a mountain stream over rocks. It's effortless; you don't even notice the miles as they pass under foot.

The resonating throb of arriving Harleys was felt deep within as it mixed with the sounds of the band as they began to warm up. Soon the music took over from the machines and as the driving bass line set the rhythm, the crowd began to move.

As the runners near the halfway point, their breathing is measured; concentration intense, the pace is relentless. Like the mountain stream as it descends, there are bumps, ripples and eddies, but the flow continues, quicker at times, slower at others but it keeps moving on.

Mid-way though the party, there are people everywhere and it's hard to move. There is a line at the grill; the cooks are just keeping up as they add more charcoal, then, throw another dozen burgers on. The bartenders were like dervishes, amid the whir of the blender, the chicka-chicka-chicka of the printer, punctuated by anonymous voices crying "Excuse me," "Send me a Bud," "That'll be $4.50," "Next." The crowd didn't realize that they were in the middle of a maelstrom; they were so close to the chaos that they couldn't see it.

Everyone was having a great time. The "power of beer" kicked in. With beer goggles on, everyone was beautiful. Laughter. Dancing. Movement. Some with practiced rhythm, others can only try. The Power of Beer. Everyone is perfect. Now is the time to concentrate, to hold it all together, to make it happen.

Twenty miles. The wall looms. Will it be there? Merciless and brutal, ready to break anyone who dares to challenge it head on. Or will you be able to go around it, reducing it to a mere detour in the achievement of the day? Your legs are tired, your breathing more labored, but your spirit is free, flowing like that mountain stream. Today, you are the mountain stream.

You started slowly, smoothly and ran easily. You kept on moving relentlessly. As the stream becomes a river, unstoppable, you also became stronger, in tune, in the zone. At twenty-two miles, you know that you will make it. Your inner strength, your determination says I will triumph. I will not stop.

The crowd has peaked. The dancers won't stop. The end is in sight, but there is still a lot to do. Close out checks. Clean up. Say good-bye to regulars. Create order out of chaos. Return to the serenity of the evening, listen to the sounds of the harbor, and enjoy the silence. Have a beer, Ahh, the power.

That was yesterday. Today it was different. One of yesterday's revelers was dead. The memory of a perfect day had turned ugly. Who was he? Why was he killed? Did he have anything to do with the band or was it just a horrible coincidence? All of these thoughts went through Jack's mind as he sat there finishing his eggs, sausage, and toast.

"Jack. Jack. Earth to Jack. Did you hear anything we were saying?" said Max.

He fumbled for words as he tried to cover. "Oh yes, of course. You remember seeing the guy there. Right? I remember him also."

"Jack, you weren't paying attention, but yes, we do remember seeing him."

CHAPTER 6

ANY THOUGHTS THAT JACK HAD had about going for a short sail in the afternoon were gone by the time breakfast was finished. Today, he would have to be satisfied with the usual Monday evening run with his club. He spent the rest of the morning doing errands and after a late lunch, stopped by the police station to see Tom.

Tom had been busy since the discovery of the body. After Jack and the girls left to go get breakfast, he went over to Courtney's to let her know what had happened and to see what she might know about the victim.

After speaking with her, he returned to the department and began the tedious job of filling out reports and organizing the investigation. When Jack knocked on his door, he welcomed the interruption. It gave him a chance to take a break from the endless paperwork involved when a dead body shows up in your town. Besides, he wanted to talk with Jack in a little more private setting. "Hey, Jack. Come on in."

"Thanks."

"Two murders in one year. Can you believe it?" Tom began.

"I know. What are the chances?"

"I've got a pretty good picture of what happened this morning. What I'd like to know is a little more about what you remember about this guy. You said that you had seen him at the Sunday reggae fest on several occasions."

Jack sat back, stretched his legs out and looked up at the ceiling. He didn't say anything for a few moments while he searched his memory. Tom watched him from across his paper-covered desk. It was amazing how much paperwork a small town could generate, but that was the nature of police work in today's world. Everything had to be carefully documented and records preserved just in case someone someday wanted to question an event or, even worse, sue the town. More time seemed to be spent covering one's ass than actually solving crimes and keeping the peace. Finally, Jack began to speak.

"He's been at Ben's several times this summer on Reggae Sundays, but I have a feeling that I've seen him there before this summer. It was that tattoo on his arm caught my attention. I just can't remember exactly when."

"I can understand that," agreed Tom.

"Other than that, he just blended in. He was quiet and pretty much kept to himself. Most of the Sunday crowd came as part of a group or to join a group. The groups pretty much remain intact, with some, but not a lot of interaction with others. They have their own party within a party. Even those people who come by themselves seem to be there to hook up. They are continually moving around, striking up conversations, using every lame line that exists, and otherwise working the crowd." He paused before continuing, "The staff refers to the whole scene as the delicatessen of life because it can be such a meat market with something or someone for everyone. There are prime cuts, choice cuts and even pimento loaf."

Tom chuckled at this description. "So, he came in by himself. Was he on the prowl as well?"

"Not really. I'd call him a watcher. He just sat, sipped his drink and listened to the band. He did this each time, until yesterday when I saw him talking to the band."

"He was talking to them?"

"Yeah, I remember seeing him go over when they took their first break. From their body language, it seemed as if they knew each other. I couldn't hear what was said, but it didn't seem like the band liked what they were hearing. After a few minutes they parted, the band went outside to chill out and he went off to the far side of the deck and sat back down on the railing."

"Did you hear what they were saying?"

"No, I was busy just trying to keep pace with the never-ending stream of empty bottles and other trash that was around."

"What happened then?"

"Not much. After their break, when they began playing again, they seemed a little tentative during the first song or two. Sometimes after a break, their singing might be a little pitchy but as soon as their voices warmed up again, they would smooth out. This time it seemed different, it was as if they were distracted. I can't really put my finger on what it was, it was just more of a feeling. I also noticed that Joshua kept looking around as if trying to spot the guy who'd approached him."

Tom interrupted, "Who's Joshua?"

"Sorry, Joshua is the guy on the steel drums. He and Percy, the bass player, are the heart and soul of the band. They started it and the other guys who make up the group will change from year to year, although the drummer, Leslie, has been with them for at least the past six years. Peter who plays keyboard is new this year."

"Okay, go on. You were saying that they seemed distracted or something."

"It wasn't anything really solid, just a feeling. Something just didn't seem right. I've known the band for a long time, and I've heard them at their best and at their worst. Something was just different, but, I was too busy to really pay much attention."

"Thanks, Jack. Do you know how to contact the band?"

"Sure. I've got their number at home. I'll give you a call later." Jack got up to leave, then hesitated. "Any word on who he was or how he was killed?" Tom shook his head and said, "No not yet, but I hope to have something back from the coroner's office in the next day or so; I'll let you know what I find out."

"Thanks, Tom. I'll call you with their number."

CHAPTER 7

THE DRIVE HOME TOOK LESS THAN ten minutes. As he pulled into the drive, Jack saw Courtney kneeling by one of the flowerbeds rooting about, a pile of weeds on the ground next to her. She looked up when she heard his truck and waved. There was a smudge of dirt across her cheek, her hair which once must have been neatly pulled back and tied up had begun to unravel and her face glistened from sweat. She was wearing overalls and an old, red tee shirt.

"Hi, Court." Jack called out as he climbed out of his truck.

"Hey, Jack." She stood as he walked toward her.

"Nice job. You pull weeds really well," he teased.

"Thanks." Then returning his tease she said, "Hey, what's this I hear about you finding a body floating in the harbor this morning? Tom came over to see me and told me the news. You know, you're giving my place a bad name. First, you find a body last winter while I'm on vacation and now you find another one."

Jack stopped her there, "First, I did not find that body last winter, Patti did. As to everything else, I just got sucked in. It was all about Max, so don't go laying that one on me."

"Details, details. You were involved then and you're still involved now. So what gives?"

"It's really pretty simple. I was down at the harbor around 7:00 just to enjoy the quiet of the early morning. I saw something floating down by the boat, checked it out and it turned out to be a body."

"Tom said that it might be someone who had been at reggae yesterday?"

"Yeah, he was. Actually, he has been at reggae over the past few weeks. I feel like I know him, but I can't put a name with him. You've probably seen him, too," said Jack.

"Say, would you like a beer or something? It's hot out here."

"Sure. I'll pass on the beer, we're running tonight, but I'll take a glass of water."

Courtney said, "Great, Come on in."

He followed her in. The cottage was small with an open floor plan on the first floor and the bedrooms and bathroom on the second floor. Jack was struck with how cool and serene it was inside. Courtney had done a great job with the place; she had a real touch. The gentle breeze blowing through the open windows was ruffling the light gauzy curtains. Slightly off white walls accented with several carefully placed bright watercolors, a few tropical floor plants, light colored hardwood floors and just the right pieces of white wicker furniture with overstuffed floral patterned cushions gave the place a clean and refreshing feel. Court motioned for Jack to sit at the small table that overlooked the back yard. She filled a brightly colored glass with ice and water and handed it to him before getting herself one as well. She sat down with him.

"There, that's better. So tell me more about this guy."

"I'm not sure there is a lot to tell. I had seen him several times on Sundays this summer. I noticed him because he seemed a little different from everyone else. You know how everyone there seems to be there to pick some one up? He wasn't, or at least didn't appear to be. He would come, have his drink and just sit there watching and listening. He didn't really seem to care about the whole scene, but he seemed to be interested in the music or the band or some combination of the two."

"What did he look like? I'm still having a hard time picturing him."

"Well, yesterday he was wearing khaki cargo shorts, a striped tee shirt and sandals; although he only had one on when I found him. He was a very light skinned black man. Short hair. Good looking, freckles and a tattoo of a snake on his arm, very distinctive. That's what seems familiar, I just don't know why. I feel as if I've seen that tattoo before, only I can't put my finger on where."

"Tom showed me a picture that Patti took of him."

"So why are you asking me what he looked like?"

"Because I really didn't look at the picture. It gave me the creeps."

"I'll get a copy from Patti for you to look at."

"I don't want to."

He ignored her protest, "I'll bring one over."

"You are such a jerk." Then changing the subject slightly she asked, "You said that he seemed to be interested in the band and their music, not so much the other extra curricular activities going on. Do you suppose that the band knows him or is involved in some way?"

"I really don't know. That was only an observation that I made, not anything that I know. I've got to call Tom with the band's number so he can contact them. Even if there is no connection, it will make for an interesting summer."

Courtney agreed. "Changing the subject again. What's up with you and Max? After all that stuff last winter, I thought that you two were finally facing reality and getting together."

Jack started to fidget. Taking a sip of his water, he turned away from Courtney's expectant gaze and looked out the window at the marsh. Memories of last winter came flooding back. He didn't find it easy to talk about such personal things. He had almost lost her. He didn't like to think about what would have or could have happened that night if he hadn't shown up at her place when he did. Franz had already killed Andy and was seconds away from catching Max when he had arrived. As a result, they had crossed several thresholds. The intensity of those experiences had forced them together, every emotion magnified by the circumstances, and they had become lovers. But now, some time had passed and, things had cooled off a little. Sanity was beginning to reassert itself into their lives.

Finally he looked back at Courtney and with some annoyance in his voice, he said, "Thanks for asking, but Max and I are just friends. There is nothing going on there. As a matter of fact, apparently there is some guy who has been flirting with her for the past few Sundays. She has her own life. Why don't you go talk to her about it?"

Courtney already knew the answer. It wasn't serious, just some light flirtation on Max's part; a way for Max to test her feelings for Jack. They had a deep friendship, but that next level, the one they had reached briefly, scared Max as much as it scared Jack and she was now recoiling from it. With a mischievous twinkle in her eyes, Courtney said, "Maybe I will." As she answered, she was thinking *Jack, you are so full of shit. You love her and she loves you. Why don't you just face it?*

"You know, you two are made for each other."

She knew that something was there and that neither one of them would face it. It was too easy to get him all flustered and being the romantic that she was, she also knew that they would work it out in their own way. Of course it might take a little nudging.

Jack stood and abruptly ended the conversation. He didn't like where it was going. Courtney sure knew what buttons to push. "Bye, Court. I think it's time for me to get going."

CHAPTER 8

JACK MADE HIS ESCAPE AND HEADED toward his apartment. Cat was lying there, taking a sunbath just outside the door. Cat had adopted him about 10 years ago and was his only true confidante. Jack knew that Cat was the very personification of discretion and wouldn't betray his confidences. He stopped to scratch her head. "Hey, Cat. You look like you're enjoying this beautiful day. That Courtney is something else. She thinks that I have something for Max and that I won't face up to it. What do you think?" Cat just looked up, threw him a couple of eye kisses and a soft mew, then curled back up. "You're right," said Jack. One more scratch behind the ears and he got up and went inside to find the band's number for Tom.

He found the number, called Tom with the information and then, looking at the clock, realized that there wasn't much time before he would meet his running buddies for their Monday night run, so he just fixed a snack and sat down to read one of his sailing magazines. He had set the alarm on his watch so that he wouldn't be late for the run and it was a good thing he did. He was a little disoriented when he heard it go off, but he quickly realized that he had dozed off while reading. It had been an eventful day. Now he was refreshed and ready for a run.

Every Monday night, they met in front of Ben's for a weekly run and after they'd go into the bar for some on tap rehydration. As Jack approached the group, he was met with a chorus of hellos and while he made the rounds, Dave was there getting everyone organized. The decision was made as to which route they would run and after a few stretches, they were off. Jack and Dave led the way up Harbor Road and onto the Boulevard.

"So Jack, how have you been?" asked Dave.

"Pretty good. Yesterday was a busy day at reggae and this morning I found a body floating in the harbor by my boat."

Dave didn't react at first to this pronouncement but then it hit him. "You what?"

"I found a body floating in the harbor this morning." Jack's casual attitude was having the desired effect on Dave.

"No shit," he said. "Tell me about it." Turning to the group behind he said, "Hey you guys, catch up, Jack has a story to tell. He found a body floating in the harbor this morning."

That announcement tightened up the pack and Jack had center stage. He began, "There really isn't much to tell. I was up early this morning and I went down to the harbor to check things out. I saw something floating next to my boat and when I checked it out, it turned out to be a body."

"Guy or gal?'

"It was a guy. He was at reggae yesterday."

"Any idea who he is?"

"No idea."

Jack tried to answer everyone's questions, but there were limitations because he really didn't know all that much beyond having found the body. As the distance increased the group spread out and soon just Dave remained with Jack.

"Dude, that's so fucked up. You all right?" asked Dave.

"Yeah, I'm fine."

"Cool."

They ran the rest of the way in silence. Back at Ben's, the group slowly reassembled and while a few left immediately, most went into Ben's for a beer. Max was behind the bar and as they came in she began pouring pitchers. The rest of the evening was spent in lively conversation about the body, training schedules, upcoming races, aches and pains. The group began to break up as the last pitcher was drained. Goodbyes were said along with promises to get together next Monday. Soon only Jack and Dave remained. While Dave waited to say goodbye to Patti, Jack went over to the bar to see Max.

"Hey, Jack. How was the run?"

"Good."

"That sure was a creepy way to start the day."

"Yes, it was. I'm sorry that I woke you up so early this morning."

"That's okay. I got a lot done today." Then she smiled and asked, "I'm off tomorrow. You want to do something?"

"Sure. Call me," said Jack. "I've got to get going. I'm beat." He didn't notice the subtle disappointment that registered on Max's face with his nonchalant response as he turned and left. As he walked home, he felt content.

Max was confused.

CHAPTER 9

THE NEXT MORNING, AFTER A GOOD night's sleep, Jack called Max and plans were made to hang out that evening. He spent the rest of the day working in his shop, running errands and otherwise keeping busy doing nothing remarkable. It was late afternoon and he was on his way back from the hardware store when he decided to stop at the station to see Tom.

"Hey, Tom," he said as he walked into Tom's cramped office.

"Oh. Hi, Jack. What's up?"

"I just wanted to see if you had found out anything else about the body."

"Actually, I have. Let me see." Tom rustled through some papers on his desk, pulled one out, looked it over and said, "I talked to Joshua last night. By the way, thanks for his number. This morning I went and saw him and showed him a picture of the body and you were right, he knew the guy. His name was Anthony Williams, but every one called him Python and he was in the band seven or eight years ago."

"Yeah. That's right. I remember him now. He sang vocals and did some percussion. Good voice. That's why the tattoo looked familiar. Python? Hunh. I don't think he was with them for the entire summer though, only a few Sundays."

"Right. Joshua told me that he had joined the band during the winter doing vocals. He had a pretty good voice and for a while everyone got along well. They had collaborated on some new songs, I guess he was a pretty good writer, but eventually egos began to get in the way. As their successes increased, so did the tension and that summer it all fell apart and he left the group. He didn't seem to know much more about him, but I have my doubts. I have a feeling that he knows more than he's telling. I'm hoping to talk to the rest of the band over the next couple of days. These band guys sure are hard to catch up with."

"I know what you mean. Their life styles are pretty . . . ah, fluid . . . shall we say."

"Fluid. That's a nice way to put it," said Tom.

After a slight pause, Jack said, "You know Tom, it's coming back to me. I remember now. He did have a kick-ass voice. The band really sounded good that summer, but there was something going on. You could feel it. There was a tension. I never asked Joshua about it and he never said anything. Even after Anthony left the band and I asked him about it, he just shrugged it off saying that that's the way it goes sometimes."

"Yeah, well I'm sure that something else is going on. I mean there were several witnesses who saw them talking on Sunday, yourself included, and Joshua was really evasive about what they talked about. If you get the opportunity to talk to them, maybe you could have more success in finding out what's going on."

Jack mulled the request over in his mind. While he heard little alarm bells going off in his head, somehow he knew deep down that he wouldn't or maybe couldn't refuse to help his friend. Those two competing voices in his head were at it again. One said, "Do it." It was a simple enough request and shouldn't be a big deal. The other said, "Run, don't get involved," reminding him that whenever Tom had asked him for a little help in the past, those easy simple requests always seemed to get out of control and turn into dangerous situations.

He remembered when he and Tom had both lived in Miami. Jack had signed onto a private yacht for a Caribbean cruise, not knowing that the owner was under investigation. When he told Tom about his plans, Tom asked him to be his eyes and ears, since the yacht's owner was the subject of one of his investigations. "I don't want you to do anything except watch, tell me what you see, and enjoy the trip," he had said. At the time it had seemed a harmless enough request. "Just observe."

Jack hadn't asked any other questions and Tom hadn't offered any further explanation about the investigation. So he went. Then, when Jack witnessed his employer execute a guest who had come aboard while they were in Belize, his observations took on new meaning. Jack realized that he could easily become fish food because of what he had seen. As soon as they returned to the U.S., Jack left the boat and while angry at Tom, their friendship was never in question. This past winter was the most recent time he had helped Tom with an investigation and came close to losing Max. Despite his recollections and reservations, Jack found himself saying, "Sure Tom, I'll talk to Joshua the next time I see him and see if I can't find out what's going on."

"Thanks, Jack."

CHAPTER 10

WHEN JACK GOT HOME AFTER HIS visit with Tom, the light on his answering machine was blinking. It was Max telling him that she would pick him up at 6:00. He was intrigued. She didn't give any hint as to what she had in mind.

A little before 6:00, Jack heard the honk of Max's car horn. He looked out the window and saw that Patti was in the car with Max. Until he saw Patti, he had been wondering what Max had in mind. His thoughts went from the innocent to the less so, which was definitely the more unlikely scenario, but there is that dark corner in every guy's mind, even if they won't admit it. He blamed Courtney for jump-starting those thoughts with her teasing and questions

He headed downstairs and as he went outside, Max and Patti came tumbling out of the car like two exuberant puppies as they ran toward him. For a split second, Jack couldn't move even though it felt like an eternity. Sensory overload. Max looked great. She was wearing khaki shorts and a short sleeved, scoop neck jersey that was stretched just enough by her breasts that it was hard not to stare, or at least take a good look. Her hair was loose and there was a vibrancy all about her. Max grabbed one hand and Patti grabbed his other, "Come on." Jack recovered and let them guide him to the car. He was too overwhelmed to resist or even say anything as they piled into Max's car, Jack in the back and the ladies up front, with Max driving and they were off. As they headed down the street, he finally was able to find his voice, "Where are we going?"

"You'll see," was the two-tone answer.

"Okay, fine. Be that way," he replied in a slightly whining tone.

All he got in return were giggles and the volume on the radio was turned up louder. *Girls Just Want to Have Fun* was playing and he thought, *How appropriate.*

It wasn't long before they reached their mystery destination. Sun and Surf Mini Golf. Jack hadn't played in years and as Patti pulled into a parking space, he saw Dave was there waiting for them. Max turned to him and said, "Tonight, we are going to kick your butts. Girls against guys." The challenge was issued and Jack's competitive side emerged.

"Not a chance in hell. Dave and I are going to give you a spanking."

They clambered out of the car and Dave walked toward them. Patti bounded over to give him a hello kiss as Jack shouted a warning, "Be careful Dave, she's going to try to put a hex on you. We've been challenged and the game is on." Dave had his hands full so his response was somewhat muffled.

Properly outfitted, putters in hand, the game began. Windmills, giant clowns, U-turns and rolling greens challenged the foursome. At the end of the first nine holes, Jack and Dave were up by two strokes. Trash talk was flying and the guys were feeling pretty confident. That's when the girls put the hammer down and the guys were done. They were subtle. They were sneaky. Whispered promises at critical moments, a wink, a nudge, a movement just as a stroke was taken all added up to defeat for the guys. When the last ball rolled into the cup and the match was over, the girls had won by one stroke. Victory was declared amidst Jack and Dave's weak protests as their claim that they had been taken advantage of fell on deaf ears. The girls just laughed and let them know that they were buying the beers. They agreed to meet down near the beach at a bar near Dave's. Patti went with Dave, leaving Jack to ride with Max.

The beer was cold and their conversations lively as they relived the evening's game. Eventually, it came to be time to call it a night. As they left the bar, Patti turned and said to Max in a voice intended to be a whisper, but loud enough for everyone to hear, "Max, I'm going home with Dave. You're on your own with Jack." She punctuated this with a wink and a grin.

"Okay," was the reply. "Come on Jack, let's leave these two love birds on their own." Patti left with Dave while Jack and Max headed for her car. Max was driving and after a few minutes of silence, Jack looked over at Max and said, "Thanks, Max. It was a great night even though you girls cheated to win the golf match."

"We did not. We won fair and square."

"Right," Jack said with just a touch of sarcasm in his voice. The rest of the ride was spent without much conversation, each keeping whatever wanted to be said inside and private.

When they reached Jack's, they endured that awkward moment when it was time to say good night. As friends it was simple, just hop out of the car, a quick "See you tomorrow," and it was over. More than friends, then an invitation to come up for a nightcap would be in order and who knew? The problem was that their relationship was neither. Except for their trip to Switzerland last winter, neither had been willing to commit to that level beyond friendship. Jack knew that his feelings for Max were real, but what he didn't understand was why he couldn't tell her so. She had certainly given him every opportunity and reason to take that step, but he always stopped short. She knew in her heart that Jack was the man for her. She had all but told him so, but it was important for her to hear from him that she was the one. She had resolved not to trap him, all she could do was give him opportunities. Now was such an opportunity. So there they sat in awkward silence. Jack's heart was racing and he felt as if he couldn't catch his breath even as he appeared calm and relaxed. Max was feeling much the same. This moment of shared indecision seemed to last forever as neither one wanted to make the first move, regardless of direction. It abruptly ended when a light came on in Courtney's cottage. The spell was broken, the final good nights were said, and it was over.

Jack watched Max drive off and he turned to walk to his apartment. As he walked he muttered to himself, "That was so junior high. Did you see how great Max looked tonight? You know there was something there. Why don't you face it?" He couldn't answer the question. There was something blocking him and he knew that someday he would lose her if he didn't act, but he just couldn't. Not now, not yet. He fell asleep wrestling with his emotions.

CHAPTER 11

SEVERAL DAYS HAD PASSED since the mini golf outing. Jack kept replaying the awkward goodbye in his mind. He wished he could have a do-over for that moment. The weather had continued to be perfect and tourists were everywhere. The bar was busy every night so there hadn't been many opportunities for time with Max. For the moment, their lives seemed to be running parallel to each other, neither able to cross over. Jack wasn't sure how to deal with this, and neither was Max for that matter.

Saturday night arrived and Jack strolled into Ben's. Patti gave him a quick wave as she disappeared into the kitchen and the cocktail waitress, Amber, flashed him a smile as she headed toward the deck with a full tray of drinks.

"Hi, Max." Jack said as he took his seat at the bar.

"Hi, Jack. Beer?" Max said when she saw him sit.

"Please."

As she placed the beer in front of him, they experienced a movie moment where for that split second, there is total silence as the two former lovers eyes meet and they realize that it's not over, but neither will admit it.

"Thanks, Max. How are things?"

"Busy." And before she could say anything else the order printer began its almost incessant chikka-chikka-vroosh-chunk as it spit out another order and she had to leave. Jack began to relax, he felt at home as he sat at the bar sipping his beer while trying to have one of those fragmented bar conversations with Max. There were enough distractions and activity that neither felt any pressure to deal with their unspoken feelings. The dining rooms were full, so parties were waiting in the bar for tables. Amber was a blur of motion as she greeted her new customers, placed their orders and served their drinks.

Jack took notice of how great Max looked as she moved about behind the bar. She was wearing a black mini skirt, which showed off her well-tanned legs. The Hawaiian print shirt she was wearing was not what would be called form fitting but it wasn't baggy either. As she worked, her breasts moved as if they had a life all their own. When she bent over the bar, her shirt would gape open just enough to tease and Jack was mesmerized. Memories of their trip together last winter flashed through his head again. He remembered the intensity and how right those intimate moments had felt. Then something changed in the bar that brought him back to the present. It wasn't apparent at first, but Jack could feel it. He looked up and at first didn't notice anything or anyone. He looked at Max and saw that her rhythm had changed. Now there was a tension where before fluid motion had existed. That's when Jack saw him.

Jack didn't know his name, but he knew his face. Jack studied him. He had been at reggae on Sundays for the past few weeks. All the women had noticed him, but he seemed to be interested only in Max. She knew it and was enjoying the attention. He was younger than Max, about six foot three, and Jack guessed about 195 pounds. There was a smoothness in the way he moved which suggested athletic ability. His amber colored eyes, a disarming smile with nearly perfect teeth, dark wavy hair with the natural highlights that can only come from time spent outdoors, all added to the effect and the capper was the way he dressed. He was neat, but not perfect. His look was a mix of pretty-boy-preppie and I'm-an-ordinary-Joe-and-this-is-what-was-clean-today. One thing was for sure, though, his clothes were not bargain basement. Tonight he was wearing khaki slacks, a blue work shirt, and sandals.

Jack had hoped to be able to talk with Max tonight and maybe smooth things over. *Shit*, he thought. What he didn't need was to have this guy here hitting on Max. This would change everything. Jack glanced at Max to check her reaction. She was trying to act cool, as if he were any other customer but she was failing miserably. He had obviously surprised her. At that moment, she glanced at Jack and caught him looking at her.

Time stood still for Max. She felt trapped. With a quick glance around, she saw that the only open seat was next to Jack. Two men, both attracted to her, and to whom she was attracted for very different reasons were about to meet. For Max, the world had gone silent and she felt as if time stopped. The printer spitting out an order on her register brought her back to the present. She turned away to grab the slip that had just printed and went to work. Safety. She could avoid the inevitable for a few more moments by hiding behind a Cosmo, a Deep Sea Martini and two drafts.

He looked down the bar, saw the only open seat and moved toward it. Seeing this, Jack wasn't about to leave, giving his unknowing rival any advantage, so he sat there, sipping his beer.

"Hi, Max. I hope you don't mind me stopping by like this. I just had to see you." Jack noted that the man's voice matched the rest of the package. There was a self-assured quality in the way he spoke. Jack also picked up a hint of an accent. He couldn't tell where it was from, but it was there nonetheless. The way he spoke and looked at Max, it was as if she was the only person in the room.

"Oh, hi, Daniel. What a nice surprise. What brings you by?"

Jack looked up a little surprised. He hadn't realized that she knew his name.

Daniel looked at Max, but before he could answer, Patti came in to pick up her drinks. She saw Jack, smiled and opened her mouth to speak, then she saw Daniel sitting next to Jack. Her smile froze. Max caught Patti's look and nearly spilled the Cosmo as she put it on Patti's tray. Without turning, she said in a soft voice to Patti. "Tell me that what is about to happen isn't happening . . . please." Patti just looked at her and almost without moving her lips whispered, "It is." With another quick glance past Max, Patti said, "I've gotta go. Good luck."

As she picked up her tray, she turned back to Max and said with a bit of a mischievous twinkle in her eye, "You know, he's really cute." Before Max could reply, she scooted off toward the dining room. Max took a big breath, put on her game face, turned, faced her two men, and moved down the bar toward them. She needed to regain some control over the situation so introductions were in order. Better for her to introduce them, than to have it happen on its own, risking a stray comment that could really ruin everything.

"Hey, Daniel. Can I get you something?"

"I'll have a beer. What's on tap?"

"We have two local beers, Red Hook ESB and Widmer Hefeweisen. Jack here is our local expert. Jack, Daniel is new to the area, could you give him your recommendation?"

Jack didn't see this coming, but he quickly recovered. "Sure. The Hefe is a light summertime wheat ale and the ESB is a little more full bodied amber ale."

"Thanks. I'll have an ESB. By the way, my name is Daniel. But I guess you already figured that out. And you're . . . uh . . . Jack?"

Jack took his offered hand with a grip that was a little firmer than normal and said, "Yeah. Nice to meet you."

"I'll be right back," said Max still working hard to maintain her composure.

She turned and went out back to get the beer thinking, *Great, first they sit next to each other and now they'll probably become drinking buddies. I am so screwed.* The pint was drawn and she returned to face them. She placed the beer on the bar in front of Daniel. "Here you go. Enjoy."

"Thanks, Max."

She turned to make her escape as quickly as possible. Patti had just returned to the bar so she went over to her.

Daniel picked up his pint and turning to Jack he said, "Back home we have a saying, 'Here's to good beer and the women who serve it.'"

Jack reluctantly raised his pint; they touched rims and with a slight edge to his voice said, "Sure. Here's to Max," while stealing a good look at Daniel before looking back at Max. Jack knew that Daniel didn't know who he was so he decided that he would learn as much about this Daniel as he could. For starters, where was home?

They drank.

Max's back was to the two men, but Patti witnessed the whole ritual and grinned.

Max leaned over the bar and whispered to her, "Tell me what they are doing. No don't. Oh, shit."

Patti took another glance over Max's shoulder and said, "Well, they are toasting to something and they seem to be getting along."

"Shit. Why does this happen to me?" hissed Max.

With a teasing tone in her voice Patti said, "Max, it's your own fault." and taking another peek over Max's shoulder she said, "He is really hot."

"I know . . . What am I going to do?"

"Well, Jack has been a little slow, maybe this will wake him up."

CHAPTER 12

THE REGISTER STARTED IT'S *chikka-chikka-vroosh-chunk* at that moment and Max had to go back to work. As she pulled the slip off the printer and began to make the drinks, she glanced over at Jack and Daniel. Jack saw her and motioned for another round. She nodded. Finishing the drinks she was working on, she went out back to get two more drafts all the while cursing the power of beer.

This was one of the worst nights that Max had ever spent in the bar. It was hot. It was busy. And Jack and Daniel sat there all night. After a chilly start, the power of beer had kicked in and soon they were talking, laughing and generally being guys, neither wanting to give the other any advantage by leaving first. They talked about just about everything that could be discussed: sports, travel, drinking experiences. World problems were solved and they even touched on religion. The only topic they avoided was Max, and except for a few furtive glances at her and a few random toasts to the "Best damned bartender on the seacoast," she was ignored.

To a casual observer, they appeared to be two good friends who hadn't seen each other for a while and were catching up on old times, but in reality, they were rivals engaged in a high stakes chess game and Max was the prize. Jack knew who Daniel was and he was wary of every move, every word he spoke. Daniel did not yet know exactly who Jack was, so at the moment the advantage rested with Jack and he was playing it cool, letting Daniel expose himself, Jack taking note and shoring up his defenses. As flattering as it was to have two very different men interested in her, it made Max uncomfortable. This was not a role that she played willingly, and yet here she was, being tugged in two directions by them, one her long time friend and confidant and the other, mysterious and tempting.

Eventually, the night had to end. Ben's was closed, cleanup was finished, and it was time to lock up. The two men were still there, neither willing to give up.

"Patti, you've got to help me." Max whispered. "They won't leave."

Patti grinned at Max and was going to say something witty but the look that Max gave her stopped her short. "Okay, you go out back and I'll get rid of them." As soon as Max was gone, Patti announced, "Hey guys, it's been fun, but it's time to call it a night."

They both looked up at Patti. "Where's Max?" they said in unison.

She repeated, "Time to go. We're closed," while ignoring the question.

Patti could be wonderfully blunt and as they gave her that beer-induced look as they processed this new information, she said again. "C'mon, let's go."

"Oh, all right, we'll leave. Say goodnight to Max," mumbled Jack. Daniel said, "Let's go, bro," and they hi-fived each other and left. Patti followed them to the door and watched as Daniel got into his car. It was a MG-TD convertible, the iconic two seat English sports car, British racing green and it fit him like a glove. He started it, the engine just purred as he slowly drove out of the parking lot and over the bridge, his taillights disappearing down the boulevard. *Nice car*, she thought.

Jack began walking home and Patti called out to him just before he rounded the corner and moved out of sight, " G'night, Jack."

He waved to her without looking back.

She couldn't hear if he said anything, she just saw the wave. What it said was, "whatever."

Max was waiting inside for her. "Thanks, Patti."

CHAPTER 13

COURTNEY HAD GONE INTO WORK EARLY. It was Sunday, there wasn't a cloud in the sky, and it was already warm outside. As she sat at her desk catching up on some office work, she paused and looked out the window over the harbor. It was so peaceful. *Jack was right,* she thought. *It really is beautiful early in the morning.*

It wouldn't be long before the hoards of reggae revelers, regulars and newbies, would begin to arriving for another crazy afternoon of rum, music and dancing. The cleaning crew was hard at work and soon the rest of the staff would begin to arrive. She glanced at the schedule and noted that even though Patti and Max had been the last ones out last night, today they were scheduled to be the first ones in. "They'll be fun this morning," she said softly to herself.

She had finished her first cup of coffee and needed a refill, so she went downstairs and headed for the kitchen. As she reached the bottom of the stairs, she heard Patti and Max arriving. "Hi, ladies. Late night?" She already knew the answer but she asked anyway.

"Mornin' Courtney. Yeah, it was," mumbled Max as she sipped from a large coffee that she had bought at the drive through. Patti was sipping an iced latte and was also pretty subdued.

"Well, look on the brighter side, you'll be out first today and you won't have to clean up the mess tonight." Courtney was trying to put a positive spin on things.

"Big whoop," was the sarcastic reply from both.

Courtney decided that the coffee had not kicked in yet. As soon as the kitchen crew got in and made them some breakfast they'd be fine. Max and Patti went to work setting up the bar and Courtney headed for the kitchen in search of more coffee.

"You okay?" Patti asked Max.

"Yeah, I'm okay." was Max's reply. She paused, and then added, "No, I'm not. Can you believe that he came in last night and sat there at the bar all night, right next to Jack? And Jack. What about him? Sitting there all night with his new drinking buddy, acting all friendly and like they were old friends and hadn't seen each other for a long time. I know Jack knows who he is. He's seen him here for the last few Sundays. What was he thinking? The bastard, he did that just to piss me off."

Patti sat there as Max went on this mini tirade. Occasionally she was able to get in a few words. "Jack didn't plan anything. He was reacting. Wouldn't you have done the same thing?"

"No, I wouldn't . . . yes . . . no . . . oh, I don't know."

The longer Max went on, the funnier it became and soon Patti was having a hard time not giggling.

"What's wrong with me? Jack and I have been friends and more for so long. We've been through so much together, is it too much to ask for a little more commitment? Then Daniel shows up a few weeks ago and begins hitting on me and Jack just ho-hums the whole thing. Now, Daniel shows up last night and sits there with Jack all night. That was the last thing I needed." She paused, then with a slight grin, she said, "Daniel really is gorgeous though, isn't he?"

Patti touched her index finger to her lips and made a sound like water on a hot pan, "Pssss. He sure is. Of course, I'm only looking because I have Dave," said Patti teasingly as she grinned while busting on Max.

"Shut up. You'd be saying 'Dave, Who?' if Daniel was paying attention to you."

"No way! He's strictly eye candy."

"Right," was Max's sarcastic reply.

It was at this moment that Courtney reappeared, just catching the tail end of this conversation. "Who's eye candy?"

Max busied herself cutting some limes, not making eye contact while Patti's eyes lit up and she began to tell Courtney the story.

"Max has this really cute guy after her. He started coming here a few Sundays ago and he's so obviously interested in Max."

"Is not," mumbled Max under her breath.

"Anyway, he came in last night to see Max and sat at the bar all night. Of course, Jack was here and they ended up sitting next to each other and became buddies by the end of the night. I had to get them to leave while, Maxie hid out in the kitchen."

"Really?" said Courtney with a grin. "Tell me more about this mystery man."

"Well, he's really cute with the most luscious amber eyes, he has dark wavy hair, a great bod, you can tell that he works out and he isn't stuck on himself. He seems really nice. He drives a really cute car, you know, one of those English two-seater sports cars. He has a slight accent and I don't recognize it but it is really sexy."

Still grinning and with a teasing tone, Courtney said, "Whew, I'm getting hot just listening to you," as she waved a napkin in front of her like a fan and looked over at Max.

Max looked up, just wishing that they would all go away. This was a problem and it wasn't funny. "You guys are making all too much out of this. Now go away and leave me alone. I have work to do."

"Touchy, touchy. Let's go. We should leave Max alone. After all, they'll both be here soon enough and she needs to get ready," giggled Patti. A truce went into effect as the pace of preparations for the day picked up.

CHAPTER 14

JACK HAD A MUCH MORE LEISURELY start to his day and he needed it. He definitely had too many beers last night. He was awakened by Cat, gently poking and prodding his cheek. It was her way of getting his attention. "Cat, leave me alone." With a soft mew and another round of pokes and prods, Jack opened his eyes. Cat, triumphant at getting him awake, mewed again and pranced across his full bladder as she made her way off the bed. Jack just groaned. He really had to get up now. His head throbbed as he made his way across to the head. After relieving himself, he looked into the mirror and it was not a pretty sight. "Ohhh," he groaned as he brushed his teeth and drank a large glass of water. Cat was still pestering him; she really wanted to start her day outside. "Okay, okay, I'll let you out. Let me start the coffee."

"Come on." Cat raced ahead of him down the stairs and was turning circles in front of the door in anticipation of release. After letting Cat out, Jack took in a deep breath of the morning air; it was clean and fresh. The recent humidity was gone. The sky was blue and it was going to be a beautiful day and that meant that the crowd at Ben's would be huge. He groaned again and went up to his coffee.

He took his first sip. Jack savored it as he sat down and looked out over the marshes through the back window.

Memories of last night flashed through his head. Max, the bar, Patti saying good night, too much beer and . . . *What was his name? Daniel. Yeah. Daniel, that was his name.* Daniel had been at reggae hitting on Max for the last few weeks. Jack hadn't paid much attention until last night because she has all kinds of guys flirting with her all the time. It's part of the act, part of being a good bartender. He slowly sipped his coffee and with each sip, he remembered more of the previous evening.

He seemed okay, but . . .

Jack always thought of Max as his, even though he never thought to tell her so.

"She knows."

Another sip and his conversation with himself continued.

"Of course she does . . . Doesn't she?"

The more he remembered about last night, the more he questioned.

Another sip.

He was there to see Max. Son of a bitch. What did he know about me . . . and Max? Does she like him? Could she really be interested in him?

He couldn't remember discussing Max at all except when they toasted her as a great bartender.

Then, as he took his last sip it hit him. *That's why Max was acting so strange. She's interested in him.*

That's when his stomach rumbled. "I need some food," he said aloud to himself. A shower, breakfast at Paula's and then he'd figure out what to do about Daniel . . . and Max.

CHAPTER 15

BREAKFAST AND MORE COFFEE WORKED wonders on Jack, and by the time he was finished, he wasn't as panicked as he had been. At Ben's today, he would be helping Jimmy out on the door, checking I.D.'s, collecting the cover and otherwise helping maintain some semblance of order. Preparations were in full swing when he arrived and the outside patio was already full of early diners.

Peggy was at her post at the hostess stand and waved as he came in the front door. He wasn't even five steps into the building when Courtney came around the corner and saw him.

"Hi, Jack. How are you feeling this morning?" She said this with a teasing lilt in her voice. Before he answered, Jack thought, *Shit, news travels way too fast around here. I wonder what stories are circulating about me this morning?*

"Good morning, Court. Great day. Should be busy," he replied.

"Definitely. How do you feel after last night? I hear you had quite the night at the bar."

"I'm all right and I don't know what you're talking about."

"Come on, Jack. You know you spent the whole night at the bar drinking beers with that cute guy who has the hots for Max."

"Oh, that," said Jack nonchalantly.

"Yes. That," pressed Courtney.

"So. He sat next to me because it was the only available seat and we had a few beers together."

"And?" Courtney would not give up. She could be tenacious when looking for information. He knew what she wanted and he decided that it would be best to play dumb, at least until he was able to talk to

Max.

"And nothing. We just talked about guy things and when the bar closed, we went our separate ways."

"And you didn't talk about Max?"

"No. We didn't talk about Max. What is this all about?"

She cracked. "Jack you must be the densest person in the world if you can't see that he is interested in Max and that she is beginning to show some interest in him. Jack, listen to me. You and Max are meant for each other. You know it and I know it and Max knows it. Everyone knows it. Face it and get off your ass and tell her so or you may wake up one day and she'll be gone."

He didn't want to have this conversation, so he said to Courtney, "Listen, today is going to be hell, I've got to get to work."

As he walked past her she said, "Fine, Jack. But remember what I said."

Having made his escape, he went into the bar and was met by looks and furtive grins from everyone. *What is with this place?* he thought. Max was behind the bar. He took a deep breath and walked over to her. "Good morning, Max. I'm sorry about last night. I hope I didn't cause you any problems."

"No. You didn't, but thanks."

Anyone overhearing her response would probably not have picked up on the strain in her voice. Jack did; his conscience wouldn't let him miss it.

"Good," said Jack as normally as he could. It was obvious that neither of them wanted to talk about last night, at least not at this moment. There was a commotion out on the deck. Jack turned to see its cause and Max looked over his shoulder. It was Joshua. He was struggling with a large speaker cabinet. This would be the first of many trips needed to get all of the band's equipment in and set up for the day's performance. Jack looked back at Max and said, "I should go help him get that stuff in."

Max nodded her agreement. They both felt relief at not having to continue their conversation. Each knew that they were avoiding the inevitable and that was just fine for now.

"Hey, Joshua!" called out Jack.

"Hey, mon."

"Need a hand?"

"Sure. This stuff don't get no lighter with age."

It took several trips before all of the equipment was in place and Jack could catch his breath. As they stood there together looking out over the harbor, Jack said, "It is gonna to be a smokin' day."

"Sure is, mon," agreed Joshua.

Then in a quiet voice, Jack asked Joshua about Python.

"Jack, mon. We've known each other for a long time, but there are some things we jus' shouldn't be talkin' about."

Jack thought this response a little strange so he pressed on, not sure where it would lead.

"Did Tom get hold of you? I gave him your number. I hope that was all right."

"Yea, mon. He got hold of me and I talk'd to him." He turned and began the process of plugging all of the equipment together. Jack took the hint and moved off to continue his own work in preparation for the crowds that were already building. As he walked off, Joshua gave him a long last look and mumbled under his breath, "I hope you listen to me and stay out of this."

CHAPTER 16

JOSHUA, WE ARE GOING TO TALK. *You're hiding something and you are going to tell me,* Jack thought as he walked off in search of Jimmy, with whom he would be working the door.

It wasn't long before they were too busy and Jack forgot about Joshua. It seemed like an endless stream of people coming in. It was hot and Jack was thankful to be standing under the yellow and white umbrella that was on the front porch of Ben's. It always seemed that there were more women coming in than men, but the reality was that the numbers were pretty much even. Maybe it was just that the women made more of an impression.

Short shorts, miniskirts and loose flowing gauzy skirts, all low slung on hips, showed off flat, well-tanned tummies with bejeweled navels. Tramp stamps tattooed on the smalls of backs that seemed to say "Open for Business" were in abundance. Topside, they were just as provocative with more than a hint of cleavage showing on most.

Bikers and their women, some young, hard and hot, and others who had had more than a few years in the saddle, streamed in. Packs of young studs, well tanned and biceped, arrived with the gleam of hope in their eyes as they surveyed the scene. Couples whose life's high point had been the Caribbean cruise last winter were there hoping to relive those moments of escape. Jack grinned. The delicatessen was open and today business would be brisk.

The tap-tap-tap-tap-boom-da-da-da-da-boom followed by the first sharp note from Joshua announced that the party had begun as they began their first number. The chikka-chikka-vroosh-chunka of the bar's printer provided a counterpoint to Leslie's drums. The whirr of the blender was nearly nonstop. The *kchick* of beers being opened, the *crootsch* of ice being shoveled into plastic cups and the clink of glass as Max and crew grabbed and replaced bottles from the speed rack punctuated by the sharp retort of an empty bottle being added to the recycling bin created their own music and rhythm. The smells of coconut oil, perfume, and now burgers on the grill, assaulted Jack's other senses. The sights, sounds, and smells of a busy Sunday created a near sensory overload and Jack loved it. Reggae Sundays had a life all their own. It was born in the quiet of a perfect morning, it had an intense, loud, active life and then it died until the next week's rebirth.

The band finished their first set and stopped for a break. No one was waiting to get in. "Hey, Jimmy, you okay if I take a quick walkabout?" Jack asked.

"Sure. Go ahead. I'm good."

He couldn't get what Joshua had said, or rather what he hadn't said, out of his mind. He had to talk to him again. The deck was crowded so it took some time to make his way around as he looked for Joshua. Neither he nor the band was there. He headed back and stepped out into the front parking lot and a quick scan netted the same result. No Joshua, no band.

"Hey Jimmy. Did you see if the band came out here after they stopped?" Jack asked.

"Yeah, they came out the gate just as you went in. They headed out back. I think that's where they parked today."

"Thanks."

Jack walked toward the back parking lot. As he came around the corner of building, he saw Joshua's van parked across the street under a tree. Next to the van, he saw that the whole band was there, gathered in a tight group having some kind of a discussion. Curious, he paused and watched for a moment. He could tell that someone else was with them and seemed to be the focal point of their attentions, but he couldn't see who it was so he moved further around the building to change his angle of view without approaching. He stopped again, standing just behind a pine tree that was by the corner of the building and that's when he saw who was with them. "What the hell?" he said to himself.

Now, more curious about what was going on than in talking to Joshua, Jack stepped back and decided to watch from his vantage point. Jack didn't need to hear what was being said, he could tell from the intensity of their body language that something serious was being discussed. And Daniel was in the middle of it. *What was Daniel doing there?*

Right then, a passing car honked its horn at some new arrivals as they prepared to cross the street. The band and Daniel all turned at the sound and for the briefest moment, Jack found himself staring straight at Daniel. Daniel saw him at the same time and their eyes locked. It lasted less than a blink, but it was all that was needed. That moment would change everything.

Jack quickly turned and headed back to his post at the door while Daniel's attentions went back to the band.

"Everything all right?" Jimmy asked.

"Yeah. Why?"

"You've just got this strange look on your face."

Before Jack could answer, a group of giggling, well-tanned and scantily dressed young women arrived and the question was lost as I.D.'s were checked and the cover collected. It wasn't long after that encounter that the band returned. As they walked past the door, past Jack, on the way back to their instruments, there was no indication that anything had transpired. Jack watched them, still wondering what was going on. There was no sign of Daniel. The music started and the dancing began again.

CHAPTER 17

THE REST OF THE DAY WAS relatively uneventful—busy and crowded—but uneventful. The band played their three sets, white guys danced, drunk women in miniskirts did the limbo and pickup lines were everywhere. The afternoon was a success. Jack didn't see Daniel again, and that was just fine as far as he was concerned. By the time the last song was played, Max and Patti had finished their shifts and were relaxing on the deck with the rest of the partygoers. Jack was walking past the bar on his way to escort some departing guests out when he overheard Patti ask Max in hushed tones, "Did you see him today?"

In a low voice, she replied. "No, I didn't. I don't think he was here."

This was a conversation he wasn't supposed to hear and he was sure the girls didn't know that they had been overheard. He noted both disappointment and relief in Max's voice in her reply.

Jack thought to himself as he moved away from the girls, *You didn't see him, but I did.*

As Jack helped finish cleaning up from the day's event, he couldn't get Daniel out of his mind.

He was so working Max last night that she didn't even realize it. "Hi, Max. I hope you don't mind me stopping by like this. I just had to see you." What a crock.

Jack replayed that scene over and over as he debated with himself.

He wants something and she seems interested.

She's not that stupid.

You're not dealing with stupid. You saw the way she and all the other girls look at him. He's good and dollars to donuts he's had lots of practice. He's done this before.

Jack glanced over at Max. Courtney was right. He needed to do something. She needed to know. *Tomorrow.* It was always tomorrow.

Daniel's attraction to Max he could understand. What he didn't understand was the feeling that Daniel was after something else.

What had been going on out back with the band?

The sunset had been spectacular because of the clouds that had gradually moved in during the day and it was nearly dark by the time the band was a packed up and ready to leave. Jack saw Joshua and Leslie standing by the edge of the parking lot looking out over the harbor. He went over. "Hey guys, great day today."

"Oh yeah, it was smokin'," said Joshua.

Leslie nodded his agreement as he sipped from the cup of tea in his hand.

"Can I ask you something?" Jack said.

"Ya mon, what's on your mind?" said Joshua as Leslie sipped.

"Remember earlier today during your first break when you were out back?"

"Ya mon," said Joshua warily.

"I was out back then and saw you. There was a guy you were talking to. Who is he?"

"What you want to know that for, mon?" said Joshua with a defensive tone to his voice. Jack noted this reaction and so he decided on a less direct tack. He didn't think that he needed to let on that he knew who he was. He wanted to see what Joshua and Leslie had to say. "I think he's been hitting on Max. I just want to know who he is and if I need to worry."

Both band members grinned and Joshua said teasingly as they relaxed a little, "Oooh Jack, man, you feeling da jealousy. Some guy chasin' after Max."

"No, that's not it," said Jack also being defensive.

"Yah, I tink dat's what it is. Jack don't want no one messin' wid his woman."

"Max is not my woman, we're just friends and I like to keep an eye out for her. So who was he?"

"He's no one, Jack. Just some guy who wanted to buy one of our CDs."

Joshua was lying. Jack knew it, but he didn't press the point, at least not now.

"So I don't have to worry about him?"

"No, mon. I tink he's just some tourist. Max is yours, Jack. You don have anyting to worry about."

"Thanks, Joshua. Good night. See you guys next week." As Jack walked away he wondered, *What is going on? Daniel's no tourist. He wasn't buying a CD. He's here for something else. What?*

As he walked back inside, he saw Patti standing alone by the bar. He was about to go over to talk to her when Leslie came in and asked, "Got a minute?"

This took Jack by surprise because Leslie didn't usually have much to say and he had remained pretty much silent when Jack had been talking to them only moments before.

"Sure."

"Let's go outside."

As they walked out onto the deck, Jack glanced back and saw Max join Patti by the bar. He'd have to talk to Max later. Leslie led Jack out to the back corner of the deck away from the building, as far from prying eyes as possible, out to where the shadows were the deepest. The clouds that only a few hours before had been all pink and blue as the sun lit them from below, hid the moon. Now, as they thickened for the predicted rain that would arrive tomorrow, any light that might have come from the moon or stars was blocked, and the world was darker than dark and Jack felt a chill.

CHAPTER 18

THE SAME INKY NIGHT THAT HID Jack and Leslie also gave anonymity to Daniel as he sat on a rock overlooking the dark ocean, listening to the surf pound on the rocks below. He needed some time to think about what to do next.

He had intended to go in and see Max today, but after Jack had seen him talking to the band during their break, his plans changed. He couldn't risk the job by getting involved in some kind of a confrontation over a woman. Not now. His employer would not understand. So he left Ben's and drove away.

He had needed to clear his head. The day was still warm when he left, so with the top down on the MG, he drove away from Ben's and away from Max. With the wind turning his hair into a tangled mess, he began to relax. He always found driving back roads, with no particular place to go or to be, truly pleasurable. As the sun began to set, clouds began moving in from the west creating an ever-changing palette of pinks and blues. As the sun dropped below the horizon, those brilliant pinks and blues turned to shades of gray and with each passing mile, the grays deepened until all that remained was blackness. He drove on following that short cone of white light that his headlights carved out of the darkness, for what seemed like moments, but in reality were hours. Eventually, the roads returned him to the ocean, where, after parking his car, he got out and walked, following the sound of the surf and that brought him to the edge of the land. There he sat, on a rock, in the dark, listening to the ocean's incessant *crraroushhh* on the rocks below as he considered his options.

He had come to Rye in search of new talent for his employer. It was supposed to be a simple job. The band that he had been told about was everything he had hoped for. They were young, naïve, and talented. Their local success had not yet gone to their heads. Ambition hadn't yet tainted them. For them, it was still all about the music. It was his job to tempt them, to make them see opportunities and to capture them.

He had done this more times than he could remember and had never had any problems. This time it was different. Two things had happened that were unplanned. Max was one. In all the years he had spent working bars and clubs searching for talent, there had been other women, but none like Max. He couldn't get her out of his mind and he found that unsettling.

The other was Python. They had met in Newport, Rhode Island. Python was a talented vocalist and songwriter looking for the big break and Daniel had been there to give it to him. Gigs materialized, CD's were recorded and released with great fanfare. There was even a New England tour. Python was hot and he owed it all to Daniel, his new best friend. While Python was all wrapped up in the rush of celebrity, contracts were written and signed; contracts that Python thought would propel him to the next level. In reality, they gave Daniel's employer all the rights to his work, past, present and future; contracts that he would not understand fully until it was too late. After all, Daniel was his new best friend who believed in him and Python trusted him.

It had all gone so well. *Damn him. Why did he have to be the one to question things? Why did he have to show up here? Now?* He knew why but didn't want to admit it. He had overlooked the fact that many years ago, Python was a member of the band he was now trying to recruit.

Daniel thought back to those days. He had done his job well and his employer was pleased and it was time for him to move on. He became more distant and increasingly difficult to reach as all that had been going so well for Python began to unravel. Gigs became less frequent and those that he played were in smaller, less well-known clubs.

Recording sessions were less frequent. It was a process calculated to fade Python into obscurity until his successes were only a memory. Most of the performers that Daniel had scammed like this figured that they had had their shot at the big time and didn't make it. They still dreamed, but had accepted the reality that it was not to be, never knowing that it wasn't them or how good their work really was or that someone else owned it.

That's when, quite by chance, Python heard about a new sound that was making it big in Europe and he recognized one of his songs and asked Daniel about it. Feigning disbelief Daniel lied and assured Python that the lawyers would look into it.

The reality was that no one would look into it, certainly not Daniel, but Python didn't know that. After all, Daniel was his friend and agent. It wasn't the first time that his employer had struck it rich in this way, it was just the first time that anyone had asked the right questions which could cause great problems. Python was now more than just a victim, he was a problem, and Daniel's employer would not tolerate problems.

Python had to be silenced and it fell to Daniel to make the arrangements. Before he was able to do that, Python vanished. His employer congratulated him on a job well done. Daniel knew otherwise. He hadn't done anything. He moved on and began pursuing this new band, hoping that a new success might help him forget about Python and the problem his reemergence could create.

All was going well until three weeks ago when Python showed up at Ben's. Daniel thought about that Sunday. He had just arrived in Rye and the band was as good as he had been told. He was considering how to approach them when he saw Python sitting alone at the far end of the deck. He didn't think Python had seen him and he wanted to keep it that way until he could get him alone, so he stayed in the bar watching from a corner table.

That same afternoon, he saw Max for the first time. The band was almost finished for the day. The never-ending line at the bar was beginning to shorten when he first noticed her. She looked exhausted, her hair was a mess, her skin glistened, a combination of sweat and spills and splashes and yet there was something about her that struck him. He tried not to be too obvious but he found it hard not to stare. He had to meet her. This job would keep him here for most of the summer and he didn't intend to spend it alone. That just wasn't his style.

The band finally finished and he decided not to talk to them until after he had taken care of the Python issue. He glanced outside. *Damn it! Where did he go?* he thought. He was still fuming about losing Python when he looked up he saw that the line at the bar was finally gone. So was she. It was not turning out to be a good day. He decided to come back another time to meet her when he was a little more focused.

As he left the bar, he turned and took one last look back for her. He didn't see her. It was at that moment the sharp crash of bottles breaking and bouncing as they hit a hard floor, came from around the corner. He looked around the corner and saw Max, an empty box in hand, its bottom having fallen out and the contents at her feet.

"Fuck," she muttered under her breath as she began picking up the mess without looking up.

He saw his opportunity and walked over. "Let me help you with that."

When she heard his rich, sexy voice she looked up and saw that there had been a witness to her mishap. She blushed, looked down quickly in embarrassment and began picking up the few unbroken bottles and larger pieces of broken glass. "No, no, it's okay. I'll get it," she mumbled. Unprepared for those eyes, the hair and that smile, she felt like a school girl who had just met the guy she had a crush on at the most inopportune moment possible.

That moment when she looked up into his face hit him like a brick—so close, caught in a moment of complete vulnerability, there was something in her expression that left him dumbstruck. Before either of them could recover enough to say anything else, others came to her rescue. A tall, older guy had come to help Max and the moment was over. Daniel left with her face etched into his memory, knowing that she was special and that he had to have her.

He returned the next Sunday, introduced himself, and they had quite a laugh over their first encounter. More importantly, his initial reaction was confirmed and she seemed to respond to him in more than just a polite arm's length way.

In the two weeks since his first Python sighting and the broken box incident, he had had no luck in finding Python, but his luck was holding with Max. Then Python was found floating in the harbor.

At first, Python's death seemed like a blessing. Problem solved. As he reflected on it, doubt began to creep into his mind. He hadn't solved the problem and he didn't know who had. Was it an accident? Was there a new player he didn't know about? He knew that his employer had little patience for failure or problems. Loose ends were not tolerated and this could be a very big loose end. Success was the only option that his employer would accept, so Daniel resolved to concentrate on the job at hand, signing the band, hoping that the Python issue would go away.

While working to sign the band, he would be able to pursue Max and he smiled. That smile quickly faded as one more problem surfaced. *What was his name? Last night, Max introduced us.* He thought hard, and then it came to him. *Jack. That was his name. He seemed nice enough, but today he saw me talking to the band.* The moment in the parking lot flashed through his head as he remembered how Jack had been watching from behind a tree and how he reacted when they saw each other. He shivered. *He was going to have to watch out for him.* This thought was followed quickly by a realization. *Max had really tensed up last night around Jack. What was going on there?*

CHAPTER 19

WHILE DANIEL SAT ON HIS ROCK pondering his problems, Jack and Leslie had their own conversation in a dark corner of the deck.

"What's up, Leslie?" said Jack after they disappeared into the shadows.

In hushed tones he replied, "Jack, you shouldn't be asking all those questions. There is some bad shit going on."

"What are you talking about?"

"Bad shit. You don't want to know."

"Yes, yes I do," said Jack.

There was a long pause, Leslie looked away then he turned back toward Jack, "Understand, we never had this talk." There was a noticeable quiver of fear in his voice.

"Leslie, I understand. Now, what's going on? Does it have anything to do with that guy I saw you talking with this afternoon, Daniel what's-his-name?"

Leslie continued to just stand there, then he turned away again.

Jack reached out and touched his arm, "C'mon, Leslie. Talk to me. Does it have anything to do with Python's murder? What's going on?" There was an urgency in Jack's voice that begged for—demanded—an answer. Leslie turned back and very slowly and in measured tones he merely said, "Yeah. Python's dead and we are in deep shit."

A thousand thoughts raced through Jack's mind as he stood there looking at Leslie. *What happened that caused Python to be killed? What does Daniel have to do with all of this?* At the thought of Daniel, Max's face flashed in his head. The way she had acted when he was in the bar on Saturday night. A voice in his head screamed out, *You asshole! Max is fallin' for this guy and you're not doing anything about it.* Before Jack could say anything else to Leslie, he heard his name being called. Turning, he saw one of the other bartenders standing in the doorway.

"Hey, Jack. We're about to lock up."

"Okay, we're coming." Turning to Leslie he said, "We're through for tonight, but you and I will have to talk again. I'll call you."

"Okay, but remember, this is only between you 'n me."

Jack let Leslie out through the back gate before going into the bar. It took a moment for his eyes to readjust to the bright lights.

"Max and Patti gone?"

"They left quite a while ago. They said to say goodbye."

"Oh," he said. Disappointment filled his heart.

As he walked down the hall toward the door, Courtney called out. "Jack?"

Surprised, he stopped and turned.

"What are you still doing here?"

"I had some work to finish. Can I talk to you for a second?"

"Sure." As he walked toward her, he began to get a queasy feeling in his stomach. Something told him he was going to get another Max lecture.

"Did you talk to Max tonight?"

No. I didn't get the chance. I was busy when she left so I didn't even get to say good night."

She stared at him.

"What?" He stared back.

"Jack, you don't get it, do you?"

"Get what?" He had a feeling where this conversation was going, but he played dumb hoping that he was wrong; he wasn't.

Not one to beat around the bush, she simply said, "You're about to lose her."

"What are you talking about?"

"You're going to lose her."

"Who?" Still playing dumb.

"Max, you idiot."

"What are you talking about?"

"You don't know?"

"No, what?"

"I guess you haven't been around enough lately to notice."

"Notice what?"

"That someone else is interested in her."

He paused. "Who?"

"I guess if you don't know, that proves my point."

He knew, or at least suspected, he just couldn't bring himself to say it. "Who?"

Exasperated, Courtney blurted out, "Daniel."

"What do you mean I haven't been around? I've been around. And why him?"

"Jack, are you stupid? I don't mean 'around' like in not here. You haven't been around for Max. She needs you."

"What are you talking about?"

"Well, for starters, how about last Tuesday when she took you to play mini golf?"

"What does that have to do with anything?"

"God, you're dense. Do you even realize how Max set that whole evening up? It was all a ploy to try and, get something more out of you than just 'Hi Max, sure I'll have a beer.' And you blew it."

He was getting more uncomfortable by the minute. "C'mon. Max knows how I feel about her, she knows that I'll always be there for her."

Before he could say anything else, she cut him off. "That's not enough. Have you ever thought to tell her?" Silence. "I didn't think so. She needs to be told, she needs to be shown. And now this Daniel is all over her and she's just mad enough at you that she might actually fall for him."

"Courtney, I've got to go." He didn't feel like getting beaten up any more. What Leslie had told him, or rather what Leslie hadn't told him about Daniel, worried him. He had noticed Max's reaction to him and he had tried to ignore it. Now he would have to face it, just not tonight, not here, not with Courtney. He couldn't.

"Good night, Court." He turned and walked down the hall and left.

She just looked at him with her mouth open as he walked out. "What the hell is wrong with him?" she said to herself as she watched him leave.

CHAPTER 20

THE SOUND OF RAIN ON THE skylight above his bed awakened Jack. The gray sky matched his mood. Gray. Gray. Gray. Cat was curled up on the foot of his bed, pressed against his leg. Unlike sunny mornings when Cat couldn't wait to get outside, when it was rainy, it was nearly impossible to wake her. Jack moved his leg away from her, she didn't move. He sat up, slumped forward with his hands cradling his head as he tried to get up enough ambition to start the day. A glance up at the clock told him that it was nearly 8:00. He groaned. "This sucks," he said aloud. The rain changed everything. Plans that he had made would need to be changed. His mood went from upbeat to one of funk.

The sound of his voice caused Cat to open one eye. As soon as she located the source of the sound, her ears twitched, she closed her eye, and promptly went back to sleep. Jack marveled at how totally relaxed and comfortable she looked. He wished that he could achieve that same level of contentment, but he knew that he would never be able to be that relaxed. All she needed was food, a roof over her head and a bed to sleep in and she was content. "It's too bad that life can't be that simple."

He made coffee and as he stood in front of the window looking out over the marsh, he reflected on the past few days.

What was up with Max? Saturday night he had gone into the bar to see her and what's-his-name showed up and he had to sit there next to him while Max got all weird. Jack knew that the guy was interested in Max, but it was not uncommon for guys to flirt with her. She would flirt back, but that was part of her job. Was Courtney right? This time the flirting did seem different. She actually seemed interested in him and that worried Jack. Courtney had been on his case about Max, Patti was on his case, even the band had said something to him about how he shouldn't take Max for granted, otherwise he would find himself watching her walk away.

Daniel. That was his name. There was something about him that bothered Jack and it didn't have anything to do with Max—at least not at first blush. *What was he doing with the band out back?* When he spied Jack watching him, the look he returned was not the look of innocent conversation. *Where had he disappeared to? He never came back in to hit on Max.* He recalled his conversation with Joshua, how closed he had become, how he didn't want to talk about Daniel, and how he had tried to brush him off. Then Leslie came back and wanted to talk in private after everyone had gone.

That's when the phone rang. As he crossed the room to answer it, Cat stood, stretched and promptly curled back up. "Hello," said Jack.

"Hi, Jack." He recognized Tom's voice. "You up yet?"

"I answered the phone didn't I?"

"No need to be so touchy. Any chance you could stop down at the station today?"

"Why? What's up?"

"I've got some information about your corpse."

"What information? And it wasn't my corpse."

"My, aren't we cranky? Come on down and I'll tell you all about it when you get here."

Jack was curious now. "What time?"

"How about noon? I'll order some lunch," said Tom.

"Sounds good. I'll see you then."

Jack hung up the phone. His mood was improving with the prospect of . . . well, something. He hoped that it would help answer some questions.

"Cat, something strange is going on."

Cat, totally unconcerned, merely did a little re-snuggle without even opening an eye and kept on sleeping.

CHAPTER 21

THE RAIN CAME DOWN STEADILY, no wind, just rain. It washed all colors away, remaking the world in shades of gray which matched Jack's mood as he left to go meet Tom. The five-minute ride to the station took closer to ten because of the rain. Jack felt damp, the result of the short walk from his apartment to the truck, so he was in no hurry to get out when he reached the station. He sat in his truck for a moment, hoping that there would be a sudden lull in the rain. His thoughts stuck on all that he had learned in the past few days. There was no lull. He leapt from his truck, sprinted and splashed though the puddles and into the station. As he shook the rain off his coat, Tom appeared.

"Hey, Jack. Thanks for coming down. Nice day, isn't it?"

"Not really."

"Well, we need the rain."

"Right."

Tom turned and headed for his office and Jack followed after hanging up his coat. Jack followed asking, "So what's up?"

"You hungry? I ordered some subs and they'll be here soon. Italian good for you?" Tom replied as he went into his office.

"Sure. That's fine. You didn't answer my question," replied Jack.

"Have a seat."

"Thanks," said Jack as he sat down looking at Tom expectantly. "So what's up? Why the big mystery?"

Tom looked across the desk at Jack, leaned back in his chair, reached out and picked up a folder, and opened it. He looked inside, then began.

"I have some background on the dead guy that I think you will find interesting as well as the coroner's report."

"Okaay," said Jack as he drew out the word.

Tom went on. ". . . Python, real name Anthony Williams, age 32, parents Jamaican immigrants who became U.S. citizens. He was born in Newport, Rhode Island, but his family moved from there to Virginia when he was in the sixth grade. They still live there. Stable family, by all accounts a good kid. Went to college, studied music, wanted to be a musician. Seemed to have some talent. Just after graduating from college, he hooked up with Joshua and joined the band on vocals. He sang with them for less than a year. That's when you first heard him. As I recall, you told me that he was pretty good. After he left the band, things get a little fuzzier. Jack interrupted again. "What does this have to do with anything?"

Tom held up his hand in a way that said, "Have patience."

"Let's see, where was I? . . . We know that he continued to work in the music business. His parents confirmed that he was living back in Newport, and that his career was beginning to take off. He was signed by a small indie label released his first CD and was beginning to show some success. Then things get a little weird."

At this moment, there was a knock on the door and the receptionist stuck her head in and said, "Lunch is here. Do you want it here or in the conference room?"

"Here is fine," said Tom.

The subs were deposited on the desk.

The smell of the subs as they were unwrapped made Jack realize just how hungry he was.

The story was put on hold as they both bit into their subs. While still chewing, Tom continued. "His parents . . . mmm, that's good."

Jack nodded in agreement as he took another bite.

"His parents," Tom started again, "told me that the last time they saw him, something didn't seem right. He just wasn't the same. He wouldn't talk to them about it. He put up a good front, but they were sure that something was wrong. Whenever they asked him about how his music was going, he would say okay and change the subject quickly. The last time they saw him was last spring and other than a couple of quick phone calls, they hadn't seen him since."

"This is all very interesting," said Jack, "But what does it have to do with me?"

"I'm getting there. I finally talked to Joshua, by the way, thanks for his number. He is one hard person to get hold of. Anyway, I finally talked to him. He was reluctant at first, but after I filled him in on some of what I had learned about Python's activities, he seemed to relax and was more willing to talk. Apparently, they had kept in touch off and on over the years after he left the band and a couple of months ago he called Joshua and told him that he had to see him. Joshua said that he sounded strange over the phone; actually his exact words were "scared shitless." He needed to see Joshua in person, but wouldn't say anything else other than he'd be up sometime during the summer, and that he had some things to take care of first. Joshua said that he was very cloak and dagger and said he'd see him whenever he made it up.

Python did finally show up. That's when you first saw him hanging out at Ben's. Apparently, they got together and Python told Joshua how his life, Python's that is, was in danger and that he should be careful as well. He didn't tell me why Python felt threatened or why he had to be careful, but I'm guessing that it had to do with their music somehow. That seems to be the only common thread between them."

As Jack listened to Tom's narrative, he began thinking about what he knew about Python, the band, what Leslie had and hadn't told him, and of Daniel. Somehow, he knew in his gut that they were all linked together, he just didn't see how.

Tom continued, "According to the coroner, he died from drowning, but there was no obvious sign of a struggle. There was some bruising on the back of his head so it looks more likely that he may have been knocked unconscious and either thrown into or fell into the water where he drowned. Or, it may have been accidental. But how do you hit yourself in the back of the head, or fall, hitting the back of your head and then land in the water and drown? And where could that happen? Doesn't seem likely considering where he was found, especially since he probably floated down to where you found him from the marsh."

Tom noticed that Jack seemed distracted. "Jack." Tom said sharply, "Jack, did you hear what I was telling you?" Jack replied, "Yes, I did, and I agree that something is going on here."

"No, Jack, I was telling you what the coroner found."

"Yeah . . . yeah, you were saying he drowned and that it looked like someone hit him over the head."

Tom leaned forward, across the desk and pushing his sub wrapper aside he said, "Jack are you all right? Is there something you're not telling me? You seem distracted."

"No, I'm okay. Sorry."

"Can I ask you to help me get some answers? I could use your help."

"Sure. Of course I will." Jack was still a little distracted with his own thoughts."

"You sure you're all right?"

"Yeah, I'm fine." He said, even though he couldn't get Daniel out of his head. He wanted to find out more before he told Tom about him. This was personal.

"Great. How's your sandwich?"

CHAPTER 22

THE RAIN CONTINUED TO FALL, having little or no effect on the thickness of the atmosphere. Jack sat in his truck, defrosters on, waiting for the windshield to clear. The grayness of the world didn't seem quite as depressing as when he had arrived. Now the rain just gave accent to the air of mystery that was swirling around inside Jack's head. Impatient to get going, he wiped the inside of the windshield with his hand, leaving a wet circle, just clear enough to look out. He shifted into gear. He decided that he needed to talk to Max.

Even though it was only late afternoon, the lot at Ben's was empty save for her car. He really wanted to talk to Max and thought that now might be a good time. When he walked into the bar, he didn't see anyone. No customers, no Max, no Patti, no one. He took a seat at the bar and just waited, still lost in his thoughts. He was brought back to the present when he heard his name called out. It was Patti.

"Hi, Jack. What are you doing here?"

"Hey, Patti. I just stopped by to see Max. Is she around?"

"No, she's off today."

"Her car's here."

This statement caught her off guard. "Oh, . . . I drove her home last night."

Jack didn't remember seeing her car in the lot when he drove by earlier in the day and his expression must have signaled to her that he suspected she was lying.

Quickly trying to change the subject she said, "Are you all right, Jack? You seem a little preoccupied."

"I'm fine. Where's Max?"

"Don't know. I haven't seen her."

He stared at her then tried again, "Any idea what she's up to?"

Patti hesitated for just a split second before answering.

"No, I haven't heard from her."

Jack had picked up on her hesitation. "Patti, come on, don't bullshit me. Where is she?"

"Jack. I can't tell you. Please don't ask."

He continued to stare at her. He was getting a bad feeling and he had his suspicions. He could tell it was killing her to keep quiet.

"You're right, Patti. It's not fair of me to put you in this position. How about a beer?"

"ESB?"

"Sure."

She drew the beer and placed it in front of him. He took a sip and looked up at Patti and said quietly. "I really blew it, didn't I?"

"Oh, Jack. You haven't blown anything yet."

"Yet?"

"You are still very dear to Max. She's just a little frustrated that you haven't been a little more, ahh, shall we say, attentive."

"Patti, you know me. It's hard for me to open up. I just thought that Max and I had an understanding."

"Jack, you are such a guy. A girl needs to be paid attention to. She needs to feel special. She needs to be reassured occasionally."

"So you keep telling me. I thought that Max knew."

"She needs more Jack. You haven't lost her . . ." She didn't say it, but Jack heard it in her pause, "yet."

Then she continued, "I don't think that that will ever be possible."

"So where is she?" he tried again.

She didn't bite. "I don't know."

"Fine." Jack wanted to believe her, but deep down inside he knew that she was lying. His gut told him that it had to do with Daniel.

Why else would she be so reluctant to tell him where Max was? Patti didn't volunteer any more information and Jack didn't ask again. He sat sipping his beer while she walked off to greet the first customers of the night. *Daniel. There was something not right about him.* Jack was concerned and he just hoped that it wasn't too late. He finished his beer, said goodbye and went home with his thoughts.

CHAPTER 23

WHILE JACK HAD SPENT HIS DAY with Tom and his thoughts, Daniel had also been busy. He left his rock when the first drops of rain began to fall. The top on his car was secured and he returned to his motel room for some much needed sleep. As his eyes closed, his day danced around in his mind. *Python, was dead—how? And more importantly, who? He thought he knew the why. The look Jack flashed him when he was taking to the band, his employers instructions, and finally Max.* As he fell into a deep sleep, the last image in his mind was of Max.

By the time he awakened, it was early afternoon. It was raining hard, but not storming. He looked out the window at the parking lot. Most of the places were still occupied. "Tough day to be on vacation," he thought. Standing there, his thoughts returned to Max. Days like this could go two ways. They could leave you feeling really alone and isolated or if you were with the right person, they could create a feeling of closeness and intimacy. He didn't want to be alone; he wanted to be with Max.

It took him a while, but he finally found her phone number. As he dialed, his heart was pounding, his mouth was dry and he could feel his face flushing. It was as if he was sixteen and calling a girl for the first time. He nearly hung up before hitting the last number, but a deep breath and a little self-chastisement allowed him to hit that number. The phone rang, once . . . twice . . . and on the third ring, she answered. "Hello." She sounded like she wasn't fully awake. The sound of her voice almost struck Daniel dumb, but he recovered.

"Hi Max, it's me, Daniel."

There was a short pause while she processed this information.

"Daniel . . . What a surprise." She didn't know whether to be excited or concerned.

"I'm not interrupting anything, am I?"

"No, I was just sitting here reading. Rainy days make me lazy."

"Me, too." he replied.

"Daniel, how did you get my number?" she asked with some hesitancy.

He didn't answer her question but asked one of his own. "Max, how would you like to spend the rest of this rainy day with me? It's not the kind of day to spend alone. I thought we could take a drive up to the mountains. I've never really been up north and I thought it might be fun."

This stopped her short. She didn't say anything while she gathered her thoughts, then she answered.

"I really can't," she said, while thinking *Of course you can. Go for it.*

"Oh, come on Max. It's pouring buckets. Surely you don't intend to sit in and read all day." He was expert at walking that fine line between begging and convincing. After another pause, she laughed and gave in. "Oh, all right."

"Great, how about I pick you up in an hour?"

"Why don't we meet at Ben's and we can go from there?" As attracted to him as she was, and as nice as he seemed, she really didn't know him very well. She hadn't given him her phone number and he really hadn't answered her question about how he got it.

"That sounds great. I'll meet you in an hour."

"Make it an hour and a half," she countered.

"Okay. An hour and a half it is. See you then. Bye."

"Bye."

When he hung up, his heart was pounding even more than before. She had said yes. That was easier than he thought it would be. Now, the question was, where to go? He went to the motel office and picked up some brochures to try and come up with an itinerary.

CHAPTER 24

AS SHE HUNG UP THE RECEIVER, she sat there in stunned silence for a moment before quickly dialing Patti's number. The phone only rang twice before Patti answered. "Patti! You'll never guess what just happened. He called me. I don't know how he got my number, but he called me. He asked me out and I said yes."

Patti was a little overwhelmed by this outburst since the phone's ringing had just awakened her.

"Max? Who called? Slow down and tell me what are you talking about?"

"He called . . . Daniel. Daniel called and asked me if I would go for a drive up to the mountains with him."

"No! Really? When?"

"Today. We're meeting at Ben's in an hour and a half."

"Max, have you thought this out. I mean you hardly know the guy. What about Jack? What's he going to think?"

"I know. But it's not like we are dating or anything. He's been kind of . . . you know . . . out there since he found that body. You're not going to tell him are you? Promise me you won't tell him anything."

"Okay, okay, I promise, but what are you going to tell him?"

"I'll think of something. But right now I have to get ready. Bye."

"Call me as soon as you get home."

"I will."

"Promise."

"I promise I'll call you as soon as I get home. Now I've got to get going. Kisses. Bye again."

"Bye."

Max hung up the phone and faced her closet. What should she wear? It was raining, but they'd be in his car. It might be cooler up north. What if they went out to dinner? While she contemplated her wardrobe options, she made a cup of tea and ate a toasted bagel with cream cheese and strawberry jelly. She didn't want her stomach grumbling. By the time she finished the bagel, she had narrowed her options. She didn't want to be too provocative, and yet she did want to catch his eye. Finally, she decided on a pair of khaki slacks that she knew made her look good from any angle, her running shoes, a pale yellow shirt, and she'd bring her rain coat and a sweater. Decisions made, food eaten, a quick shower, hair, nails, makeup. By the time she had finished and given herself a good review in the mirror, it was time to get going.

The rain was not letting up, so the drive to Ben's was slower than normal. Deliberately, she hadn't left herself enough time to get there on time. A few minutes late was good. It was early afternoon and there weren't many cars in the lot on this rainy afternoon. As she turned into the parking lot, she scanned the other cars looking for his. His was on the far side of the lot. She drove over and parked next to it. Before she could get out, he had jumped out of his car, opened an umbrella and came around to her door. Seeing this, she thought that there were some things about first dates that always happened. Car doors being opened were one of them. As the door opened she said, "Thank you, Daniel. You didn't have to do that. You're getting soaked."

"It's okay, I won't shrink. Come on, get in before you get soaked."

"Thanks." He walked her around to the passenger side door of his car, opened it and she slid into the passenger seat. He closed the door and while he went around to get in himself, she looked around. She had never been in a car like this before. It was tiny, the walnut dash was pitted and scarred and yet glowed with a high gloss finish. As she looked out the tiny windshield, she noticed how the rain made the dark green hood shine and shimmer. It seemed so long. The seats were leather and there was a coziness to it that made it the perfect car for this day. His door opened and he tucked the umbrella behind his seat and then squeezed himself in behind the wheel and quickly shut his door. Her warmth had begun to fog up the windows and his completed the job. She looked over at him, rain dripping off that dark, wavy hair of his. As he turned the key in the ignition, he looked back at her with those amber eyes and said, "Thanks for coming."

She replied, "Thanks for asking."

As the engine roared to life, he looked at the fogged windshield and said, "It'll be a moment before we can see enough to leave." Then he twisted around and pulled a towel out from behind the seat and offered it to her.

"No thanks, I'm fine."

"You don't mind if I do?"

"No, of course not."

He faced straight ahead and began to dry his face and hair, Max glanced over at him. She didn't intend to stare, but she couldn't help herself. He was better looking than she had remembered and the way he matter-of-factly toweled off affected her in an unexpected way. She quickly looked away and blushed. What had she gotten herself into?

When he finished, he used the towel to wipe off the windshield, turned and tossed the towel behind the seat. He looked at her, smiled, and then without a word, shifted into gear and drove off.

She was about to ask him to stop and let her out when he said, "You know, I've never been to the mountains here in New Hampshire. Have you?" Before she could reply he added, "Sorry, dumb question, of course you have."

"No, it's not a dumb question," she replied, "I have, but it's been a while and I don't know them very well."

"Perfect. That will make this into an adventure for both of us."

It was late when they returned to the parking lot at Ben's. Her car was still there and the lot was empty. The rain had finally stopped but the pavement was still wet. When he turned the engine off, they could hear the surf crashing on the jetties, overlaid with the peeps of marsh frogs and crickets that were still celebrating the rain. They turned toward each other and simultaneously began saying, "Thank you, it was such a wonderful day." Max giggled first and Daniel laughed. He said, "You go first."

"No, you," was her reply.

"Max, I had a wonderful day. Thank you."

"I did, too. Thank you."

He leaned toward her. She didn't pull away and their lips met. It was a gentle kiss, a tease. Her heart was pounding and she dared not breathe as she waited for another. Instead, he reached over, brushed his fingers across her cheek and while looking deep into her eyes whispered, "Thank you for a wonderful day."

Before she could reply, he opened his door, got out, went around the car and opened her door for her. He offered her his hand as she climbed out and then they were standing there, face to face. She looked up at him and he down on her. They embraced and kissed again, this time a little deeper and longer.

Max pulled away, trying to catch her breath. "I've got to get going."

Daniel's heart was pounding in his ears and he was also trying to catch his breath.

"Yes, we should both get going."

He opened the door on her car for her and then closed it slowly after she got in. She started the engine, looked out the window at him, gave a little wave and drove off, leaving him standing there next to his car.

As Max drove off, her mind was in a jumble. The day had been perfect, despite the rain. Daniel was a perfect gentleman. He was funny and spontaneous and just too good to be true. Then she thought about Jack and she began to feel guilty for having enjoyed the day so much.

CHAPTER 25

JACK LEFT THE BAR AND WENT HOME. Patti had lied to him. He was sure of it, but he also knew that he would never accuse her of doing so. Cat was waiting for him, insisting on supper. He fed her, opened a beer, sat down and looked out the window. There were so many thoughts and emotions bouncing around in his head that his mind was blank. So there he sat, beer in hand, staring out into the darkness at . . . at what? He didn't know. He must have fallen asleep, because he suddenly jerked himself conscious. His beer was warm and undrunk in his hand and the clock read well past midnight.

"Enough of this bullshit," he mumbled as he got up, poured the beer out in the sink and fell into bed. As he lay there fully awake, his thoughts turned to Max. She had been his best friend almost from the moment they first met. Back then she was too young, or so he thought so he became her family, her brother, her father, her uncle. He had been through this before whenever she began dating someone new. It always hurt, but not like this time. This time it was different. He had saved her life last winter. They had gone to Bern, Switzerland together so that she could claim her inheritance and they had crossed the line. It had been so right there. Why had it become so different here? Since their return, it was as if they had to conform to everyone's expectations, not to their own. They had changed. Their relationship had changed. They would always be there for each other, but now there was a new force working its way into their lives. Daniel. Jack knew it, although he didn't want to face it, at least not yet, not openly. There was something about him that worried Jack. It was just a feeling, but he was rarely wrong whenever he felt it.

CHAPTER 26

AS SOON AS MAX GOT HOME, she called Patti. Patti was still up and was waiting for the call. She would have killed Max if she hadn't called.

"Oh my god, you won't believe what a day I've had." gushed Max.

"Tell me everything. What was he like? What did you do? What did you talk about? Did he kiss you? Tell me . . . tell me."

And Max did. They talked for nearly an hour when Max finally said, "Patti, I've got to get some sleep. I'm really tired and it's late."

"Okay, I'll let you go. I'm so excited. Oh, I almost forgot to tell you. Jack stopped in this afternoon looking for you. He saw your car and when I told him that I had taken you home last night, I don't think he believed me. He seemed a little upset."

"How upset?

"Well upset in a depressed sort of a way, not the 'I'm pissed and I'm going to do something stupid' kind of way."

Max was silent for a moment.

"Max, you still there?"

"Yeah Patti, I'm still here,"

"You all right?"

"Yeah, goodnight."

Patti heard the connection go dead as she said, "Goodnight."

As Max sat there, her elation was consumed by guilt. Jack knew. This situation wasn't new, but this time it was different. Their relationship was closer than many committed couples. They had met when she moved to the seacoast all those years ago. Neither was comfortable with a dating relationship due to the difference in their ages, so a deep friendship had developed. They grew to love each other, as family, not as lovers. That had changed last winter when he had saved her life. They both had realized how dear to one another each was. In Switzerland, they had been in a strange romantic place, outside of their normal world, and it was just the two of them. It had been an intense, passionate, emotional two weeks. After their return home, under the constant scrutiny of all their friends, things slowly reverted back to the way they had been before, only now there was the memory of Switzerland.

In the past, whenever Max had begun dating someone new, Jack would be hurt, in a brotherly, protective sort of way and when things went badly, he was always there to help her pick up the pieces. She knew that this time it would be different and she didn't know what to do. Sleep, that healing balm, was slow in coming and when it finally took her, it was a troubled sleep.

CHAPTER 27

ONE NIGHT SEVERAL WEEKS INTO his cruise, anchored in a small unnamed cove somewhere on the coast of Maine, clarity came to him. Jack knew where he had to go and what he had to do to find the answers. At dawn, he pulled up his anchor and set his new course.

The sunrise on this crisp fall morning had promised a spectacular end to his journey to Newport, and it was. Now with the sun beginning to set, after passing Brenton Reef Light and leaving the string of red buoys to starboard, he entered the East Passage as he made the final approach to Newport Harbor.

The anticipation of arriving somewhere new was exhilarating and his fatigue was forgotten. The water is deep as East Passage threads between Aquidneck Island to the east and Conanicut Island to the west. The contrast between the two shores is striking; to the east, man dominates the landscape with manicured lawns and stately mansions that have pushed Mother Nature to the edge, where she holds on with acres of wild roses. The western side of the channel belongs to her. Craggy rocks pounded by the incessant surf provide a constant reminder of what once was.

Both shores were deserted except for the ever-present gulls. There were no throngs of tourists lining the shore to witness Jack's arrival. The summer tourist season in Newport had ended. Jack could tell that the winter haul out had begun by the number of empty moorings. Many of the remaining boats were stripped of sails and were just waiting patiently for their turn to be pulled out of the water, out of their natural element. No longer would they be beautiful and alive, free to bob and sway with the wind and water. Restrained and exposed, they would endure the cold winter, waiting for that day in the spring when once again they would touch the water and return to life.

He anchored near Fort Adams, just to the south of the Ida Lewis Yacht Club. Even though there were plenty of moorings available, tonight he preferred to anchor. Tomorrow he would contact Olde Port Marine Services and arrange for a mooring closer to town. They also provided a launch service so going ashore would not be a problem. Securely on the hook, his anchor light on, he made one turn around *Irrepressible* making sure that all was in order, paused to marvel at the sunset then descended into the cabin for some food and drink.

Opening a bottle of red wine, he filled two glasses. One was for himself, that one he'd drink, the other was an offering to his boat and to the sea. He raised his glass and looking around the cabin said, "*Irrepressible*, you're a good boat, thank you." He took a sip.

Then, picking up the second glass, he climbed up into the cockpit and as the last moments of light faded, he left the cockpit and stood by the stays where he raised the glass, held it out over the water in a gesture of salutation, paused reverently, and poured some of it into the water then drank the rest.

Jack didn't consider himself a particularly superstitious person, but where the sea was concerned, he was cautious. Unlike the land, which is pretty much unmoving and constant, the sea is alive, always in motion, never the same from moment to moment. Thousands of years of experience had taught mariners to respect the sea, and if some of that respect seemed like superstition, then that was fine with Jack. It was mere common sense to cover all of one's bases.

He returned below and he scrounged through the ice chest for some food. The wine began to take hold and he suddenly realized just how tired and hungry he was. There wasn't much left in the cooler; a piece of leftover roasted chicken, some bread and a small piece of Brie would have to do. As meager as his dinner seemed, it was sufficient and delicious. After he finished eating, he cleaned up what little mess there was, doused the cabin lights, took the bottle of wine, and went back up into the cockpit where he proceeded to sit, sip, and think.

It amazed him how peaceful everything was. There wasn't as much boating traffic now as there would have been in the summer, but Newport was still a busy harbor surrounded by a busy city. As he sat there drinking his wine, he could barely hear voices and laughter in the distance, punctuated by the clinking of glass as others on shore were enjoying this perfect evening. There was only the faintest breeze rippling the water's surface, making the reflections of lights from shore twinkle like the stars. Boats never sit still; even at rest, they are always dancing. Tonight, for Jack, it was a slow sensuous dance. *Irrepressible* was seducing him. His eyes grew heavy from the wine and his mind began to drift into the mosaic of dreams. She made him feel safe and secure. He was in the womb of a soft enveloping bed, with overstuffed covers. He could feel his lover next to him, her head resting on his shoulder, their skin just touching, so smooth, so warm. The scent of her hair was intoxicating.

CLUNK! The sound of the empty wine bottle falling onto the cockpit sole awakened him from that other lovely place. It took a second for him to realize where he was. It was cold and dew covered everything. It was late; the voices from shore were gone and there weren't so many lights twinkling on the water's surface. Jack picked up the empty bottle, staggered down into the cabin and climbed into his berth.

CHAPTER 28

IT WAS DIFFERENT DOWN BELOW. In the cockpit, you were exposed, vulnerable, the sounds of the world around you were ever present. Below, it was different. There was a feeling of closeness, of security and safety. It was a retreat back into the womb where the sounds of the outside world were muffled, replaced by the soft gurgling of water against the hull of the vessel that protected you.

As Jack lay in his berth, sleep returned and with it dreams and memories. He was bathed in the heat and fragrances of the Caribbean. Marie was beside him and he was at peace. Then there was an explosion, a loud sound and she was gone. The emptiness in his heart was crushing. Then Tom appeared and saved him from himself by bringing him north, to New England. It was as if he had been given a new life. Tom. Courtney. Then there was someone else in the dream.

At first he couldn't see who it was. It was Max. Then, as time passed she came to him and he to her. It was as if Marie had chosen her for him. Peace had returned to his life, but that peace was short lived. Another force became present, a dark force. At first he could only feel it, then slowly it took hold of Max and began to pull her away. Jack was powerless, paralyzed as he watched that force take form and seduce Max.

He broke free.

CRACK! A sharp pain ran from his forehead down through his neck and shoulders. His head smashed into the ceiling above his berth and reality transcended his dream. He fell back and lay there trembling and breathing hard as the dream which had been so clear and real began to disintegrate. The only image that remained clear was that of Daniel.

This wasn't the first time Jack had had this dream. Each time, he had seen Daniel's face, although usually his awakening wasn't quite so violent. As the pain in his head lessened, he drifted back into sleep.

CHAPTER 29

FOUR WEEKS HAD PASSED SINCE HE had split the breakwaters and sailed out of Rye Harbor. At the time of his departure, he had no intended destination, only the need to get away. He turned left and sailed north up the Maine coast. He needed time, time alone to figure out what he could or should do. Sailing, like running, was an escape for Jack. Though unlike running, where the almost self-hypnotic rhythms of his footsteps on the pavement and his steady deep breathing would allow his subconscious to wander, often helping him solve problems and make decisions, sailing had an added dimension: it was healing.

Each passing day he felt more whole again. The pain of losing Max was still with him, but he was beginning to come to terms with it. He had begun to understand that it wasn't Max or Daniel or anyone else. He had only himself to blame and he had to accept that.

Max, Daniel, Python's death, the band, advice from Courtney, advice from Patti, all crowded his thoughts, especially Daniel. *What was it about him?* That question haunted him.

It was more than just the fact that he had stolen Max away. It was something else. The longer Jack sailed, the more certain he became that under that polished veneer of the handsome, likeable, too good to be true person that everyone saw, there was a different Daniel, a dangerous Daniel. Max was in danger and Jack felt that he was the only one who knew it.

Irrepressible had taken care of him after Marie's death and had made him whole again. When he sailed out of Rye, his hope was that she would be able to work her magic again. For four weeks, his world measured thirty-nine feet by ten and a half. No longer was he the moving object in a static world, but rather the constant in a fluid, moving world where no two moments are alike.

While Jack's conscious self was continuously busy with the job of sailing, his subconscious was free to roam. The ever-changing textures, sights, and smells were like spices in a stew of memories, swirling and sloshing, mixing and remixing until some connection was made, until something unexpected appeared. That night, anchored in that isolated Maine cove, he tasted the stew.

Irrepressible had worked her magic and now he was asleep, anchored in Newport, Rhode Island, knowing what he was going to do. Max, Python's murder, Daniel and the band were all tied together like some Gordian knot and it was up to him to untie it. This is where he would start.

CHAPTER 30

SUNLIGHT STREAMED THROUGH THE portlight and slowly swept back and forth over Jack's face like a prison spotlight as *Irrepressible* swung on her anchor. With difficulty, he pried his eyes open, the light burned into his throbbing head and for a moment he had no idea where he was or how he got there. Slowly it came to him. He was in Newport; he had arrived last night. He drank too much wine and his head hurt. As the sun made another pass across his face, he raised his arm to shield his eyes and in doing so brushed his forehead, which sent a wave of pain through his head. Clarity returned. Last night's dreams flashed through his mind. He remembered sitting up quickly only to be driven down by the cabin ceiling. Nature was calling, so he carefully sat up. That's when he felt the full impact of last night's wine. He would have lain back down except that he really had to pee. Gingerly he stood and swayed. "Whoa," he said.

The high-pitched whine of a small outboard assaulted his ears. Before he made it into the head, its wake slapped the topsides of his boat and the swaying increased. He still felt woozy. Steadying himself, he looked out and saw a very small dinghy with two large people in it arriving at their destination: a large red-hulled sloop moored about a hundred feet away. Its sails had already been stripped. Jack watched them climb onto the sloop and disappear below. Haul out time in the fall always made Jack a little melancholy. It signaled the ending of the warm days and pleasant sails and was the harbinger of winter. He knew that he would be doing the same soon. One last glance at the sloop and he made his way into the small head and peed.

He took a look into the mirror and mumbled, "You look like shit." A splash of cold water in his face, then, he brushed his teeth. As he forced a hairbrush through the bed-headed, wind-tangled and salt-tinged mess on his head, he winced as the brush hit the bruise on his head.

"I need coffee," he mumbled as he left the head.

As the coffee brewed, Jack climbed out of the cabin and up into the cockpit. Goosebumps appeared on his arms as the coolness of a crisp fall day washed over him. Everything was covered with early morning dew so he stood in the center of the cockpit rubbing his arms and turned slowly, surveying his surroundings and thought, *I hope he's around. It'll be good to see him again.*

He was John Burney. They had met many years ago at Ben's. John had been on his way down Maine when the weather had turned sour and he sailed into Rye Harbor to wait out the storm. Jack met him in the bar. He was cold, wet and tired. Jack recognized a kindred spirit and became his self-appointed host and they became instant friends. John had intended for his stay to be only a day or so, but it stretched into a week, as the weather was slow to clear. Jack's place became John's home away from home as Jack invited him to crash there until the storm passed. Days were divided between preparing for the continuation of his trip and more mundane tourist activities. Many nights were spent sampling the nightlife around the seacoast. John was an accomplished musician. He played blues harmonica and on several nights out, he jammed with some of the local bands. The weather finally cleared and with promises to keep in touch, John sailed out of Rye Harbor.

CHAPTER 31

THE SMELL OF FRESH BREWED COFFEE wafted up from the cabin. Chilly, Jack retreated below for a sweater and his coffee. The smell alone made him feel better and that first sip was heavenly. Sweater on, he grabbed a towel, his coffee, and went back outside, dried off a seat and sat down to slowly start the day.

His thoughts drifted back to the events that had brought him to Newport. Ben's had had a busy summer season. The weather had been almost perfect except for a few late summer rainy days. It was one of those rainy days when Jack knew that he was beginning to lose Max. Daniel had asked Max out and she went, but that wasn't where it all started.

It was that Sunday, several weeks after Python's death, when he had wanted to talk to Joshua about Python. He found the band out back talking with Daniel. Daniel caught him watching and their eyes locked for just a split second. It was then that he had known Daniel was trouble.

He began hitting on Max and she fell for him. In the past, whenever Max had fallen for someone new, she and Jack had always remained close. She would talk with him about her new man and he would listen. Those others had never seemed a threat to Jack. He always knew they would fade away in time. Daniel was different. This time it felt different.

What was this power he had over her?

The closer that Daniel got to Max and the more accepted he was by her friends, the more certain Jack became that Daniel was involved with everything that had gone on. Jack couldn't stand by and watch so he stayed away from Ben's as much as possible. It had seemed that whatever he did, it was wrong. His frustration had grown each time she went out with Daniel until it had become nearly impossible even to talk to her. Her happiness and his misery seemed to wax and wane in synch.

Every Sunday Daniel was there, waiting for Max to finish work and they would go off together. Tom's investigation of Python's death had stalled. Little more had been found out beyond what Tom had told him on that rainy day. The band wouldn't talk about Python. Jack finally quit asking; it wasn't worth the animosity that was growing between himself and the band. Daniel's continued interest in the band didn't go unnoticed. Often when the band would take a break, Daniel would disappear from his usual spot in the bar. At first, this didn't seem unusual, as everyone after a few beers had to heed nature's call. It wasn't until Jack had seen him out back with the band a second time that he became more suspicious.

What the hell was going on?

The final straw for Jack was when he found out that Daniel had asked Max to accompany him to Boston for some charity ball or something. He had spent the day helping his friend Terry installing a new engine in a boat. Terry was the local mechanic and from time to time, Jack would help him out when he needed another pair of hands. It had been a long day and he was hot and tired. Out of habit, he stopped at Ben's on the way home for a beer. Max wasn't there. She had the night off and Courtney was in the bar.

"Hey, Jack. You look beat. What have you been doing?"

"Hi, Court. I was helping Terry install an engine in a boat down at the marina."

"Who's Terry?"

Before she could say anything else, he added, "You remember him. Tall, good looking guy, soft-spoken, southern accent. He's stopped in a few times. I know I introduced you."

She still had no clue who he was talking about, but it was easier to pretend she did. "Oh yeah, I remember him. Nice guy." Then abruptly changing the subject she said, "Have you seen Max lately?"

Jack didn't like this turn in the conversation, but he was trapped. Courtney had been on his case ever since Daniel began showing interest in Max to get off his ass and go after her. Courtney knew he loved her and she kept telling him that Max loved him. Jack had tried, but his efforts always seemed too little and too late. The drama of the situation was inflamed by all of the girls at Ben's. Daniel was the hot new guy and they all wanted him, but he was interested in Max so they had to be content to live out the fantasy through her, so the affair was encouraged. At the same time, they knew Jack was the true blue nice guy who was being pushed aside. It was all too soapy and juicy to leave to the actual principals to work out.

"Jack, did you hear me?

He looked up. "Yeah, I heard you, and no, I haven't seen her lately."

"You haven't heard, have you?"

Now Courtney was feeling awkward. She had assumed that Jack knew about the invitation and she just wanted to be a friend in case he wanted to talk about it. Now she realized that he was clueless and she had to be the one to break the news.

"Well, uh, I thought you knew."

"Knew what?" Jack was beginning to get a little annoyed.

She inhaled, then let it all out and said. "I thought you knew. I'm sorry. Daniel has asked Max to go to a big charity ball down in Boston in a few weeks. Everyone is all excited. You know how they all get."

This hit Jack like a sucker punch. He tried to act as if it didn't really matter and he was okay with it. Courtney knew different. And before he could say anything she continued. "Jack, it's not too late, you know. Go talk to her."

It was a few moments before Jack said anything. Finally, he turned to Courtney and said, "Thanks, Court. I know you're trying, but I don't think that anything I say at this point will make much difference." He threw back the last of his beer, stood, tossed some money on the bar and walked out without saying anything else. Courtney felt like a real shit for telling him and could only sit there watching him go.

Jack didn't remember the short ride to his apartment. There were too many emotions and thoughts going through his head. Inside, Cat mewed, asking for supper. Jack fed her and then he sat down, numb from what Courtney had told him. Cat jumped into his lap. He scratched Cat's head and she curled up, purring loudly, content.

That was when he decided to leave. It wouldn't be forever, just until he could get things sorted out in his head, to find some answers. Jack continued to work at Ben's until the end of the summer out of friendship and loyalty to Courtney. She had been there for him twenty-five years ago when he first arrived in Rye and he felt that he could never fully repay her for that support. They had many long conversations about Max and she, too, was worried, although she never said as much to Jack. When he told her he was planning to take off for a while on *Irrepressible*, she understood and offered to take care of Cat for him.

CHAPTER 32

HE WAS BEGINNING TO FEEL BETTER, but he needed more coffee. As he stood, he looked over at the red sloop. The dinghy was still trailing patiently off the stern. Jack assumed that the two people he had seen board were still below since he saw no one on deck. He studied her lines. She was a handsome vessel and she looked fast, even while sitting on a mooring. The people on the red sloop reappeared, climbed over the side into the dinghy, started the outboard and cast off. As they motored past, waves and nods were exchanged. He went below, refilled his cup and returned to his seat in the cockpit.

Sheltered from the breeze by the canvas dodger, the sun was warm and despite more coffee, he closed his eyes and was quickly transported back to Switzerland. Even though it had been less than a year, it felt like a lifetime ago. Max was with him. There were small cafés, intimate dinners, he could almost feel her touch, her smell, and the joy of being with her. He smiled, then a gull cried out, waking him as if he had been slapped.

It took a moment for him to regain the present, then his thoughts drifted as he relived that day in Rye when he knew it was over.

He had stopped by Ben's to ask Courtney something, what he couldn't even remember. As he turned the corner into the bar, he saw that the staff was gathered around the bar and something or someone had their attention. For a split second, things were as they had always been as he asked, "Hey everybody, what's going on?"

The collective sucking of breaths and following silence told Jack all he needed to know. Patti turned toward him and as she did he saw Max. She didn't move. She was standing there, still as a mannequin. Jack gazed at her and she was all that he saw. It was as if there was a spotlight on her and the rest of the room was dark and silent. The little black dress that she was wearing was stunning in its simplicity. Thin straps flowed over her shoulders, to the low cut bodice that revealed just enough of her perfect breasts to tease and promise. Its length was short enough to high-light her legs without exposing all of their secrets. Jack had never seen Max like this before and he was speechless. There was a calm self-confidence in the surprised look on her face.

For a split second, their eyes locked and they connected as only former lovers could, then the moment was over. Max blushed and the slight rosy flush that extended from her neck down to her breasts only made her all the more desirable. That's when Jack saw it. She was wearing the diamond. The diamond over which Jack had saved her life, the diamond that had led to those days of bliss in Switzerland. The diamond was strung on a thin gold chain that hung just above her breasts as if it were a beacon signaling "Come to me." Before anyone could say anything, before that moment, which felt like an eternity ended, Jack turned and left. He knew then that she was lost to him and that he needed to get away. That time seemed so long ago and at the same time it felt as if it were yesterday.

He shook his head forcing those memories back, back and out of his conscious mind. It was still too painful to relive those memories, even though he cherished them. To distract himself, he began inspecting in detail the cockpit of the boat, anything to refocus his thoughts. He spun a winch drum, listening to the pawls click. He visually followed the main sheet as it went from traveler to block and back again and then he tried to count how many coils there were in it as it hung from the end of the boom. He tried to convince himself that these were good mental exercises, but he knew better. He was getting into a funk and it would be a fight to get out of it.

"Come on, asshole, stop being a whiney bitch," he said to himself. Finishing his coffee, Jack began to plan his day. It was a beautiful day and there were many things that needed doing. As he began to make a mental list, his stomach rumbled. Food instantly went to the top of the list. He went below and only came up with a few granola bars. He ate one while he poured a third cup of coffee. It would tide him over, but was no substitute for a full breakfast.

Hunger is always a good motivator, so he began to make preparations to move the boat to a mooring where launch service would be available. First a call on the VHF radio on channel 68 to the marine service that rented moorings and provided launch service.

Their response was immediate. A mooring was available. He was given directions and as soon as he was secure, they would come out to finalize arrangements and transport him to shore.

Within the hour, he was standing on land for the first time in weeks except for a few quick trips ashore in the dinghy during his travels. First, he needed a real shower, then breakfast. Once his personal needs were taken care of, he would call John. Along with his towel and clean clothes, he also packed his running things. A run might be just what he needed later in the day. Three weeks on a boat can be a little confining and it would be good to stretch his legs.

CHAPTER 33

THE PHONE RANG SEVERAL TIMES before a cheerful voice answered. "Good morning, John's Boat Store. May I help you?"

"Yes, is John in?"

"He is, may I ask who is calling?"

"I'm an old friend of John's and I'd like to surprise him. Could you just get him for me?"

"Sure," replied the voice, not quite as cheerful now.

"John here." He sounded just as Jack remembered him.

"Is this John Burney?" Jack disguised his voice. He wanted to yank John's chain a little.

"Yes." John replied slowly. His voice betraying the fact that he didn't recognize the caller.

"I've just sailed into Newport and I need some help and on good authority I've been told you are the man to talk to." As Jack made this statement, he let his voice return to normal.

There was a pause on the other end of the line then John said, "Jack? Jack Beale. Is that you?"

"Yeah. It's me."

"Where are you? What have you been up to?"

Jack cut him off. "I'm here in Newport. I sailed in last night anchored out and picked up a mooring this morning."

"Why didn't you call and let me know you were coming?"

"I couldn't."

"You couldn't?"

"This trip wasn't planned, it just sort of happened."

He paused a moment before asking, "What's up?"

"I need your help."

"Where are you? I'll come get you."

"I'm down by Bowen's Wharf. The launch service dropped me off."

"Great. I'll be right down. You hungry?"

"No, I'm good. Before calling, I caught a shower and some breakfast."

"You should have called. I would have picked you up and you could have showered at my place and Jenny makes a great breakfast."

"Jenny? Who's Jenny?"

"Oh I didn't tell you?"

"No, you didn't. But then it's been a while."

"It has. Sit tight. I'll be right down to get you. It'll take me fifteen minutes or so to get there." John said.

"Great. See you in a few."

Jack hung up, looked around and began thinking about how he would kill the next fifteen minutes.

The area was filled with shops, and they were all beginning to open for the day. Jack decided to just walk around and watch the city waking up. He always found this time of the day the most interesting in any city he visited. There was a friendliness and optimism that was unique to the first moments of the day that didn't seem to exist at other times.

As he walked around looking in shop windows, he couldn't help but notice all of the handbills and notices posted everywhere for different bands, performers, and performances. Jack knew that Newport had an active music scene as evidenced by the jazz and folk festivals, but he hadn't realized that the local scene was so active. There was one utility pole in particular that was covered with these notices. Layer upon layer of them. The oldest covered up by the new. It seemed that only age and weather would remove them. It was a living history and Jack was fascinated. He stood there, reading the pole when one old, weather torn notice caught his attention. All that was visible were the words "The Marlinspike presents Python—March 15. . . ."

He froze. He remembered what Tom had told him of Python's past. It had to be him. There couldn't be any other performers by that name. He took his pocketknife out and began prying staples out of the pole, carefully removing the more recent notices, slowly working his way toward his objective. He was so intent on what he was doing that he didn't hear the car pull up next to him. As he peeled off the last layer, an anemic beep beeping followed by a voice calling out his name broke his concentration. He turned. The beeping and the voice came from an old VW Bug convertible stopped right behind him at the curb. The top was down and inside was John. "Jack, get in before the traffic backs up."

"Hey, John. Be right there." He was not so careful in removing the rest of the notice and it ripped, but he did keep the information he wanted. The Marlinspike was the name of the club. John hit the horn again so Jack grabbed his bag and with notice in hand hustled over to the bug, threw his bag into the back and climbed into the front seat. "Hey, man. It's good to see you. You look great," said John.

"Thanks, you too."

"What's that you got?" said John nodding toward the paper in Jack's hand.

"Nothing really. I just saw an old notice with a familiar name on it. I was curious."

John didn't say anything else as he worked his way through the traffic and the tight one-way streets, Jack took a closer look around the car; it was a vintage bug and it sounded and looked its age. You could see where rust had been patched, the seats had a few tears in them and it was the most awful shade of green.

"Nice car. Where did you ever get this? It looks like it's on its last legs."

"Yeah, I know. It's not mine. It's Jenny's."

"Who's Jenny?"

"I'm sorry. We live together. I met her one night at the club I play at occasionally. Wait till you meet her."

"So you're still playin' the harp?"

"Yeah. Still playin'. It keeps me sane. No money in it, so I haven't quit my day job, that's what the store is for, but I still love the music. So what brought you down here? It's a crazy time of year to be out cruising."

Jack paused before answering. "It's a long story."

Before he could say more John cut in. "A woman, right?"

"How'd you know?"

"Had to be. Only a woman could make someone go to sea this late in the year." He looked over at Jack.

"Hey, keep your eyes on the road," said Jack as the bug began to swerve into the other lane.

John yanked the wheel to the right and turned his eyes back to the road. "That sucks."

"So where is this club where you're playing?" said Jack changing the subject.

"Smooth, Jacko. I get it. You don't want to talk about it now, there's plenty of time for me to get it out of you. I'm playing at the Marlinspike. As a matter of fact, I'm playing there tonight."

The Marlinspike. Stunned, Jack looked down at the notice he had taken off the pole and read it now. It said, "Release Party for local singer/songwriter Python. March 15." Jack looked at the name of the club again. The Marlinspike.

"Hey, John." Jack said, "You know a guy named Python?"

"Yeah . . . yeah I do. Great vocalist and songwriter. He was here for quite a while, then he hit it big and signed a contract with a publishing house and he was on his way. He had a big release party at the club. That's where I met Jenny. You know, it's strange, he seemed to just disappear after that. Haven't seen him since."

"I don't think you will. I found him floating in Rye Harbor this past summer."

This statement of Jack's caused John to hit the brakes and swerve off the road.

"Did you just say what I think you just said?"

"Yep. He's dead."

CHAPTER 34

FOR THE REMAINING THIRTY MINUTES that it took to get to John's place, Jack talked while John drove and just listened. John and Jenny lived as far out of town as you could get on the island. Located at the end of a narrow road that had been paved once but now was rutted and dusty, it wound through a forest of Christmas trees. Then, abruptly, there were no more Christmas trees and the road turned into a gravel drive which ended in front of John's house.

The house looked like it had been an old carriage house at one time. It was two stories high with well-weathered shingles, large windows with dark green shutters accenting the white trim, and a red tin roof. Out front, there were flower gardens and even though they had pretty much gone by, Jack could tell that they had been well tended.

As they pulled in, John tapped the horn, its anemic beep sounding as awful as the car looked. Jack was silent as John parked the old green bug near the front door. "Well, here we are." John's voice broke the silence.

"This is incredible," was Jack's almost whispered reply.

John hopped out of the car at the same time a young woman came around from the side of the house to see who had arrived. When she saw that it was John, her face lit up and she waved. She had long auburn hair pulled back into a loose ponytail. She was wearing loose well-worn overalls with a white tank top tinged with sweat. Green rubber gardening clogs completed the outfit.

Jack, still seated in the car, watched her walk toward them. She had a smudge of dirt on her cheek and her face had the glow of someone who had been engaged in some vigorous physical activity. Her tanned arms glistened and they, too, were brushed with dirt.

"Hey, Jenny," John called out as soon as he saw her walking toward them and he went toward her. As they came together, he gave her a hug and a kiss, both of which were enthusiastically returned in kind. He then turned and still holding hands they walked back to the car. Jack opened the door and got out as John said, "Jack, I'd like you to meet Jenny. Jenny, Jack. Jack is an old friend who just sailed into Newport from Rye, New Hampshire." She extended her hand and Jack took it saying, "It's nice to meet you. Your gardens are beautiful," *and so are you,* Jack thought.

"Hello, Jack. Welcome. Any friend of John's is a friend of mine. Can I get you anything? Coffee, a drink of water? A beer?" Her voice was warm and friendly and exuded confidence and Jack immediately felt as if he had known her forever. Jack thought to himself that John had done well.

"No, I'm all set."

"Well then, I'm going to leave you two, I have some bulbs to finish planting out back." After another quick kiss to John's cheek, she turned and walked back into the direction from where she had come. John was grinning and Jack noted that the view from the back was as enticing as the one from front.

"So what do you think?" asked John.

"About what? Jenny or the place? Or both?"

"Both actually, but I meant Jenny."

Jack paused a moment before answering. "John, I've only just met her, but she seems to be everything a guy could want. I'm looking forward to getting to know her better. You done good."

"Thanks. Come on, grab your bag, we'll put it inside then I'll show you around."

Jack grabbed his bag and followed John inside. The inside was not what Jack had expected. He wasn't sure just what he expected, but it was not what he found. The first floor was one large room and it was filled with plants. They hung from the ceiling, they were on the walls and some very large floor plants divided the room into areas.

"Wow!" exclaimed Jack.

"Yeah, I know, it's kind of overwhelming. Jenny really likes plants. In the summer, a lot of these are outside and the room is kind of empty. Now she's moving them in and things can get a little crowded."

Jack could see that on the back wall there was a wood stove and it was near the kitchen area. "You never struck me as a plant kind of guy. I assume this is all Jenny," said Jack.

"You got that right. If I were taking care of them, they'd all be dead in a week."

How'd you meet Jenny?"

"Well, like I told you. I was at this big release party for Python." He paused, then before continuing with his story he said. "Tell me about how you found him. You know, he was a terrific talent and a really nice guy."

"I will, but first I want to hear about Jenny," replied Jack.

"Okay. So, I was at this release party at the Marlinspike. Most anyone in the local music scene was there. Have you ever been to the Marlinspike?"

"No. Never heard of it until today."

"Well, I'll take you over there. It's this really cool place over in Jamestown. Nothing fancy, but the guy that owns it is really into music so he always has someone playing there. Occasionally, there'll be a really big name playing. I don't know how he gets these people, but it's really cool. The place has an outside patio and on a warm summer night, you can sometimes hear the music all the way over here."

Jack cleared his throat and interrupted. "Do you have a glass of water?"

"Oh, sure." John went over to the fridge and got out two bottles of water and handed one to Jack. The both paused and took sips.

John then continued, "So I was at this party, eating the free food and beginning to get buzzed. The drinks were free too. Anyway, there was some band playing, we were all waiting for Python to show up to perform some of the songs that were on his new CD. It was hot inside, so I stepped out for some fresh air and that's when I met her. Or more accurately, she met me. I had just finished talking with some of the guys I play with and was standing by the railing, looking out over the water, enjoying the view when she came over and stood next to me. It wasn't crowded or anything but I could feel her presence. She didn't say anything and I glanced over at her. It must have been more that a glance because she turned to me and said, "Can I help you?" Man, was I embarrassed. I must have turned a thousand shades of red. I think I said something dumb like "Water's really calm tonight." She just stared at me silently for a moment and then said, "I'm sorry, I didn't mean to embarrass you. My name is Jenny and I came over here because I wanted to meet you." And then she held out her hand. I think I just stood and stared at her for a moment before taking her hand. Finally, I took her hand and shook it and again said something that must have been really dumb. I don't remember what, but she laughed, not in a mocking way, but in a very nice way and that was it. It was her laugh that got me. The rest of the night was a blur of great music, too many drinks, and the next morning I woke up with her next to me and we've been together ever since."

Jack just stood there grinning. "You sly dog."

"So what about you?" asked John. "You sail down here without any notice, show up on my doorstep and you tell me that Python is dead. What gives?"

"It's a long story."

"I've got time. Let's go outside and enjoy the rest of this nice afternoon. There aren't too many of them left."

"Fine by me."

The two men stepped out the back door onto a small patio. John nearly bumped into Jack because he had suddenly stopped and was staring out over the most amazing array of plants and gardens that he had ever seen. In the center of the patio, there were four chairs clustered around a table. The chairs were all different shapes and sizes and painted in bright colors. In contrast, the table was made from some old planks held together by some iron straps and was unfinished and weathered. What it originally was Jack couldn't tell, but it matched the chairs perfectly.

Clusters of pots were filled with plants of every shape and size and were arranged in such a way as to create an intimate setting while still being exposed to Mother Nature. Out back, he could see Jenny working in one of several other gardens that were connected by stone paths leading from one to another.

The gravel drive which continued past the house came to an end at an old barn. The barn doors were open and inside he could see a boat.

"Nice place, John. Did you do all of this? You don't strike me as the type."

"Nah, it is all Jenny. She has the green thumb, I just do the heavy lifting."

"Don't you work at the store anymore? You still own it, don't you?"

"Yeah, I do. I have a young couple working for me who pretty much run it, so I don't have to be there all the time. Working with Jenny is a lot more fun." He grinned as he said this and Jack picked up on it.

"John, you're whipped," he said with a touch of envy in his voice.

"Maybe. But now tell me your story," motioning to one of the colored chairs on the patio he said, "Sit."

Jack began. "Well, early in the summer, I had gone over to Ben's to enjoy the quiet of the early morning harbor and saw something down in the water by my boat. When I got down closer, I found that it was a body and that body turned out to be Python. I didn't recognize him at first even though he looked familiar. Eventually, I remembered who he was because he had played with the reggae band that plays at Ben's on Sunday afternoons. That had been a few years ago, but I still recognized him, mostly from that tattoo on his arm. The police didn't get too far in the investigation other than basic background and that's how I found out he had been in Newport."

John interrupted at this point. "Okay, that makes sense, not his death, but how you knew him. You're not a cop. Why are you here?

"Do you remember Max?"

"She was that really attractive red-headed bartender at Ben's, right?"

"Yeah, that's her."

"What about her?" pressed John.

"Last winter, she and I became a little more than friends. Actually, there was a dead body found in the ice floes in front of Ben's and she became involved. I ended up saving her life, we went to Switzerland and, well, we became more than just friends."

The look on John's face said it all. "Slow down a bit, Jack. There was another murder at Ben's last winter?"

"Yes."

"And Max became involved?"

"Yes."

"And you saved her life and became lovers?"

"Well, yes, sort of."

"Jack, this could take a while. Would you like some lunch and a beer?"

"That'd be good." Jack welcomed the break from his interrogation. He really didn't like talking about all of this, but he realized that he was going to have to and he needed to.

John made sandwiches for all three of them and then called for Jenny to join them. John and Jack grabbed all of the lunch stuff and headed back out to the patio. Just as they were putting everything down on the table, Jenny came around the corner. "This is great. I was beginning to get really hungry and to have two cute guys waiting on me—what more could a girl want?"

"Don't flatter yourself," said John with mock derision.

She pouted and posed in a way that made Jack hold his breath for a split second. *Goddamn*, he thought. She was incredibly sexy and in that same moment, he really missed Max.

"Jenny, pull up a chair. Beer?"

She nodded and sat across from Jack and next to John.

John handed her a beer and passed the plate of sandwiches to her. She took a half and slowly took a bite all the while watching Jack. Jack realized that she was staring at him and he found it a little uncomfortable. John broke the tension when he said, "Jack was just telling me quite the story. Do you remember Python?"

Jenny swallowed and said, "Yes, how could I forget him? We met at his big release party."

"Well, Jack found him dead in Rye Harbor this past summer."

"What!" She nearly choked on the sip of beer she had just taken. Her gaze intensified as she looked more deeply at Jack, her eyes asking the questions before her voice could.

John continued before she could speak, "He was just telling me about another dead body that was found in Rye Harbor last winter and how it led to his affair with Max the bartender and I suspect that that has something to do with why he is here. Right, Jack?"

By now Jenny couldn't speak, she just stared at Jack. Jack sat back and in a quiet voice said, "That's about it." His mind seemed to be elsewhere and for a moment, all three of them just sat in silence, chewing and sipping.

Jenny finally found her voice and was the first to speak. "I'm so sorry."

"Sorry for what?" replied Jack.

"It's obvious that you are either running from or searching for answers to something. Whatever it is, it's painful to you. I don't know why, but you are here and we are here for you."

Jack just looked at her, stunned by her prescience and wondered how she picked up on all that. He had hardly spoken with her and John's telling of the story was sketchy at best.

John saw the look on Jack's face. "Jack, she does this to me all the time. It's kind of spooky, but she's usually right. That's one of the reasons I am so in love with her."

Jenny blushed slightly and continued to gaze at Jack.

"Well, she's not too far off the mark."

"I knew it," murmured Jenny.

The rest of the afternoon was spent in small talk. Jack wasn't ready to open up and John and Jenny were too polite to pry.

CHAPTER 35

TRAFFIC TO JAMESTOWN WAS SLOW and they arrived at the Marlinspike a little later than intended. As soon as they got inside, John left Jenny and Jack. He was late and the band had already started to play and he had to join them. While Jack stood there looking around, getting a feel for the place, Jenny left him to go look for a seat. It was crowded and noisy and had a more common man feel than Ben's.

Larger than Ben's, there was a pretty good-sized stage straight in from the door and Jack saw John climbing up and taking his place with the band. There were mismatched tables throughout the room and off to the right of the stage there was a grouping of overstuffed chairs and a couch. The bar was opposite and to the left of the stage. Jack counted more than a dozen bar stools, all occupied. There were two bartenders who were a blur of motion taking care of those at the bar and the waitresses who were picking up drinks.

As Jack watched them, he thought back to the summer and those reggae Sundays at Ben's. He couldn't help but compare them to Max and company. *They're good,* he thought, *but as good as they were, they were not as good as my girls.* He caught himself, *My girls?*

That was when Jenny returned. She had to lean into him and almost shout into his ear to be heard. "I've got a coupla' seats, come on." As she turned to go, Jack finished his survey of the room while noting which way she headed. There were doors at the far end of the bar that led out onto the patio. Jack could see that if the doors were opened those outside would get a good view of the band. Tonight, they were closed. Past those doors was a corridor that ran past the stage with a sign indicating that the restrooms were that way.

He turned and caught sight of Jenny over by the couch. She turned and he could see that she had expected him to be right behind her. It took her a second to spot him in the crowd and when she did, she waved him over. Jack had had no problem spotting her and began moving in her direction.

Tonight, she was a different Jenny from the one he met in the afternoon. Gone were the overalls and clogs as were the dirt smudges on her cheeks, and the tangled hair from hours spent in the garden. Tonight, her long auburn hair hung straight down over her shoulders and it shone. Her skin had a healthy fresh glow, from the combination of sun and having been scrubbed clean. She wore only enough makeup to accent her dark brown eyes.

She was wearing a tight black top that had long sleeves and a high collar. It had a tear drop shaped cutout that ran from over her right shoulder and curved across the top of her breasts, exposing just enough to tease, as if that were needed.

Her form fitting, low riding designer jeans with a silver studded belt showed off her flat, tanned stomach which was further accented by the shiny jewel that adorned her navel. Her already tall five foot ten frame was boosted even taller by the spiky heels of her fashionable shoes. To Jack they looked uncomfortable, but she moved naturally in them and they did complete the look. In short, she was smokin' hot and he wasn't the only one to notice. For about the bazillionth time, Jack found himself marveling at John's good fortune.

As he approached, he saw that she had found space on the couch for them. She sat down just as he got there and she patted the space next to her, and he sat. There was no doubt in Jack's mind that Jenny dealt with the world on her terms. He should have been intimidated, but he wasn't.

"This place is great," said Jack.

"It really is," she agreed, "And the music's not bad either."

The cocktail waitress appeared and they ordered drinks. Jenny had a

Cosmo and Jack, a beer. Nothing much was said while they waited for the drinks to come. Jenny seemed focused on the music and Jack continued to watch the bar. The drinks arrived and Jack proposed a toast, "To John Burney, a truly great harmonica player."

"To John," replied Jenny and they clinked rims.

It wasn't long before Jenny looked at Jack and said, "Tell me about why you are really here in Newport, Jack Beale."

Strangely, the question didn't really surprise Jack.

He probably would have been more surprised if she hadn't asked. He took another sip of his beer while he organized his thoughts and then he began.

"Jenny, I have to tell you up front that I don't really know why I'm here. I'm looking for something. I'm not sure what, all I know is that I feel like I'll find some answers here."

"Well, why don't you start by telling me about Max."

Jack sat back and began telling her about the body that was found last winter in the ice in front of Ben's. It wasn't long before he sensed that he was losing her. She had asked about Max and he was telling her about a murder.

"Jack, I think you are avoiding my question. I want to know about Max. Who is she? What does she mean to you?"

"I know that's what you want, but it isn't an easy answer. I have to tell you the story from the beginning so you'll understand. This isn't easy for me and somehow it's all wrapped up into one big mess. I'm sorry."

Before he was able to go on, the band took a break and John came over to the couch.

"Hey guys, how are you liking the show?"

Jack welcomed the break from Jenny's questions. "You guys really sound great. It's been a few years since you were in Rye and you sat in on some of those jam sessions. You haven't lost a lick and I even think you sound better."

"Thanks, Jack. I hope Jenny hasn't been too hard on you. We both are concerned and want to know what's going on. She insisted on getting first crack at you."

"Ah, so that's it. You guys are going to play good cop/bad cop on me, hoping I'll cave."

Jenny waved the cocktail waitress over and ordered another round then looked at Jack and said in a slightly teasing way, "Jack, that's not fair. We're not going to gang up on you, we're going to ply you with truth beer and you will be powerless."

They all got a good laugh at this and when the cocktail waitress brought the drinks, they laughed again. After she had left, John said, "I sure hope she didn't think that we were laughing at her. Drink up."

John had to return to the stage, leaving Jack and Jenny on the couch. Jack was definitely feeling more relaxed and Jenny was as tenacious as ever. "Okay, Jack, continue with your story."

He did and by the time the story reached Switzerland, it became harder for Jack to continue. Jenny was touched and she could see his torment. "Jack, I think I'm beginning to understand. If you don't want to tell me any more tonight, that's okay. I want you to know that I'm here and I'm a pretty good listener if you just need to talk."

Jack stopped and looked at her. "Thanks, Jenny. Maybe another time, because if I continue now this whole night will become a real downer."

"I understand," she said. Then, she leaned toward him and gave him a small hug.

They sat in silence for a couple of minutes and finished their drinks. The waitress saw the empty glasses and before she reached the table, Jack caught her eye and signaled for another round.

Jenny looked over at Jack and said, "Let's change the subject. Tell me about Python."

This was easier for Jack to talk about because he wanted some information in return. He began, "Well, this past July, I was down at the harbor early one morning just enjoying the quiet of a day's beginning. I saw something floating down by my boat. It looked like a log, I really couldn't tell, but when I checked it out, it turned out to be a dead body. I recognized the tattoo on his arm and further investigation by the police determined that the body was indeed Python. I knew him from quite a few years previous when he sang vocals with the reggae band that plays at Ben's on Sundays in the summer. I don't remember much about him except that he was one hell of a singer."

"I still can't believe that he's gone," said Jenny.

"Yeah, it pretty much sucks."

"Have the police found out who did it or anything?"

"Nah, other than determining that he had been in Newport and had a burgeoning career, they really don't know anything, but you know, it was strange. He had been hanging around in Rye for several weeks before his death. I saw him talking to the band several times but they won't talk about it. As a matter of fact, I saw him talking to them the day before I found him and there seemed to be some tension. I tried to talk to the guys and they just brushed me off. It was as if they couldn't or wouldn't talk about it. It was really strange."

Jenny agreed that that seemed strange. Jack noticed that she was really thinking about what he had told her and he got a sense that she might know something more. Before he could pursue his questions, and before she could try to get anything more out of him, the band finished for the night. John rejoined them and they ordered one more round before the bar closed. Jack couldn't help but notice how much into John Jenny was. *Good for him* thought Jack for the billion and oneth time.

CHAPTER 36

THE NEXT MORNING, NO ONE WAS moving very fast. After they had left the club and returned home, a bottle of wine was opened and then another and then another. For the rest of their conscious hours, they talked, opined, commentated and argued about almost any topic imaginable. The power of beer was in full effect even though they were drinking wine. Eventually they ran out of wine and energy and called it a night, although it was more like early morning.

Jack was the last one up and as he made his way to the kitchen area, the smell of coffee was in the air. Looking out, he could see that the morning was more fall-like than the day before. The sky was clouded over and it looked cold outside. The wood stove was burning and the heat that radiated from it felt really good. He didn't see anyone else around, but he knew that at least one other person was up as evidenced by the coffee and the wood stove. He poured himself a cup, found some cream and sugar and was just taking his first sip when he was startled the sound of a door closing, followed by a voice from behind. It was Jenny.

"Good morning." She didn't sound fully awake either and had that same sexy, smoky, I-just-woke-up-voice that Max had at the start of the day. Memories flashed. "Mornin'," he replied as he turned toward the voice. She was standing in front of the wood stove warming her backside, holding a cup of coffee. She was wearing flannel pajama pants and an old sweatshirt. "How are you feeling?" she asked.

"Just peachy," replied Jack as he took another sip of coffee and studied her.

"You look like hell."

He wanted to say to her that she did too, but it wasn't true. Even with a bad case of bed head, no make-up and eyes that reflected a serious lack of sleep and too much alcohol the night before, she was still incredibly beautiful. So instead he said, "Doesn't look like a very nice day today."

"It's not. I was just outside checking to see if there had been any frost on my plants; it looks like they're okay."

"That's good. Where's John?"

"He had to go to the store early this morning. He was nice enough to light the stove and make the coffee before he left."

"Good man," agreed Jack.

By now the coffee was beginning to kick in and he continued to look at Jenny. This time she noticed and said to him, "Is everything all right? You keep staring at me."

Busted. With some embarrassment, Jack stammered out his reply. "No, everything is fine, I'm sorry, I didn't mean to stare, but I've known you for less than twenty-four hours and I feel as if I have known you forever." What he didn't say was that he was totally mesmerized by her. Yesterday, she was the gardening earth mother, then last night the hot clubber and this morning . . . well, he didn't know what label to put on her but he felt really comfortable in her presence, not unlike how he used to feel around Max. He pulled a chair closer to the stove and sat down. Jenny didn't move, so there they were, both cradling their coffee cups in hand, staring blankly into nowhere, lost in private thoughts, letting the fire in the stove warm them. They remained like this for several minutes until Jenny broke the silence. Softly she said, "Jack, tell me about her. Last night you got as far as telling me about how you had ended up in Switzerland with her. I want you to know that what you did was pretty amazing, saving her and all."

He wanted—needed—to talk and so he began. "We went to Switzerland together. The bank, out of embarrassment I suppose, paid for everything. It was late February/early March. Not a really pretty time to go anywhere, but with Max everything seemed to shine. There were no outside pressures, just the two of us. We sat in small cafés for hours, we talked and walked and made love. Honestly, I had never felt that close to anyone in a very long time. I didn't want it to end and I don't think that she did either. But we had to go home."

Jenny interrupted at this point and asked, "You didn't tell me. What was in the box? What almost got her killed?"

"I'm sorry. Along with some family pictures and papers, there was a large, uncut diamond. With the help of the bank, we were able to find the company that her great-grandfather had founded. It had been sold shortly after his death to one of the diamond cutters who had worked for him for many years and now his son ran the company. He was most helpful. It was decided that the uncut stone would be split into three separate diamonds and he would cut and polish the largest for her in exchange for the two smaller stones. That seemed to be the right thing to do. Splitting and cutting diamonds takes time and it was not ready by the time we had to return home. I had never seen it until that night when she was getting ready to go to some fancy event with Daniel and I stopped by Ben's. She was modeling her dress for all the other girls to see and she was wearing the stone. It was a teardrop shape and hung from a fine gold chain around her neck. When I saw it, too many memories came flooding back and I knew I had to leave. I stayed through Labor Day, but then I left."

Jenny had been listening intently, letting Jack tell the story in his own way at his own pace, but now she interrupted. "Jack. Who's Daniel? Why did you let him take Max away? It sounds like there was so much going for the two of you."

"Jenny, that's a whole 'nother story and it will take some time to tell. Can we continue this later?"

"Of course. Are you hungry?"

"I'm starving. Any ideas?"

Right then John came in bringing with him a blast of cold air from outside. The day was still overcast, cold, and raw.

"Damn, it's getting cold out. What's with you two? The morning is nearly over and you're still in your pajamas. Lazy sacks of shit." This last statement was said with a chuckle.

"John, Jack was just telling me more about why he is here so stop being such a self-righteous asshole. Just because you got up early and went to work doesn't mean that we haven't been busy. As a matter of fact, we were just talking about getting something to eat." Jenny scolded him. "What would you say to some pancakes?"

"That sounds good to me."

Jack nodded in agreement so Jenny headed to the kitchen area to begin the pancakes. Jack just looked at John with a look that said, *You've fallen into it and you don't even know it, you lucky bastard.*

Jack got up and offered to help. He was put in charge of cutting up some fruit and setting the table. John joined him. He didn't want Jack to get all the credit.

Some really good smells were beginning to fill the air and as the two guys worked on preparing the table, Jack looked over at John and said, "Do you have any idea how lucky you are?""

"I do," said John. "Do me a favor and don't tell her."

A wink and the deal was sealed.

Pushing back from the table after eating way too many pancakes, Jack asked, "Are there any running groups around here? After this settles some, I need to go for a run. Too many weeks on the boat and then last night, I need to stretch my legs."

CHAPTER 37

NEITHER JOHN NOR JENNY WERE RUNNERS and Jack found their discussion of his request quite entertaining. After some time John, remembered that Nigel, who played bass in the band, was a runner so a call was made. After the obligatory small talk, John asked, "Any chance you're going for a run today?"

There was a short pause while Nigel processed this odd question from John. "Yes. Why do you ask?"

He knew that John wasn't a runner and couldn't imagine why he was asking this particular question.

"Would you like some company?" asked John.

There was silence on the line.

"Nigel. Are you there?"

That's when the laughter began. Finally Nigel choked out, "I'm sorry, for a minute I thought that you asked me if I wanted company on my run."

"I did, but not me. I have a friend visiting. You probably saw him at the club last night with Jenny and me. He's a runner and would like to get out and stretch his legs this afternoon. I had no idea what to suggest to him so I called you."

Nigel's laughter subsided with the explanation. "As luck would have it, I missed my run this morning. I'd love the company."

"That's great. What time?"

"Around four. How about we meet at the Y?"

"Great. Four. We'll be there. Thanks, man."

"No problem. After the run, I'll bring him back to your place."

John hung up the phone. "Okay, Nigel is looking for company and he'll meet you at the Y at 4:00. I have to go out then so I'll drop you off and after he'll bring you back here."

CHAPTER 38

JACK STOOD OUTSIDE OF THE Middletown YMCA, shivering in the chilly fall air, his bag on the ground at his feet. It was still overcast and the breeze made the forty-nine degree temperature feel much colder. He checked his watch again just as a small Japanese car pulled up, honked and parked. The driver got out and waved Jack over. "Hi, I'm Nigel. You must be Jack." They shook hands. "I'm sorry to have kept you waiting."

"No problem, I just got here."

"Did John just leave you here?"

"He was going to wait, but I didn't want to hold him up so I told him to take off."

"Look, throw your stuff in the back of my car and we'll get going. There's a bit of a breeze blowing today so I thought we might run through what we call the Newport hills. It's the most sheltered run on a windy day. I think you'll like it."

"Fine by me. Lead the way."

A few quick stretches and they started. Nigel set an easy conversational pace and they warmed up quickly. The early miles were spent getting to know each other. It quickly became a small world tour. Even though they had never met before, there were enough shared events and acquaintances that they agreed that they must have met each other at some time in the past.

Nigel was curious, "What brought you to Newport this time of year? John said that you sailed here."

"I did."

"I'm not a sailor, but isn't this the wrong time of year to be out sailing?" said Nigel.

"Sort of,"Jack continued, "I had some personal problems and I needed to get away for a while."

Nigel didn't respond to this last statement for a half-mile or so, and then he asked, "A woman?"

"Why did you ask that?"

"I've had enough problems with women in my life that whenever anything goes sour in someone's personal life, I always assume a woman is behind it somehow."

They ran in silence for another quarter of a mile when Jack broke the silence this time and in a labored voice said, "Yeah, well, you are right."

Jack hadn't run in several weeks and now his legs and lungs were beginning to feel the layoff. Nigel sensed this and backed the pace off a bit until it was comfortable again, then he said, "That's too bad. Do you want to talk about it?"

"Not really. John and Jenny have been grilling me since I arrived."

"'Nuf said. John also told me that you were the one who found Python dead last summer."

"Yeah, that would be me."

"Do you mind telling me about it? I was his bass player a while back and he was a good friend."

"No, not at all." Jack began his narrative. "I first met Python six, maybe seven years ago. He sang vocals for this reggae band that played on Sunday afternoons in Rye. He only sang with them for a short while . . . less than a year. Then he left. I remember that he had an incredible voice. I hadn't seen him again until this summer.

Nigel interjected, "That must have been just before he moved to Newport. He showed up here about that long ago. He made the rounds singing with several bands and eventually ended up with his own group. A lot of what he did here was original work."

"When he was in Rye, they did some of his original songs. They were pretty good as I remember."

"He was good."

Jack continued, "Anyway, this summer he showed up on several Sundays to see the band. I didn't get a chance to talk to him because it was always so busy, but I did notice that he mostly kept to himself and just sat and listened. One day, I saw him talking with the band while they were on a break. I remember because after the break, the band seemed agitated and I didn't see him again until the next morning when I found him face down, floating in the harbor."

"Does anyone know who killed him?"

"No. The police hit a dead end. Other than who he is, how he died, and the fact that he was living down here in Newport for the last few years, they don't have much. He drowned, but there was a nasty bump on the back of his head. I was asked by our town detective to try and help get some answers from the band, but they wouldn't talk to me either."

Nigel had been silent through most of Jack's narrative and the Y was in sight. They ran in silence the rest of the way. By now, it was nearly dark and streetlights were coming on. The orange glow of the streetlights gave an eerie look to the steam radiating off the two runners, making them look like demons just arrived from hell.

CHAPTER 39

JACK SPOKE FIRST AND HELD UP HIS HAND. "Thanks, man. That was terrific." as they high-fived.

Nigel replied, "No problem, thank you. Listen, how about a beer? There is a good sports bar near here where we go sometimes after running for some rehydration."

"Sounds great to me."

They retrieved their clothes from Nigel's car, went into the Y, showered, changed and headed to the bar.

It was very much a typical sports bar with televisions everywhere, and an animated crowd. They found a booth and as they sat, Nigel motioned to the bartender for a couple of beers. Jack said, "Nice place, reminds me of a bar at home."

The beers arrived and Nigel picked his up and offered a toast in Jack's direction, "To running, may it always keep you fit in body, sound of mind, and young in spirit."

Jack replied, "To running." They clinked rims and sipped their beers.

As Nigel put his beer down, he said to Jack, "You know, it's strange."

"What's strange?"

"Python's death. I mean here you have a guy who seemed to have it all. He had a dream, he had talent and it was all working for him. Then he ends up dead. How does that happen?"

"I don't know, although I think maybe something else was going on."

"Why do you say that?"

"Well, first Python shows up. He's an old friend of the band and he just sits and watches them play for a few Sundays, then when I see them talking it doesn't look like a friendly reunion. He ends up dead and several weeks later when I bring up the subject with Joshua, he warns me off. About the same time that Python showed up, this other guy, Daniel, shows up."

Nigel interrupted. "Who's Joshua and who's Daniel?"

"Sorry. Joshua plays the steel drums in the band. He and Percy, the bass player, started the band years ago. Daniel, he's another story. He showed up about the same time as Python. At first, he seemed more intent on hitting on Max and since that happens all the time I didn't pay much attention to it. I figured that after a week or two, he would move on when he discovered that she wasn't interested. It didn't work out like that. He kept coming back and she began to respond to his bullshit. That was bad enough, but when I saw him talking to the band, things got weird."

Nigel stopped Jack. "You're losing me. Who's Max?"

"Max is . . . or was my best friend who bartends at Ben's."

Nigel couldn't help but notice that a quiet sadness had crept into Jack's voice when he made that last statement. "Tell me more about this Daniel."

"Like I said, Daniel's this guy who started showing up on Sundays about the same time as Python. He was . . . I don't know . . . All the girls were gaga over him. He was too smooth, tall, athletic, dark wavy hair. The girls loved his eyes. They were all drooling over him, but he only seemed interested in Max. She's always being hit on by the drunks on Sundays . . . I didn't really pay attention. No big deal, or so I thought. Then she went out with him and got her friend to cover for her. She obviously didn't want me to know."

Nigel stopped Jack. "I don't mean to pry, but is Max the reason you took off?"

Jack sipped his beer and looked at him, and said quietly, "No offense taken. Yeah, that and some other stuff."

"That sucks." Nigel had had his share of heartbreak and he thought he understood what Jack was going through. He could tell that Jack wanted to talk about it, but he was more interested in Daniel so he asked again. "So what about this Daniel?"

"Yeah, Daniel. Understand that I'm not a fan of his."

"Understood."

"Remember I said that I saw Daniel talking with the band?"

"Yeah?"

"I was looking for Joshua during one of their breaks. I wanted to talk to him because earlier he kind of blew me off when I asked him about Python's death. Something wasn't right. When I finally found him, he was out back with the entire band and they were having some kind of an animated discussion with someone. Something told me I shouldn't go over, so I watched from a distance until I saw who they were talking to. It was Daniel. At one point, he looked in my direction and saw me. The look he gave me was strange and unnerving. I turned and went back inside and I didn't see him again the rest of the day."

"That's bizarre."

"It gets weirder. That night, after the band was packed up, I went over to chat with them. You know, say hello, talk about the day, nothing serious. I was curious what was going on with Daniel and when I asked, they said that he was just some guy who wanted to buy some CD's. I knew that was bullshit but I didn't press the point. Later, Leslie, the drummer, came back and we had a private conversation and about all he would say was that there was some bad shit going down and that I should stay out of it. He wouldn't say more, but I'm sure it has to do with Daniel."

Nigel nodded and the two new friends each raised their pints at the same time and drank. "So tell me about Python's death again."

"Not much to tell. He showed up out of the blue and hung around for a few weeks. I never really spoke with him. Then, the day before he floated up dead, I saw him talking with the band."

"Any idea what they talked about?"

"None."

"The police have no leads?"

"None that I'm aware of other than the fact that he drowned and had a bump on the back of his head."

More silence. More beer.

CHAPTER 40

FINALLY, NIGEL ASKED, "This Daniel, did he have a slight accent?"

The question caught Jack by surprise. "Yeah, How did you know?" Now it was Jack's turn to sit and stare, questions flooding his mind.

Before answering, Nigel flagged down the waitress and ordered another round. There was no doubt that this conversation would need more beer.

She brought over the beers, grabbed the empties and asked if they would like anything to eat.

Nigel looked up at Jack, "You hungry?"

"Yeah, I am."

"Me too."

The waitress, who was still standing at the table asked, "What would you like?"

Nigel ordered first, "I'll have a grilled chicken sandwich with fries."

She looked over at Jack and he said, "I'll have a burger, medium rare, and fries."

She thanked them and went to put the order in.

"You know, sometimes you just need a good greasy burger with fries," said Jack. "Now, why did you ask if he had an accent?"

"He sounds too much like a guy that was hanging around down here maybe a year or so ago, just about the time that Python was signing contracts and his career was taking off." He paused for a sip.

That got Jack's full attention, forcing him to quickly swallow his beer before he choked. "Really?"

Nigel swallowed, took another hit off his beer then he started. "Like I said, it was about a year ago. Python was beginning to make an impact on the local music scene here. He had started his own group. He was performing five nights a week and wherever he played, there was a full house. He ruled the club scene here in Newport. Then this guy, Charles, who sounds like your Daniel, started hanging around Python. He said he was an agent for some small independent music-publishing house and they wanted to sign him to a contract. They wanted to get a CD out right away. They were really eager, looking back, maybe too eager."

Jack had been listening intently and now spoke. "So this guy shows up all hot to sign Python. So what's the problem?"

"That's what I'm getting to. The guy was smooth, and as I recall, he looked a lot like how you described Daniel. But there was something about him that didn't feel right. He was completely likeable and yet I found myself really suspicious of him. He was just too smooth, too good to be true. Despite my gut feeling, I fell for his pitch the same as Python and everyone else. Let's face it, local guy makes it big, of course you'd be excited. Everyone was excited. You know how it is. Well anyway, Python signed the contract; they produced his first CD and threw a big party for him. It was really cool."

"Do you think we could be talking about the same guy?" asked Jack.

"I really don't know, and besides, what are the odds?"

"I have no idea, but there does seem to be an awful lot of coincidences."

"I agree."

The food came and the rest of the evening was spent talking about running and less weighty matters.

CHAPTER 41

BY THE TIME NIGEL DROPPED JACK off at John's place, John and Jenny had already gone to bed. He had questions for them that would have to wait for morning.

Monday morning came much too soon for Jack; however, by the time he got up, John and Jenny had already been up for hours. As he wandered into the kitchen area a chorus of "Good morning, sunshine," greeted him. Jack just looked at them, mumbled a return greeting and accepted the cup of coffee that Jenny handed him. As Jack took his first sip, he realized that Jenny had prepared it just the way he liked it, light and sweet. *How did she know?*

John must have caught the look on his face and said to him, "Don't ask, she just knows. So how was the run?"

"The run was terrific, Nigel's a cool guy. After the run, we went out for a few beers and some food and played the small world game."

"I just don't get this running thing," said John.

"Well, in some ways it's like sailing. It gives you some time alone when no one can bother you and it's great for thinking and clearing your head."

"I still don't get it."

As Jack finished his last sip of coffee, he looked at both John and Jenny and asked, "Do either of you remember the guy who signed Python to his contract?"

"Yeah, Charles. Why?" asked John.

Jenny also nodded yes.

"Tell me what you remember."

"Sure, but why?"

"Humor me."

John started, "Well, the one thing I can tell you was that he was smooth."

Smooth . . . There was that word again.

"He showed up one night while Python was sitting in with my group. After we finished for the night, he came over and introduced himself and told Python that he was an agent for this publisher who was interested in his work. Well, it was late and guys like this are always coming around, so Python kind of put him off by telling him that he had to leave immediately that night and that he was going to be out of town for the next few days. Usually, that would be the end of it. But it wasn't. Charles showed up five days later at one of Python's performances. So Python sat down and talked with him after the show. He seemed like the real deal. Like I said, he was really smooth. He didn't push too hard but he was always there, very friendly. It was easy to forget that he was on business and not a friend."

Jack interrupted John at this point. "What did he look like?"

Before John could answer Jenny spoke up. "He was gorgeous. He was tall, well built, he had this dark wavy hair and the most amazing almost amber eyes."

Jack continued to look at Jenny very intently.

She sucked her breath in and held it for a moment. Her eyes opened wide. "You think it's him. You think he's Daniel, don't you?"

That's exactly what Jack was thinking. There was no proof, just that old feeling that you know something to be true even though you have no logical reason to. He replied, "Maybe," all the while thinking how extraordinarily perceptive she was.

John rejoined the conversation at this point. "Who's Daniel? What am I missing here?"

Jenny looked over at him and matter-of-factly said, "He's the guy who stole Max from Jack, and that's why he is here."

John looked at Jack. Jack looked back at John and then at Jenny. Jenny looked at Jack and said, "Right?"

Jack surrendered. "Right." As he continued to look at her he thought to himself, *How does she do that?*

John spoke up again, still obviously a little confused. "Let me make sure I get this. Max is with a guy named Daniel."

"Right," answered both Jack and Jenny in unison.

"What makes you think he's the Charles who offered Python a contract?"

Jenny looked over at John. "John, stop being so dense. This Daniel was smooth, tall, handsome, had dark wavy hair and amber eyes. That description matches Charles to a T."

"I didn't know that you took such note of him," said John.

"I didn't tell you because it was nothing, but I saw him at several of the gigs he was at before the release party where we met. He was hitting on me. And I must say, he was pretty hot."

"You didn't tell me this before," said John.

"I didn't think that it was relevant. I said he was hot, but the vibe wasn't there. It was flattering, yes, but no vibe. You, on the other hand, have the vibe in spades," said Jenny teasingly.

John blushed at this last comment.

Jack, who had been listening to all of this now, butted in. "Okay, can we get back to this Charles?"

"Sure," John and Jenny said at the same time.

Jenny picked up the story, "So this Charles started hanging around Python. He was at performances, he was always there giving him props, stroking his ego until Python began to believe that he was his best friend in the whole world. Before long, Python had signed a contract with his publishing company. Everything snowballed from there. The CD was produced and the release party was totally kick-ass. Locally, Python was a god, you know, local boy on the way."

"It was pretty intense," agreed John. "Python was always going somewhere, meeting someone, doing whatever Charles wanted him to. As sales of that first CD began to wane, Python was eager to do another."

"And that's when Charles began to become scarce. It was subtle. He didn't leave, but he became harder and harder to contact and Python became increasingly pissed off and anxious. As a side note, Python was not the only pissed off person. Charles had left a long line of conquests all over Newport."

"Did Python ever check the guy out?" asked Jack.

"He did, but not until it was too late," said John.

CHAPTER 42

"UNTIL WHAT WAS TOO LATE?" asked Jack.

"Well, as Charles began to be increasingly difficult to reach, Python became more persistent in his efforts. He left messages, he called the record company, and he talked to the women that Charles had been seeing. Nothing. Once he found a message on his machine from Charles, but it was vague, he didn't leave a number and never called again. He even got Nigel to help him."

"Nigel? The guy I ran with yesterday?"

"That's him. He's a lawyer. They didn't find much. Charles didn't exist as best they could tell. The company had recently been sold to another company without anyone knowing. That one was an offshoot of an offshoot of an offshoot, and anything significant or important either was nonexistent or so buried that they came up bupkis. Python didn't talk to anyone about it much, so most of what I know is second or third hand. Let's face it, he was embarrassed. Then early this summer, I heard that he had found out something—I don't know what, no one did, not even Nigel, but from the grapevine it sounded like he was going to go after Charles and the record company. Then he up and left and we haven't seen him since."

Jack sat there absorbing all of this new information. He was more convinced that ever that Charles was Daniel and that he was involved in Python's death somehow.

Jenny chimed in at this time. "Jack, I can tell that you think they are the same person. I do, too. If I were you, I'd really be concerned about Max. If she's getting mixed up with this guy, it can't be good. I saw what he did to women around here. You'll need to be there to pick up the pieces, if there are any pieces left to pick up."

Jack looked at Jenny. She had done it again. She seemed to know exactly what he was thinking. He said, "Jenny you're probably right, but before I go running off I need to find out a little more. I need to talk to Nigel again. Can I have his number?"

"Fine, suit yourself, but don't blame me when you get back and find she's gone." He was given the number and John and Jenny left the room so he could have some privacy for his calls.

CHAPTER 43

JACK MADE THE CALL AND TALKED with Nigel. He didn't find out much more than he already knew. Nigel had kept notes throughout his investigation and he said he'd copy them for Jack. Maybe Jack would be able to find something that he couldn't. Then Jack made several phone calls. The first was to Tom. After the usual small talk, Jack told him what he had found. Tom was appreciative. "Thanks Jack. You know, you really should consider being a PI. You have a knack for it. I'll see if I can find out anything else with the information you've given me."

"How's Max?" Jack asked.

"I thought you'd never ask. That Daniel is quite the smooth talker. He has convinced her to go with him to the Caribbean." Before he could say anything else, the line went dead while Jack dialed another number.

He let it ring for what seemed like several minutes. There was no answer. He made a third call. This time it was picked up on the second ring and he heard Courtney's voice. "Hello."

"Hi, Court. It's me, Jack."

"Jack, where the hell are you?

"Court . . ."

"Do you have any idea what's going on here? You had better get your sorry ass back here as fast as you can."

"Court . . ."

She finally let him speak. "Court, I'm in Newport. I ended up here because . . . well, I can't explain it easily, but somehow I knew I'd find some answers here. I have. Is Max all right?"

"Max is not all right. You left and she took that as a sign. She went with Daniel to that fancy dinner in Boston. It must have been something because she didn't come home until late the next night and by then, he had asked her to go to the Caribbean with him. She said yes. They left a few days ago."

"Tom just told me that he had asked her. He didn't tell me that she actually did it."

"Well, she did. You really fucked this one up, Jack."

"You don't have to tell me that. I know it."

"Well, I am going to tell you that over and over because you are so dense. You fucked up."

"Okay, I got your point."

"You fucked up."

"Court . . . I get your point."

"Do you? Because you really fucked up."

"Court, enough."

He cut her off before she could make her point again. "I'll be home in a couple of days. I can't leave the boat down here and it looks like there will be a few good days coming up. Bye, and thanks for being such a good friend."

"Bye . . . fuck up" was the last thing he heard as he hung up the phone.

CHAPTER 44

AFTER HANGING UP, it took Jack a few minutes to compose himself. He felt as if he had just sprinted a mile. The adrenaline was flowing and he felt breathless and as if he was going in ten directions all at the same time. Jenny peeked around the corner to see if he was off the phone. She had been trying to hear what was going on, albeit unsuccessfully, and when she didn't hear any more conversation, that's when she peeked. Seeing that he had hung up the phone, she came in and quietly asked, "Is everything all right?"

Jack's silence and the look on his face told her more than his words. "Yes . . . uh, . . . No. You were right. She's gone."

"Gone?" said Jenny with surprise in her voice.

"Gone," said Jack, flatly.

"What do you mean gone?" said Jenny.

"Just what it sounds like. She's gone. He asked her to go to the Caribbean last week and she went."

"Oh, Jack. I'm so sorry. I never thought that it would come to that." She paused, then taking a deep breath she said, "Oh God, what if he's got something to do with Python . . ." her voice trailed off.

Before Jack could react to Jenny's question, John came in. Jenny looked over at him. She was the one with the adrenaline surge now and said, "John, Max is gone. She's run off with Daniel the murderer to the Caribbean and we have to help Jack get her back."

"Whoa, slow down a sec. Jack?"

Jack looked at them and said, "First, there is nothing to suggest that Daniel is a murderer, but apparently after I took off sailing, Max took that as a sign that I was not interested. He was there being mister smooth and caring and asked her to go to the Caribbean with him."

Under her breath Jenny said, "Oh, Jack, you really fucked up."

"I heard that."

"Sorry," said Jenny. Then she went on, "But come on. We know that Daniel and Charles are the same person."

"No, we don't," said Jack.

She was not to be deterred. "While here in Newport, he went by the name of Charles, the description matches Daniel's. We know Charles was a womanizer and Daniel really scooped Max up."

It was John's turn now, "That proves nothing."

Jenny continued, "After Python released his CD, Charles became very scarce. Nigel and Python found out that the publishing company he signed with had been sold and swallowed up and there was no sign of it. I think Python found out something else and didn't tell anyone what it was. I think he either followed Charles up to Rye or he went there to warn his friends. When he found Charles there, who was now calling himself Daniel, he confronted him, they fought and he was killed. To cover his tracks, Daniel distracted everyone with his relationship with Max. She was a convenient excuse for making his escape." She said all of this in one breath and as she finished, John gave her a sharp look and sheepishly she said, "Sorry."

John then said, looking at Jack, "Jenny's a little exuberant, but is there anything we can do to help you?"

Jenny's story really wasn't that far off from what Jack was thinking, although he didn't say so. Instead, he answered John's question. "Yes, there is something you can do to help me. It's a big favor, but I need to get back to Rye. I can't leave my boat here, so would you be willing to help me sail her back to Rye? With two of us, we could go nonstop and Jenny could drive up and meet us, then give you a ride home."

"No problem," said John and Jenny agreed. "It looks like we have a pretty good weather window right now so the sooner we leave, the better."

The rest of the day was spent provisioning and preparing for departure. Jack collected the copies of Nigel's notes from him and promised to keep in touch. The decision was made to leave that night; there was no sense in waiting

CHAPTER 45

"DID YOU SEE JACK BEFORE HE LEFT?" Courtney asked casually. It was late and she was helping Max close the bar. Even though it had only been a few days since Jack's departure, it was the first chance that Courtney had had the opportunity to talk with Max alone.

Max, who had been restocking the bottled beer, stopped what she was doing,

"Uh. No. He left?"

The slight quiver in her voice and the way her shoulders tensed answered more than her words.

Oh God, thought Courtney. *She doesn't know.*

Then Max turned, and asked, "Where did he go?"

Now it was Courtney's turn to feel uneasy as a thousand thoughts rushed through her head. *How much should she say? She had known that he was planning to leave for a while after the summer ended. How could Max not have known that? What did she know? She guessed not much, but she had to have known that something was up.*

"I don't really know, He didn't tell me. But he's on *Irrepressible.*"

"Did he tell anyone where he was headed?"

"Not that I know of."

"No one?"

"If he did, it wasn't me." replied Courtney.

"When? When did he leave?" A soft panic was beginning to creep into her voice.

"Only a couple of days ago. It was just after he saw you modeling your outfit for the ball."

"You have no idea where he went?" There was both anger and disappointment in her voice.

"No idea."

Max stared at her silently as the past few weeks flashed through her mind. *They had all been about Daniel. He would send flowers for no reason. He would call and say that he just wanted to hear her voice. The trip to the mountains, and then the invitation to the gala.* She sucked in her breath as the realization hit her. "Oh, my God," she mouthed the words and sat down, her face ashen as she remembered. *Jack had walked in that day when she was showing everyone her outfit for the ball and she was wearing the diamond. Their eyes met and then his lowered as he stared at the pendant. His gaze only lasted a moment, but it was enough. Then he turned and walked out.*

Courtney's voice brought her back to the present. "I really don't know where he was going. Listen, it's not your fault. Jack's a grown man. He's seen this happen before. He just needs a little time. He'll be back. Besides, as cute as Daniel is, he's not Jack."

"Court, it's not that simple. This time it's different. Daniel is so. . . . I can't describe it, but he makes me feel so good, in a way that no one else ever has, not even Jack."

Courtney looked at Max intently. That last statement took her by surprise and before she could say anything, Max continued.

"I know that Jack and I have something special." She paused as if she had said too much.

Courtney watched as she searched for words. "Last winter . . ." then her voice trailed off and she turned away.

"What about last winter?"

Max remained silent. Her back was to Courtney, her shoulders shuddered slightly and as she sniffled, Courtney could tell that she was wiping her eyes.

"Max?"

"I'm okay." Then with a final deep breath she turned back to face

Courtney. Her face betrayed the strength in her voice. "He didn't have to leave. He should be here."

"I know. I just think that right now he needs to be away. He'll be fine."

"Thanks."

Courtney gave her a kiss on the cheek and said, "We all love you, Max. Everything will work out. Now enough of this. You have a party to get ready for, so eat some chocolate and buck up."

During the final two days before the ball, Max didn't see much of Daniel. He did call, but he said that he had to take care of some business. He never told her what his business was nor did she ask.

CHAPTER 46

"YES. YES, I UNDERSTAND," he said quietly, and then the line went dead. Slowly, Daniel hung up the phone and sat down on the edge of his bed. If he wasn't worried before, he was now. His employer was impatient and expected results. The call he had just received made that perfectly clear.

Daniel began pacing back and forth as he replayed in his mind the just-ended conversation. While it hadn't been said directly, he knew that Python was causing the most concern and he needed answers. What had Python been up to? Why here? Why now? And most importantly, who killed him? As he considered the situation, he decided that first he needed to get the band signed. Maybe, just maybe, that might buy him some time.

He sat down on the edge of the bed and began to check off in his mind what he had done so far to reach his goal. Whenever he started a new job, part of his routine would be to get to know the bars and clubs where his target played. That part was easy and he had done that. Then, he would work on getting to know the band and becoming a recognizable member of their following. Done. Part of his routine was to hook up with a hot member of the opposite sex who was also a fan. He was good at this part and it usually included some great sex as a side benefit. It had become a game and a welcome release for all the tension and stress generated by the con he was implementing. The more challenging the conquest, the better. He prided himself on always winning. He grinned as he lay back on the bed.

That's when he began thinking about Max. She was different. She didn't fit the profile of his usual conquest. When he saw her for the first time that Sunday afternoon, he knew she would be the ultimate prize.

She wasn't one of the typical fans that would follow a band. She was a bartender. She had just finished her shift and it was obvious that she was tired and couldn't wait for the day to end. Her face glistened from the heat and her hair was a mess, but there was something else about her that caught his attention. He tried to put it into words, but they wouldn't come. Daniel blushed as he remembered how anxious he had felt when he was ready to leave and she had disappeared from sight and he hadn't found a way to meet her yet.

It was at that moment he heard the loud crash of bottles dropping and smashing on the floor out in the hallway. He looked around the corner and there she was, empty box in hand, with a pile of broken glass at her feet.

"Her eyes. It was her eyes," he said softly as it came to him as he relived that moment. He remembered going over to see if he could help. He remembered how his voice had startled her and when she looked up at him with those green eyes, he knew instantly and they betrayed her as well.

That look only lasted a moment as others came to see what had happened. "Jack." Daniel sat up and suddenly he wasn't thinking of Max. He stood and began pacing and talking out loud to himself. There was something about Jack that worried him. "What was with him? He and Max seem to have something and yet he's never challenged me. Why?" His thoughts drifted, *He saw me talking to the band.* Then aloud, "No, he was watching me talk to the band."

He stopped when he said that. It was as if a light was turned on in a dark room and in that first split second everything was seen, then as your eyes adjusted to the light you realized that you didn't recognize anything in that room. Clarity and confusion swept over him.

His thoughts returned to Max and he smiled. The more he got to know Max, the more his feelings had changed. At first, he had seen her as a prize in a game of sexual conquest that he played with each new job. Then that night in the bar after the broken box incident when he met Jack officially for the first time, the game suddenly became more challenging. Seeing Max's reaction to their meeting told him that Jack was more than just her friend and right then he decided that that would make Max an even sweeter prize. Game on.

Now, he was about to claim that prize. She was going to Boston with him to the big charity event. He knew that they would not return that evening. He had it all planned out. Having done this many times before, he knew how it would end, but two things troubled him. The first was Max. She was no longer a simple prize to be won and then left in the trophy case of memories. He really cared for her and was both scared and elated by the prospect of a future with her in it. More troubling was that his victory was by default. Jack had given up and sailed away without so much as a word to anyone, leaving him unchallenged. *Why? Why would Jack do that?* Not knowing the answer worried him and that feeling of unease returned. He needed to hear Max's voice for reassurance, so he reached for the phone.

CHAPTER 47

THE PHONE RANG IN MAX'S HOUSE and she practically leapt off the couch to get it, hoping that it would be Daniel. Before answering it, she paused and took a deep breath. Scolding herself, she said aloud, "Will you stop acting like a fool? Take a breath, let it ring and be cool." On the third ring, she answered.

"Hi, Max." It was him. Her heart raced and she could feel her face flush. She loved that sexy accent of his. She still didn't know where it came from, but it worked.

"Oh . . . Daniel, it's you." She tried to not sound too eager and was failing miserably. "Where have you been for the last few days?"

"I've been away on business. Did you miss me?" he teased.

"Of course. What kind of business?"

"Are you ready for tonight?" He had no intention of answering her questions.

That did it. She could tell that he wasn't going to talk about where he had been so she stopped asking. "Yes, I am. What time will you pick me up?"

"Well, the ball starts at 9:00, and we don't want to be too early so I thought that dinner first would get us there fashionably late. How about 7:30?"

"Sounds great. I'll see you then."

"7:30 it is. Ciao."

Max sat there, holding the phone in her hand for a moment before hanging it up. She had so many thoughts racing through her head. Some were unspeakably private and made her blush while others were more serious. *Why was he so secretive about his business? Where had he been for the last few days? And where was Jack . . . her best friend in the whole world? Jack with whom she had so much history. Jack who seemed to have conceded her to Daniel. Where was he?* Granted, much of this was of her own doing. Jack was safe, Daniel was mysterious, and maybe a little dangerous and oh, so sexy. She loved his attention. Her reverie was broken when the phone rang again. This time it was Patti. "So, has he called? Tonight's the night. He should have called."

"Patti, will you slow down. He just called. He's picking me up at 7:30."

"Are you excited? I'm practically wetting my pants thinking about it."

Max was trying to sound cool and very matter-of-fact. "Patti, take a chill pill. It's just a date . . . with the sexiest man I've ever met . . . and we're going to a charity ball in Boston! No, I'm not excited."

"What if he doesn't bring you home?"

Max just made a little humming sound in the back of her throat, somewhere between a tune and a moan.

"Gotcha," said Patti. "I'll see you later."

It was 7:15. Patti had been at Max's for the past two hours, helping her get ready. As she fastened the clasp on the necklace, she looked over Max's shoulder at her reflection in the mirror. She thought: *if I were a guy, I'd spend the whole night with a hard on.* What she said was, "Max, you are absolutely gorgeous. You're not coming home tonight."

"Patti," Max said firmly. "Stop that. I will be home."

"Right," said Patti with more that a touch of sarcasm.

One more look in the mirror and the doorbell rang. Both women froze, turned and looked at each other. "It's him. How do I look?" said Max with a slight quiver in her voice.

"You look fabulous. Now wait here. I'll get the door."

She opened the door. It was Daniel and for the briefest of moments, neither moved nor spoke. She, because he looked hotter than any man she had ever seen, and behind him was a gleaming black limousine with the door being held open by the driver. He glanced at Patti, then looked past her with those amber eyes as they searched for Max. Her palms started to sweat and her throat went dry. Finally, she managed to croak out, "Hi, Daniel. Max is just about ready. Won't you step in?"

"Thanks, Patti."

He stepped through the door and waited while Patti headed down the hall to Max's room to get her. She had to close the door behind her when she went in and leaned against it. Her face was flushed. Max looked at her and asked, "Are you all right?"

"Oh . . . my . . . God. I need a cold shower. He is so gorgeous. There is a limo outside waiting. Max, you are so in trouble."

"Patti, it's only Daniel, you've seen him before." She was trying to be the calm one now.

"Not like this I haven't."

"Okay, one last look." She turned slowly so Patti could do a final inspection.

"You look fantastic. No one will be able to take their eyes off of you two tonight."

"Let's go."

Patti opened the door and led the way.

When she entered the room, Daniel had his back turned to them. He turned as soon as he heard their footsteps. Patti took another deep breath, and stepped aside. Max, now exposed to his gaze, inhaled when she saw him and thought to herself, *Oh, my God. Patti was right. I'm in trouble.* She froze, not daring to breathe. Her heart was pounding in her ears and her mouth went dry. She tried to swallow but couldn't.

The look on his face said all that needed to be said. She watched his lips move, but could only feel the resonance of his deep baritone voice, then his sexy accent came though and she heard the words. "Hello, Max. You look absolutely stunning." He paused then asked, "Shall we go?"

Finally, she managed to say just above a whisper, "Hello, Daniel . . . Yes, let's." Turning to Patti she flashed a smile and Patti knew all that she needed to know. Max would not be home tonight. "Bye, Patti." With that, she turned and they left. Patti flopped on the couch and just sat there grinning.

CHAPTER 48

THE EVENING WAS A BLUR. The ride to Boston, dinner at an exclusive intimate restaurant that exceeded its reputation and the ball itself. It was a Cinderella evening. Daniel was a natural dancer and his skill made Max better than she ever thought she could be. The final song of the night was being played. As they held each other dancing to *As Time Goes By*, Daniel softly whispered in her ear. "Will you spend the night with me?" Max looked up at him and after a moment, whispered back, "Yes." Daniel just smiled back at her. She saw a smile of tender feelings. But that smile was as much a smile of victory as it was genuine.

The entire evening had been just what Max had dreamed of. In a word, it was perfect. In the hotel suite, they drank champagne, savoring each moment. It wasn't awkward. It wasn't rushed. It wasn't embarrassing. It was just two people totally focused on each other. They kissed, and then gently he turned her away from him. Softly, he kissed the nape of her neck and slowly, tenderly, unzipped the back of her dress. She shuddered slightly as it fell to the floor. She leaned back into him, his arms wrapped around her and he held her tight. His grip loosened and ever so tentatively, he cupped her breasts in his hands, holding them as one might the most fragile of objects. Then slowly, he ran his fingertips over her hard nipples, her knees felt weak and she leaned back into him again and he held her. She could feel his breath on her neck. His lips just touched her ears. She exhaled slowly, eyes closed, savoring his touch on her bare skin.

She turned to face him and his arms dropped to his side as she slowly peeled off his shirt and loosened his pants and they joined her dress on the floor. Her fingertips explored him, as if reading Braille, and he shuddered. She leaned into him and when their bare skin touched, it was electric. As they touched and explored each other, their labored breathing would be interrupted by moments of total silence, breaths held, so as not to interfere with the intense pleasures that they unleashed upon each other. Time stood still. When sleep came, it was deep and contented as they lay in each other's arms.

Morning came and with it, renewed passion. This time it was more urgent, more vigorous, like two animals in rut; the counterpoint to the previous evening's point. When they were finally exhausted, they slept again.

Not fully awake, Max was still in that place somewhere between sleep and consciousness, where dreams and memories flow freely—where nothing makes sense and yet everything is understood—when she rolled over. Her arm fell onto cold, empty sheets. It took a moment for the panic of disorientation to subside and for her to become fully conscious. The last twenty-four hours, Daniel, Jack, Switzerland, and pleasures never felt before all whirled and swirled, coming together and flying apart in the mosaic that the mind creates as it sorts and processes just before waking. There was only silence as she sat up, looked around the room, and realized where she was. She blushed. "Daniel?" she said as she remembered last evening. "Daniel?" she said again, a bit louder. And again, she was greeted with silence. Getting up, she walked around the room, noticing that there was no sign of him at all. No clothes, nothing, then she saw the note on the table. Her heart was pounding as she stared at the piece of paper, dreading what she might find written on it. She picked it up and finally was able to take a breath as she read:

Dear Max,
Has anyone ever told you how beautiful you are when you are sleeping? I didn't have the heart to disturb such perfection. I will be back soon.
Yours,
Daniel

Where had he gone?" Her mind raced through possibilities, then she blushed again as she thought about the last evening and felt a rush of heat. "I need a shower," she said to herself.

She took a long, hot shower, cleansing away the physical reminders of last night's love making, leaving only its memories. As she emerged from the bathroom, she stroked her hair with a brush provided by the hotel; her skin, a fresh scrubbed, rosy, pink created a sharp contrast to the whiteness of the thick, soft, robe that she was wrapped in. She stopped. On the bed were some boxes that weren't there before. "Daniel?" she called out. As before, there was only silence. The boxes all bore labels from the exclusive shops in the lobby of the hotel. An envelope was on the top of the pile. Her name was on it and it was in Daniel's handwriting.

> Max,
> I took the liberty of having the hotel send up some clothes for you. I know you weren't expecting to stay over. I hope I got the sizes right. Last night's outfit is a little formal for what I have in mind this afternoon. Back soon.
> Daniel

Max just stood there, all pink in the thick white robe and stared at the pile of boxes on the bed. "What the hell?" she mumbled to herself as she began opening the boxes and found underwear, bras, slacks, shirts and sweaters. There were several of each item to choose from. She checked the tags. The sizes were right. The underwear was sexy in a practical way. Whoever shopped for these clothes knew what they were doing. As she tried on different outfits, she pictured Daniel consulting with the clerk, deciding which ones would be perfect. *Nah. No guy is this good,* she thought as she shook her head. *He just had one of the hotel's personal shoppers do it for him.*

Her stomach was beginning to rumble as she dressed. She chose some basic khaki slacks, a light green and white blouse that was the perfect shade to go with her hair and a light fisherman's sweater. As she did the final mirror check and ran the brush through her hair, she heard the door. "Daniel?" she said again.

This time instead of silence, she heard his softly accented voice. She flushed. "Max, did you get the clothes I sent up? I hope I got the sizes right."

She stepped out and she said, "Yes, you did. They are perfect."

He looked at her and said, "Wow, you look terrific." At the same time, he congratulated himself. He hadn't lost his touch.

She went to him and they embraced. It was a shorter hug and kiss of greeting, rather than a prelude to passion. As they released each other, he said, "Are you hungry? I am."

"Yes, I'm starving."

"Good, then let's go."

CHAPTER 49

OUTSIDE THE HOTEL, THERE WAS A SMALL sandwich shop. It provided a sharp contrast to the elegance and formality of the hotel, but the food was honest and really good. Max had a cup of chowder and a grilled chicken sandwich. Daniel had creamy mushroom soup and a corned beef sandwich. Their lunches were filling and after the previous night's activities, they had both worked up pretty good appetites. As they finished, Daniel signaled for the check and said, "We have one more thing to do before I take you home."

"What?" asked Max.

"You'll see." He paid the check and they walked out onto the street. Arm in arm they walked, oblivious to others sharing the sidewalk until a man rushed out of a nearby doorway and bumped into them, causing them to separate. After the appropriate apologies, the man and Daniel shook hands and parted. Max watched all of this unfold, not thinking anything unusual about it. What she didn't notice was that the man had pressed a piece of paper into Daniel's hand when they shook. Daniel just put it in his pocket and tried to act as if nothing had happened. Inside, he was in turmoil. There could only be one reason for that to have happened. His employer was not happy with him.

The surprise that Daniel had for Max was an afternoon Duck Tour of Boston. They were alternately like two little kids on a school field trip, giggling, teasing each other and then like lovers, embracing and stealing kisses.

It was the perfect ending to a perfect weekend and Max never knew that something might be wrong, but every time Daniel reached into his pocket, he felt that piece of paper. It wasn't until they had returned to the hotel that he finally had the opportunity to read it without Max's knowing. All it said was, " We have to talk."

Those four words, four simple words would change everything. In the best-case scenario, his employer would want to send him on a new job as soon as he finished with the band at Ben's. They were close to signing and then he would be able to move on. This seemed to be the most unlikely option. Maybe Python's death was making his employer nervous and he wanted to find out how he was cleaning that mess up. *Possible*, thought Daniel, but his employer was not known for tolerance of sloppy work. Additionally, Daniel did not know who killed Python. He wondered if his boss knew something he didn't. It seemed unlikely, but . . . He paused as a third possibility came to him sending a shiver of fear washing over him. They would meet and he would end up like Python. This was a definite possibility. It was in that moment he knew he had to disappear and he wanted Max to go with him. He was certain that his employer did not know about his boat in Belize.

As they walked out of the hotel, Daniel had one more surprise for Max. Casually, he said to her, "I want you to come with me to Belize."

Max stopped and looked at him, not sure that she heard him correctly. "Belize? What are you talking about?"

"I have a sailboat there, and well, I want you to come with me."

"Daniel! What are you talking about?"

"I have to go to Belize for a while and I want you to come with me."

"You have a sailboat in Belize?" asked Max incredulously.

"Yes."

"You know how to sail?

"Yes."

"Why didn't you tell me this before?

"Didn't seem necessary," he said with a smile.

"This seems to be a fairly significant piece of information to not seem necessary."

"What can I say. . . . so will you go with me?"

"Maybe," said Max, " When?"

"Right away."

"Define right away." Now, Max was getting a little twitchy. This kind of thing had never happened to her before and she wasn't sure exactly how to act or what to say. So she asked, "What's your boat's name?"

"*I Got d' Riddem*"

"That's an unusual name for a boat."

"Will you go with me?"

CHAPTER 50

IT WAS LATE ON SUNDAY NIGHT when the limo pulled up in front of her house. All the lights in the house were on and Patti's car was in the drive.

Before the driver could turn into the drive, Max said, "Uh oh, Patti's here. Have the driver leave me off at the bottom of the drive."

Daniel started to say something but Max cut him short. "Please."

Daniel could see that it would do no good to argue, so he signaled the driver to follow her wishes. Then he turned to her and said, "You haven't given me an answer."

"I have been thinking about your invitation all afternoon. I can't believe that you want me to just drop everything and go off to Belize with you."

"Max, I know that it's a lot to expect, but sometimes you just have to jump without looking and trust fate that everything will be okay. You are very special. I won't pressure you, but I would like an answer sooner than later." Then he leaned toward her, placed his hand on her cheek and gently guided her to him and he kissed her. It was soft and gentle. It was perfect.

That did it. Max moaned softly and said, "Yes. I'll go with you."

Another kiss and she got out of the car. Daniel helped her with her packages and said, "Are you sure you don't want me to help you carry all this up to the house?"

"Yes, I'm sure. Will you call me later?"

"You know I will. Get some sleep."

"I'll call you tomorrow."

"Goodnight."

She watched him drive off, and then picking up the packages at her feet, she began walking up the drive. That's when Patti came bounding out.

"Max! Where have you been? I was starting to get worried. What's all this?" Before Max could respond, she continued, "So, how was the weekend? Was it just fabulous? What was Daniel like? I want all the details."

"Patti, slow down. Let's go in first."

"No. Tell me . . . Tell me," she pleaded.

Max smiled and kept walking with Patti following like a puppy excited to see its master, her pleading becoming more incessant. "Come on. The suspense is killing me. Tell me all about the weekend."

When the door closed behind them, Patti suddenly stopped and stared at Max. Max looked back at her and said, "What?"

"Those clothes, you didn't take any with you." She slowly circled Max, taking note of every little detail and then she looked at the label in the sweater that Max was wearing and softly exhaled. "Whoa. Do you have any idea what you are wearing?" Max really didn't. She never paid much attention to those kinds of things. She just knew that it was a nice sweater. Patti began looking more closely at everything Max was wearing. "They are fabulous, where did you get them? Did he take you shopping?"

"Not exactly."

"What do you mean, 'Not exactly'."

"Well, he had them delivered to the room."

"He had them delivered to the room? Stop right there. Back up. You had better start from the beginning."

"Okay, but this could take a while."

The two of them sat up until sunrise talking.

CHAPTER 51

MAX WAS EXHAUSTED AND SLEPT UNTIL NOON. When she finally awakened, Patti was gone and she was alone with her thoughts and memories. As soon as the coffee was brewing, she scrounged through the fridge and found a left over pastry.

With coffee and danish in hand, she sat down on the couch and began to relive the weekend. Now she was alone and could be more analytical. So much had happened in the past two days, she needed to sort it all out. Daniel was everything she had imagined and then some. He was so perceptive. He knew all the right things to say and all the right things to do. Everything he did was about her and for her. She had never felt pressured. He made her want him. He was the sexiest, most caring, sensitive, wonderful man she had ever met. In short, he was too good to be true.

As she sat there sipping her coffee, she finally admitted to herself what she hadn't acknowledged consciously before: she knew very little about him. She started checking off in her mind what she knew about him. *For starters he had to be wealthy. His clothes, his car, a boat in Belize. And that shopping trip? Those clothes were just what I would wear, and all of the sizes were perfect, even the underwear. That's just not normal.* Then the question returned. *What do I really know about him?*

She now started pacing around the room and her thoughts became words as she argued with herself.

"I know what I'm doing. Jack's gone. He didn't have to leave, but he did. You shut him out. Daniel showed up and you shut Jack out."

She stopped and considered what she had just said. The impact of her spoken words hit her like a slap in the face. The act of speaking her thoughts made them seem so much more real. A tear spilled down her cheek. *Jack hadn't even tried,* she thought. She paused, sniffled and then said aloud with resolve, "So now I'm moving on."

With that statement, her thoughts returned to Daniel and the weekend they had just spent together. She circled the couch again, saying nothing, and then she stopped, grinned, and blushing said, "Shit, I'm going to do it." Then almost as an afterthought, as if she needed to justify her decision, she added to no one but herself, "Max, you're a big girl. The most amazing man you have ever met wants you. Go for it. You may never get this chance again. Sure it's a risk, but few of life's truly great moments are risk free."

CHAPTER 52

THE PHONE RANG, ITS RING ENDING her moment of decision. On the second ring, she picked up the receiver. "Hello?"

"Welcome back, Max." It was Courtney. "How was the weekend?" The way she said it, Max had a feeling that she already knew the answer. *Damn that Patti.*

"Hi, Court. It was fabulous."

"Will you be around later? I've got some things to talk to you about."

"Sure, I'm up but, I still need to get showered."

"That's fine. How about my house, say five o'clock? We can have cocktails."

"Great. See you then."

Max hung up the phone and winced. *She knows,* she thought.

Five o'clock was several hours away, so Max lay down for a short nap. She jerked herself awake after what felt like only a few minutes, looked at the clock and saw it was 4:15. She jumped up and headed for the shower.

It was just a few minutes after five when she pulled into the drive at Courtney's. A twinge of melancholy flooded through her as she looked up at Jack's place. She missed him, but he was gone. She got out, took a deep breath and went to the door. Courtney must have seen or heard her pull up because she opened the door just as she reached to knock.

"Come on in, Cinderella, I want to hear all about it," Courtney said with a chuckle.

"Hi, Court," and she gave her a hello hug. Even though Max was an employee, they were also close friends and tonight was about friendship. Cat came over to greet her and Max scratched her ears and thought about Jack for a moment. Before the door shut, Cat ran out.

"Drink?" said Courtney as she closed the door.

"Sure."

"How about a Cosmo?"

"That sounds good, thanks."

Motioning toward the refrigerator, Courtney said, "There's some cheese in the fridge and there are some crackers on the counter. Why don't you get them while I whip up these drinks?"

Max put together a plate of cheese and crackers, Courtney finished making the drinks and they sat at the table, sipping their drinks in silence while looking out across the yard, past Jack's place and out to the marsh as the day began that slow transition to night. The sky was beginning to glow with shades of red and purple and orange. The drinks were delicious and the two women began to feel their effect. Courtney looked over at Max as she sat looking out toward Jack's place and wondered, the she said, "So, tell me about the weekend."

Max was snapped out of her thoughts and turned toward Courtney, and a slight blush came to her face, partly from the drink and partly from the question and the memories it evoked. "It was unbelievable. I have never been with a man like Daniel before. He makes you the center of the universe. The ball was incredible and he can dance, and I don't mean the old drunk white guy dance. I mean he can really dance."

"Was he as good in bed?" Courtney had a way of being totally blunt at times.

Max blushed. "Courtney," she said taken by surprise by the directness of the question. She knew that it was going to be asked, she just hadn't expected it so soon.

"Yes, he was." That kind of direct question needed a direct answer.

"And?"

"Okay, so after the ball he took me to the Lennox Hotel where he had a suite reserved." Max's face reddened as she offered just enough information to satisfy Courtney while keeping the details private. "But, even more remarkable was the next day. While I slept, he went shopping and bought me some clothes since I hadn't packed an overnight bag. Right down to my underwear and he got it all right. Sizes, styles, everything."

"No shit." said Courtney. "Sizes, everything?"

"Everything."

"Can you have him go shopping for me? I'd like to see what he would come up with."

They laughed and finished their first drinks.

While Courtney made another round she said, "So what is this I hear about him asking you to run off with him to Belize?"

Patti had spilled the beans.

"Yeah, he did," replied Max a little sheepishly.

"Are you going?" asked Courtney as she handed Max her new drink.

Taking a sip first, Max said. "Yes, I am."

"When?"

"I don't know exactly, but it sounded like Daniel wanted to leave soon. Do you hate me? I don't want to screw everyone at Ben's."

"Max, I could never hate you. Am I disappointed? Yes. Selfishly, I don't want to lose you. You're my best bartender. Personally, I am a little worried. Jack is in a total funk. I don't know where he has gone off to, other than he sailed out of the harbor just before the weekend. And I'm worried about you. Do you really know what you are getting yourself into?"

"Court, I love you. You're right about everything, but something tells me I have to do this. Don't be angry, please."

"I'm not, honey." said Courtney as both of their eyes welled up with tears. They hugged.

Tender moment over, Courtney said, "A boat in Belize?"

"Yeah, he told me it was a catamaran, and that it's name is *I Got d'Riddem.*"

"Really. Do you know where Belize is?"

"Sort of. It's in Central America, I know that much."

"I just saw a show on the Travel Channel and it was on Belize. It looks really cool. It has the second longest barrier reef in the world, and they speak English because it used to be British Honduras but is now independent. It is quite the hot spot to visit."

"Now I'm getting even more excited."

The rest of the evening was spent on girl talk. It was close to midnight when Max finally got home. Throughout the night, she went through moments of certainty about what she was about to do and then there would be moments of doubt. In the end, she felt that going with Daniel was the right thing. Her answering machine message light was blinking. She pressed the play button and heard his voice. "How about we leave the day after tomorrow? I'll call you in the morning. Oh, I almost forgot. Do you have a passport?" Then the message clicked off.

Day after tomorrow. Whoa, that's fast. At least I still have my passport from the trip to Switzerland, she thought. That triggered a brief memory of being with Jack in Bern and caused a sharp pang. The moment passed and she went to sleep thinking about what she would take, and how long they would be gone.

CHAPTER 53

THE PLANE WAS BEGINNING TO DESCEND and through the window she could see jade green water surrounding an island. "That's Ambergris Caye," said Daniel. Soon Caye Caulker came into sight, followed by Caye Chapel. They were low enough to make out some white specks on the water that must have been sails. The plane banked right, turning away from the water leaving Hicks Caye, Porto Stuck, and North Drowned Caye in the distance. Green jungle, red roofed houses and neat, square shrimp ponds came into sight as the final approach to the Philip Goldson Airport began. The 737 dropped onto the runway, reversed engines and hit the brakes, finally coming to a stop at the end of the runway. A short taxi to the gate and they had arrived in Belize.

Daniel let out a quiet sigh of relief. He had managed to elude his employer before his unannounced departure. He knew that when his employer found that he was gone, his life would probably be worthless. He had messed up the Python affair even though the result should have been acceptable. He had been unsuccessful in signing the band at Ben's and had ignored his employer's request for a meeting. Each event itself was worthy of his employer's wrath, but all three? His employer was not known for tolerance. It was possible that Python's death was unrelated to him or his employer, but neither could take the chance. Loose ends would have to be tied up one way or another

If he had never met Max, maybe things would have been simpler, but he had met her, and he had become obsessed with her. He might even love her. He wasn't sure about that. He didn't know who had killed Python, but he could guess. His success at convincing her to go to Belize with him was as much about his powers of persuasion as it was to protect

Max. It wouldn't have been hard for his employer to link Max to him, and if he had disappeared alone, she would have been available as leverage. She didn't know how lucky she was to be here with him.

The flight crew opened the door and a blast of hot humid air hit them as they walked down the ramp. Max had never exited a plane this way. She had never walked across the tarmac. She looked around, taking it in; every sight, sound and smell a new experience. Daniel calmly guided her along, explaining to her what would happen next. They passed through immigration and then customs with no difficulties and then got straight into the line at Tropic Air to check in for their flight to Ambergris Caye. Max had never flown in a small plane before and her anxiety was heightened by all the activity of check in. To her it was chaos, people and luggage seemed to be everywhere, but it proceeded at its own pace and soon they only had to pass through one more security checkpoint.

Once inside the departure lounge, Daniel escorted her to the far corner to Jet's Bar. If the whole experience of the last few days wasn't enough, Jet was the topper. The aged proprietor greeted everyone he encountered as if they were a long lost friend. His voice was like nothing Max had ever heard before. If Louis Armstrong had a raspy voice, then compared to Jet's he had the pure clear voice of a Pavarotti. "Charles," he croaked when he saw him. "It's been a long time."

"I'm sorry, my name is Daniel, but it's nice to meet you."

"Sorry, you look like someone else I know." He paused and looked confused. Then he asked, "Can I get you and your friend one of my famous rum punches?"

"No, thanks." Daniel said, "How about two Belikins?"

"Belikins it is," and he tipped them upside down into plastic cups. Daniel handed one to Max and then he looked at her. "Max, I've never met anyone like you. Here's to us in paradise."

She looked at him and said, "Charles?"

He just shrugged his shoulders and lifted plastic cup for a toast.

They touched rims and drank.

The flight to Ambergris Caye only took fifteen minutes and Max was like a kid in an amusement park. It was another first for her. Daniel was like one too, enjoying it through her, even though he had done it many times. Finally they were there. It was official. They were in Belize. After collecting their luggage, Daniel ushered her across the cobblestone paved street to their hotel while dodging taxis, bicycles and golf carts. Immediately, she felt the magic of San Pedro. Daniel had tried to explain, and she had tried to imagine what he was talking about, but until she was there she couldn't fully understand. Now, she got it.

Daniel had booked a room at the Sunbreeze Hotel for a few days before they would move onto *I Got d'Riddem.* Daniel felt it was a better way to ease into the Belizean rhythm, and besides, after a day of travel, an air conditioned room and a shower would feel good. Even though Max had sailed with Jack and she had some idea about sailing, she had never actually stayed on a boat for anything more than just a night so the hotel idea sounded good to her. It had been a really long day of traveling and Max was dead tired. Daniel had some business to take care of, so he left Max at the hotel while he went out.

CHAPTER 54

HIS FIRST STOP, ALFONSO'S. Alfonso was a local fisherman who, along with working as a tourist snorkel guide, also took care of Daniel's boat for him. Daniel and Alfonso had met years ago when Daniel had been in Belize on a job, a job that resulted in him buying the boat. They were younger and more carefree then and Daniel ended up saving Alfonso's life in a diving accident. They became close friends, each willing to do anything for the other. Daniel kept his personal life separate from work and he was pretty sure that his employer did not know about the boat, but he never knew for sure. He couldn't take any chances, especially after his latest, and only, failures.

Alfonso was down at his dock, which was on the south side of the island, away from town. His own boat, a long, shallow draft boat with a raised bow and bench seating all around, perfect for taking lots of tourists out snorkeling, was tied up next to *I Got d'Riddem.* He was bent over what appeared to be a new outboard motor and as Daniel approached, he could hear lots of clanking and swearing. "You know, if you talk sweet to them, they respond better," said Daniel.

Alfonso froze for a moment without looking up and said "Charles?" Then he stood and turned with a big smile and said, "Charles, why didn't you tell me you were coming down?"

Daniel jumped down off the dock and into the boat and they did the man-hug and back slap. "I wanted to surprise you, and call me Daniel."

"Daniel? Why Daniel?"

"I'm down here with a very special lady and she knows me as Daniel. I'll explain the whole story to you later."

"Sure . . . uh, Daniel," he replied with a wink and a smile.

"Listen, I'm not really supposed to be down here right now. My boss is a little pissed at me so I decided to take a short vacation without him knowing. He'll probably find out soon enough, but I hope to be out of here before he does. My friend and I are going to sail south, and spend some quality time together. I need you to keep an eye out in case anyone shows up looking for me."

"You know I'll help you in any way I can. So who's this lady?"

"Her name is Max."

"Whatever happened to that other lady you brought down here?"

"You must be thinking of April. She was fun, but that was about all she was. Max is different. You'll see when you meet her."

"And when will that be?"

"I was thinking about a trip out to Hol Chan and Shark Ray tomorrow afternoon. How about it?"

"I'll pick you up at two. Where are you staying?"

"We're at the Sunbreeze. We'll wait at the dock."

"Great. Now, when do you want to leave on *d'Riddem*?"

"The day after tomorrow would be great. Do you think you can you have her ready?"

"Sure, no problem."

"Can you provision us too, say, enough for two weeks?"

"No problem, man. I'll have my sister help with that. *D'Riddem* will be ready."

"Thanks." As Daniel turned to leave, he stopped and in a quiet voice repeated his request for anonymity. "Alfonso, remember, I'm not here. If anyone shows up asking about me or my boat and you hear about it, let me know."

"No problem, man. You know I have a large family. They live all up and down the coast, we'll keep an eye out for you. Don't worry."

"Thanks, Alfonso. See you tomorrow afternoon," and he turned and left.

Alfonso watched him go, wondering, *What has that boy got himself into now?*

CHAPTER 55

MISSION ACCOMPLISHED. Daniel returned to the hotel looking forward to a shower and maybe a power nap before dinner. When he got back to the room, Max was not there. Instead, there was a note saying that she was at the pool and would return soon. He smiled, stripped, turned on the shower, purposely keeping the water temperature cool. Standing there, the cool water cascading onto his head, down his shoulders and over his body, he could feel all the stresses of a long hot day of traveling begin to disappear. Just as he finished soaping his hair and head so he couldn't open his eyes he heard the shower curtain being drawn aside. "Max?" he said.

"Hi, I just got back from the pool and heard the shower running. I thought you might like some company." With that she stepped into the shower and pressed up behind him wrapping her arms around him, hugging him. "Oooh," she said as she felt the cool water now flowing over her body as well. "You're nice and warm."

"Mmm . . . " he moaned. Daniel probably held his head under the water to rinse the soap out off his hair and eyes a little longer that was necessary. The pleasure that he was experiencing from feeling her warm, slippery body pressed against his backside and her arms encircling him just needed to be savored. Slowly he turned, faced her, and wrapped his arms around her. They kissed deeply, becoming one as the cool water ran over their faces and over their now completely entwined bodies.

After, they dried each other off, then gently fell onto the bed and slept until hunger forced them awake. The restaurant was still open and after a couple of Blue Iguana's from the bar and dinner, sleep once again beckoned.

CHAPTER 56

THE NEXT MORNING, after a leisurely breakfast, Daniel rented a golf cart and took Max on a tour of this little piece of paradise called San Pedro. Eventually, Daniel turned off the road and drove down a long drive at the end of which was a large house. He stopped the cart behind the house and motioned for her to follow him as he walked around toward the front. It appeared that no one was home, and as she followed him silently, she wondered where they were, and why, but she didn't say anything. She just followed. When they reached the front of the house, she stopped. The view took her breath away. In the distance was nothing but the jade green water they had flown over on the way to San Pedro. There was a long dock running out from the shore and at the end was a beautiful white sailboat. The yard in front of the house was neat and filled with flowers and palm trees. Daniel had stopped and was looking out toward the boat. She stepped up next to him and whispered, "Is that your boat? Where are we?"

"Yes, that's her, and this is Alfonso's place. He takes care of my boat for me, and I'm guessing he must be out on a snorkel trip. He takes visitors out to dive and snorkel on the reef. Come on." He took her hand and they began to walk down toward the dock. Walking down the dock toward the boat, Max marveled at it. She had never seen anything like *I Got d'Riddem'*. She looked like a water bug, all gleaming white with a dark band around the cabin masking the cabin windows. "Daniel, she's beautiful," said Max.

"Come on aboard, my lady," he replied, as he offered her his hand, helping her climb onto the boat. She looked at him, not knowing what to say. He said, "Go ahead, Max, walk around, check her out."

She went forward first. There was a net stretched between the hulls that looked like a trampoline, and she could imagine lying there as they glided across the jade green sea. Returning aft, there was a gray inflatable dingy hanging from the back of the boat. The cockpit spanned nearly the full width of the boat. There was a raised seat in front of the steering wheel on the right side of the cabin. On the left, there was a table and a seat that went all the way around the cockpit. Next to the steering wheel in the center was a sliding glass door, which Daniel had already opened. "Come on in, I'll show you around your new home."

Max stepped in to the main cabin. On the right was the galley, in the center a large table and on the left a navigation station and the electrical panel. On each side, there were steps that went down into each of the hulls. *This is nothing like the Irrepressible*, she thought. What she said was, "So where do you sleep?"

"Come," said Daniel as he led the way down the stairs on the left side of the boat and turned right. There was a cabin with a double size bed. "This is our cabin, unless we choose to sleep out on the trampoline or in one of the other cabins." To the left of the stairs was the head. It was twice the size of the one on *Irrepressible* and very light and airy. Daniel led her back up into the main cabin and then motioned for her to go down the stairs on the other side. There were two more huge cabins, one forward and one aft. All she could say was. "Oh my god. This is awesome!"

When she came up, Daniel had already gone back out into the cockpit where he was sitting, enjoying the moment.

"When do we leave?" asked Max.

"Tomorrow. In the meantime, we need to get you outfitted for snorkeling because we are going to Hol Chan with Alfonso."

"What's Hol Chan?" asked Max,

"It's an underwater reserve that is a snorkeler's paradise. You've snorkeled before?"

"Of course." She didn't add that it had only been in a swimming pool, not the ocean with real fish.

"Great. Alfonso is going to take us this afternoon." Daniel didn't tell her about Shark/Ray Alley. He thought that it would be better as a surprise.

That afternoon, Max saw things she had only imagined existed. It was like swimming in an aquarium. Alfonso was at his charming, entertaining best and he never missed an opportunity to give Daniel the look that all guys recognize, that said, *You lucky bastard.* After a little more than an hour in the water, they climbed back into Alfonso's boat. Max was shivering so Daniel rubbed her with a dry towel and then he let the sun complete the job. That's when Alfonso announced, "Okay, let's go to Shark/Ray Alley. "Max looked up, first at him and then at Daniel. The look on her face was a combination of confusion, fear, and curiosity. "What did you say?" she said.

Both men were grinning from ear to ear. Alfonso spoke first, with mock surprise in his voice and said, "Didn't Daniel tell you we were going to go swim with sharks?"

"NO!" was her emphatic reply as she gave a look that threw daggers at Daniel. He just sat there grinning.

"Max, it's okay. They're just nurse sharks and quite harmless. You might even get to hold one."

This was too much for her. She put her hands over her ears and looked down. Whatever she said was drowned out by the sound of Alfonso's motor as they raced off to Shark/Ray Alley. By the time they got there, the shock had worn off and she was now curious. Revving his engine and throwing chum in the water brought a swarm of sharks to the boat. "Go ahead, jump in," said Alfonso. She whipped around to glare at him and before she could say anything, she heard a splash as Daniel went into the water. He was surrounded by sharks and rays who couldn't have cared less about him. Alfonso shooed at her with his hands, "Go on. Get in. I'll be right behind you. I won't let anything happen to you."

She looked at Daniel in the water, said, "What the hell?" and went overboard. She swam straight to Daniel and clung to him. If she was going to be eaten, he was going with her. Alfonso joined them and he brought a shark over for her to touch. Somehow, he made everything feel safe. She touched it. She touched a ray and she even held a small shark and he took her picture. Daniel could have watched her all day. She was like a child, totally free and uninhibited in her wonder at what she was doing.

It was 4:30 when Alfonso dropped them off at the same spot where he had picked them up earlier. He said that he would have his cousin, who was a taxi driver, pick them up at the hotel the next day at noon. Daniel and Max walked slowly back to the hotel, stopping at BC's Beach Bar for a celebratory beer. As they sat down, the bartender came over and said to Daniel, "Hey, Charles. Long time."

Daniel looked up at him and said, "I'm sorry, you must have me confused with someone else. My name is Daniel," as he offered his hand."

Obviously confused and a little embarrassed he said, "Sorry, man, you look so much like a guy I know. Nice to meet you, Daniel." They shook hands. "Can I get you something?"

"No problem, it happens to me all the time. We'll have two Belikins."

"Charles, again?" Then teasingly Max said, "Do you have an evil twin or something else I should know about?"

Daniel started to answer just as the beers arrived and the bartender said, "These are on me. Sorry again."

"Thanks."

Charles was forgotten as they sat sipping their beers, relaxing, looking out over the water watching the billowing clouds out over the sea begin to turn pinks and yellows from the sun setting behind them. Max sensed a tension in Daniel. He was looking down the beach, at what she couldn't tell. "Daniel, are you all right?"

He hesitated for just a moment before answering, taking one more look down the beach, "Yes, I'm fine. Why?"

"I don't know. It's just that all of a sudden you didn't seem to be here. What were you looking at?"

"Nothing, I was just thinking about how great the next few weeks will be."

Max wasn't convinced. Something in his response didn't feel right. It passed quickly enough and she forgot about that moment as they began to relive the days snorkel trip. The rest of the evening was magical. Dinner at the Blue Water Grill, a walk on the beach, then collapsing into each other's arms followed by long, slow lovemaking, and finally, the deep sleep that comes only after a perfect day.

CHAPTER 57

AT NOON, ALFONSO'S COUSIN ARRIVED at the hotel to take them to the boat. The ride only took fifteen dusty, bumpy minutes. *D'Riddem* was all provisioned and ready to go by the time they arrived dockside. The engines were warmed up, ice was in the ice chest and the refrigerator was all cooled down. Max went aboard put her things below and began taking stock of the provisions. Alfonso seemed to have thought of everything. There was plenty of rum, beer, fruit juices, eggs, canned goods, pastries from the bakery and even a small key lime pie.

Before Daniel went on board, Alfonso took him aside. "Hey man, my cousin who just brought you here picked up a new arrival at the airport yesterday while we were out snorkeling."

"So?"

"Well, it may not be anything, but he just didn't fit. You know, when you are dealing with gringos every day, you learn a lot about reading people and he said that something just didn't seem right about him."

"What did he look like?"

"He was tall, thin. His eyes were close together and he had a mean look about him. He also didn't have any luggage, only a small case."

A chill went down his spine. "Thanks, Alfonso. He doesn't sound like any one I know, probably just one of those people," said Daniel trying not to show any reaction. *Could his employer know? He couldn't know about d'Riddem . . .*

"No problem. Now listen, as you go south, I have many cousins and all you have to do is say that you are a friend of Alfonso's and they will help you in any way possible."

"Thanks, I'll remember that."

Max had just climbed off the boat and came over and put her arm around Daniel and said, "What are you two talking about? Everything looks great. Thank you, Alfonso."

"It was my pleasure," said Alfonso. Then looking at Daniel he said, "What are you waiting for? You shouldn't be sitting here talking to me when you could be out sailing with this beautiful lady."

Max blushed and Daniel said, "You're right, my friend. Let's go. Alfonso, thanks."

Daniel turned and climbed on board and immediately began the final preparations for departure. Before Max could turn to join him, Alfonso touched her arm. In a quiet voice as if he didn't want Daniel to hear, he said, "Can you do me a favor?"

"Well, sure."

His voice remained low and his face seemed to cloud over for the briefest of moments. Then with a slightly forced smile he said, "When you get to Placencia, can you take this letter to my sister, Nancy?" He handed her a small white envelope while glancing at the boat as if he didn't want Daniel to see him doing this. "She'll be easy to find. She's the pie maker. If you need anything, don't be afraid to ask her. She'll help you."

Max took the envelope from him and replied. "Of course, I'd be happy to." She slid the letter into her pocket, not sure what the mystery was all about. As soon as she did, the look on Alfonso's face changed as if he felt a sudden relief. She smiled and said, "Thank you again, Alfonso."

"For what?"

"For that incredible trip yesterday and for all your work getting the boat ready."

"No problem. It's my job."

"I think it's more. Thank you."

Before anything else could be said, Daniel shouted, "Hey! Will you two quit gabbing? It's time to go."

Alfonso helped her step up onto the boat, then untied the lines and cast them off. While Daniel steered a course down the narrow channel toward deeper water, Max stood there, waved farewell to Alfonso, and watched Ambergris Caye become a memory.

CHAPTER 58

THE SUN WAS HOT, the sky was blue with white puffy clouds, and the northeast trade winds were blowing them toward Caye Caulker and points south. The water was like nothing Max had ever seen before. She was mesmerized. It changed colors continuously from a jade green to bright almost whitish blue-green where the bottom was sand, to darker green where the bottom was covered with turtle grass. Passing clouds cast deep blue shadows that danced across the surface.

Max went below while Daniel steered to clear water. As they exited the channel, she reappeared wearing a black string bikini with a tube of sunscreen in her hand. "Will you be able to help me with this on my back?" she asked as she began to spread it over those exposed parts of her body that she could reach. She was so totally absorbed in what she was doing that she didn't notice Daniel gazing at her, thinking how incredibly sexy she was. Her skin was a milky white with just a blush of color and Daniel said to her, "Be really careful down here in the sun, especially in the middle of the day. You'll crisp up in no time and then we'll both be miserable."

"Thanks for the warning. I'm ready whenever you are."

Daniel pressed the button that activated the autopilot and waited a moment while it took control. When he was satisfied that they were tracking correctly and that the course ahead was clear, he climbed out of the helmsman's seat and took the tube from her. He squeezed some lotion into the palm of his hand. It was warm. "Unhook your top so I can get your whole back." She reached back, unhooked the strap and leaned forward, not bothering to hold her top to her breasts as she braced herself against the table. The gentle motion of his hands rubbing the warm lotion on her back felt as good to her as it did to him. Her eyes closed and she moaned softly. He smiled and remembered to breathe. As soon as her back was well coated, he stood and took note of their course. Max re-hooked the straps of her top, adjusted the front and asked if he would like her to put some on his back. "I thought you'd never ask," he said.

He peeled off his shirt and she began rubbing the warm lotion over his back. He was naturally darker than she was, but the sun could still cause him to burn if he wasn't careful. She loved the way her hands slid over the gentle undulations of his firm muscles. It was hard for her to decide which felt better, him rubbing lotion on her back or her rubbing it on his.

When she finished, he made one more course check then went below. He returned wearing a pair of quick dry shorts, picked up the tube of lotion and began to spread it over the rest of his body. She watched him and tried not to be too obvious as she did so. The day was hot, but the heat she was feeling didn't come from only the sun.

Putting the tube of lotion down, Daniel announced, "Time to get the sails up and turn off those infernal engines."

"Okay. What do I do?" said Max.

"This first time I will have you steer the boat while I handle the sails. Next time you hoist."

"Okay."

Daniel turned off the autopilot and slowed the engines until they had just enough way on to maintain control. He had Max stand at the helm and take the wheel. "It's just like steering a car. The boat will go in the direction you turn the wheel. Just do it slowly, you have to feel the turn. It happens slower than a car. Try it, see how it feels."

She tried several turns. It wasn't all that different from *Irrepressible* only the boat was so much wider. Max found herself smiling from ear to ear. "Okay, I'm ready, let's get those sails up."

Turning the boat into the wind, Daniel went forward to the mast. He had already unfastened the strap that kept the boom from swinging when they were not sailing. The sail cover was unzipped and he shouted back to Max, "Are you ready?"

"Go for it," was her reply.

Max held the boat into the wind and Daniel began hauling on the main halyard. The sail had full battens and from the effort that Daniel was putting into it, she could tell that it was a heavy sail. For the last foot or so, he had to use the winch to fully tighten the sail's luff. Satisfied that it was tight enough, he returned to the cockpit breathing heavily and sweating as much from the effort as from the hot sun. Max wasn't sure that she'd be able to tackle the sails, and anyway, she'd rather watch Daniel.

"So now begin to turn to starboard slowly so we can head to our destination." There was a soft whomp as the sail filled. Since their course was taking them south, it would be nearly a downwind run. Daniel pulled the throttle controls into neutral and the trade winds began pushing them south. The loud whistle from the engine panel signaled that each engine was shut down and silence took over as soon as each key was turned off. Now only the soft swish and gurgling of the water passing by the hulls remained. The sky, the clouds, and the incredible color of the water had Max transfixed. Sailing had never been like this before. There was very little motion, they were just gliding and as she looked all around them, there were no other boats in sight except far off in the distance the spray from a fast moving water taxi could be seen.

"Time for the jib." Daniel eased the furling line and the wind pulled the sail out. Standing next to Max, he trimmed it so it was full and pulling. She found herself continually comparing *d'Riddem* to *Irrepressible.* They were so different and yet they were the same. Caye Caulker was just about dead down wind making the sailing slow and easy. "What's our destination?" asked Max.

"We're only going as far as Caye Caulker and should be there within the next two hours," replied Daniel. Caye Caulker was only about ten miles or so south of Ambergris Caye and he continued to let Max have the helm, until they were more than halfway there. What had at first looked like a bar code on the horizon soon became a solid line and now could clearly be seen to be a land mass. Daniel took the helm so that she was free to move about and feel *d'Riddem.* Max walked forward, stepped onto the trampoline and lay down. The water swooshed and gurgled below her and she thought, *It must be like being a bird, gliding just above the waves.* Rolling over she looked back at Daniell at the helm. She could only see his head and he was smiling the same way she was.

CHAPTER 59

AS THEY NEARED CAYE CAULKER, Max returned to the cockpit and stood by Daniel. He explained to her that Caye Caulker was a long skinny island and this northern part that they were gliding past was mostly mangroves and few people lived there. It was divided from the southern part by a cut, which was created by storms, effectively making two islands. They would be anchoring in a natural harbor off the backside of the settlement. Coming around the last point, the settlement village came into sight. Daniel started the engines and left them idling as they continued to sail into the harbor. The harbor was U-shaped, open to the west and the sunset. It appeared deserted except for a few boats that had not moved in a very long time. They were sporting beards at the waterline and all had the look of abandonment. At the dock, there was a barge with a propane truck on it tied up and Max could see activity there. The generator station could be heard droning on and there were only a few houses on the water. "It's kind of deserted isn't it?"

"This is the back side of the town. It's a better place to anchor but it's not real pretty except for the sunset. The other side, facing the reef, is pretty active," replied Daniel.

"What's that pink place?" she asked.

"That's probably the nicest resort on the island. It's called the Iguana Reef Resort. When we go ashore, we'll take the dinghy to their dock and walk into town. They don't mind and they have a nice bar there for watching the sunset."

Daniel had Max turn the boat into the wind, while he furled the jib and then dropped the mainsail. Max had never seen a sail come down so fast and neatly stack itself in the zippered sail cover. Daniel returned to the helm and pointed out to Max a light spot of bottom, explaining that it would be sand.

"That's where we will drop the hook, in that sandy spot. The darker areas are turtle grass and sometimes it is hard to get a good set in the grass, although here it shouldn't be a problem."

Max guided the boat to the spot and as forward motion stopped, Daniel lowered the anchor and paid out enough chain for a five to one scope. Then he did something she had never seen before. There was a line attached to each end of the catamaran's forward crossbeam. It had a hook in the center of it and this Daniel attached to the chain, then he let more out until the boat was riding on this rope. When he was finished, he returned to the cockpit and she asked him about the rope and what it was for. "That's called a bridle, and it is there so that the boat is pulling on it rather than on the windlass. Being tied to each end of the crossbeam the way it is, it also steadies the boat and she won't swing back and forth as much," explained Daniel. "Don't worry, by the end of tomorrow, this will all be second nature to you."

The port engine was shut down, but the idle on the starboard one was increased and he turned on the refrigeration, explaining how they would have to cool it down twice a day, for an hour in the morning and again at night. A celebratory beer and a quick swim off the back of the boat, then a fresh water rinse off occupied refrigeration time. Finally the timer clicked, turning off the refrigeration and Daniel shut down the engine as the sun began to drop to the horizon. They sat there, Max leaning into Daniel with his arms around her and watched the sun dip below the horizon.

"That was incredible," said Max in a soft voice.

"Are you hungry?" asked Daniel.

"Yes."

"Good. Let's go ashore and find some food."

"What should I wear?" Max asked.

"Things here are pretty casual. Shorts and shirt are fine, bare feet are not a problem although I would suggest something on your feet. We'll be doing some walking."

They dressed, turned the anchor light on, locked up the boat, lowered the dinghy and putted over to the Iguana Reef. The dinghy secured, they walked across the hotel's raked sand yard and past the bar where some of the guests were sipping blue drinks with umbrellas.

"Charles! Charles!" a voice cried out. They both turned to see where the voice was coming from and saw the bartender walking toward them. "Charles, how have you been, man?"

Daniel gave him the blankest look he could while Max looked from one man to the other.

"I'm sorry, were you talking to me?" said Daniel. With this statement the bartender stopped and looked at him quite puzzled. "Charles?" he said again.

"No, my name is Daniel. You must have me confused with someone else."

"Sorry, man. You really look like this guy I know named Charles and I saw you come in on his boat."

Daniel laughed at this. "That must be it. I charter my boat out occasionally and whoever this Charles was, he must have been a charter on the boat. I must have one of those faces because I'm always having strangers come up to me thinking I'm someone else. My name is Daniel," and he extended his hand.

The bartender extended his hand and said, "Michael. Sorry again for the mistake."

Max had been closely observing all of this. This was the third time on this trip that this had happened. Something didn't seem quite right, once or twice, maybe, but three times? Her thoughts were interrupted by Daniel's voice, "Michael, I'd like you to meet Max."

"Oh, hi Michael," and she stuck out her hand which he took into his.

"It's a pleasure to meet such a pretty lady. I'm sorry for my confusion. I have to get back to the bar. Perhaps I'll see you both later." And with that, he turned and left.

Max looked at Daniel.

He looked back with the most puzzled look on his face. "What?" he said.

"You know what . . . Charles," she said with some irritation.

He looked into Max's eyes and said, "Look Max, I'm as confused as you. I have no idea who this Charles is or why everyone thinks I'm him." He paused, and then continued with a whispered urgency in his voice as if speaking the unspeakable, "He must be an international man of mystery. You know, like in the movies when the unsuspecting tourist is mistaken for some spy or something and he becomes the unwilling hero in some life and death struggle over world domination." Then he smiled at her.

She continued her look, and then she, too, smiled.

Then they both laughed.

"You're probably right, mister unwilling hero. Let's hope we're not involved in something we don't know anything about. I just want to be with you."

"I'm sure it's all just nothing. Come on, let's go eat," said Daniel.

With that, they walked out of the front entrance of the Iguana Reef, pausing to watch a half dozen or so barefoot kids kicking a ball around on the hard packed sand and sparse overgrown vegetation that served as the local football pitch. In the remaining light the goals could be seen at either end of the field. Once all new and white, now they slumped from age, rust was taking over the paint, but they still defined the playing field. They walked around the game and headed toward Front Street. The walk was only a couple of hundred yards at best, past small houses on stilts with doors and windows open, spilling their light out onto the street and allowing glimpses into their spare interiors, aqua painted walls, an occasional framed picture on the wall and from some, music could be heard. Few seemed to be home and it seemed as if the entire population was out on the street, enjoying the cooler night air.

They reached Front Street and stopped to look and decide which way to go. People were walking, bicycling, standing and talking, kids running and playing. Some had places to go, purposeful in their stride or if they were on a bike, the way they zigged and zagged around and passed those engaged in less urgent pursuits. Sunburned tourists, some wearing backpacks, recently returned from their day's activities, could be seen looking at menus posted on the street, debating and discussing where to eat. Stray dogs and little children ran around in packs, carefree, all wrapped up in their own worlds and oblivious to all that was going on around them accented the mix. It was vibrant, it was alive, and it was not San Pedro.

It was San Pedro twenty years ago. In many ways, it was still a sleepy little fishing settlement, in others, it was every bit as modern as any city at home. There were restaurants, street vendors, stores and even an Internet café. But it wasn't like home. The scale was different. It was smaller, more human. It was touchable. There was connection, not anonymity. On closer inspection, you were reminded that it was an island, dependent on barge, boat and plane for everything. Stores had shelves full, but of only a few items. There were ever-present signs reading "... due in tomorrow". There was an optimism and a spirit that Max had never felt before. It was how a frontier town must have been in the early days of the west back home. Growth would come in fits and starts, leaving a society that more closely resembled a multi-textured fabric created from what was available than a planned, carefully designed and woven cloth.

They turned left and walked north. On their right, lining the beach were dive shops and other water sport vendors, each with their own dock running out into the water. Some were well maintained and others not so, still showing the effects of past storms. Boat traffic continued, even after dark. Out beyond the shore, beyond the boats, was the reef. It was the great protector of the shore from the sea. It was a thin white line now just visible as the moon rose in the ever-darkening night sky. The rustling of the palms and sea grape trees muffled the constant roar of the surf crashing on the reef as they swayed in the ever-present sea breeze. A fine sand dust blew everywhere and shopkeepers were constantly sweeping it from their floors.

There was one section in the middle of the beach that served as a sort of park. There were small palapas for shade, grills for cooking, and volleyball nets. Across from this park was a stone wall, behind which were some long unfinished buildings. On the wall and behind there were dozens of cats; young cats, mature cats, yellow ones, black ones, tigers. Max had never seen anything like it. They stopped to look and first one cat jumped onto the wall, then another and before long there were a dozen cats on top of the wall, all vying for their attention. Max was speechless as she scratched kitty heads. Daniel explained, "This is where Carlos the cat man lives. He takes in cats, provides sanctuary for them from the dogs and islanders who would hurt them. He feeds them, he gets them spayed and neutered and gives them medicine when they are sick." At this moment, a small man wearing a red tee shirt and khaki shorts came out of the small house that was in the back of the property. Max looked at him and thought that with his small round glasses he looked a little like Gandhi. "That's Carlos," said Daniel as he approached and said hello to them in broken English. Daniel didn't worry as Carlos never remembered names. It was an hour before they were able to pull themselves from Carlos and his cats. Max had fallen for one little tiger in particular who had only one eye. She called him Squint.

Not too much further down the street was a restaurant called Don Corleone's. It was Italian and decorated with movie posters and pictures from *The Godfather*. Daniel guided Max in and they were seated near the open front so they could feel the breeze and watch the world go by. Wine was served and Max looked at Daniel over her glass and said, "Well, Mr. International-Man-of-Mystery, tell me about where we are going." Obviously she had not forgotten about the last "Charles" incident.

"South," he whispered as he glanced around the room as if he were making sure that they had not been followed.

"South?" said Max.

"Shhh. Not so loud, the walls might have ears."

Max now joined the game and in a loud whisper while also glancing about she asked, "Where to the south?"

Once again he had deflected her curiosity, this time by getting her to play the game, Max not suspecting that it might not turn out to be a game. Daniel leaned forward, looked deep into her eyes and over his glass of wine said softly, "We are going to sail south and eventually we will end up in Placencia."

"Placencia?"

"Placencia."

"Why there?"

"For one thing, I think you'll like it. If you think that Caye Caulker is what San Pedro was like twenty years ago, then in Placencia we will go back another twenty. I want you to feel this country. I want you to love it the way I love it. I want you to be safe." He didn't mean to make that last statement, it just came out. She looked at him questioningly, "Safe? Safe from what? Daniel, you're making me nervous."

He reached across the table and took her hand. His voice was warm and soothing. "Max, I didn't mean anything by it. I was still playing the part of the International-Man-of Mystery and it seemed like the thing to say. I do want you to see Placencia, though. Alfonso has a sister there. She is expecting us and it should be a lot of fun."

"Okay, but no more games."

"No more games."

The rest of dinner was spent with Daniel telling Max about past trips to Belize and why he felt so at home here. After some dessert and strong coffee, Daniel paid the bill and they headed back down Front Street toward the Iguana Reef where they had tied the dinghy. People were still out, but it was much quieter and peaceful. The day was nearly over.

Max slept the sleep of the dead. The whine of a powerful outboard motor followed by a slight shaking sensation and the sound of water sloshing against the hull woke her. A bright light was passing back and forth across her face. She pried her eyes open and for a moment she wasn't sure where she was. Then, as the boat swung back, the sunlight streaming in through the forward hatch passed over her face again. A warm breeze washed over her and she remembered and smiled.

He was already up and she wondered what time it was. That's when the smell of fresh brewing coffee wafted down to her. Her smile broadened as she thought about Daniel and how right everything felt. Even though it had only been a few days, she was already losing track of time and it felt like forever. Another whiff of coffee was all it took for her to get up. The floor creaked when she stood on it. *"No sneaking up on anyone on this boat,"* she thought to herself. She went up the steps into the main salon that was empty save for the pot of coffee on the stove. Then she heard, "Good morning, beautiful." The voice came from the cockpit outside. Looking outside, she saw Daniel lying in a hammock that he had slung under the bimini. He smiled at her and lifted his cup in greeting. She poured herself a cup of coffee and went out to join him.

"Good morning. How long have you been up?"

"Since sunrise."

"What time is it?"

"A little after 6:30."

She looked at him with a somewhat surprised look on her face. She couldn't remember the last time she had seen such an early hour voluntarily. She said, "It looks like another beautiful day in paradise."

He smiled and she walked over to him and gave him a good morning kiss, then she sat down at the table and took a sip of her coffee. Neither said anything as they enjoyed the moment. "Where are we going today?" asked Max.

"South. There's no hurry and I thought we'd spend the night in the Drowned Cayes. From there we'll be able to see the lights of Belize City."

"Will we have any company?"

"Probably not."

"How romantic." She smiled, looked over her shoulder at him and went below. Daniel followed.

CHAPTER 60

TWO NIGHTS LATER AND A WEEK after Max had left with Daniel, Jack guided *Irrepressible* through the breakwater at the entrance to Rye Harbor. Homecoming, after a voyage, no matter how long or short, always seemed so full of hope and promise with friendships to renew, tales to tell, and the comfort one felt when arriving home. Tonight was different for Jack. There was no comfort. Yes, he was glad to be back, but he was returning to a different place. The one person he cared about the most was gone. The darkness of the harbor matched his mood. Most of the pleasure boats had already been hauled out for the coming winter. The party fishing boats were gone, the whale watch boats were gone, and the main dock had been hauled out, its sections stacked in the parking lot like huge dominoes. Even some of the fishing boats were gone. Its emptiness mirrored the emptiness he felt. John felt it, too. Such emotional and physical fatigue overcame them as they tied *Irrepressible* to her floats that they didn't leave the boat and just fell into their berths. Morning would arrive soon enough.

While they slept, clouds moved in and they awakened to gray skies and drizzle, but at least it wasn't windy. A cold, raw, dampness penetrated everything and everywhere. Even hot coffee had little effect. They finished securing the boat and walked to Jack's place, collars up, shoulders hunched with hands in their pockets, trying to maintain what little warmth they had. As they walked up the drive, past Courtney's, Jack heard a door open and Courtney's voice. "Jack?" He stopped and turned toward the voice, said "Hi, Court."

"Can you come in for a minute? I have to talk to you." It wasn't a greeting, it was a summons.

"Sure, just a minute."

She closed the door as Jack turned to John and said, “Listen, you go ahead, get a shower and warm up. You know where everything is. I have to go talk to Courtney for a minute.”

“Sure, and I’ll give Jenny a call.”

Jack turned and went back to Courtney’s, opened the door, and went in. It was warm and dry and comforting and he could smell the coffee brewing. She was over by the stove with her back to the door and him and she didn’t even turn around. Cat looked up from her spot on a big poufy pillow on the couch.

“Hi, Court. What are you doing up so early?” asked Jack as he went over to scratch Cat’s head. She started purring and curled up again. It was too early for her.

“Coffee?” she asked and then turned toward him.

“Yes, thanks. You didn’t answer my question.”

She picked up one of the cups she had been pouring, walked over and handed it to him. Then she stood and watched as he added cream and sugar and took his first sip. Finally she spoke, “Ever since Max left, I haven’t been able to sleep much. I’m worried about her.”

“She’s all right isn’t she?

“Yes, as far as anyone knows. We haven’t heard from her. Daniel seemed to be a really nice guy and he certainly did treat her like a princess. He was always kind and considerate, it’s just that it was all so sudden. I mean, she only met the guy a short while ago.”

“Court, you don’t have to tell me. All I have been thinking about for these past few weeks was Max, how I screwed up, and this guy . . . you know, I have a feeling that he has done this before.”

“What are you talking about?”

“He was part of why I was in Newport although I didn’t know it at the time.” Courtney had a puzzled look on her face. He continued, “You remember during the summer when he first started showing up on Sundays?”

"Sort of."

"Well, I do. He showed up just after Python did. Then, one Sunday, several weeks after Python's death, I saw Daniel talking to the band out back. He saw me watching them and when our eyes met, I got a weird feeling. As soon as they finished and the band went back to play, he disappeared."

"So what does any of this have to do with Max?"

"I'm trying to get there. Through all of this, Daniel was hitting on Max and I didn't handle any of that very well. When I saw her showing off her dress that night in the bar, something snapped inside and I had to get away, so I left."

"Jack, you're babbling. What does any of this have to do with Max?"

"I'm getting there. So I ran away, or rather sailed away. While sailing, all these different events kept rattling around in my head and for some reason, I felt that answers would be found in Newport."

"Now you are really making no sense."

"Let me continue. Python had come up from Newport. It just seemed like a starting point and my friend John lives there and he's a musician."

"John?"

"He's the guy you just saw me with. You remember him. He sailed into Rye a few years back. I took him in and we became friends."

"Okay, I remember him now."

"Well, I got to Newport, got hold of John and met a friend of his, Nigel, who's a runner. He's also a musician and they both knew Python. I told them what had happened to him and they told me what he had been up to in Newport. He was quite the hot property. CD's released, contracts, all that stuff. A guy named Charles had signed him and then disappeared."

"So?"

"So this Charles sounds exactly like Daniel. He had hit on John's girl friend, Jenny. She'll be here later today. You'll really like her. Jenny filled in some other parts of the story for me. The long and the short of it is that I think that Daniel and this Charles are the same person. I think he worked some kind of a scam on Python. Python found out something and followed him here and ended up dead. I suspect that Daniel was involved in Python's death, and now he has disappeared with Max."

Courtney sat there looking at Jack. She was speechless. Finally, she spoke up. "Jack, that is a bizarre story, but on some level it makes sense to me. Have you told Tom any of this?"

"I've talked to him briefly and I'm going to see him later this morning. What can you tell me about Max's departure?"

"Well, they left only a couple of days after that weekend at the big charity event. It was awfully sudden. That must have been some weekend."

"Do you know where they were going?"

"Yes, they were going to Belize. He has a boat there or something."

"Belize?"

"Yes. That's what she said."

Now it was Jack's turn to sit in silence as memories of a time long ago and nearly forgotten flashed through his head; a time before he had met Maria, before he had come to Rye, a time before Max. He remembered how beautiful Belize was and how he had sworn to himself to return there someday. A promise he had buried deep in his memories after the cold-blooded execution he had witnessed while a part of the crew on *The Raven*. Now, he knew he would finally return. He just hoped that he wouldn't be too late.

"Jack . . . Jack. Are you all right? I kind of lost you for a minute there."

"Um, yeah, I'm okay. Listen Court, I have to get going. I want to get cleaned up and I have to go see Tom." He stood and gave Cat another head scratch. She didn't even look up this time. "Cat seems to like it here."

"Yes, she does. I've totally spoiled her."

"Thanks."

"Okay. You go, but come by later. I'd like to see your friends."

As he left her house, the drizzle had turned to a light rain. Not the soft warm rain of spring, but the cold, biting rain of the fall. He hurried down the drive to his apartment.

In less than an hour, they were walking into Paula's for some breakfast. The usual cast of characters was there and Jack had to make the rounds saying hello and answering questions about where he had been. The one subject not asked about directly but which everyone wanted answers about was Max. Jack deftly avoided the subject and when it became obvious that no answers were forthcoming, he and John were able to eat their breakfasts in peace. "Did you get hold of Jenny?" asked Jack.

"Yeah, I did. She'll be here by noon. I gave her directions to Ben's and she'll meet us there for lunch."

"Good. When we finish, I want to go and see Tom. I have copies of Nigel's notes for him."

"He's the detective you told me about?"

"Yep, that's him."

CHAPTER 61

THE RAIN CONTINUED TO FALL, harder now than when they had arrived for breakfast and there was no indication that it would end soon. The temperature was far enough above freezing that there was no chance of the rain turning to snow and yet it felt as if it could. With the wipers clapping and the defroster blowing as hard as it could, the view out the truck's windshield was limited at best. The drive to the station was slow. The road had become a silver gray ribbon, mirroring the grayness of the sky, with no visible lines or markings.

Tom had just arrived minutes before Jack and John did. He was still wearing his wet coat when they walked in.

"Jack!"

"Hi, Tom."

"When did you get in?"

"We sailed in late last night." They shook hands and Jack then introduced him to John.

"Come on in, take your coats off. Damn but it's cold out today. Welcome to paradise."

Jack and John took their coats off and hung them on the coat tree that was near the door and then followed Tom into his tiny cramped office. His desk was still a mass of papers and files.

"Well, I can see you haven't accomplished much since I was last here," chided Jack.

"Paperwork. It's endless. No sooner do I clear a few cases then I have more to replace them. Most of it is pretty minor, but the paperwork is the same. Listen, why don't we go into the conference room? It's not much bigger, but at least the table is clear."

"Sure. Fine by me." said Jack; John just followed.

As soon as they were seated around the table, Jack handed Tom Nigel's notes. "These are for you."

"What's this?"

"These are Nigel's notes. He's the guy I told you about in Newport who was helping Python try to find out what happened to his music career."

Tom took his time looking through all of the pages. Finally, he looked up. "God, what a mess. I never realized just how nasty the music business was."

"Were you able to find out anything else here after I called you last week?" asked Jack.

"Actually, yes. After you called me I went back to the band and had another talk with them. At first, they were just as uncooperative as they had been when I first talked to them. Then when I filled them in on what you had told me about Python's experience in Newport, they were a little more willing to talk."

"What did they tell you?"

"It sounds like the same story, only the names have changed. This Daniel Cummings had approached them. He was all hot to get them to sign a contract with the music publishing house he represented. Sun Soul Records was its name. At the same time that he was talking to them, Python had showed up and warned them to be careful. He said that the guy who was talking to them was the same guy who had been his contact in Newport, except that his name was Charles. They were going to get together later so that he could tell them more about what he had found out. He never showed and then you found him floating in the harbor. They freaked, wouldn't talk to anyone and they wouldn't sign the contracts."

"Besides the fact that this Daniel or Charles was the same guy, did they tell you anything else?"

"Nothing. They said that he was a little too pushy and the last time they saw him, he seemed a little nervous."

"When was that?"

"The last time they had talked was shortly after Python's death. It seems that this Daniel was all wrapped up in scoring with Max. He must have been successful because she left with him a few days ago. It almost seemed like he was working two different scams at the same time."

Tom regretted what he had just said to Jack as soon as he said it. "Sorry."

"That's okay. I deserve it."

The rest of the morning was spent going over the information that Nigel had given Jack. John was able to give both Jack and Tom a crash course in how the music business worked and the kind of money that could be involved. Neither one of them had had any idea how high the stakes were.

When John finished, silence filled the room and Jack felt as cold and gray inside as the weather outside. His thoughts were jumbled. *There was no proof, yet he was convinced that Daniel and Charles were one and the same, and that he had sucked Python in, in Newport, then had moved on to Rye where he was working the same scam. Python had followed him to Rye and ended up dead. What did Python know? Did Daniel kill him or did someone else? One thing was for certain, whomever Daniel worked for was invisible. Did Daniel even know his employer? What was Daniel's interest in Max? Why did he take off with Max and why Belize?*

Tom was the first to break the silence. "I don't think there's much more for us to do here today. I'm going to contact my friend at the FBI and see if they have anything that might help us."

John looked at his watch and said, "Jack, it's after noon and Jenny should be getting to Ben's soon, if she's not there already. We should go."

Jack looked at his watch, "You're right."

The three men stood. Goodbyes were said and as Jack and John put on their still damp coats, Tom thanked them and said he'd be in touch later. He hoped he would be able to find out something before the end of the day.

It was a quiet ride to Ben's, neither one of them saying much. As they pulled into the parking lot, they saw Jenny's green VW. "I can't believe she drove up here in that," said Jack.

John just grinned, "I know what you mean, but I've learned that some things you just accept with Jenny and you don't question."

The rain had slowed to a drizzle, but they still hurried inside. It was warm and felt like home. It had been a while since John had been in Ben's, but it was just as he remembered. As they walked down the hallway, the hostess smiled at them before turning and escorting another couple into the dining room. John and Jack looked into the bar and saw Jenny, Patti, and Courtney sitting by the wood stove, obviously engaged in a serious conversation. Jenny had her back to the door and didn't see them come in. As they walked over, Courtney looked up and saw Jack. Before she could say anything, John was leaning over from behind Jenny to give her a kiss on the neck. Startled, she jumped and turned around and instantly her face softened as she said, "John . . . you startled me." He grinned and then they all began talking at the same time.

"Hi, Babe. You been here long?" asked John.

"Jack!" said Patti as she stood and gave him a hug. "It's about time you got back here. Where have you been?"

Before he could answer, Courtney said, "Hi, Jack," then turning to John said, "John, it's good to see you again."

Jack replied, "Hi everyone, I see you have met Jenny. Patti, this is John."

"Hi, John."

Then Courtney turned back to Jack. "Jenny's been filling us in on this Daniel character and what happened to Python in Newport. I think Max is in trouble"

"Slow down, Court. There's an awful lot we don't know. We just finished meeting with Tom and gave him some new information. I think that we'll have to wait for him to see where that leads."

"Wrong, Jack. You need to go, now."

"Go where?"

"You dumb shit. Belize."

"Fine. But, other than Belize, we have no idea where she is. Has anyone heard from her?"

There was silence all around the wood stove and Courtney glared at Jack.

CHAPTER 62

OVER A LEISURELY BREAKFAST, Daniel and Max watched Caye Caulker wake up. A barge arrived with a propane truck on its deck and that was swapped for a dump truck. One of the water taxis arrived from Belize City, discharged some and picked up others as it headed to San Pedro. As it sped off to the north, Daniel said, "There goes one of the weeble boats." Max looked over at him. "What?"

"I'm sorry, I call the water taxis weeble boats because they look like those kids toys, you know the song—'Weebles wobble but they don't fall down'."

She looked at him as if he had lost his mind then after a pause, she said. "I suppose I do see the resemblance, but how do you know about Weebles?" He just didn't seem like the kind of guy who would know about kid's toys.

"Max, I don't live in a vacuum. I do watch TV and I am in the music business. It was a catchy jingle. Give me a break."

Several of the dive tour boats had gone past them to fuel up for the day's trip to the reef. The concept of going slow didn't exist and as their wakes hit *d'Riddem,* Max was thankful that she was on a catamaran as she watched other single hulled boats rock back and forth while *d'Riddem* just shimmied gently.

Together they washed the dishes, tidied up the boat and when there wasn't anything else that had to be done, they looked at each other, each realizing that that there was nothing that they had to do at that moment and they smiled. "So what now?" asked Max.

Daniel was stopped by the simplicity of the question, and then he said, "I don't know." There wasn't anything that they had to do. Yes, they were going to continue sailing south, but without any sort of timetable.

"Fine. While you figure things out, mon capitaine, I'm going to work on my tan." And with that Max turned and went below, returning a few minutes later wearing another string bikini. This time it was a floral pattern that was every bit as sexy as yesterday's black one.

He tried not to be too obvious as he studied her every curve. She looked in his direction and he blushed as he realized that he had been caught staring. "Here, make yourself useful," she said with a teasing lilt in her voice as she handed Daniel a tube of sun screen and turned her back to him. He took a deep breath and could feel his heart starting to pound as he squeezed some lotion into the palm of his hand.

As he rubbed his hands together to spread the lotion onto each of them, he glanced down at his hands to make sure the shaking he was feeling wasn't too obvious. They appeared steady so he began to gently rub the lotion on her back. Any sensation of shaking that he was feeling went away. Slowly, gently he rubbed the lotion onto her back. He took his time, enjoying the pure sensual pleasure of it and his thoughts wandered.

She was perfect. As he rubbed the lotion on her back, he convinced himself that his escape was a success and that he could now be truly free. He was beginning to slip into island time where the day began with the sunrise and ended shortly after sunset. Gone were the pressures of life back home where performance was crucial and failure was not an option. Here, the only worries were those that existed in this small world called *I Got d'Riddem.*

"Thanks." Her words snapped him out of his thoughts.

"No problem."

"I'll be up front on the tramp. If you need me, you know where to find me." Then, before he could respond, she grabbed her towel and book and headed forward.

He needed her all right, but there was plenty of time for that later.

Now he needed to decide where they were sailing to next and how he was going to convince her that he intended for this to be more than a short vacation. He didn't intend to return and he wanted her to stay.

CHAPTER 63

"BELIKIN TIME," HE CALLED OUT TO HER.

"Pelicans? Where?"

"No, Max, Belikin time. Belikin Beer. It's eleven o'clock and on *d'Riddem* eleven o'clock is Belikin time. Would you like one?"

She nodded and swam back to the boat. Max had been swimming behind the boat in an attempt to cool off after a strenuous morning spent lying on the trampoline when Daniel had called out to her. As she climbed up the swim ladder and began to wring out her hair, rivulets of water ran off her already slightly pink body.

"Use the hose there to rinse off with fresh water. I'll get you a towel," he said pointing to the opening where a hose peeked out near the transom.

"Thanks."

As she pulled it out and began rinsing off, he stopped and watched. First her hair, then her shoulders, back, arms, and finally her legs. *Max, I am so glad you're here with me,* he thought. Turning away, he went to fetch her a towel and the two beers. Returning with beers and towel in hand, he stood in the cockpit and watched her again. Her back was to him as she wiped the water off her arms and legs with her hand. He flushed and just as she turned, he pressed the cold beers to his stomach, sending a shock through his system ending the stirrings he was beginning to feel. She climbed up into the cockpit and he handed her the towel, which she draped over her shoulders, and he handed her a beer. "To us and Belize," he said, tilting his beer toward her.

She didn't say anything. She just looked deeply at him and slowly put the bottle to her lips and took a sip.

His thoughts were inside her bikini, but an even more urgent voice told him that it was time to move and continue their journey south. There would be time enough later for what he had in mind. And besides, the anticipation would only enhance the pleasures yet to come. "How about lunch before we leave?" he said.

He caught a flash of disappointment in her eyes before she replied, "Sure, that sounds great."

The rhythm was beginning. Daniel marveled at how quickly and naturally Max took to the routine. Lunch finished, sun block on, engines on, release the boom, make sure the dinghy was secure, swim ladder up, release the main sheet, hoist the mainsail, get off the bridle, haul up the anchor and sail off. All done with engines in idle. The port engine was only needed to operate the windlass so it was shut down first. The starboard was left in neutral and revved up to charge the refrigeration and with that they were off. As they left Caye Caulker harbor and turned south, Caye Chapel came instantly into view.

"What's that island?" asked Max.

"That's Caye Chapel. It's a private island golf resort, very expensive and they don't encourage visitors."

"Oh," said Max as she watched it slide by through the binoculars.

"Next stop Porto Stuck."

"Porto what?"

"Porto Stuck. It's a narrow pass just to the west of Montejo Caye. Look at the depth gauge. Pretty much all of our sailing north of the Drowned Cayes will be in seven to fifteen feet of water. It's just one big swimming pool."

Bar codes were coming into view on the horizon and Max scanned them with the binoculars. They would soon fill in and became more solid lines before becoming trees and Cayes. There was a sail in the distance and she studied it. It was one of the local fishing or cargo-carrying boats. Most were around twenty-five feet long, their masts were not tall, but the booms were really long. There was a small jib and on the back, a large outboard motor for those times when the wind was either contrary or nonexistent. Mostly, they just sailed at their own pace. Water taxis could be seen in the distance and all boats going south or coming north had to go through Porto Stuck.

Finally, the refrigeration was charged, the engine shut down, and only the gurgle and swoosh of the water passing under and between the hulls was heard. Max went to lie on the tramp up forward, Daniel sat at the helm, letting the auto pilot steer and just watched the world go by, lost in his own thoughts.

As they neared Porto Stuck, Max stood and before coming aft, held onto the A-frame that braced the crossbeam and gazed forward as if she were a figurehead on some Spanish galleon. Daniel smiled as he studied her. *My God, she is beautiful,* he thought. For that moment, the events that brought him there were forgotten and he truly believed that this was his future, totally free, with Max. She turned and began making her way back to the cockpit and as she did, she shouted to him, "I'm thirsty, how about a Belikin?"

She was glistening from a combination of sweat and sun tan lotion and there was a glow about her that once again he was finding irresistible. He began to regret the self-control he exhibited earlier before leaving Caye Caulker. Retrieving two beers from the fridge, he again held them to his body in an attempt to shock his system out of the lust that was beginning to overcome him. He shivered and returned to the cockpit just as she arrived and he handed her a beer. "Thanks."

He resisted the urge to take her right then, as there was only enough time to enjoy the beer before the auto pilot would have to relinquish control to him for the passage through Porto Stuck. He proposed a toast to Porto Stuck and adventures beyond. Bottles clinked and they drank.

The passage through Porto Stuck was uneventful except for the boat that passed them in the center of the cut. It wasn't one of the water taxi boats, but rather a local boat commonly used for fishing and maybe small sight-seeing tours. It was long and narrow, the bow raised and was steered from a pedestal near the rear. Engines on the tour boats are usually large and fast, and this one was no exception. The boat was painted black which was unusual and there was no name on it. Its only occupant gave *d'Riddem* a hard look as he passed by. Daniel hadn't seen him coming up from behind. "What the hell?" he said under his breath as the boat sped past.

Max was startled as well and she had to catch her balance as the wake hit them. Daniel didn't get much of a look at the driver, but something just didn't feel right, the boat had passed too close and too fast to be accidental. As the black boat disappeared from view in the direction of Belize City, Daniel and Max just looked at each other in stunned silence. Finally Daniel said with a grin, "Wasn't that exciting?" but there was something about that boat that bothered him.

Max just looked at him in disbelief. "Do they always drive like that?"

He didn't want to alarm her, "Nah. He probably just had a fight with his girlfriend or something, nothing to worry about." Even as he said these words, he wasn't convinced.

Safely through Porto Stuck he set a course a little bit west of south toward Swallow Caye. "Over there is St. George's Caye," said Daniel pointing further over to the left. "It was the sight of the great Battle of St. George's Caye in 1798 between Spanish forces and the English settlers. Had the Spanish not been defeated, then Belize would not be what it is today. There's a book down below about the battle and it's a pretty good read. It really gives a pretty good picture of what life probably was like then."

"What's there now?"

"There are some private homes, a small resort and a British Army R&R facility. We're going to bypass it today but someday I'll take you there. Over to the right of St. George's are the Drowned Cayes. They are a series of mangrove cayes, with some terrific anchorages." Pointing almost straight ahead, just off of the port bow, he said, "That's Mapp's Caye. We'll sail around it and turn more toward the south east, run down the Ships Bogue; it's a narrow channel between Swallow Caye, there straight ahead, and the Drowned Cayes."

Pointing forward and to starboard Max asked, "Is that Belize City?"

"It is. We'll see the city lights in the distance when we anchor for the night."

It had been a little over an hour since they had passed through Porto Stuck when they began to carve a long slow course change around Mapp's Caye, turning to the south and into the Ships Cay Bogue. As they made the turn, Daniel started the starboard engine. The sound startled Max. "Is everything okay?" she asked.

"Everything is just fine. I just want to charge the refrigeration now so that when we get on the hook, we can shut down and enjoy the silence."

Max finished her beer and moved over next to him and put her arm around him. Daniel pointed to the right, "There, that's Swallow Caye. It's a manatee reserve surrounded by some really shallow water, but the channel we're in is quite deep, but narrow."

It would only be another hour or so before they were safely anchored and he smiled in anticipation of a secluded anchorage and the reward for his earlier patience. As they exited the channel, they continued sailing south only a mile or so off the Cayes, but to Max, they looked like one continuous line of mangroves. When they were opposite the Stake Bank, another mangrove caye surrounded by shallows to the west of the Drowned Cayes, Daniel began to turn easterly, closing the distance to the Drowned Cayes. Now Max could begin to see inlets and divisions between them. Finally, he pointed ahead and said, "That's where we'll anchor for the night."

It was a deep cut going far into the mangroves several hundred yards wide. As the distance closed, the other engine was started, the sails were dropped and furled, and Max watched the depth gauge slowly go from twenty five feet down to twelve feet, where it stayed. They motored far enough in to be secluded, but not so far as to be invisible to someone passing the inlet. Daniel explained that if they went too far in, mosquitoes could be a problem if the breeze dropped. The anchor was lowered and set and the engines shut off.

At first, total silence filled the late afternoon and neither spoke, as if afraid to be the first to disturb it. Then, slowly, a new canvas of sounds, the sounds of nature, began to fill the air. The soft rustling of the wind as it blew through the mangroves, the occasional cry of an unseen bird and the splash of a fish feeding near the shore. As the sun dropped lower in the sky and the bimini no longer blocked its rays, it felt as if a giant spotlight was upon them and they could feel its final heat. "Max, give me a hand dropping the shade screen."

They released the ties that held it rolled up to the back of the bimini and as soon as it fell into place, the cockpit felt cooler. It was an aqua color and was made of a mesh fabric so you could see through it when you looked directly at it, but from an angle it appeared solid. "That's better," said Daniel. "It's time for a drink. Would you like one?"

"Sure."

While Daniel went into the cabin to make the drinks, Max continued to absorb the subtle splendor that surrounded them.

As Daniel returned to the cockpit with two brightly colored plastic goblets in hand, he didn't see her right away then he heard a splash. "Max?"

"I'm out here."

Placing the drinks on the table, he looked around the sunshade and saw only her head as she treaded water. That's when he saw her bikini lying on the last step of the transom by the swim ladder. He grinned and found himself blushing and his heart pounded as he watched her swim back to the boat. Her body, even though visible under the surface, was hidden just enough by the waters distortion, like an otherworldly sea nymph. "The water feels great. Why don't you join me?" she called up to him.

She didn't have to ask twice. He dove in and as he surfaced, he looked around for her. She wasn't there and for a moment confusion and panic washed through him. Then he heard her giggle and turning around again saw her climbing up the swim ladder onto the boat. He watched as she pulled out the fresh water hose and rinsed off, then picking up her bikini from the deck she disappeared into the cockpit. He remained in the water for a few more minutes in an attempt to bring his excitement under control.

When he finally emerged from the water, rinsed off and climbed into the cockpit, he found her sitting at the table sipping on her drink. He saw that she had slipped into a loose fitting cotton top and shorts and it was obvious that that was all she had on.

"This is delicious," she said to him.

"They are, aren't they?" Then as he began to dry off, it was her turn to watch him and her thoughts strayed. As the sun began to touch the horizon, they rolled up the shade screen and watched its final decent.

When the sun finally disappeared, Daniel said, "I'll be right back." Max continued to stare out over the water, watching the lights of Belize City come on.

Daniel returned shortly wearing light weight drawstring pants and a long sleeved cotton tee shirt. He saw that she had finished her drink. "Would you like another?"

"Sure," and she handed him her goblet. As he made two new drinks, his thoughts were of Max and his anticipation of pleasures soon to come. Then, the black boat they had seen earlier flashed through his mind and for a moment a darkness overcame his thoughts. Something about that boat bothered him. He couldn't put his finger on it, but it was there.

He jumped and that dark thought vaporized when he felt a touch on his shoulder.

“Sorry, I didn’t mean to startle you.”

“You didn’t,” he lied, then picking up the two drinks he turned and handed one to her. Again he toasted her. “Here’s to us and Belize.”

She nodded and smiled, they touched rims, and then they sipped together before returning to the cockpit to watch the lights of Belize City sparkle in the distance. Other than an occasional squawk from a bird in the mangroves, it was silent save for the sound of the wind.

Max’s thoughts were divided between the past, and the life and friends that she had left behind, and the unknown future. She didn’t know when she would be going home. Those things had not even been discussed. So far this entire adventure had been about the present and that’s where most of her thoughts were. Daniel was everything she had imagined a prince charming would be and the present just felt so right.

CHAPTER 64

AS FAST AS THE SUN HAD SET, hunger now began gnawing at them. Dinner was prepared, consumed and cleaned up along with another round of rum punches. As the last dish was put away, Daniel said to Max, "Come with me, I want to show you something." He grabbed a blanket, turned out all but the masthead anchor light and went forward to the trampoline. Max followed. It didn't take long for their eyes to adjust and the shape of the shoreline could easily be seen in the starlight. Daniel spread the blanket out on the trampoline and sat on it while motioning for Max to join him. She did, and they lay back and looked up at the heavens. "Oh my God, it's beautiful. There are so many more stars here than at home," said Max.

"There aren't, but I agree, it does look that way," Daniel identified stars and pointed out constellations to Max and she created a few of her own. The constant night breeze of the trade winds was cool, and it wasn't long before the edges of the blanket were pulled tight around them, wrapping them in a warm cocoon. Daniel could feel the heat of her body and she his, as they lay there next to each other in the dark, near silence of the night. They melted together and after a time, he could hear a subtle change in her breathing. It became softer and more regular. He could feel her body relax as she slipped into sleep. He smiled as he enjoyed the perfection of this moment and soon his eyes closed and sleep overcame him as well.

Suddenly, Daniel sat up with a start. He had no idea how long he had been asleep and he wasn't sure if it was something in his dreams that woke him or if it was something else, but his heart was racing as he looked around at the dark shapes of the mangroves.

The motion startled Max awake and she sat up as well. The panic of disorientation consumed her as she flailed her arms trying to get free from the blanket that was holding her. As her arms became free, she realized where she was, calmed down and found her voice, "What's going on?"

Daniel held his finger to his lips and softly shushed her as he stood, slowly turning, making a 360° turn. He saw nothing. Max's heart was pounding and now the solitude of the quiet anchorage was scaring her. She stood and joined him, whispering, "What's happening?"

He put his arm around her shoulder. "I don't know. Something woke me up."

"There's no wind," she said softly.

Now he saw that the water's surface was like a mirror. The breeze had stopped so the silence was that much deeper. He whispered. "That must be it. It's late."

"How do you know?"

Looking up at the stars he said, "The stars have moved."

"Oh."

Another bird squawked, and Max instinctively pressed herself to him and wrapped her arms around him. He could feel her heart pounding in sync with his. He wasn't convinced that the lack of wind was what awakened him, but he didn't say so. The breeze began again and Max shivered. He picked up the blanket, draped it over her shoulders and said, "Come on, let's go inside." Clutching the blanket around her shoulders, she followed him back to the cockpit. There she looked at him and asked, "Everything's all right, isn't it?"

"Yes, everything's fine," he said in his most reassuring voice. It was true for the moment and it didn't feel like a lie, but at the same time he knew that he wasn't being completely honest either. He would explain it all to her, when they were truly safe.

"Good." He could hear the sleep in her voice. "I'm tired, I'm going to bed." She turned and went inside.

"I'll be right down." He is nerves were still on edge. He wanted to take another look around and he needed some time to think, so he went back out into the cockpit. Nothing seemed to be out of place. He left the cockpit and starting on the port side, he walked slowly in a clockwise direction around the boat, studying the water and the shoreline. Everything seemed normal. He listened, but heard only the wind whistling through the rigging and the rustling of the mangroves. As he completed his walk around the boat, nature was calling so he went down the stern steps on the starboard hull to relieve himself. The steps were wet with dew. He froze, his eyes straining to see through the shadows, his imagination working overtime. He listened for any sound that might betray the imagined visitor. For a moment, he thought he saw a movement near the shoreline where the inlet met the channel. He froze and barely breathing, he studied that spot. Nothing. Finally, satisfied that they were alone, he heeded nature's call and then returned to the cockpit where he sat and fell asleep until sunrise when his dreaming was interrupted by Max touching his shoulder and he jerked awake.

"Did you spend the whole night out here?"

"I must have fallen asleep. After you went down below, I was too awake to sleep so I thought I would just sit and enjoy the night and I guess I was more tired than I thought."

"Is everything all right?"

"Of course. Why?"

"I don't know. That was pretty weird last night and yesterday after that black boat went by you seemed, well . . . distracted."

"Max, you are the only distraction in my life. Trust me. Things couldn't be more perfect. Now, how about some coffee?"

"That would be good."

He got up and went into the galley to put some water on while Max stayed out in the cockpit, lost in her own thoughts. She asked herself if she was doing the right thing. Then Daniel returned with two steaming cups of coffee and her doubts vanished.

CHAPTER 65

JACK AND JOHN JOINED THE GIRLS in front of the wood stove at Ben's and over lunch, the discussion of Python, his death, and Daniel/Charles continued. Jack was content to let the others carry the conversation. He was lost in his own thoughts about Max, Daniel, Belize and how he would get her out of harm's way. First he had to find her, then he had to hope she wanted out, otherwise he would look like a complete fool. The drizzle had stopped by the time Jack, John, and Jenny left the bar and went over to Jack's. "Listen guys, you make yourselves at home, I need to go for a short run." Jenny gave him a look to which John put the words, "You're nuts, man."

"Maybe. Maybe not. It helps me think." Nothing more was said while Jack changed. When he was ready, he put on his reflective vest and said goodbye. It wasn't yet dark out, but it would be soon.

The roads were still wet and car headlights reflected off of any remaining puddles. His pace was slow and easy. He wasn't warmed up enough to begin pushing it and he just enjoyed these early miles to feel his body as it began to loosen up. By the time he turned up Washington Road, he was feeling relaxed and in the groove and his mind began to drift as the running became automatic. He turned onto Brackett Road and headed north.

He remembered those years when he had been in Belize. *It was beautiful, but totally undeveloped. What was it like today? Why did Daniel take Max there? Why not the Virgin Islands, Hawaii, Alaska, Europe? There were so many places he could have taken her. Why Belize? What was his role in Python's death? Did he even play a part? Was his interest in Max purely personal or was she becoming a pawn in something larger?*

By the time he had returned to the boulevard near Wallis Sands, he didn't have any specific answers to the questions in his head, but he knew what he was going to do, he just hadn't figured out all the logistics. It would be several days before he would be able to leave for Belize. That time would give Tom a chance to see if he could come up with anything new based on the information he and John had given him. He would also spend some time doing some research on Belize and he needed to talk to Leslie again. He hoped that maybe Max would contact Patti, giving him a starting point for his mission. Having decided all this he, picked up the pace and just as he reached Ben's, the rain started again.

Wet, but refreshed, Jack walked from Ben's to his apartment. As he went up the drive, past Courtney's, he noticed that her curtains weren't drawn and he could see John and Jenny inside. They were drinking some wine, laughing and seemed to be having a good time. He was beginning to feel the chill now so he didn't stop. First, he wanted to get into a hot shower and some dry clothes and then he would go over and join them.

As he finished his shower, he saw that the light was flashing on his answering machine. He pressed the play button. There was only one message. It was John, "Hey, Jack. We're over here at Courtney's. Come on over and join us."

Jack finished dressing and once more went out into the cold fall rain. It was a quick dash to Courtney's and he didn't get too wet. He knocked and then went right in and was greeted by a chorus of "Hellos" and "How was your run?" A glass of red wine was offered, which he gratefully accepted and before long pizzas were ordered. As the evening progressed and empty bottles began to line the kitchen counter, laughter, silliness and song overcame the day's somber beginnings. For a few hours at least, Courtney's became a refuge of happiness. By the time the last bottle was emptied, Jack was asleep on the couch.

It was agreed to let sleeping Jacks lie, so John and Jenny said their goodbyes and holding onto each other for support, wobbled their way back to Jack's apartment. Courtney found a blanket, spread it over Jack and then sat down in the overstuffed wicker rocking chair across from the couch. A wine induced melancholy began to overcome her as she sat there, watching him sleep, thinking and blaming herself for what had happened. *Last winter it was so perfect. Jack and Max had finally gotten together. They belonged together. How could I have let things get to where they are today? Jack shouldn't be alone, sleeping on my couch. He should be with Max.* Her eyes began to well up with tears and as the first one spilled over and ran down her cheek, she sniffled and blew her nose.

"Don't blame yourself, Court. It's not your fault."

The sound of Jack's voice startled her and she quickly turned away from the gaze of his barely open eyes and wiped her arm across her face, trying to wipe away the tears. When she turned back with a big sniffle, he had fallen back asleep.

She stood, went over to the couch, adjusted the blanket and barely touching her lips to his forehead, she kissed him as a mother would kiss a sleeping child and whispered, "Good night, Jack."

By sunrise, the storm had passed. Courtney's house was flooded with sunlight, which belied the cold temperature outside. Jack pried his eyes open and just lay there as his body slowly woke up. At first he was a little disoriented about where he was, then it began to come back to him. He sat up and his head spun briefly, but that passed quickly. His whole body felt like lead. Looking around the room he saw the remains of last night. Empty pizza boxes, empty wine glasses on the table, and a row of too many empty wine bottles on the counter. Standing on unsteady legs, he gathered the wine glasses and put them in the kitchen sink. Coffee was next on the agenda. He always drank instant, but he knew that Courtney preferred brewed. It took a few minutes for him to sort it all out and get the coffee going.

Next stop, the head. A good piss, some cold water on his face and a rinse of mouthwash and he felt a little better. The mirror didn't lie, however. He still looked like hell, and until he could get home and shower, that wasn't going to change. Leaving the bathroom, the smells of fresh brewing coffee came at him and he breathed in the welcome aroma.

The coffee wasn't quite finished so he picked up the remains of the previous evening. Empty bottles in the recycling bin, wine glasses in the dishwasher, and by the time the coffee was ready, all was cleaned up. He poured himself a cup, found some cream in the fridge and with his properly whitened and sweetened coffee, he sat down at the kitchen table to savor that first cup of the day while looking out over the salt marshes.

Before he finished his coffee, he heard a shuffling behind him and he turned to see Courtney gingerly walking across the room toward him. She was all wrapped up in a large, red, bathrobe. "Coffee . . . Jack you are my hero."

"Good morning, sunshine." Standing, he motioned to her and said, "Here, sit down. Let me get you a cup. Black?"

"Yes. Thanks."

He handed her the steaming cup of black coffee. She cupped it in both hands and inhaled its aromas before gingerly taking her first sip. "Ooh, that's good. Thanks."

Jack poured himself another cup, sat back down and neither said anything for several minutes.

Courtney was the first to speak. "You're going after her aren't you?" It was as much a question as it was a statement.

"Yes."

"When?"

"Soon."

CHAPTER 66

THE REST OF THE MORNING was spent recovering. It helped that the sun was out. By the time Jack returned to his apartment, John and Jenny were up and having their coffee. They wanted to spend the day exploring Portsmouth and the seacoast and that suited Jack just fine. After more coffee, showers and breakfast, they were ready to leave. It was agreed that they would meet at seven o'clock in the bar at Ben's. Jack watched them drive off in Jenny's green bug.

The first thing he did was place a call to Leslie. Jack hadn't talked to him since that night at the end of the summer, out on the deck. Their conversation hadn't been lengthy, but more had been said by what wasn't said than by what was said and Jack needed to talk to him again. He had had a lot of time to think about all that had transpired, but he couldn't quite put it all together. He hoped that Leslie would be more talkative this time and help him. The phone rang several times before he heard Leslie's distinctive voice answer. "Hello."

"Leslie, it's me Jack."

"Jack, man, how you doin'? It's been a while."

"Yeah, it has."

"What's up?"

"Leslie, I need to see you."

" 'Bout what?"

"I'd rather not talk over the phone. Can I come see you?"

Jack caught a slight hesitation in Leslie's voice before he answered. "Uh, sure man. When?"

"How about this afternoon?"

His previous hesitation now became more pronounced, if not cautious. "This afternoon? What's the hurry?"

"It's about Max," blurted out Jack. As soon as he said that, he regretted it. Jack didn't want to tell Leslie the real reason for his call for fear that he would not be willing to talk and he needed some answers.

The caution and hesitation that Jack had heard in his voice was now replaced with concern. "Max? You mean that beautiful bartender you been sweet on all these years?"

"Yeah, that's her . . ."

"What's the problem, man?"

"Leslie, can we please get together?"

"Sure. I'm playing at Jimmy B's tonight. Why don't we meet at five o'clock," then he added, "You can help me load my equipment in."

"Sounds good. Where is Jimmy B's?"

"It's in Newburyport, just off the main drag in an old warehouse."

"Five o'clock it is. See you then." Jack hung up the phone. He had a few hours to kill so he decided to visit Tom to see if he had turned up anything new.

Tom was busy at his desk when Jack arrived and waved him in, motioning for him to sit in the only chair in the room.

"Hey, Jack, I'm glad you're here, I was just going to call you."

"Timing is everything. Have you had a chance to do anything with what we gave you yesterday?"

"Actually, yes. I have found out some things. You know, that Nigel was good. He ought to be a cop. He found out more than he thought he did."

"Really? What?"

"The music business is even more cut throat than John described to us yesterday. It seems that anyone involved is either the prey or a predator. There are virtually no nice guys. Mostly, the musicians are prey. That's not to say that some of them don't do very well, some do extremely well. Some have honest agents and sign with legitimate companies. But so many others are just taken advantage of. Python fell in the latter category. I was able to take the information that Nigel provided and go a little further with it. It seems that he was not the only one who had been taken advantage of by what seems to be the same organization. At least that's how it looks."

"Oh?"

"Well, I talked to a friend in the FBI's fraud unit and he told me about this music scam that has been going on for years up and down the eastern seaboard. They know who some of the lower and midlevel players are, but they haven't been able to find whoever was behind it, let's call him Mr. Big. It looks like your instincts were right, Daniel is involved and may be a key player, but he's definitely not the top guy."

Jack stared at Tom and took a deep breath. "You're shitting me."

"No, I'm not. It seems that Python's contact was Charles Gowings. Daniel's name was Cummings. Cute, huh? Comings and goings."

Jack just shook his head.

"Well, anyway, like I said, this was going on all up and down the east coast. The specifics of Python's case matched the files of several dozen other bands. Most of what the FBI does know came from an informant, Daniel's predecessor, only he's dead. They assume that he was discovered and, well, let's just say that Mr. Big is not a very nice person. For whatever reasons, most of the victimized bands haven't been too cooperative, but with what Nigel found out, it seems plausible that this Daniel, or Charles or whatever other names he may have used, is involved big time." Tom paused and looked at his notes before continuing. Jack was silent.

Tom continued, "Here's what we know. The way the scam works is that they find good local bands who have developed a solid local or even regional following. Then Daniel, or maybe someone else like him, approaches the band. He portrays himself as an agent for a publishing house that will be their steppingstone to a national audience. Apparently, he's quite convincing. To this point, it's all legit. The performer signs on, a CD or two gets produced and released, the performer gets paid some royalties, gets some air-time, and they think that they're on their way. Then Daniel, or whoever he was at the time, would become increasingly scarce and harder to reach, eventually disappearing altogether as he moved on to a new band. In the meantime, the publishing company that the band had originally signed with would be sold and resold until they effectively became invisible, disappearing along with the rights to the band's works. They even found one case where the band's name had been trademarked overseas and someone else had become them. In other words, their identity was stolen."

Jack interrupted at this point. "But couldn't they sue or something?"

"They could, but the cost and time involved generally makes that an unrealistic option."

"Okay. I see how a band could get screwed, but these are local bands and they never hit it big. Whoever is doing this isn't in it just to screw bands; what's in it for him?"

"You're right, Jack, it's not about screwing local bands. It's about some serious money."

"Explain."

"Like I said, these companies are sold and resold, each time becoming an ever smaller part of a larger whole, making it really hard to trace them, eventually ending up part of some foreign music company. This company—or maybe companies—now has a huge catalog of material that they now own. Material from this catalog is then mined for possible hits. A song would be recorded by some local band and released overseas in a different market. Some of these songs become hits and all the royalties from them then go to whoever holds the rights."

"So if Daniel is the guy setting all of this up, why haven't they grabbed him?"

"They want Mr. Big, the guy behind it."

"They have no idea who he is?"

"Apparently not. The FBI thinks that he is foreign, but they really don't know. It's possible that Daniel doesn't even know who he is."

"Why do you say that?"

"Well, most of this information was gathered from Daniel's predecessor and like I said, he's dead. The FBI has been watching Daniel, looking for an opening, but so far there hasn't been one and now he has left the country."

"That's incredible. So Daniel is the guy who gets it all started," said Jack finally.

"It would seem so."

He was stunned and his head was spinning with questions. *If Daniel was as involved as Tom had suggested . . .* He finally asked, "Do they think Daniel killed Python?"

"They don't know."

"But they think he might have."

"From the information you gave us, it seems likely that Python found out something he wasn't supposed to know and that got him killed, making Daniel a very real suspect or fugitive depending on your point of view."

Jack sat and thought about this for a few moments, and when he broke the silence he said, "Tom, I'm going to meet Leslie this afternoon. With what you've told me, maybe I can get something more from him."

"Good, it's worth a shot."

Before getting up, Jack looked across the table at Tom and said, "Tom, we know that Daniel took Max to Belize. I'm going after her."

"Jack, don't do anything foolish."

"I won't."

CHAPTER 67

JACK PLANNED TO TAKE ROUTE 1-A south, all the way to Salisbury Beach, just over the Massachusetts border, where he would turn west and rejoin Route 1 for the final few miles to Newburyport. The sun was beginning to set as he drove along the beach and he thought back to last winter when he was chasing Franz Stokel. That seemed a lifetime ago. There was little traffic so he made good time. Before he knew it, he was crossing the Merrimac River into Newburyport. He took the first exit, turned left and drove into town. Jimmy B's wasn't hard to find and it was early enough that parking was equally easy to find.

"Hey, Leslie," Jack called out as he approached the restaurant and saw him struggling with a large speaker cabinet. "Need a hand?"

"Jack, good to see you. Yes, I could use a hand. Grab hold of that side; we're going into the bar on the left."

Between the two of them, it only took three more trips to get all of his equipment inside. "Thanks, man," said Leslie as he put the last piece on the stage. "So what's up?"

"Let's go sit down over there," said Jack, motioning to an empty table in the far corner of the room.

They sat and the bartender came over and asked them if she could get them a drink.

"Tea would be good," said Leslie and Jack ordered a beer.

"So Jack, what's up? You said it had something to do with Max."

"Do you remember last summer after Python's death and you and I had that conversation out on the deck? You told me that the band was in deep shit and I should butt out."

A dark look came over Leslie's face. Warily he replied, "Yes, I remember that."

"I haven't spoken to anyone about that evening, but I need to know some things from you."

Leslie picked up his teacup and took a sip, his eyes boring into Jack. Jack could see his shoulders tightening. There was the barest hint of a tremble in his hand and his tone became wary, defensive. "Like what things?"

"Leslie, Max has taken off with Daniel. They are in Belize and I think she's in danger and doesn't know it. I need your help."

He swallowed the sip of tea he had just taken, and exhaled softly as he put the cup down. Some of the tension left his shoulders and the hard look in his eyes softened as he said, "That's rough man. But, why me? What can I do to help?"

"Tell me about Daniel. What was going on last summer?"

The tension returned. He took another sip of tea. He didn't say anything at first, and then he took the cup from his lips, leaned forward slightly and in a hoarse whisper said, "Jack, I shouldn't do this, but we've been friends for a long time. Can I trust you to keep this conversation between us?"

"Yes, if it helps get Max back."

He looked around the room. Save for the bartender, they were still the only ones in the bar. Jack watched him intently, wondering why he was so secretive. Leslie leaned forward, his forearms on the table, teacup between his hands and he began. He told Jack how Daniel had approached the band. He wanted to represent them. He would promote them and with his connections he could get them gigs all over New England. They would be playing in larger clubs, for more money and maybe even open for some national acts. He would get them into one of the top recording studios in Boston to professionally produce a CD. It almost seemed too good to be true. All he needed to start it all was for them to sign a contract with Sun Soul Records, the company he represented.

"Did you sign?" asked Jack.

"Not immediately. None of us had ever heard of Sun Soul Records, but Daniel was convincing and Percy wanted to sign immediately. Joshua was a little more cautious and I wanted to find out more as well. That was when Python showed up. We hadn't seen him in years, so it was quite a surprise. We all got together one night at Joshua's place and drank and smoked and jammed. It was like old times. He filled us in on what he had been up to and it sounded great. He had put out some CD's, he had played bigger venues and negotiations were in progress for him to be the opening act at a concert in Boston. We were blown away by his success. That's when he dropped the bombshell."

"What happened?"

"Well, we were all pretty high and all of a sudden he got all weird and stuff. He started going on about how it had all been a scam, how he overheard a conversation he shouldn't have heard and how after that things began to go wrong. The opening gig fell through. Bookings fell off and the publishing house he had signed with became increasingly hard to contact. As a matter of fact, the guy who signed him pretty much disappeared off the face of the earth until Python saw him here."

"You're losing me. Can we back up a little? Why was Python up here in the first place?"

"Well, like I said, he had been having all this success and all of a sudden nothing was happening so he decided to get away to put his head back together and ended up at Ben's. I guess a friend of his, another musician who was also an attorney, had been helping him in trying to find out what was going on and whatever they found out really upset him. He never told us exactly what. Anyhow, he didn't know that we were still playing there, and that's how we got together."

"Okay. So he shows up at Ben's, you all get together after at Joshua's and he tells you about his recent success and subsequent problems."

"Right."

"Go on."

"Well, like I said, Python saw the guy who had signed him at Ben's. That guy turned out to be Daniel, although he knew him as Charles. This turned into a big fight between Percy and Python. Percy didn't want to believe any of this and Python kept insisting that we had to stay clear or we'd get screwed. It was ugly. Finally, Joshua got everyone to settle down and we agreed that we would confront Daniel and find out what was going on. Python agreed to stay out of it until we had a chance to talk to him, and took off as soon as this was decided, but Percy was still really pissed. Joshua and I spent another hour or so trying to get Percy to chill out. He finally seemed cool, so we all went home.

"The next Sunday we met Daniel out back during one of our breaks. It wasn't pretty. Joshua told him what we had heard, and of course he denied all of it. Tempers got a little hot and after we went back to play, he disappeared. I hadn't seen Python at all and it was the next day that he was found dead. We didn't know who had killed him, but we suspected that it might have been Daniel and we didn't want to become involved."

"So you just decided to say nothing and that's why you told me to back off?"

"Yeah."

"Do you think he did it?"

"Jack, I just don't know. Joshua was pretty pissed at Python and I could tell that Percy was too. This opportunity was what they had been waiting for and for Python to tell them that it was a scam was rough."

"What about you?"

"It would have been great, but I'm happy with my life where it is, so I could take it or leave it."

The two of them continued to sit there, and for several minutes not much was said. Jack thought about what Leslie had just told him and it fit with what he already knew, although he didn't tell him so. It did seem that Daniel might have murdered Python, but there was just no proof. Jack finally broke the silence. "Hey man, I've taken up enough of your time. You have to get set up for tonight so I'm going to get going."

"That's cool."

"If you see Joshua or any of the other guys, say hello for me."

Leslie looked at Jack. "Sure. Take care and good luck. I hope you find each other."

They shook hands and Jack left.

Jack had a lot to think about as he left Newburyport and headed back to Ben's to meet up with John and Jenny. When he pulled into the parking lot, Jenny's green VW Bug was already there and he wondered how long they had been waiting. He found them in the bar, well into their drinks and judging from the volume and quantity of laughter, he guessed that those were not their first. The rest of the night was spent just having fun and little was said of Max, Daniel, or Python.

CHAPTER 68

BREAKFAST FOLLOWED COFFEE as the sun rose in the sky. It was going to be another perfect day of blue skies, white puffy clouds, and it would be hot. While Max cleaned up the remains of breakfast, Daniel went below and changed into cooler shorts and a tee shirt. He returned topsides when the galley was clean and Max was on her way down to change. While she changed, he began to prepare to get under way. The engines were started, the main was prepared for hoisting and he brought in enough anchor chain to disconnect the bridle. "What should I do?" Max asked.

He glanced back to the voice. "Keep us into the wind, I'm going to haul up the main and then we'll get the anchor up and we'll be on our way." Max was a quick study and in no time they were free and heading out toward the channel under the main sail only. Daniel finished securing the anchor while Max steered the boat. Daniel finally returned to the cockpit and got his first look at Max's outfit du jour. Two days ago, she had worn the black bikini, then yesterday a flowered one and today it was a floral maillot. *Damn*, thought Daniel and he smiled. The engines were put into neutral, then the port one was stopped and the starboard one was left running to charge the refrigeration. Daniel couldn't wait to shut it down when only the sounds of sailing would remain. As they reached the channel Max looked over at him and asked, "Where to, my captain?"

"Turn to port and steer a heading due south."

"Aye, aye. South it is."

Daniel ran the jib out, trimmed it and their speed picked up noticeably. He noticed that Max was grinning from ear to ear as she stood at the helm. He found himself smiling also, reveling in the perfection of the moment. His plan was to stop at Rendezvous Caye for lunch and a snorkel. Then they would anchor in Bluefield Range for the night. There were few other boats in sight, only some local fishing boats far off in the distance. They were alone. They stayed maybe a mile off from the Drowned Cayes and soon Water Caye, the last Caye before the main shipping channel to Belize City, was in sight. As they reached Water Caye, the markers for the deep channel could be seen and Max watched the depth sounder as it rapidly plunged to one hundred sixty-five feet. As they passed Water Caye, she asked about the small stand of palm trees that were due east. "That's Goff's Caye." Then pointing more southeast, Daniel said, "That small Caye with the lighthouse on it is English Caye. It marks the southern side of the entrance through the reef. Further south is Rendezvous Caye, our destination for lunch."

"Where is Rendezvous?"

Pointing off the port bow Daniel said, "It's over there. Let me get you the binoculars. You really can't see it yet without them. Would you like a Belikin?"

"Yes, please."

Daniel noticed that the refrigeration timer had stopped so he called back to Max to shut down the starboard engine, which she did. Then with binoculars in one hand and two ice cold Belikins in the other, he returned to the cockpit. He put the two beers down on the table, handed the glasses to Max and took the wheel so she could look for Rendezvous. After a quick check of course and sails, he set the autopilot and reached for his beer.

"I think I see it," said Max still staring off to the southeast. "It's just a speck."

Daniel didn't respond as he sipped his beer, lost in his own thoughts.

Satisfied with having located their destination, Max placed the binoculars on the table and picked up her beer. Due south and straight ahead was a large caye. "What's that?" Max asked pointing at it.

"That is Middle Long Caye. Not much on it other than a few fish shacks. We'll be leaving it to starboard and when we are nearly at the end, we'll turn to port and go out to Rendezvous Caye."

Daniel took over the helm and Max headed for the trampoline. Lying there, she was mesmerized by what she saw. Rendezvous Caye was a small, uninhabited, sandy spit populated by a dozen palm trees, some sea grapes, several resting pelicans and gulls. In a word, it was a cliché. The water surrounding the Caye varied from deep blue where the coral dropped off and the water is deep to an almost blinding blue-white over sandy bottom where the water was only a foot or so deep. They were securely anchored just before one o'clock and once again it felt as if they were the only people on the earth.

The sun was merciless. The only clouds to be seen were far out to sea, the only shade was under the bimini and the only true relief, in the water. Max was the first one in and Daniel was close behind. Even though the temperature of the water was quite warm, it felt cool against their overheated skin, causing them to suck in their breaths momentarily. In a matter of moments, the chill was gone and so were their clothes. The water was crystal clear and fish swam by, totally unconcerned with the two naked bodies that had become one.

Refreshed and exhilarated, they climbed back onto the boat, rinsed off with fresh water and then dried off with the sun's help. Having satisfied one hunger, their attentions were turned to satisfying the other. Wrapped in just their towels, Daniel uncorked a bottle of Pinot Grigio and with some bread, cheese and fruit it was a simple, yet perfect lunch.

"Daniel, will we stay here tonight?"

"No, this isn't a good overnight anchorage. We're going to anchor at Bluefield Range." He turned and pointed to the southwest. "It's just over there behind that next Caye."

By the time they had finished the wine, the sun was beginning to set and it was time to go. Towels were exchanged for dry clothes and since they didn't have too far to go, the sails would stay furled and they would motor to their new home for the night. It took just over an hour to get there and they entered through the southern entrance.

Bluefield Range was an anchorage formed by three mangrove cayes. It was open to the north and south with the western side formed by a single caye which has a small resort on it's southern tip. The other two Cayes formed the eastern side of the anchorage. The water lacked the clarity that they had experienced at Rendezvous Caye. It was more of a milky jade color and they anchored in fourteen feet of water. For the third night in as many days, they were alone. The resort even looked abandoned.

Looking over at the collection of brightly colored boxes that were built on piers over the water, Max asked, "Is that really a resort?"

"If you use the term resort in a very broad way. It's a little primitive, but I've heard that there are groups that stay there. I've never seen anyone staying there, but I have seen the caretaker so I know it's not abandoned." Rum punches in hand, they sat and watched the sun as it began to set. There were towering clouds off to the west, over the mainland, and they were beginning to turn shades of rose and gold. It was like nothing Max had ever seen before.

"I wish Patti were here to photograph this." The Bluefield Resort was now just a collection of silhouettes in front of the brilliant colors of the sunset. "Do you have a camera? I forgot to pack one."

"Sorry, I don't have one, and I didn't say anything to Alfonso so I doubt that he put one on board."

"I haven't seen one."

"That's okay. We'll have our memories and they will be all the more special because they will be just ours."

"I guess, but a few pictures would be nice."

Daniel could hear the disappointment in Max's voice.

"I've always been satisfied with my memories and never had much need for pictures." This last statement was not entirely true. At home, he took pictures of the bands he signed all the time. It was a great tool. It was just here that he didn't want a camera. He didn't want to have any evidence of his trips to Belize posted on anyone's refrigerator. He was pretty good at hiding his tracks; false names and passports did a pretty good job of that, although this time too many people had called him Charles and that made him nervous.

"Well, I'll just have to write to Patti again and tell her about it."

This last statement caught Daniel by surprise. He hadn't thought about that possibility. "What did you say?"

She started to reply but before she could say anything else, the silence was broken by the high-pitched sound of a very powerful engine and the pounding of a hull going over the water at a high rate of speed.

"What the . . ." His sentence was cut off by the sight of a boat moving very fast on the channel side of the resort heading south. When the boat had traveled far enough to clear the coral reef that extended south from the resort, it began carving a turn around the reef and headed toward *d'Riddem.* In the diminishing light, Daniel couldn't see the boat clearly, but that didn't stop the uneasy feeling he had.

"Max, will you do me a favor?" She was watching the boat as well. "Will you go down below for a few minutes?"

She looked away from the approaching boat and at him. Something in the tone of his request surprised her. Then as she began to open her mouth to speak, he cut her off. "Go below . . . now!"

The boat was rapidly closing the distance and Daniel could see that it was jet black. He couldn't tell how many people were on board, but he didn't want them to get a good look at Max.

His unease was increasing. He shot Max another look. She wasn't moving. "Now!" he hissed at her.

Surprised by his tone, she froze and stared at him. She saw a hardness in his eyes that she had never seen before. No longer were they the soft, warm amber that she loved. They were like black ice, cold and lifeless. She shivered.

The whine of the black boat's engine was getting louder and he could now hear the sound of its hull slapping the surface of the water as it raced toward them. He quickly diverted his gaze from Max to the boat and then forcing himself to remain calm, he looked back at Max with those warm eyes and said, this time a little more softly, "Please."

Still frozen in silence, Max glanced at the boat, then back at Daniel and moved slowly toward the cabin entrance.

Just as she disappeared inside, the black boat slowed suddenly and angled toward *d'Riddem.* It was the same boat that had passed them as they had gone through Porto Stuck and as before, there was only the driver on board. As he guided the boat closer, Daniel was able to get a good look at him. He was just over six feet tall, with thin narrow hips, broad powerful shoulders and well muscled arms. His physique was made to look even more impressive by the loose camouflage pants and tight, black, tank top he was wearing. His hair was shoulder length and in small neat dreadlocks. As he idled past, the two men stared at each other. No words were spoken. No one moved. Then Daniel saw him push the throttle arm forward, the engine roared to life and the black boat leapt forward. It weaved around the shallow bar in the center of the anchorage, continued north, eventually turning west out into the channel and disappeared into the ever-increasing darkness.

CHAPTER 69

SILENCE RETURNED TO BLUEFIELD RANGE. Max peeked her head out from the cabin and stared at Daniel's back. He was still looking in the direction that the black boat had gone.

"Daniel?"

There was no reply. Motionless, he continued to stare out into the gloom.

"Daniel! What is going on?"

He didn't move or reply.

Max came out of the cabin and touched his shoulder. "Daniel . . . is everything all right?"

He jumped slightly at her touch, turned and faced her. His eyes were no longer dark and cold, but neither were they the warm, sexy eyes that she had fallen for. Now there was something new. Concern? Fear? Apprehension? She wasn't exactly sure which, but it was unsettling.

"I'm sorry Max," he said softly. He went to put his arms around her, but she pulled back, staring at him.

"Daniel, I don't know what is going on here, but I think you owe me an explanation," she said firmly.

It was somewhere between a command and a request, and he said, "I know. Sit down."

She didn't move.

His voice softened. "Please."

Max sat down still looking at this new Daniel.

He sat across from her and quietly said, "First, let me say that I'm sorry."

"Sorry for what?" She didn't like the way this was starting.

"Before I tell you anything else, I have to ask you something."

"Okay," she said slowly.

"Just before that little incident, when we were looking at the sunset and talking about cameras, did I hear you say that you would have to write to Patti again?"

Puzzled by this question, Max paused before answering. "Yes. I sent a letter to Patti just before we left on the boat."

Now it was Daniel's turn to pause, then he said, "That explains a lot."

"What explains a lot? Daniel, what's going on here?"

"Max, you are an incredible, trusting, independent woman. I've never met anyone like you before. That's why I am crazy about you and why I want you here with me."

"Daniel, I feel much the same, except that you are starting to scare me and I don't like it."

"Max, I have to ask you to trust me. I'll tell you everything, but first we need to leave this place."

"What do you mean we have to leave? Why? What's going on?" A hint of panic was beginning to creep into her voice. Ignoring her pleas, Daniel got up from the table and started the engines.

Max sat in stunned silence, then she, too, got up. She grabbed his arm. He turned and faced her and before she could say anything else the same steely, cold tone returned to his voice. The darkness hid his eyes, but she didn't need to see them. "We are going to take the channel straight south to Placencia tonight. Please help me with the sails and the anchor." No explanation, no reassurance, just a cold statement. With that he headed forward.

It took another moment for all of this to sink in. Max was frightened, but she dutifully took her place at the helm while he hoisted the main sail and then raised and secured the anchor. As soon as he finished, he came back and took the helm and guided *d'Riddem* out of the anchorage, south past the reef that extended off the end of the caye, then west, into the channel, before heading south again.

The clouds that had made the sunset so spectacular rapidly covered the sky. Daniel noted that there would be no moon or starlight this night, making it that much darker. That was just fine with him. The wind was now from the north and increasing. *Those clouds must be the leading edge of a Norther,* he thought. They were common during this time of year and would bring with them strong winds, cool temperatures and rain. As they headed south in silence, Daniel was thinking about the coming night. Max sat at the table and wasn't sure whether she was more scared or pissed off.

Daniel asked gently, "It's going to be a long night. Could you see if you can rustle up some food?"

"No."

The bluntness of her reply caught him by surprise. "Max . . ."

She shut him off. Anger won out over fear. "What the hell is going on here? Why did we leave so quickly and why are we sailing after dark? I thought it was too dangerous."

"Okay. Okay. It's okay to sail down the channel at night. The water is deep and there isn't anything to bump into. Why we left so quickly is a little more complicated."

"Try me."

He didn't say anything for a few moments as he searched for the right words, then he said, "I think that my employer is after me and he may try to kill me."

Now it was Max's turn to pause while she processed his last statement. "What the hell are you talking about?"

"Max, what I'm trying to say is that I think that he has found us . . . uh, me and if we don't disappear quickly, we may disappear permanently."

Now fear took over. "Daniel, That's not funny. Now really, what is going on?"

"Max, I just told you. I think that my employer is after me."

"Daniel, that's not good enough. What do you mean he's after you? You're in the music business. Its not like you're in the mob or something."

He hesitated.

"You're not, right?"

"No, I'm not in the mob."

For a moment she felt relief. Then she held her breath.

"So?"

"Max, I am in the music business. My job is to find good local talent and to jump start their careers."

"So what's the problem?"

"There's more."

She could see that he was getting uncomfortable. "Go on," she persisted.

"My job was to scout local bands that showed promise. I would get them a contract with a publishing company, one of the many that my boss owned, then I would help them professionally produce a couple of CD's and get them released with a lot of fanfare. With the exposure I would create, their notoriety would begin to grow. I'd book them into larger venues than they ever thought possible. They'd open for even bigger acts. My job was to engineer their success. Once I had brought them to a certain point, I'd move on. That's what brought me to Rye and to you."

"I'm not understanding how this turns into your fear of your employer? It sounds like you were just doing your job."

He paused again staring off into the now inky darkness. The steady whooshing sound as *d'Riddem* flew south before the ever-increasing wind seemed amplified by the blackness of the night. "Max, when I came to Rye this past summer to sign the band, I expected that it would be just another job. That is until two things happened: I saw you, and I can't explain why, but I became obsessed with you. Max, I've never felt this way about any other woman in my life."

She listened and heard what he was saying, but her questions weren't being answered. He was doing it again. He was shifting the focus away from himself and directing it toward her. It was as if he was casting a spell over her.

As taken as she was with him, she was beginning to acknowledge things about him that she had sensed before, but while in the throes of infatuation wouldn't face. Now, she began to face them. Too many people had greeted him as Charles. Charles who? What was with that black boat and his reaction to it and why the sudden departure? And most importantly, why did he think his employer was out to kill him? Max listened, then with frosty resistance in her voice she said to him, "You said there were two things that happened in Rye. This first one we will leave alone for a while, what was the second one?"

"The band. Things were going as planned. I had met them, we had several meetings and I was beginning to convince them that I would be able to give their career a big boost. They were getting close to signing with me when Python showed up. He changed everything. He recognized me because I had signed him in Newport. His career didn't take off quite as he expected and he blamed me. We never actually talked, but he must have talked with the band because it wasn't until after his arrival that they became very nervous and all of a sudden began backing away from the deal."

He paused a moment before continuing. "Then, he turned up dead in the harbor. The guys in the band got it in their heads that I might have killed him."

"Did you?"

"No. Max, I swear to you I had nothing to do with his death."

She wanted to believe him, but she still had a feeling that he was not telling her everything. "So who killed him?"

"I don't know."

"Well, who do you think killed him?"

He remained silent and she watched him. The wind continued to increase, as did the motion of the boat. Unseen waves came from behind and rushed past *d'Riddem* and Max could feel the boat surge forward. As the wave passed, there was a moment of calm before the next one pushed them on. In the faint red glow of the cabin's night light, Daniel looked like some kind of other worldly demon, his hair blown and tangled and his gaze straight ahead staring into the darkness. Max's fear was tempered by her growing anger and as she waited for his answer to her question, she found herself wishing that Jack were there. She shivered.

Daniel turned and saw her shiver. It was beginning to get cold and he knew that it would be raining soon. "Max, why don't you go inside and put something warmer on? You look cold."

He spoke in that soft, caring, gentle voice that belonged to the man she had fallen for and for a split second she forgot her anger and fear . . . and Jack. It was at that moment a large swell caused the boat to lurch suddenly and she was snapped back to the present. She felt stupid. She had been too easily swayed by his silky voice and comforting manner. He had just told her that he was suspected of murdering a man and that killers were chasing him. She shivered again.

"I think I will." She got up and headed into the cabin to find a sweatshirt. Once inside, she thought that even though he may be a liar and who knows what else, he was sailing the boat. For now, she was entirely dependent on him. She turned back and asked him if he would like one, too.

"Yes, I could use one," she returned in a sweatshirt and sweatpants. She handed him his sweatshirt, he took it, smiled at her and said, "Thanks." Max didn't say anything. She just sat back down at the cockpit table and watched him. Neither made any attempt to rejoin the conversation as they sat there, each lost in their own thoughts.

I Got d'Riddem was a good boat. She surfed and sailed south before the approaching storm taking care of her two occupants. Max fell asleep, her head on the cockpit table while Daniel continued to steer. He could have used the autopilot, but he needed to be doing something physical as he considered his options. Suddenly, Max sat upright with a start. She looked about, caught in that twilight between sleep and full awareness, expecting to see Jack, but it was Daniel she saw instead and she realized that she had been dreaming. She couldn't remember what the dream was about, but what she did remember was Jack comforting her and making her feel safe.

Her stomach rumbled. It had been nearly ten hours since their leisurely lunch at Rendezvous Caye. The adrenaline rush of their quick departure from Bluefield Range had worn off. Daniel's subsequent revelations coupled with the storm they were running before suddenly came crashing down on Max. She felt faint and needed to eat.

She got up from the table, Daniel looked in her direction and said, "You all right?"

"Yeah, I'm going to get something to eat," then without any thought she asked, "You want anything?"

"Sure," was his short reply.

Max went inside, put some water on for coffee and pawed through the refrigerator. She pulled out some bread, peanut butter and guava jelly and began making sandwiches. By the time they were made, the water was boiling. She dropped a tea bag in a cup and filled the cup with boiling water for herself. While it steeped she stuck her head out and asked him, "Coffee?"

"Yes, black."

Max returned to the cockpit with his cup of coffee, her cup of green tea and the sandwiches. He remained at the helm so she passed him a sandwich and his coffee. They ate in silence, each lost in private thoughts, while *d'Riddem* continued to carry them south. After eating,

Max went inside and put away the remaining food before returning to the cockpit table with her tea. She sat there, holding it, absorbing its remaining warmth while sipping occasionally and watching Daniel.

"Why haven't you been honest with me?"

"What?"

"Why have you lied to me?"

"Max, I have never lied to you."

"You've kept secrets from me. That's the same thing."

"No, it isn't. I would have told you eventually. The time just hadn't seemed right and it wasn't necessary."

"Eventually? Wasn't necessary? You didn't think that it was necessary to tell me that you might be suspected of murder? What were you going to tell me eventually? 'Oh Max, by the way, now that we are far away from home, I might be a fugitive, and, oh, yes, I almost forgot, my boss might want me dead also.'"

"Come on, Max. It's not like that at all."

"It's not? Then what's it like? If it's not like that, then why did we leave in such a hurry to sail all night in this shitty weather? Tell me Daniel, what's it like?"

Daniel could tell that he was not going to win so he just looked at her, said nothing, and then silently returned to sailing the boat. Max, feeling better for having confronted him, also realized that she was not going to get any answers. Besides, she was tired and still cold so she decided to go inside. Her last thought as she disappeared into the cabin was that if he wasn't going to talk to her, he could just sail the boat by himself.

CHAPTER 70

DOWN BELOW, CURLED UP IN HER BUNK, the sounds of the storm and the rocking, surging, motion of *d'Riddem* as she raced south made sleep nearly impossible. The noise of waves thumping and crashing against the bottom of the bridge deck, the whoosh of the water against the hulls as they alternately surfed and plowed through the waves and the constant whine and roar of the wind were terrifying, but her anger trumped her fear so she lay in her berth, eyes wide open and her mind in overdrive.

She felt betrayed and alone. She began thinking back over the short time she had actually known Daniel. He had seemed so perfect. He was gorgeous and he always made her feel so special in spite of the fact that she was older than all of the girls at Ben's and he certainly could have had any one of them. But he had wanted her. Everything had always been about her and as she remembered, she smiled. Now she wasn't so sure. The revelations of the past few hours showed him to be a totally different person, one that she could not completely trust. She wasn't afraid of what he might or might not do to her. She was afraid of the others. Those unknown shadows he was running from and who may or may not see her as a complication. With those thoughts running through her head, fatigue eventually won out and sleep came.

The front finally passed at daybreak and as the winds calmed, so did the seas. Daniel was finally able to set the autopilot and leave the helm. Before going below, he scanned the horizon. The sky was still overcast, water and sky sharing the same shades of gray. Satisfied that they were alone, he went below. Before going into the head, he quietly looked in on Max. She was peacefully asleep and he just watched her for a moment.

The reflection that stared back at him from the mirror in the head was not pretty. His hair was windblown into a tangled mess and his eyes reflected the stress of sailing all night with no sleep. As he splashed water on his face, he studied the stubble on his cheeks and chin and decided that a beard might be a good idea. Finishing his ablutions, he returned to the helm for another look around. They were still alone and Placencia was about five miles ahead. They had just passed Jonathan Point and were nearly at False Caye. He needed coffee so he went back inside to begin heating water.

Daniel didn't see the small boat with its lone occupant coming out from behind False Caye. It wasn't until he heard the squeaks and moans of the water beginning to heat in the coffee pot that he noticed the boat. He grabbed the binoculars and without leaving the cabin so he could remain unseen, he studied the boat. It was similar to the black boat, only smaller, the hull a well-worn white. The engine was not as large and so its approach not as rapid or threatening. The driver appeared to be a local fisherman and it was possible that he wasn't even interested in them and that he would just pass them by. His coffee water was starting to boil when he saw the driver of the boat waving in their direction.

Daniel, coffee in hand stepped out into the cockpit and waved back. He noted that it would take a few minutes before the boat would catch up to them, so he stood there sipping his coffee while studying the boat. Daniel watched the man in the boat intently, looking for any sign of threat or danger. He saw none, only a smiling Belizean fisherman. "Good morning!" the driver shouted to Daniel as he came alongside, carefully matching his speed to that of *d'Riddem* and staying just far enough away so that the two boats wouldn't touch.

"Good morning," Daniel warily returned the greeting.

The fisherman was short and stocky, powerfully built with dark copper skin, his face indicated a Mayan heritage. A gold tooth flashed as he talked. Daniel guessed that the man was in his sixties although he could have been much younger. He wore an old tee-shirt and shorts made from cut off pants. As he maneuvered his boat, Daniel noticed that he seemed to have six fingers on his left hand although he couldn't be certain and he didn't want to stare. There was a mask and snorkel, spear gun, and a lobster hook in the bottom of his boat. "My cousin Alfonso told me to watch for this boat. You must be Mr. Charles."

It was at that moment that Max stepped into the cockpit behind Daniel. He was unaware of her presence until he heard the fisherman say, "Mr. Charles."

Daniel jumped, not expecting Max and almost spilling his coffee in the process, turned and said, "Max, good morning."

"Mr. Charles," she repeated with ice in her eyes and voice.

He turned back to the man in the boat hoping to avoid her wrath although he could feel her presence. "What's your name?"

"I'm Ramón, but everyone calls me Digit," and he held up his left hand showing Daniel that there was indeed an extra finger.

That caught Daniel by surprise and he tried not to stare. "Nice to meet you . . . Ram.. ah, Digit. My name is Daniel, not Charles, and yes, I do know Alfonso. How is he?"

Digit looked confused over the names. Maneuvering his boat closer, he looked about for the pretty lady he had seen a moment before. "Alfonso is fine."

With Max standing behind him, Daniel was not able to explain anything to Ramón so he asked, "Do you have any fish for sale?"

Digit, still confused, replied, "No, not yet, but I will have some later."

"That's great, we are going to Placencia and will anchor off of the fuel dock. Will you come by with some later?"

"Sure. I'll see you later."

"Great," said Daniel, then he waved as Digit turned away from *d'Riddem* and sped away shaking his head in puzzlement.

"Holy shit, six fingers," he said to himself. As he turned he found himself face to face with Max. She had the same icy glare as before and it went right through him and he knew instantly that she wasn't interested in discussing Digit's six-fingered hand. "Max . . ."

Before he could say anything else, she cut him off. "Daniel, or Charles, or whoever the hell you are, you still have a lot of explaining to do. I need some answers, or I'm off this boat as soon as we hit land."

"Okay, Max. We're almost there so how about as soon as we are anchored. I tell you everything."

Silently, she went forward and sat on the trampoline.

The excitement that Max should have been feeling about arriving in a new port had been replaced by the anger she felt toward Daniel and the fear of not knowing what was going on. She watched the shore as they approached the cut between Placencia Caye and Placencia Settlement. It was all sandy beach, dotted with palm trees and a collection of brightly painted cube-like houses raised up on stilts. There didn't seem to be any large hotels. All the docks with dive boats and water taxis, and all of the hustle and bustle were missing. It wasn't at all like San Pedro or even Caye Caulker. A few children playing along the water's edge, some men fishing, and pelicans diving for food, seemed to be the only activity. Even though it was still early in the day, Max had a feeling that it wouldn't get much livelier. As they sailed through the cut, she was transfixed by the quiet. Daniel's voice brought her out of her reverie.

"Max, we need to anchor. Can you please come here and take the helm? I'll show you where we want to anchor, and . . . well, you know the drill."

Max took the helm and listened to his instructions without saying a word. She just nodded her understanding. It didn't take long for them to be securely anchored in about twenty-five feet of water and a couple of hundred yards from shore. They were only the seventh boat in the anchorage. Three of the others were catamarans like *d'Riddem*, only larger. They were part of a fleet of charter boats that were based there. Of the other three boats, only one appeared to be seaworthy. The remaining two appeared abandoned. Beards of seaweed around their waterlines said that they hadn't been moved in a very long time. Tears in faded canvas dodgers, empty jerry cans tied to not very secure looking lifelines, and the patina of neglect left questions about how they came to be there and what had happened to their owners.

CHAPTER 71

SECURE ON HER ANCHOR, *d'Riddem*, faced the Placencia waterfront. Max studied it. From left to right, there was a small dock with a dive shop on it, a bar, the end of the road, the fuel dock, two more dive shacks and the fisherman's co-op. That was about it. A few taxis were parked facing the water with the drivers waiting for the first visitors to arrive. Placencia Settlement was on the end of a long narrow peninsula and Max was looking at its tip.

Daniel returned to the cockpit and Max glared at him. She said nothing.

"Sit down, Max." She did.

He sat across from her at the cockpit table. She continued to glare at him and finally he spoke in that deep honey voice that she had found so compelling.

"Look Max, I'm sorry. I'm sorry that I have involved you in things you know nothing about. I'm sorry that I haven't been totally honest with you. Sometimes I'm even sorry that I ever met you, because you deserve better. I'm so sorry."

He took a breath and she continued to stare, resisting the power of that voice. Her eyes conveyed the questions he would have to answer. He continued. "Max, when I first saw you working behind the bar at Ben's last summer, something happened to me. It's hard to explain. I just knew that I had to have you. In my job, I met beautiful women all the time and I had discovered how easy it was to take them and use them and you were going to be the next notch. Then I met you and all that changed. You weren't going to be the next notch, you were different and I became blind to common sense and reason. I wasn't as focused as I should have been on my job. When Python was found dead, I panicked. I realized too late that I was in trouble. Instead of doing the smart thing and disappearing, I continued to suck you in. I never should have done that. I'm sorry. I dragged you down here thinking that I could just ignore the past or at least run away from it. I can't. My employer won't forget and as a result I have put you at risk and that was never my intent."

Max listened to what he said in silence and almost bought it again. He was good. He knew what to say and how to say it without ever really answering the questions. She became increasingly mad at herself for being such a fool. Why hadn't she listened to Courtney . . . and Jack? Guilt was now setting in as she thought about how she had shut out her closest friends. They were her family and she had cast them aside. What did she get in return? Some of the best sex she had ever had? Sure. The romance of being whisked away to a tropical paradise on someone's yacht? Yes. But, at what cost? Her friends? Her life? What had she been thinking? How shallow could she have been? She looked at him and said, "I have some questions for you. Who are you? Daniel, or Charles, or are you someone else altogether?"

He looked down at the table. "I'm both. My real name is Charles Daniel Cummings. Depending on where I was working, I would use either Daniel or Charles. That's why everyone down here calls me Charles."

That settled, she continued staring at him and with a cold steady voice she asked, "How many others? How many other woman have you brought down here?"

"Just one. She was no one, just a fling."

Max continued to stare, other questions going through her head, "What happened to her?"

She really wanted to know about his job, about the black boat, who he was running from, but first she needed to know where she stood, hence the questions about his other conquests. "Max, please believe me when I say that she was the only other woman that I ever brought down here. Let's just say that it didn't work out and we went our separate ways."

She found it hard to believe that she was only the second woman he had ever brought down here. She could see the discomfort in his eyes and was about to ask him about what was going on, when a shouted hello interrupted them. It was Digit. He had returned and was pulling up to the back of the boat. His gold tooth flashed as he smiled and held up two perfect red snappers. Max turned and went inside. She really didn't want to see anyone else at the moment.

Daniel helped Digit tie up to *d'Riddem* and invited him aboard not expecting him to accept, but Digit, being naturally curious, climbed on board with fish in hand. Daniel took the fish and went inside to put them on ice. Curious about everything, Digit made himself at home and began exploring *d'Riddem.* He went forward and gingerly stepped on the trampoline, grinning from ear to ear he looked down at the water through the netting. He stood by the mast and studied its winches and many colored lines, tracing each one, trying to understand what it might do. He had never been on a boat like *d'Riddem* and he was fascinated. He had returned to the cockpit and was standing at the helm, holding the wheel when Daniel returned. "What do I owe you for the fish?"

Digit, standing at the helm, just looked at him and with a grin said, "Today nothing. Any friend of Alfonso's is a friend of mine."

Daniel looked at him wondering what to make of this curious little man. Before he could say anything else, Digit began peppering him with questions. "My cousin asked me to keep an eye out for this boat and that a Mr. Charles with his lady would be on it. He asked me to help you if you needed anything. Why did you call yourself Daniel? Will you be staying in Placencia for very long? Where's your lady friend?"

Even though he was feeling trapped and he didn't feel like talking,

Daniel was getting a good feeling about Digit. Some people you just knew you could trust and he felt that Digit was one of those people. He replied without answering all of Digit's questions, "I'm not sure how long we will be staying. Thank you for the fish."

"Is your lady friend all right? She didn't look too good."

Daniel's answer was half true, "She's fine. She's lying down. It was a long overnight sail and it was a little rough. She's tired."

Then in a very quiet voice and with a wink of his eye, Digit asked Daniel, "Are you hiding from her husband or something?"

"No, it's nothing like that."

"Then why should I call you Daniel? I know you are Charles."

Daniel was beginning to get a little testy. Digit wasn't taking the hint, so this time Daniel's answer was considerably sharper. "Look Digit, I have had a very difficult couple of days. It's complicated and I'm not sure that it is any of your business."

Max, who had been down inside her cabin and had been straining to hear their conversation had now moved up into the salon. She was still out of sight, but she could hear clearly what was being said.

Still flashing his gold tooth smile, but with a kind of hurt puppy look in his eyes he said. "It's okay. My cousin told me that you were a special friend of his and that I was to help you in any way I could. That's what I'm here for. If you don't want to tell me your secrets, that's okay. Just remember, if you need anything, just ask." With that, he got up to leave.

Daniel stopped him and said with some resignation, "You're right Ramón. My name is Charles. Actually it is Charles Daniel and this beautiful lady only knew me as Daniel so right now she's a little upset with me. If you could go along and call me Daniel, I'd appreciate it."

"Sure, no problem." He paused expecting Daniel to offer more, but there was only silence. Then as he turned to go down the stern steps, Daniel spoke to him again.

"Listen, Ramón, can I ask you a big favor?"

"I told you, Alfonso asked me to help you in any way I could so go ahead and ask."

Max moved closer to the door, still trying to stay hidden while staying close enough to hear.

Daniel lowered his voice and looked around before speaking. "Up north we were bothered by a guy in a fast black boat. I have a feeling that he is working for someone who may be after me."

Digit inhaled. "Her husband?"

"No, I wish that it were that simple. No. I used to work for this man. I couldn't finish a job for him and I'm afraid that because of that, he's after me."

"What did you not do?" asked Digit in a voice barely above a whisper.

Just as Daniel was about to explain, he saw Digit's focus shift to somewhere behind himself. Daniel turned. It was Max.

Curiosity had gotten the best of her and she had silently stepped out of the cabin to hear Daniel's explanation.

He turned, and startled to see her said quickly, "Oh Max, there you are. Are you feeling better? This is Ramón. He's a cousin of Alfonso's. He's just brought us some snapper he caught earlier today."

"How nice," said Max, stepping forward and around Daniel, extending her hand to Digit. "Mr. Ramón, it's a pleasure to meet you."

Daniel looked at her, wondering what she was up to.

Digit took her hand and held it a little longer than necessary. While looking deep into her eyes, he said in a voice just above a whisper, "Alfonso was right. If there is anything you need, just ask." Then in a louder voice, "It's nice to meet you, but please call me Digit. All my friends do."

Releasing her hand he turned to leave and as he stepped down the stern steps and into his boat she said to him. "Mr. Digit . . ."

He turned and corrected her, "Digit, please."

"Digit, would you mind taking me ashore? I really need to stretch my legs."

This took Daniel by surprise and before Digit could answer he said, "Max, let's not impose. I'll take you ashore in a few minutes. I need to go as well."

Digit looked at Max and she flashed him a look. He then looked over at Daniel, then back at Max before saying, "No problem."

"Max . . ." Daniel reached out for Max's arm, she pulled away and glaring back at him said in a strained voice, "I'd like to go ashore immediately. You can meet me later."

Daniel knew that if he protested further, things would get ugly. Not wanting to make a scene he gave in and said, "Okay, I have a few things to take care of on the boat. How about we meet at the Pickled Parrot in a couple of hours?" He thought that maybe some time ashore might give her the chance to settle down and then maybe he could do a better job of explaining things to her. Doing so in a public place might also be an advantage.

"That's fine. I'll see you later. Let's go."

Max brushed past Daniel and climbed into Digit's boat and they headed to shore, leaving Daniel wondering what he would do next.

CHAPTER 72

JACK WANDERED INTO BEN'S shortly after opening, said hi to Peggy, and took a seat at the bar. He was still feeling the effects of last night's revelry so he ordered a coffee and asked for a menu. Both were delivered and he asked if either Courtney or Patti were around.

"They're around somewhere."

Just then a great deal of noise came from the kitchen, screams and thumps, giggles and a lot of running around. It got Peggy's attention, so she went into the kitchen to investigate. There were more screams and squeals followed by the sound of the kitchen door slamming open and Patti and Courtney came stampeding into the bar. Patti was waving something in her hand. "Jack! Jack! I'm so glad you're here."

"Why? Did you just win the lottery?" He wasn't sure that he had ever seen the girls so excited.

"Better!" she shouted waving what he could now see was a letter in his face. "It's a letter from Max!"

"What's it say?"

"I haven't opened it yet."

Jack's heart was beating in his ears. He looked at Patti trying not to appear too anxious. "Well, are you going to open it?

"Okay, okay. I'm opening it." With collectively held breaths, Courtney, Jack, and Peggy watched as Patti ran her finger through the envelope, tearing it open. She took out the letter and as she started to read she handed the envelope to Jack. He looked it over. The return address was a hotel, The Sunbreeze in San Pedro, Belize, but the postmark was from Dallas, Texas only a couple of days ago. Curious. The pounding in his ears was subsiding and he turned his attention to Patti reading the letter.

Courtney broke the silence, "Come on Patti, what's it say?"

Patti waved a hand, as a way of silently saying, "Just a minute, let me finish."

"Patti," Courtney said again.

Looking up, Patti said, "She's in paradise. They arrived safely, they've gone snorkeling on the reef, swam with sharks, and are about to leave on his boat."

"May I see that?" asked Jack.

While Courtney and Peggy pressed Patti for more details, Jack took the letter and in a world of total silence where the only sound was his own breathing, he read.

Dear Patti,

I'm mailing this to you just before we set sail for Placencia. This place is unbelievable or as they say here "unbelizeable!" I have never been anywhere quite like this. The people are so friendly and nice—especially Daniel's friend Alfonso. He takes care of his boat when he is not here and he also takes people out snorkeling.

You would love it. Our hotel is right on the beach and even though it is across the street from the airport, you'd never know it. There is a pool, an open-air bar and restaurant that look really nice. Right next door on the beach there is a little tiki hut bar named BC's that is so cool. Our flights went well, no delays, and we were here by 2 pm. Daniel wanted to check on the boat so while he did that, I sat by the pool and had a Panty Ripper—lots of rum and pineapple juice. It seems to be the official drink of San Pedro. The colors of the water are like nothing I have ever seen before. I can only imagine the pictures you could take.

I slept like a log that first night and got up early the next morning and walked along the beach while Daniel slept. The feeling you get down here is—well I can't really describe it—but you feel like you are at home. That morning we went to the boat and I met Alfonso. He is really cute, married though. Daniel's boat is called I Got d'Riddem. It's a catamaran and it's beautiful. There are three cabins, head, full kitchen and a hammock. Anyway, after seeing the boat, Alfonso took us to Hol Chan Marine Reserve and Shark/Ray Alley where we snorkeled and then saw tons of nurse sharks. I even got to hold one. Can you believe it? Me, holding a shark? The fish are amazing, I can't even begin to describe how beautiful they are.

Daniel is such a gentleman. He wants me to see everything and do everything. I must be the luckiest person to be here with the original, because I think he has a twin. Several people we have met have greeted him as Charles even though he says that he has never met them before. We've had a few good laughs over this. It's like being in some spy thriller. Dinner that night was fantastic. I walked the beach again this morning and now I'm sipping coffee in the bar finishing this letter to you. I see Daniel waving at me. We're heading for the boat to begin our sail south.

Love and Hugs,
Max

P.S. Say hi to everyone for me. How's Jack?

As he finished reading the letter, he gradually became aware of his surroundings again. The girls were still chirping like a flock of birds and as he looked up, they stopped and looked at him. "Well, it sounds like she's having a good time." He tried to sound as dispassionate as possible. He handed the letter back to Patti, stood, and said, "I've got to get going."

"Jack, are you all right?" Courtney asked.

"I'm fine, I just have some things to take care of." With that, he left the bar.

He went outside, got into his truck, but before starting it and leaving, he just sat there for a few minutes lost in his thoughts. Something didn't seem right. At least now he knew that Max was safe. That much was clear from her letter and he now knew where she was or at least where she had been within the past few days.

That bastard. Max had said that people kept calling him Charles. He's good, Jack thought. He squeezed the steering wheel with both hands and said softly to himself, "Daniel, or whoever you are, you don't deserve her."

Tom and Leslie had described a very different person from the one Max thought she was with. One thing was certain: he was a very good con man operating in a shadowy world where bad things could and did happen to people. It seemed possible that he may have killed Python even though there was no evidence yet to prove it. Jack thought back over his conversation with Leslie. Something was missing. What hadn't Leslie told him? Without thinking, he turned the key in the ignition, the engine started, and he drove out of the parking lot remembering that Max had asked how he was at the end of the letter and that gave him hope as he headed toward the police station. He needed to talk with Tom, then he would go home, book flights to Belize, and begin his search for Max.

CHAPTER 73

THE RIDE FROM *D'RIDDEM* TO SHORE took less than a minute. Digit tied up on the side of the fuel dock, helped Max out of the boat and asked if she needed any help.

"No, I just need to go for a walk . . . Yes, there is one thing you could help me with. I have something for Nancy the Pie Maker. Do you know where she can be found?"

"Sure, I know her, she's my cousin." Punctuated with much arm waving and gesturing, he directed her to Nancy's. "Go up the road a short ways and across from the soccer field you will see a sign for the Pickled Parrot. Turn right and follow the path past the Pickled Parrot to the sidewalk. Head down the walk and just past the orange and purple house that is next to Cecilia's Guest House, turn left and you will find Nancy's place."

"Thank you, Digit."

"If you need anything, just ask. You seem like a really nice lady," and with that, he climbed back into his boat, started the engine, backed away from the fuel dock and headed off to the west. The cloud cover was beginning to break up and whenever the sun shone through, its heat could really be felt. Beads of sweat began to form on Max's face. The difference between being on the water, even just anchored a short way out, and being on land was striking. She stood there on the dock for a few moments, glanced back at the boat, touched her pocket to make sure the letter was still there, then turned her back to the boat and Daniel and walked toward the shore. She wasn't sure exactly what she was going to do after she delivered the letter. Deep in the back of her mind, she knew that she would have to face Daniel at some point. The anger and hurt that she was feeling was pushing her away from him.

As she stepped off the fuel dock and onto the land, she couldn't help but notice that this was where the road ended. It was a cul-de-sac where southbound traffic turned and became northbound traffic. Maybe it would become a turning point for her as well. There were several taxis parked near the dock and one of the drivers called out to her to see if she needed a ride. She declined and began walking. As she started up the road, on her right she heard the chattering and squawks of parrots and parakeets. Right where the cul-de-sac became a road there was a large cage filled with birds. She walked over and stood watching them for several minutes before continuing her journey.

There was no sense of a defined town center, just a few shops and restaurants. Not too far up the road on the left was the soccer pitch. It was as rough as the one on Caye Caulker and yet there were kids playing on it, oblivious to its condition. Ahead she saw what appeared to be a grocery store. It was a plain windowless building that looked more like a warehouse. A truck was out front and some men were unloading boxes of canned goods and paper products. This was no San Pedro.

Before she reached the store she saw the sign for the Pickled Parrot pointing down a sandy path. She turned and followed the path. The sand was soft and the path was shaded by some large palms providing some welcome relief from the hot sun. The Pickled Parrot was only a short way down the path. It was a thatched roofed building. The path side was open with only a railing separating the tables from the path. Against the opposite wall was the bar. There was a large chalkboard above it, listing drink specials and there were a dozen or more seats around the bar. It was empty except for one woman who Max took to be the bartender.

Max continued down the path and came to the sidewalk. Save for the main road, this was the only paved surface in Placencia. Wide enough for two and starting at one side of the cul-de-sac near the fishing cooperative, it ran north for about a mile through the center of the settlement. On either side were all of those colorful cube-like houses that she had seen from the water as they had approached the harbor. Max began walking up the walk, looking for Cecilia's and the orange and purple house. As sleepy and quiet as Placencia Settlement appeared to be, Max noted that most of these houses seemed to have some kind of business as well. Snorkel tours, small guesthouses and souvenir shops predominated.

The sidewalk took her past the school and she could hear lessons in progress through open windows. She was never completely alone on the sidewalk. She did pass other tourists and her greetings were returned with many different accents. She tried to imagine where they were from and why they were in Placencia. Most seemed to be European—Swedish, German, Spanish.

One couple caught her attention. They had that backpacker look about them: simple well-chosen and well-worn clothes, shorts, tee-shirts, sandals. Alternately holding hands or with arms around each other, they walked as one. They were in their own little worlds totally focused on each other, oblivious to their surroundings. Max thought that they must have either been honeymooners or just on a lovers' holiday. It hadn't been too many days ago that she and Daniel had been like that. Now she didn't know. Cecilia's Guesthouse and the orange and purple house came into sight, so she began looking for the path to Nancy's. She found the sandy path and began following it toward Nancy's. She didn't notice that a lone man was watching her.

Only a few steps down the path and even before she saw the sign, she knew which building was Nancy's. Then she saw the sign. It was attached to the railing that wrapped around the front porch. On the left side of the sign was a pie with a slice missing, the missing slice was on the opposite side and between the two it simply said Nancy's.

Max stopped and studied the building. The colors were salmon pink with blue trim and shutters around lime green windows and a red tin roof. Wide stairs led up to the center of the front porch. Hanging under the eave of the covered porch were pots of pink and blue flowers. The door was in the center of the building with a large window on either side and to the left of the door, there were two wicker chairs with brightly colored fabric seats and a small table. Just outside, at the bottom of the stairs, lying in the sand were several of the local dogs, their noses twitching from the smells of freshly baked pie.

Patting her pocket one more time to make sure that the note was still there, she climbed the stairs. As she stepped onto the porch, two little children ran giggling out of the shop and let the door slam behind them. Max went in. The inside was painted white and felt light and airy. There was a glass display case with at least a dozen pies, some whole and some with slices missing. There was a bell on the counter with a sign that said, "Ring for service."

Before ringing the bell, Max inhaled the aromas and looked over the pies in the case. Her stomach began to rumble. Before she could ring the bell, a woman came out of the back carrying a freshly baked pie.

"Oh, hello, I didn't hear you come in."

"Hello, I just came in as those children left."

She put the pie on the counter top before opening the back of the display case. "Oh, them. Those little devils are my brother's kids. How may I help you?"

"You must be Nancy."

"Yes."

"My name is Max. These pies look delicious."

"Thank you. Did you just arrive? I don't think I've seen you before."

"Yes . . . yes, I just arrived."

"Where are you staying?"

"I'm actually on a boat. We arrived this morning and are anchored out in front of the fuel dock. I just needed to get off the boat for a while," said Max as she looked down into the display case again, studying the pies.

There was silence for a moment, then as Max looked up Nancy asked, "Trouble?"

"No, not really . . . More of a misunderstanding."

"Ahhh," said Nancy, now looking at Max more closely. She could see that Max was exhausted and she noted that she wasn't wearing a ring. Max caught the look and without thinking, she just blurted out, "I'm with a man who I have just found out isn't who I thought he was."

Nancy took a deep breath and before she could say anything, Max's eyes welled up with tears and she sniffled. Nancy came around from behind the counter and put her arm around her.

"Now, now, everything's going to be all right."

Max reached into her pocket, looking for a tissue or something to wipe her tears with when her fingers touched the note. She was about to take it from her pocket when the door to the shop opened. Both women instinctively turned toward the sound. A man stood in the doorway. He was tall and lanky. Close-set eyes peered at them from over the dark shadow on his face. His sunburned skin explained why it had probably been several days since his last shave. His clothes, while appropriate for the tropics, were sweat stained and just didn't seem right on him. He looked uncomfortable and didn't say anything at first. He just looked at the two women with dark, soulless eyes. Max quickly turned away and with a last sniffle, she left the note in her pocket and wiped her eyes on her sleeve. Nancy greeted the man who stood in the doorway. "Hello. May I help you?"

He didn't answer immediately, but rather looked around the shop as if memorizing every detail. Then in a slow, measured voice that made lie of his words he replied, "Yes. I'm sorry for interrupting, but earlier, I noticed that the young lady there came ashore from one of the sailboats anchored in the harbor. I was going to approach her then, but I didn't feel right doing so and then she walked off. By the time I had convinced myself that it would have been all right, she was out of sight. Then when I saw her come in here, well, here I am. I know this is presumptuous of me, but I just arrived and was wondering if her boat was for rent."

This request seemed a little odd, but then tourists mostly were a little odd. Nancy just looked at him not knowing what to say. Max, having wiped her tears away, took a deep breath, turned, faced him and said, "Our boat really isn't for rent."

The man silently stared at Max. Their eyes met for what seemed an eternity and even though it lasted no more than a blink, it was enough to send chills through Max and she looked away.

Nancy's voice filled the room, "There is a company over by the fuel dock that rents boats. They would probably be able to help you."

Max recovered and added, "Yes, I believe that is right. I'm sorry that I can't be of more help to you, but we just arrived ourselves."

After one last look at each woman he said, "Thank you, I'm sorry for bothering you."

Then he turned and left the shop. The sharp slap of the door shutting behind him broke the silence of held breaths. Both women turned and looked at each other, then at the same time, they burst out laughing, releasing the tension that both of them had been feeling. "That was weird," said Max.

"He sure was one strange gringo. I can't imagine him on a boat. Would you like a piece of pie?"

"Yes, please. I didn't realize how hungry I was until just now."

Nancy cut two slices of mango/pineapple pie, handed them to Max and said, "Take these out onto the porch. I'm going to get us some tea."

It seemed too hot for tea, but Max didn't argue. She went out onto the porch put the two plates of pie and two napkins on the table and sat down in one of the wicker chairs. Nancy came out with a small tray that had two cups and a teapot on it. After placing it on the table, she took the other seat. Without saying a word, she poured a cup of tea for Max and handed it to her, then she poured herself a cup. Only the sound of the breeze rustling the palms, an occasional bird squawk and the faint sounds of children playing in the distance gave texture to their silence.

The aromas of freshly baked pie and hot tea triggered memories of outdoor cafés in the cold Swiss air last winter with Jack. Her eyes began to well up again. Nancy saw this and softly said, "What's wrong?"

That did it. Max began to sob. She put her tea down on the table so she wouldn't spill it and told Nancy all about Jack and Daniel and sailing and strange men and by the time she was finished her tea was cold. She wiped her eyes with her napkin. That's when she remembered the letter in her pocket. "I'm so sorry, I almost forgot. I said I would deliver this to you," then she reached into her pocket, pulled out the letter and handed it to Nancy. Nancy took it, opened it and silently read it. When she finished, she refolded it and placed it on the tea tray. Max looked at her and asked, "Is everything all right?"

As if in deep thought, Nancy replied, "Yes. Yes, everything's going to be all right."

Max thought the answer to be a little odd, but she didn't pry, feeling that if Nancy wanted her to know what was in the letter, she would have told her. They finished their pie and now cold tea without much conversation, each woman lost in her own thoughts. Max spoke first. "I must be going. I had agreed to meet Daniel at the Pickled Parrot and besides I've taken up far too much of your time and you have been too kind. I mean, you don't even know me and I show up here unloading all of my troubles on you."

"Don't be silly. You needed someone to talk to and I was here. In his letter, Alfonso asked me to take care of you. I'm here if you need me. Everything will work out."

They stood and hugged goodbye.

CHAPTER 74

MAX LEFT FEELING MUCH BETTER and headed toward the Pickled Parrot to meet Daniel. Still angry and frightened, she wasn't sure what she was going to say to him. She decided to see what he had to say first. Nancy's was about the same distance from the road as it was to the sidewalk so instead of walking back toward the sidewalk, Max went in the opposite direction which took her toward the main road. Before, when walking through the settlement on the sidewalk, she had found it easy to forget that Placencia was a bustling community. The road divided Placencia into two sides. The ocean side was the original settlement with the famous mile-long sidewalk. This was the side shown in all of the tourist brochures and if it had been at home, they would have called it a historic district. The other side of the road was the lagoon side and Max decided to explore it before meeting Daniel. She was procrastinating and she knew it.

She crossed the main road and followed one of the side streets out toward the lagoon. It wasn't as neat and tidy as the beach side. Instead of white sand, red clay dominated. She thought that Boston had nothing on Placencia when it came to potholes as she zigged and zagged down the road. It was a good thing that there were so few cars here because they, too, had to drive a slow zig zag course, making the concept of lanes moot. Now she understood why all the cars and trucks were covered with mud splatters and dust. There was a greater variation in the houses on this side as well, the only common trait being the fact that they were up on stilts. Some were beautifully landscaped with lush gardens and some even had grass yards while others were surrounded with dead vehicles, rusting appliances, boats, and other remains of the modern world. The street that she began her walk on soon turned south, parallel to the road. At its end, she had to decide between right and left. Looking left, she could see the soccer pitch at the end and that meant the road and the Pickled Parrot. There was a sign indicating that to the right she would find the Coral Reef Bar and Grill. Curious, she chose right.

As she walked on, she noticed that the mangrove-rimmed lagoon was to her right. The further down the road she went, the spit of land she was on became narrower. She could see that to her left any houses that she passed had views out over the water. Once she even thought she could see boats at anchor, although she couldn't be completely sure without climbing through someone's garden and yard. By the time she saw the sign for the Coral Reef to her right, the lagoon had turned into more of a canal and she saw several small boats slowly motoring past.

The heat was getting to her and her throat was parched. She needed something to drink. The Coral Reef Bar and Grill was like many places she had seen—thatched roof, a bar in the center with tables to the sides on varnished hardwood floors. Walking up to the bar, she noted that the decor was simple and the place had a nice feel to it. She didn't see anyone at first and the coolness of the shade provided some relief as she took a seat at the bar. As she looked around, she saw that across the canal there was a large building under construction. Her concentration on the building was interrupted by a deep rich voice behind her, "Hello, may I help you?"

She turned with a jerk, and was faced with the largest man she had ever seen. He must have been six foot six inches tall and probably weighed three hundred pounds. His skin was ebony black, he had short-cropped hair that was graying around the edges, eyes that sparkled and a smile a mile wide that showed pearly white teeth. "I'm sorry, I didn't mean to startle you."

"That's okay. Are you open?"

"Yes. Would you like something"

"Yes, yes I would. Do you have anything that is really cold and refreshing, something fruity?"

"I know just what you would like." He turned, walked behind the bar. She could hear the clink of ice in a glass. He returned with a tall, frosted glass in his hand. As soon as he put it on the bar in front of her, a ring of water formed on the bar from the condensation dripping off the glass. He motioned for her to try it.

The glass felt good in her hand. She took the straw in her mouth and sucked on it. It was sweet, it was tart, it was cold and refreshing. "What is it?" she asked as she put the glass back on the bar.

"Do you like it?"

"Yes, it's perfect, what is it?"

"It's fresh squeezed lime juice with a little sugar and water."

She took another sip. "It's really good."

"My name is Tiny," he said, extending his hand across the bar toward her."

She returned the gesture. "Max."

"Max. What an interesting name. Are you here by yourself?"

"No. I'm with a friend. Actually, I am supposed to meet him at the Pickled Parrot. I just needed some time to myself."

"When did you arrive?"

"We arrived early this morning. We are on a catamaran anchored out in the harbor."

"Really? Where did you come from?"

"We started out in San Pedro and, well, here we are."

He was silent for a moment while he absorbed this information, then he asked, "Will you be staying long?"

"I really don't know. I may be leaving soon. I just don't know." Max took the final sip from her glass and made that sound that you get through a straw when there is no more liquid to be sucked up.

"Would you like another?" asked Tiny.

"No. I'm all set. What do I owe you?"

"It's on me. Welcome to Placencia. If you need anything, I'm always here."

"Thanks. It was nice meeting you." She started to get up, then paused and asked, "What's that building across the channel? It looks like it will be really nice."

"That's going to be the base for one of those charter boat companies. They seem like good people and it should be good for Placencia."

She took one more look at the new building, turned back to Tiny and thanked him again. Then she began the walk back toward town, back toward Daniel.

CHAPTER 75

THE RIDE TO THE STATION TOOK less than five minutes. Jack was relieved to see Tom's car in the parking lot. "Hey Tom, got a minute?" he said as he knocked on the door frame of Tom's office. Tom looked up from the paper he was reading. "Hi, Jack. Sure, come on in." As Jack sat down in the chair that Tom had motioned toward, he glanced around the cramped office. There were piles of folders everywhere, each with some kind of a report inside. Every time he entered Tom's office, he had the same thought, how can a town this small and quiet generate so much paper?

"So what's up?" asked Tom as Jack settled into his seat.

"Patti just got a letter from Max."

"Really? Is she all right?"

"Yeah, she sounds like she's having a great time."

Tom picked up on the way Jack answered and knew that it was killing him. "So where is she?"

"You know she went to Belize. They ended up in San Pedro on Ambergris Caye. It's a small island on the north end of the reef. Apparently that's where Daniel keeps his boat and they are planning to sail south. By now they are probably on the way since the letter is a few days old. She did say that they went snorkeling and she held a shark."

"What?" interrupted Tom.

"She said that she held a shark in her arms while on a snorkel trip. Go figure."

"That's amazing. So what else did she say?"

"Well, it sounds like people down there know Daniel as Charles since he has been called that several times. She asked him about it and he always had an answer and so it didn't sound like it was an issue."

"That guy is such a player."

"Yes, he is. I talked with Leslie yesterday."

"How did that go?"

Jack paused a moment before continuing, "It was interesting. He pretty much corroborated what we already knew. He was working on signing the band, but it didn't happen." He continued and told Tom the story that Leslie recounted.

When he finished, Tom looked at him intently and said, "So when Python told the band about what had happened to him in Newport and that Daniel was the same guy who had screwed him, only in Newport he was known as Charles, he and Percy really got into it."

"That's what Leslie told me."

"Then, Joshua, who had been a little more cautious from the beginning, got them to settle down and Python left, with Percy agreeing to confront Daniel the next day."

"Yeah."

"And Python ended up dead the next morning."

"That's about it."

"Leslie's role in all of this?"

"Leslie told me that he could take it or leave it. The decision really was up to Joshua and Percy. He stayed out of it as much as he could. That was when he and I had the conversation on the deck and he told me to stay out of it."

"What conversation?"

"I didn't tell you?"

"No, you didn't."

"Well, it was after the body had been found. Daniel was beginning to hit on Max. I had seen him and the band talking and I was wondering what was going on. I asked, hoping to find out something about him and all I got was silence. Leslie came to me as we were closing Ben's and we had this short conversation. He told me there was some bad shit going on and that I should stay out of it. Actually, his exact words were "Python's dead and we are in deep shit." That's all he would say and he left. I really didn't give it much thought then, but now . . . after what he just told me I'm wondering . . ." he paused.

"Jack, why didn't you tell me about this when I first started the investigation?"

"Tom, I'm sorry, but at the time I was going through some personal stuff and I guess I must have forgotten."

"Forgotten! Jack, cut the bullshit."

"Listen, that was when Max was beginning to get involved with this Daniel and I was being a jerk. I let her get away and my personal problems got in the way. I'm sorry if I wasn't thinking clearly."

"Well, not much I can do about that now, so tell me, what do you think? Is it possible that someone in the band killed him?"

"I don't know. Maybe. Percy was pretty upset . . . I guess anything is possible, but no, I really have no idea."

"Okay, so listen, Jack. I'm going to have to talk to Leslie, and then I am going to talk to the other two guys again." He paused before continuing, "Changing the subject, now that you know where Max is, are you going to do something stupid like go chasing after her?"

"Tom, I'm not sure what I am going to do right now." He lied, he knew exactly what he was going to do. As soon as he got home, he was going to book a flight to Belize.

"Okay. I'll let you know what I find out. But be cool, don't do anything rash."

"I won't." He stood, they shook hands and Jack left.

It didn't take Jack long to get home, turn on his computer and book the flight.

CHAPTER 76

MAX BEGAN WALKING BACK TOWARD town and Daniel. She followed the road straight until it ended at the soccer pitch. There were a dozen or so young men kicking a ball around so she stood and watched them for a few minutes before turning left and walking around the north side of the field. When she reached the road, she stopped and looked around.

The grocery store was right in front of her and there was an ever-changing group of people just outside the store. The empty handed new arrivals would stop to talk before going into the store, as would those leaving with the day's groceries in hand. This knot of people almost seemed to have a life of its own. She was so wrapped in thought about what she was going to say to Daniel that she didn't notice the man who had come into Nancy's earlier in the day standing to the side, alone and empty handed, watching her. Crossing the road diagonally to her right, she headed for the path that led to the Pickled Parrot. Her heart began to pound. She wasn't sure what she was going to say or do. She wasn't even sure that she wanted to see Daniel, but she knew that she had to. As she crossed the road and turned down the path, the man who had been watching her left the store and followed her.

It was a slow walk down the path because of the deep sand, but that didn't matter, she was in no hurry. When she reached the entrance, she saw Daniel sitting at the bar talking with the bartender. She stopped, took a deep breath then went in. At the sound of her footsteps on the wooden floor, Daniel turned. He smiled. She wished that he hadn't done that. The effect of his smile was like a narcotic and she had to consciously remind herself why she was there. As she drew near, he said, "Hi Max. How was your walkabout?"

Trying to remain distant she replied, "It was fine."

"Come, sit down. Let me get you a drink."

She sat.

Turning to the bartender, he said, "How about a rum punch for my friend and I'll have another as well?"

The bartender began making the drinks and Daniel turned toward Max, looked deeply into her eyes and said in a soft voice, "Max, I'm so sorry. I wish that we could start over." She began to say something, but he just put his finger softly on her lips and said, "Shhh." His touch was soft and it sent a shiver down her spine and she felt her lips tingle all the way to the back of her tongue. *Damn it,* she thought.

"Max, hear me out. You have to believe me when I say that I have never met anyone like you. I've done many things in my life that I'm not real proud of. I've lied, I've cheated, I've done things only I will ever know of. That was fine until I met you. You've changed me, I want to make a new start and I want you with me."

It was at this moment that the drinks were delivered and Max was grateful for that. She was almost beginning to believe him and the interruption was like a splash of cold water in the face.

"Thanks," he said to the bartender.

Max picked up her drink and took a long sip. It was cold and refreshing and was one of the best rum punches she had ever had. She made a mental note to ask the bartender for the recipe. As she put her glass down on the bar, she said, "That's a good rum punch."

Daniel was about to begin speaking again, but as he looked into Max's face he saw that the spell was broken. The moment had passed. He would have to try again later. "Yes, it is good, isn't it?"

The next moment was a little awkward as they sat there sipping their drinks, neither knowing what to say next. Suddenly, Max saw Daniel's expression change and his attention was no longer on her. She turned to see what he was looking at, but all she saw was the man from Nancy's walking slowly by. When Max turned, he gave her a small wave and nod of recognition. She started to wave at him and return his gesture, but before she could, he had moved out of sight. She turned back and faced Daniel.

"Max, do you know that man?" he asked, his attention still focused behind her.

She didn't answer immediately. She stared at Daniel's face. Those cold hard eyes that she had seen for the first time when the black boat approached in Bluefield Range were back. A chill went through her.

"No. I don't know him, but I did talk to him for a few moments earlier. He seemed nice enough, but kind of strange."

"You talked to him?" There was an edge to his voice.

"Daniel, what's going on?"

Again, he ignored her question and posed his own. "Where did you see him and what did you talk about?"

"Daniel, you're scaring me."

"Max, what did you say to him?"

"I was in a store and he came in saying that he saw me come ashore. He was curious about chartering a boat and asked if ours was available."

"What did you tell him?"

"What do you think I told him?" Max was beginning to get a little short tempered with him now. Her fear was being overtaken with anger and resentment. She continued, "I told him that we had just arrived and that the boat was not for hire."

"What else?"

"Nothing. That's all. The shopkeeper told him about those other boats that may be for charter and he left. What's going on?"

Daniel sat looking at her saying nothing.

"Daniel, talk to me. What's going on?"

"I think I've seen that guy before. Remember when we were in Boston and a man bumped into us on the street as we were on the way to the Duck Tour?"

"So?"

"He passed me a note requesting that I contact my employer. I ignored the invitation. Then, Alfonso told me that his cousin, the taxi driver, saw someone who didn't seem to fit and from his description, that was the guy. Now he's here. It's not a coincidence. Max, I'm sorry for getting you involved."

Max stared at Daniel in disbelief.

"Do you remember when I was trying to explain my job to you?"

Max just looked at him and took a long sip of her drink. "Yes, but you never really finished. That's why we are here. So are you going to tell me or what?"

"It's complicated."

"Try me."

"Okay. I told you who I am. I explained about my business and how I didn't finish the job I started in Rye and how my employer is not really pleased with me."

"You told me that much, but you didn't really explain anything."

"Max, I'm trying. A lot of what I am going to tell you is based on my gut feelings and what I know has happened in the past. My employer, who I have never met or even seen, is a very private man who will not tolerate mistakes or disloyalty. I'm sure that he saw my attraction to you as a form of disloyalty, and the fact that I did not get the band signed as a failure."

"Okay, he's a paranoid control freak. Why don't you just walk away?"

"It's not that simple. You don't just walk away from him. My predecessor tried that and ended up wearing cement boots. I knew what I was getting into and that was fine, until I met you."

Max was still trying to make sense of all this. It all seemed so bizarre. *Did people like that really exist?* "Okay. So you didn't sign the band, big deal. You're not going to talk to anyone, why would you? You can just stay down here and he'll never see you again."

"No, Max, it's not that simple. There is more to it than that."

"Like what?"

"Python."

"Python?"

"Yes, remember he was murdered? I'm sure that I'm a suspect and if I wasn't before we left, our departure probably made me one."

"But you didn't kill him. Your employer must know that."

"True, but I will be wanted for questioning and that's way more attention than he would ever tolerate. He can't take the chance that other questions would come up."

"Other questions?"

"Yes, questions about my job, who I work for . . ."

"What does any of that have to do with Python?"

"I don't know, but I am pretty sure that he knew something that he shouldn't have and that's why he was killed. He was a loose end. My employer did not know what he knew and gave me the job to find out and then to take care of it."

"What do you mean take care of it?"

"Don't ask. Think what you want, but don't ask. May I continue?"

"Fine. Continue."

"Before I came to Rye and before I could find out anything, he disappeared. Then he showed up there to my surprise. I thought that I would be able to take care of everything all at the same time. Take care of Python and sign the band. It didn't happen quite that way. Python talked to the band before I could get to him and I don't know what he said to them, but I know the result. They balked on signing and then he ended up dead."

"That must have made your employer happy."

"It didn't. We didn't know what he had told the band. I began to see the signs and I decided that what would be best was for me to disappear."

"So I became a convenient excuse to disappear?"

"Max, it wasn't like that at all."

"Well, if I wasn't an excuse, then what am I?"

Daniel hesitated for a split second, looked away, then looked back at Max before responding. She studied him, waiting for his reply. "Max, you are the reason I am quitting the business. You are the reason I am down here, trying to start over. I can't explain it any better."

She heard his words and wanted to believe them, but something wasn't right. Too much had happened in the past twenty-four hours and in the previous week for her to just accept his words blindly.

"Max, I know that I haven't been completely honest with you. I couldn't be before, now I see that I must if I'm to keep you. I love you."

She watched him as he spoke and in spite of what he was saying, his eyes were telling a different story. Somehow she knew that in the end he would leave her if it meant saving himself.

"Daniel, stop right there."

He stopped and looked at her.

"Daniel, stop before you say something we will both regret. You are not in love with me. You may say you love me, but a man like you could not love someone in the way that is forever."

"Max . . ." he started to speak again, but she cut him off.

She went on, "You know all the right things to say and do that make a woman feel like a princess. I never thought that anyone could make me feel the way that you made me feel, but something is missing, something that I . . ." By now the sun had almost finished setting and darkness and shadows surrounded the bar. She thought she saw a flicker of light out in the shadows where there should have been none.

"What?" asked Daniel as he turned and looked in the direction of her gaze.

"Oh, nothing. I thought I saw something move."

"Probably just someone walking past or a cat chasing lizards."

He turned his attention back to her, but before either one could say anything, a boisterous group came in and took over the remaining seats around the bar. They had apparently just returned from a day out on one of the dive boats and were excitedly recounting their experiences. Needing a little more privacy, Max and Daniel quietly got up and moved to a table away from the bar and nearer to the shadows. As they settled into their new seats and before anything could be said, Max stopped, reached out and touched Daniel's arm and in a whisper said, "He's out there watching us."

"Who?" replied Daniel and he started to turn.

"No, don't turn, just look at me. I think it's the guy we saw earlier, the guy you think might be following us. I only got a glimpse, but I think he's out there."

Silence followed as Daniel stopped his turn and looked deep into Max's eyes. She in turn was straining to penetrate the darkness. "I don't see him now."

"Are you sure?"

"No, but I'm pretty sure. . . . I don't like this."

"It'll be all right. If it was him and if he is following us, he's after me, not you."

"So what happens if that's so and he gets you?"

"He won't."

Max wasn't completely convinced. They still had much to discuss, but that mood was broken so they sat there and finished their drinks in silence, while listening in on the tales of deep sea adventure being told by the group at the bar.

CHAPTER 77

FLIGHTS BOOKED, JACK STRETCHED OUT on his couch and looking up through the skylight, watched the sky change from day to night. He must have fallen asleep because the next thing he knew, there was a pounding on his door. He glanced at his clock and saw that several hours had passed. He got up just as his door opened and he heard Courtney's voice calling up from the bottom of the stairs.

"Anybody home? Jack, are you up there?"

He snapped on a light, which answered the question before he could say anything and he heard footsteps coming up the stairs. "Jack, what are you doing?"

"Nothing. I just woke up, I must have dozed off."

"Good. We just found out that the band is playing up in Dover tonight and we're going to go get something to eat and then go see them."

"Who's we?"

"Patti, Dave, me and you."

"Okay, give me a half hour to get cleaned up. Where should I meet you?"

"Over at Ben's, in the bar."

"See you in a few."

The band was well into their first set by the time they walked into the bar where they were playing. They took the last table that was open and ordered a round of drinks. Patti was the first to say it and everyone agreed, as good as the band was, it just wasn't the same as being on the deck at Ben's on a summer afternoon. That brought a round of reminiscences and speculations about Daniel, Max, their trip to Belize, and finally Python's murder. As the conversation became more animated, Jack became quieter. Courtney saw this happening and in an effort to regain levity, she asked Jack to dance. He balked at first, then gave in. The band saw them, and with smiles and nods they said hello. When the set ended, Courtney returned to Patti and Dave while Jack stayed behind.

Joshua was the first one off the stage, followed by Leslie. Jack noticed that Percy hung back.

"Jack, 'tanks for coming. How you been?"

"Good. You guys sound as good as ever."

" 'Tanks," said Joshua.

"Have you been playing much this winter?"

"Some, but not like the summer."

Leslie joined in and said, "So who is still there from the summer? Is Max still around?"

Jack looked at Leslie with a look that said, *You know the answer to that. Why are you asking?* He paused before answering and realized that the others must not know about their recent conversation and he decided to play along. "Most of the full-timers are still there, but Max is gone. She took off to Belize with Daniel."

Joshua looked surprised, "Daniel?"

At this, Percy, who had been hanging back not saying much moved closer, suddenly interested, but still silent.

"Yeah, can you believe it?"

"That sucks. I thought you two had something going on," said Joshua.

"I did too. I thought that we understood each other. Then Daniel showed up this summer and began hitting on her and she fell for it. It all got out of control after the murder, and now she's run off with him."

Percy now spoke up for the first time. "I bet he ran off because he killed Python and she was a convenient excuse."

Where did that come from? wondered Jack. He looked over at Percy and said, "Now, what would give you that idea?"

Percy now seemed a little uncomfortable and fumbled with his words. "I don't know. I mean he tried to sign us and then Python tried to talk us out of it and he ended up dead. I'm just saying that maybe he did it. Do the police have any ideas?"

"I'm not sure," said Jack still not sure what to make of Percy's reaction.

It was at this moment that Courtney returned. "Hey, guys! You sound great, I can't wait until summer. Can I steal Jack back?"

"Sure," said Joshua. Leslie reached out and shook Jack's hand, "See you, man." Percy nodded his goodbye.

As they walked back to the table to join Patti and Dave, Courtney asked, "What was that all about?"

Jack just shrugged and said casually, "Oh, we were just talking about last summer." He was still wondering about Percy's reaction. It was strange, but he wasn't going to worry about it tonight. The rest of the night was spent dancing and drinking, but Max was never far out of Jack's mind. He was thinking about what he was going to do when he got to Belize in two days.

CHAPTER 78

IT WAS LATE, THE DIVING GROUP finally left, and it was time for Max and Daniel to leave as well.

"Max, are you coming back to the boat with me?" asked Daniel tentatively. He didn't think that she had any other options, but he had to ask the question.

"Yes, I am. But I won't sleep with you."

"That's fine," said Daniel, ever the gentleman. If nothing else, he was patient when pursuing a woman, and because of this, he usually got what he wanted in the end. He was sure that all would be forgiven soon enough.

As they left the Pickled Parrot, Max looked around nervously, trying to see if that man was still watching them. She didn't see any sign of him but she still felt as if eyes were on them. Daniel seemed unconcerned and that gave Max a small sense of security. The dinghy was still tied up where Daniel had left it and the ride back out to *d'Riddem* was uneventful. Little was said and sleep came rapidly and deeply.

By the time Max had awakened, the sun was well up in the sky. Daniel greeted her with a fresh cup of coffee.

"Good morning. Did you sleep well?" he asked in that deep, sexy voice of his. For a moment Max forgot about the events of the past few days, looked at him and said, "Yes."

"Good. You needed it."

As the coffee began to kick in and Max became more awake, she began to go over in her mind what had happened. Daniel could see that she was somewhere else as she sat there so he asked, "Penny for your thoughts?"

"I was just thinking about home and wondering what everyone was doing." This was only partly true. She was worried about what was going on here and she was thinking about Jack, wishing that he would all of a sudden show up and take her away.

"Is there anything you would like to do today?"

"I hadn't really thought about it. You're the expert, what are the options?"

"Well, there are lots of things we could do. We could just go for a sail. Not to anywhere in particular, just go sailing. We could arrange for a trip to Monkey River Town to see the howler monkeys. We could just hang out here doing nothing. Regardless of what we decide, I think that we should go into town and get some breakfast first."

"Breakfast sounds like a good idea. Let's start with that and then we can decide. And we still have some talking to do."

"I know. I'll get the dinghy ready and we'll start with breakfast."

Placencia Settlement had already begun its day by the time they reached the dive shop dock. The sound of air tanks clanking together as they were prepared for the day's first trip greeted them. A half dozen tourists were in the shop pawing over masks and flippers as they eagerly waited for their departure. Max climbed out and stood on the dock, leaving Daniel in the dinghy to tie it up. All of her senses were alive as she took in all of the sights and sounds. Finished, Daniel joined her and she suddenly said, "Look. Over there, coming into the fuel dock. Isn't that Digit?"

"Yes, I think you're right."

"Daniel, I want to go over and say hello to him."

"Sure, go ahead. I'll be right along." Daniel went into the office to make sure that there was no problem leaving the dinghy there.

Max went ahead and even though it was only a short walk over, had Digit not been talking with some other men at the end of the dock, she might have missed him. As she got closer, Max saw that he was about to walk off toward the co-op so she waved and called out a greeting. Digit turned in the direction of her call. He saw her, stopped and waited for her.

"Max, how are you doing today? Better?"

"Yes, much better. Thank you for your kindness yesterday."

"No problem, all I did was give you a ride ashore."

"Well, it was nice of you."

It was at this moment that Daniel caught up to them. "Everything all set?" she asked turning toward Daniel.

"No problem leaving the dinghy there. They'll keep an eye on it," he replied. Then turning toward Digit he said, "Mornin."

Digit's return greeting, while pleasant, didn't have quite the same level of warmth with which he had greeted Max.

Daniel continued, "Say, Max and I were looking for something to do today, do you have any ideas?"

"Why don't you go on a snorkel trip?"

Daniel looked at Max when he replied, "No, we would like to do something different, something a little less touristy." Then he looked at Digit as he continued. "You know, as many times as I've sailed down here, I've never explored the mangroves between here and Monkey River. You must know your way through there. Would you be willing to take us?"

This request took both Max and Digit by surprise. Max was the first to say something, "That sounds different. Is that something that you could do?" she asked turning toward Digit.

He looked at both of them, obviously thinking about his reply, then he said, "Well, I'm not a registered tour guide, but I do know those mangroves. Sure, I can do that."

"Great," said Daniel. "We need to get some breakfast and then some things from the boat. How about you pick us up out on the boat in say, two hours?" Then almost as an afterthought he added, "Figure out what would be fair to charge us for your time and let me know how much."

"That'll be fine," said Digit. "I'll pick you up on your boat in two hours."

Max smiled at him, "Thanks, Digit. Sounds like fun." With those words they parted, Max and Daniel heading toward Wendy's Restaurant while Digit walked toward the co-op.

CHAPTER 79

JACK HAD BREAKFAST AT PAULA'S. All of the regulars had already come and gone so he was able to eat with few distractions. He was still bothered by the way Percy had acted last night. He seemed wary and sullen until Daniel's name had come up. Then he had become more interested, even suggesting that maybe Daniel had killed Python. Why had he suggested that? That comment seemed to have come out of the blue. Why did Leslie play dumb about Max running off to Belize when they had talked about it down in Newburyport? It all seemed strained and strange to Jack. By the time he had finished eating, he decided he would stop by and see Tom and tell him that he was going to Belize.

* * *

Tom looked up from behind a stack of papers when he heard the knock.

"Hey, Tom. Got a minute?"

"Sure, Jack. Come on in. What's up?"

Jack sat in the hard backed chair that faced Tom's desk and made himself as comfortable as possible. "Tom, I'm going to Belize. I'm flying down to Miami tonight and then tomorrow I'm flying to Belize. I thought you should know."

"Okaayy," said Tom drawing out the word. "Do you really think that's a good idea?"

"Yes. I have to see Max. I just have this feeling that things may not be as perfect as they sounded in her letter. Besides, I don't trust Daniel. From what we've found out, I find it hard to believe that he's been truthful with Max."

"Fair enough. But do you know where she is?"

"I know where they stayed when they first got down there so I have a starting point. I'm sure I'll be able to find her."

"What are you going to do if you find her?"

"When. When I find her, well . . . I'll just have to play that by ear."

"Then, I guess all I can say is good luck."

"Thanks, Tom. I just wanted you to know."

Jack stood to leave, then he hesitated, "I almost forgot. Last night we went up to Dover to see the band."

"How was that?"

"It was fun, but I have to tell you it was a little weird at the same time."

"How so?"

"Well, I was talking with the band during a break and Leslie asked me about Max like he didn't know anything."

"And he did?"

"Yes, I had just seen him and told him the whole story about Max going to Belize with Daniel and yet last night he brought it into the conversation like he didn't know anything."

"Interesting."

Then Percy, the bass player, who had been really quiet, and I would almost say sullen, jumped into the conversation. It was like he didn't want to see me, but then as soon as Daniel's name came up, he became real interested and even suggested that he was the one who killed Python. It just seemed a little weird to me. It was probably nothing but it just struck me."

"Maybe I should have another conversation with him."

"Probably not a bad idea. Well, I gotta go. If I don't see you again before I leave, I'll see you when I get back."

"Will there be any way to contact you if the need arises?"

"Don't know. Bye."

Jack turned and departed, leaving Tom scratching his head, thinking about what Jack had just told him.

CHAPTER 80

BREAKFAST FULFILLED A NEED, since both Daniel and Max were quite hungry, however, conversation was sparse and at best polite. Daniel was trying hard to salvage things with Max, but she was still too upset with him to cut him much slack. As they finished, Max suggested that they get some food for lunch before going back to the boat to wait for Digit. Daniel paid the check and they walked in silence toward the store.

The sun's rays beat down mercilessly from a cloud-free sky. The buildings of the settlement blocked any cooling breeze that was present and the road's pavement reflected the heat back up. By the time they reached the store, both Max and Daniel were bathed in sweat. Max stopped and said to Daniel, "There's somewhere I want to go before we leave. Why don't you take care of things here in the store and I'll meet you at the dock?" With that, she turned and continued up the road, leaving Daniel standing in front of the store.

Her pronouncement and departure was so sudden that he wasn't even given the opportunity to respond. Finally, he shrugged his shoulders and mumbled under his breath to no one, "Fine. See if I care."

Max continued up the road and then took the turn to Nancy's. She was going for two reasons, one, she wanted to get some pie for lunch and two, she just needed to talk. Even though she had only just met Nancy, she felt comfortable with her and somehow knew, deep within, that if things really went badly with Daniel, she could go to Nancy for help. As she walked up the stairs, she could feel the breeze from the water and the relief was immediate. She didn't see the pair of eyes watching her as she went into the shop.

"Hi Nancy," she said when she saw her.

"Oh, hi Max. How are you today? You look hot, would you like something to drink?"

"You are a lifesaver. Yes, please. It is so hot today."

"Yes, dear, it is, but up here there's a breeze and it's not so bad. You just have to learn to slow down."

"You're right. I haven't completely adjusted yet."

"How are things with that man of yours?"

"Okay, I guess." Max would have been happy spending the afternoon here, but she had agreed to spend the afternoon with Daniel exploring the mangroves with Digit as their guide. She began looking over the different pies that were in the display case.

"You guess? That doesn't sound too promising."

"Well, I mean, we have talked some and this afternoon Digit is taking us out in his boat. I think it'll be good to do something like that. Maybe we'll be able to reconnect."

"Digit's my cousin. He's a good man. You'll have fun. So what can I get you?"

"I'd like some pie for our lunches. The piece you gave me the other day was so good. Do you have any of that?

"Yes. That's Digit's favorite."

She cut three slices and wrapped them in waxed paper and placed them in a box, which she carefully tied up with string. "Here you go." She handed the box to Max. "Everything will be fine. You'll see."

"Thanks, Nancy. I'm sure you're right," and she turned to go.

As she opened the door, she stopped and turned as she heard Nancy say, "Max, I want you to know, if there is anything you need, anything at all, come back here." This was said with such sincerity and feeling that Max knew it was meant from deep within.

"Thank you again," said Max as she turned to go.

"Remember, anything. Anything at all. I'll be here. Now you get going. You don't want to keep Digit waiting."

Nancy followed Max out, the door slapping shut behind them and she watched Max walk toward the sidewalk where there was more breeze and it was cooler than on the road. As Max disappeared from sight, Nancy saw the man from the day before, who had come into the shop asking questions, step out from behind a small building and begin to go in the same direction that Max had gone in. "That's strange," Nancy said aloud.

The walk toward the waterfront was much cooler than walking along the road. As she headed for the dive shop where the dinghy was tied, she saw Daniel sitting in the shade by the tourist center waiting for her. He had several plastic bags at his feet and he stood and waved when he saw her. As she walked toward him, once again she was conflicted. He was so gorgeous and memories flashed though her head that made her blush, then something snapped her back to reality. The hurt of his deceptions returned and her step slowed slightly. When she was only a few steps away, he said, "Did you get whatever you wanted?"

"Yes. I have a treat for us. You'll see soon enough."

He bent down and picked up his packages and as he stood, he paused and a dark look came over his face as he stared past Max.

"Are you all right?" asked Max as she turned, looking in the same direction as his gaze. She saw nothing.

"Yes, I'm all right."

"What were you looking at?"

"Nothing. I just thought I saw something, but I didn't. Let's go. Digit will be showing up soon."

This answer didn't satisfy Max. She knew that something had happened and it worried her. Another deception. Another lie. *What was going on?* she wondered. As hard as Daniel tried to appear relaxed, something had obviously upset him. Nothing further was said on the way back to the boat and as soon as they were aboard, Max went below to gather her things before Digit arrived. She hadn't paid any attention to what Daniel was doing, assuming that he was doing the same, but when she came up from her cabin, he was standing in the cockpit, binoculars in hand scanning the shore. "Daniel. What are you doing?"

The sound of her voice startled him. Quickly putting down the binoculars he replied, "Nothing." Before Max could say anything else he added, "I have to get my stuff," and abruptly left the cockpit and disappeared below. As soon as he was out of sight, Max picked up the glasses and looked in the same direction he had been looking. At first, she didn't see anything unusual. The taxis were lined up by the water's edge, tourists were going in and out of the tourist information center and everything seemed quite normal, then she saw him, the man from the pie shop. He was near the co-op, sitting in the sand, binoculars slung around his neck like a tourist not knowing what to do with his time.

While Max studied him, he raised his binoculars to his eyes and began scanning his horizon. He began looking away from them and then he slowly began to rotate toward *d'Riddem.* Max was transfixed, watching him slowly turn in their direction and before she could react they were in each other's sights. Max quickly looked away. Had she not turned away, she would have seen him quickly lower his glasses, stand and move out of sight.

Max jumped at Daniel's touch. She hadn't heard him come up behind her. "Anything interesting?" he asked with just a bit of an edge to his voice.

Lowering the glasses and turning toward his voice her initial reply was "No." As Daniel reached for the binoculars, she relaxed her grip on them, letting him take them from her, she changed her answer. "I think I saw that man watching us. What's going on?"

Daniel calmly raised the glasses to his eyes and scanned the shore. "I don't know what you mean Max. What man? I don't see anyone." His voice was relaxed and reassuring.

"Bullshit. You know exactly what man and what I'm talking about."

"Max, I'm afraid I don't."

"Yes, you do, and I want . . . No, I need some answers. Don't do this to me, Daniel."

He stood there looking at her, trying to remain calm and unconcerned. "Max," he said softly.

"Something is going on and I want to know what," she demanded.

"Max, nothing is going on," he said fighting to keep his voice calm. He turned to step into the salon to put the binoculars away.

"Daniel," she said. "I want the truth," anger filling her voice.

He paused, and without turning he said, "Max, you are overreacting. Now let's just get ready. Digit should be here shortly."

That did it. He couldn't see the look in her eyes because his back was still turned to her, but if he had, he might have reconsidered. She reached out and grabbed his shoulder. That's all it took. He turned sharply and faced her as soon as he felt her touch. Those warm, tender eyes that had once melted her heart flashed a darkness that was as cold and dangerous as black ice. In that moment her anger fled, replaced by fear. His jaw muscles showed strain as he clenched them in restraint. "Don't ever do that again," he said in slow measured tones. He continued, "Nothing is going on. Don't ask again. Now, I suggest that we get ready."

A cold shiver went down her spine. She had only seen that look once before in her life and that man had been trying to kill her. They stood there, not moving, silent, staring deep into each other's eyes. That's when Digit showed up.

"Hello!" his cheerful voice called out. "Is everybody ready?"

Daniel and Max continued facing each other. Max had her back to Digit and Daniel forced a smile. "Hi, Digit. We'll be ready in a few minutes."

"No problem." He tied his boat to the stern of *d'Riddem* and let it drift back while he busied himself with tidying things up in preparation for his guests.

Max brushed past Daniel and went into the cabin. Daniel turned and followed her in. "Max, come on. I'm sorry." His voice was all honey and dripping sincerity.

She stopped. He could hear her sniffle. Then as she turned toward him, she wiped away a tear that had run down her cheek. Taking a deep breath she said, "You're sorry! I'm the one who is sorry. I'm sorry that I ever met you. Something is going on. I don't like the way it's changing you and I don't want any part of it. Before things go any further, I think it would be best if I just get off the boat."

Daniel stood there looking at her. Anger, hurt, pride, and the realization that he might never see her again washed over him. "Max."

"Stop. Don't say anything else. I'm getting off the boat. I'll have Digit take me ashore. You stay and sort your life out. Who knows? Maybe there will be a time in the future when we can be together, but I know that now is not that time." With that, she turned and went down into her cabin to get her things. Daniel just stood there. He knew she was right.

While she was below getting her stuff together, he went outside and called to Digit. Digit pulled his boat up close to *d'Riddem* and Daniel leaned over to talk to him so he didn't have to shout. "There has been a change of plans. I'm sorry but, I don't think that we are going to be able to go out with you this afternoon." Digit looked up at him in surprise. "No problem, I hope."

"No, Digit. No problem. Whatever I owe you for your time just tell me."

Digit cut him off. "No charge. We'll do it another time."

"Perhaps. Thank you. Can you do me one last favor?"

"Sure, man. What can I do for you."

"Would you take Max ashore and help her find a place to stay?"

Digit looked up at Daniel, this was not what he was expecting.

"Sure, man. No problem. Is everything all right?"

"Everything is fine. Max just needs to go ashore."

It was at this moment that Max reappeared with her backpack in hand. "Daniel, I'm going to leave my large suitcase here. I have enough stuff for a short while. I'll come back later to get the rest," she said with forced civility.

"Okay. I'll see you later, then."

Daniel stood there, his focus so totally on watching Max leave with Digit that he didn't see the other pair of eyes watching him with equal intensity.

* * *

While Max was moving ashore, Jack was finishing his packing and preparing to leave for the airport. As he was loading his suitcase into his truck, Courtney came out of her house. "Hey, Jack."

"Hi, Court."

"When's your flight?"

Looking at his watch, he said, "It leaves in about three and a half hours. I want to get going in case I hit the late afternoon traffic. Those roads by Logan can be brutal."

"Why didn't you fly out of Manchester?"

"I couldn't get the flight I wanted. As it is, I had to book the first half of the trip today and the rest tomorrow."

"That sucks."

"I agree."

"Jack, be careful and bring Max home safely."

"I will, and I hope to, but time will tell."

* * *

The bell on the door clanged, announcing another customer. It had been a busy day despite the heat. When Nancy emerged from the back room, she was startled to see Max standing in the doorway. "Max!" she exclaimed. "I thought you were going out on the boat with Digit this afternoon."

It was at that moment she saw Digit standing out on the porch behind Max. Confused, she started to say something else, when she saw the backpack in Max's hand. Max had neither moved nor spoken. "Oh honey, what happened?" and she began walking around the counter toward Max. Before she had even taken two steps, she could see Max's eyes filling with tears and then the sobs began. Max dropped the backpack and accepted the hug from Nancy, her tears streaming down her cheeks. Nancy looked out at Digit, her eyes asking the question.

"There has been a change in plans, and Max will need a place to stay for a few days," said Digit.

Nancy gently eased her embrace and feeling this, Max withdrew her arms from around Nancy and wiped her eyes as Nancy held her by the shoulders, looking deep into her eyes.

"I'm so sorry. I didn't know where else to go."

"There, there dear. It's okay. Come. Come in and sit down. I'll go get some tea." Then in Digit's direction she said, "She'll be fine. I'll have her stay here with me."

"No problem. I'll see you later then," and with that he turned, went down the stairs and was gone.

Max was beginning to regain control after the flood of tears and started to say, "I . . . I can't ask you to take me in. Could you just recommend a place for me to say?"

"Max, you didn't ask me if you could stay here. I told you that you were staying here with me. Now, sit there while I get the tea."

* * *

Meanwhile, out on *d'Riddem,* Daniel prepared to leave. It was time. The man she had just seen, the man who he knew was there was one of his employer's "problem solvers." Daniel now knew that those encounters with the black boat were not random. It would only be a matter of time before it reappeared, bringing with it the help that the man on shore was obviously waiting for. He had to leave as soon as it was dark and try to get away. As he made his preparations, he kept beating himself up for being such an asshole to Max. She deserved better and he should never have let his feelings for her cloud his judgment. Back in Rye, he should have been content with his conquest and left it at that, but no, he had to fall for her. He thought that he could leave his old life behind, and start over with her. He had always known deep inside that this was just a fantasy. He just didn't want to admit it. Now both he and Max would have to pay. He knew what would happen to him if he was caught and he hoped that she would be considered irrelevant and by that irrelevance be safe. In the remaining daylight, he scanned the shore one last time, didn't see anything or anyone. Soon it would be dark and he would slip away.

* * *

The flight to Miami was uneventful. After checking in to his hotel, Jack went down to the hotel bar, ordered a beer and a burger and sat there thinking about what lay ahead.

CHAPTER 81

DESPITE THE HEAT OF THE DAY, which was now beginning to dissipate, the tea was strangely refreshing, and as Max sat there sipping it with Nancy, their silence spoke volumes. Max was the first to speak, "Nancy, thank you. I don't know what I'd do if it weren't for your kindness. I'm not sure how I can ever repay you."

"Hush, there is nothing to repay."

"No. There is. Here I am, a perfect stranger. I show up on your door step and you accept me as if we had been friends our whole lives when we only just met."

"Max, do you remember the letter you gave me from Alfonso?"

"Yes."

"You know that he's my brother."

"Yes."

"Actually he's my half brother, but we're very close. In his letter, he told me that Charles was sailing to Placencia with a beautiful young lady. He told me that you knew Charles as Daniel and that I was not to call him Charles. He also said that Charles seemed different from when he had been here before. He felt that something wasn't right. He didn't want to see you get hurt and that if you needed any help, I was to help you."

"I don't understand. Why would your brother do this?"

"He would do anything for Cha… Daniel. Years ago, Daniel saved his life in a diving accident and since then they have been almost like brothers."

"But why his concern for me?"

"I don't really know. You'll have to ask him yourself. All I know is that he asked me to help you if you needed it. You do, and I'm here. You'll stay with me for as long as you need to."

"Well . . . I still don't understand, but thank you."

By the time they had finished their tea and conversation, it was dark. Max helped her close the shop and they left, walking first toward the sidewalk and then turning north, away from the anchorage, away from lies and deception, away from Daniel, and toward Nancy's home. It took them about fifteen minutes to reach Nancy's.

Her house was similar to her shop. It was raised up on stilts, palm trees were all around the house and their fronds rustling in the breeze added to the ever present sound of waves breaking on the beach. A stairway led up to a porch that wrapped around three sides of the house. The ever-deepening darkness changed the bright colors that the house was painted into muted subtle shades of tinted gray.

While Nancy went in and turned lights on, Max stopped and leaning against one of the posts that held up the porch roof, she gazed out over the sidewalk, past the beach, and over the calm sea. The moon was rising and its silver shadow was like a road stretched out for her. If she could have floated on air, she could have followed that road to the horizon and beyond. Her thoughts went back to those first perfect days that she spent with Daniel in San Pedro and then on the boat. Everything had been new and magical, now . . . now she didn't know what was going to happen. Those days of bliss seemed like a lifetime ago, even though only a few days had passed.

Her thoughts were interrupted by Nancy's voice calling from inside. She turned and went in. The house was warm and welcoming. She entered into a large room that was the full width of the house. The inside walls were white, not a stark blinding white but a softer, warmer white. The windows and doors were framed in wood, finished to accentuate their natural colors and varnished to a glossy shine. There were two doors on the back wall. One was open with wonderful aromas beginning to waft out and she could hear Nancy in there clanking pots and pans.

There were framed photographs on the walls. The majority were black and white although some were in color. They were mostly scenes of daily life in Placencia and as she slowly worked her way around the room looking at each picture, she noticed that the same subjects were in many of them. It was at that moment Nancy came back into the room carrying two tall glasses filled with ice and an orangey-yellow liquid that looked so refreshing. Their outsides were dripping with condensation and there was a big straw sticking out above the rim. "Here, try this," she said as she handed one to Max.

"Thanks. Who are all these people in these pictures?" she asked before taking her first sip.

"They're all my family."

As Max sipped on her drink she continued to stare at the pictures. "This drink is wonderful. Who took these pictures? They are amazing. What is in this drink?"

"Well, the drink we call a Smilin' Wide because when you drink them, you begin to smile wide."

"Daniel made me something similar on the boat, but I like yours better," said Max.

"As for the pictures, Digit's wife took most of them. She's a pretty good photographer."

"She's better than pretty good. Does she do this professionally?"

"No. I know what you mean, though. She should, but she doesn't feel that she's good enough."

Max sipped and continued looking at the pictures. They were more than just family pictures. Somehow she managed to capture something deeper in each image. Max felt as if she were being allowed a glimpse into each person's soul.

Turning and facing Nancy she said, "I have a friend at home who is a pretty good photographer. If she saw these pictures, she would be blown away. They are incredible."

"You may be right, and I agree that they are good, but Manuela is very modest and would never do anything like that."

"Well, she should."

Max was almost finished with her drink and she looked at Nancy and with a grin said, "You're right about these drinks, they do make you smile."

"Would you like another?

"Yes, thank you."

Nancy took her glass, turned and headed back toward the kitchen. Max followed her. There was a strange hissing sound coming from the room that accompanied the most wondrous aromas. "What's that noise?"

"That's my secret weapon. I like to cook with a pressure cooker. It's much faster than regular stewing and in the heat down here, the less time I have to spend in a hot kitchen the better. I do that enough all day."

"What are you cooking?"

"Garlic-lime chicken with potatoes."

"Sounds yummy."

While she was telling Max about the chicken, she was also making the Smilin' Wides: ice, two kinds of rum, coconut and amber and then orange juice and pineapple juice. A dash of coconut finished the drink. Max took note of the ingredients, thinking that when she got home, she'd have to introduce everyone to Smilin' Wides.

Nancy handed Max her fresh drink and said, "It won't be long before dinner is ready. Let's go back out front."

Max followed Nancy out to the porch and they sat together on the swinging bench that hung from the rafters. The moon was higher in the sky, darkness was complete and the palms and surf continued their steady schwooshing. Other than an occasional voice out in the dark or the bark of a dog, it felt as if they were the only two people in the world.

Max broke the silence, "Nancy, can I ask you something?"

"Sure."

"Have you always lived here?"

Nancy looked at her in a questioning way.

"I mean, you're different."

Nancy looked at her again, still puzzled.

Max began to get flustered. "That didn't sound right. Let me start again. I realize that this is my first time here and I probably have some preconceived notions about the people here, but you're a little different. Your shop, your home, the way you are, just don't seem to fit what I would expect."

"Max, you are both right and wrong. Placencia is my home. I was born here, my family lives here, and I grew up here." She paused and then continued. "There wasn't much here. Placencia was just a small village. Almost everyone fished for a living. It wasn't like today. One day, this huge sailing yacht anchored here. No one had ever seen anything like it. I don't know how big it was but to me it looked like the whole village would have fit on it. Its hull was black and it had two masts that seemed to scrape the clouds. Its name was painted in gold on the back. *The Raven.* I remember that because I wasn't quite sure what a raven was."

A distant bell rang in Max's head as Nancy continued.

"One of the boat's crew had come ashore looking to buy some lobsters. I was on the beach with my father who had just returned from a day of fishing, and he had some really big lobsters in his boat. The man from the boat came up to us and asked if we would sell him the lobsters. I just stared at him. He was a good looking man with kind eyes and you could tell he was a nice person. When he looked at me, I turned away and tried to become invisible, but I was fascinated and kept glancing at him while he negotiated with my father. Finally, they finished their business. We would bring the lobsters out to the boat later and he turned to leave. I don't know why, but at that moment, as he turned to go, I spoke up and asked him what the name of the boat meant. I'm not sure who was more surprised, my father, the man or me. He stopped, turned and said that a raven was a big black bird that was a scavenger. My father, embarrassed by my outburst, pulled me away and told me to run home and tell my mother that we were going to take some lobsters to the people on the big black boat and that we would be back soon. As I turned and left, I could hear my father apologizing for my outburst and the man laughed it off."

"I went home and told my mother where we were going and since she and I had been baking bread that morning, I took several loaves of bread back with me to see if they would like any. When my dad and I got out to the boat, I was really nervous and when we climbed up onto the sailboat, my heart was pounding. Part of me was excited and part was scared. We climbed up and I looked around for the man who had talked to us on shore. I didn't see him and this older man came over to us. The way that everyone acted, I assumed that he was the owner. My father showed him the lobsters and then told him that I had baked some bread earlier in the day and he wanted to know if he would like some of that as well. He did and had another man on his crew pay us."

"We were about to climb back down into our boat when he asked if we would like a cool drink. My father wanted to leave, but I hesitated and said yes before my father could shush me. The older man then called out to someone to bring us something cold to drink. He was the man we had met on shore and as soon as he delivered the drinks, the older man thanked him and dismissed him. We drank our drinks and we left, feeling very rich and important."

Nancy paused, took a sip from her drink and then jumped up and went inside. Max followed her into the kitchen wondering what was wrong. "Is everything all right?" she asked.

Nancy began fussing with the pressure cooker, steam was hissing and when it stopped, she twisted the lid open and the most amazing aromas came out. She looked up with a smile, and said, "Everything is fine. I had just realized that dinner was finished and I didn't want it to burn. Can you pass me that large bowl over there?"

Max did and Nancy dumped the contents of the pot into the bowl. Pieces of chicken, most falling off the bone, potatoes and the most wonderful smelling broth filled the bowl. She handed it to Max and asked her to take it out to the table. Seeing that both drinks were nearly finished she asked, "Would you like another?"

"Yes, that would be good."

"I'll go make some more."

After depositing the bowl of steaming chicken on the table, Max returned to the kitchen. Nancy had just pulled some bread from the oven and placed it in a basket, which she handed to Max. "Here, take this out. I'll get the drinks and I'll be right out."

Max put the bread on the table and returned to the kitchen in time to watch Nancy make the drinks, noting the ingredients once again. The first two drinks were beginning to have the desired effect and the smells from the chicken made her stomach rumble. She hadn't realized just how hungry she was.

"Let's go eat," she said as she handed Max her third drink of the night.

Dinner was fabulous. Max had never eaten anything that tasted as good as this chicken did. Sopping up the broth with the bread was almost better that the chicken. While they ate, there was lots of laughing and chitchat about nothing of great importance. Their plates finally empty and stomachs full, Max looked at Nancy and asked, "So finish the story. What happened after you left the man's boat after selling him the lobsters and the bread?"

"Sure, but let's clean up this mess first, then we can sit." There was more small talk and lots of giggles as the two women, now feeling the effects of the Smilin' Wides, cleaned up and put away the mess from dinner. As the last plates were dried and put in their cupboard, Nancy made two more drinks, handed one to Max and motioned for her to follow her outside onto the porch where they sat again on the swinging bench, one at each end, leaning against pillows facing each other. The evening had cooled down and after the heat of the kitchen it almost felt cool. The breeze continued to rustle the palms and the ocean's ceaseless *kashwoosh* on the beach created the most soothing backdrop.

Nancy was the first to speak, "You know Max, until you asked me about my past I hadn't given it much thought until tonight. You get busy with life and you are always going here, doing that, living in the present and looking toward the future, that you forget to sit and remember the past. I had almost forgotten about that big black boat and the man who owned it until you asked me how I got started baking."

Max sat silently as Nancy continued.

"The morning after we had sold them the lobsters, two men from the boat came into town looking for the person who had baked that bread they had bought. My father was out fishing for the day, but I was home with my mother, baking some more bread when they found me. I was surprised and flattered, to say the least, that someone who was as rich and powerful as he must have been, I mean to have such a boat, would want to buy the bread that I baked. We had just baked a fruit pie and they bought that as well. My mother and I were all excited after they left. They had paid us much more for the bread and pie than we ever would have thought possible."

"After they had gone, my mother and I started over again baking some bread and another pie for ourselves. I was so excited that I went down to meet my father when he returned from fishing. As soon as he came ashore, I began to tell him about the bread and the pie. As we walked home together, we passed two of the men from the black boat. They recognized us and stopped to talk. One of them was the man who had given us the cold drinks and he asked if I might have another pie that he could buy. He wanted this one for himself and some of the other crew. We sold him a pie and we never saw them again."

"I guess that this was my beginning because after that I did everything I could to learn about baking. I read anything I could get hold of. I talked to anyone who was visiting to see what they might know about baking and I continued to bake and sell what I baked, especially to tourists."

"Years later, a man came to Placencia on vacation and took an interest in my baking. As it turned out, he owned a famous restaurant in the United States and he asked me to go there to work for him. I knew I would go, but it was hard convincing my parents. Eventually, they let me and I spent five years in the States."

Max was feeling the effects of too many Smilin' Wides, a good meal and the hypnotic background sounds of rustling palms and the surf. Her eyes were losing the battle, slowly closing, her mind drifting to faraway places. Nancy's story telling had become slower as she too was feeling the same effects. Max, though fading fast, heard the part about going to the states and asked "Where?"

"Boston."

Max was instantly awake. "Boston!"

Nancy was startled by Max's reaction. "Why are you so surprised?"

"I guess I shouldn't be, but I live about an hour north of Boston, in Portsmouth, New Hampshire and I grew up in Connecticut, just to the south."

"Small world. Maybe I baked something that you ate at some time and neither one of us knew it. Maybe we were fated to meet here," Nancy said with a smile.

"Maybe."

"Listen, I think we have both had enough to drink and I need to go to bed. Come, I'll show you where you are staying, then if you want to sit up you can, but I'm done in."

“Sure,” Max replied and followed Nancy inside. She went down the hallway that was next to the kitchen door. Nancy pushed the door to the first room on the right open and said, “Here’s your new home. My room is next door and the bath is at the end of the hall.”

Lying in bed, alone in the dark, Max became conscious of just how tired she was. Her limbs felt like lead and her eyelids grew heavy. Wondering why *The Raven* sounded so familiar, she sank into a deep sleep.

CHAPTER 82

A DOG'S BARKING FIRST PIERCED the veil of sleep and then Max heard a rooster crow, birds chattering and she could feel the warmth and brightness of the sun on her face. Slowly, she opened her eyes and was greeted by a new day in a strange bed. She sat up too quickly, and her head spun wildly, so she lay back down slowly and while waiting for the spinning to stop she wondered, "Where am I?"

She lay back down and it came back to her, bit by bit; Smilin' Wides, dinner, the sounds and fragrance of a tropical night and then . . . her dreams. She began to remember her dream, it seemed so real, and made perfect sense when she was in it, but now as she tried to remember, it was too fragmented to make any sense at all. She remembered floating in the warm sea. Daniel was with her, then he was gone and she was alone. A black boat appeared on the horizon and was speeding towards her and as it drew near she could see Daniel on the boat. The boat stopped near her, but she could neither swim towards it nor away from it. All she could do was stare at it. Daniel was looking at her, she called out to him, he didn't reply, he just looked at her with a look of fated resignation as if he were leaving and there was nothing either one of them could do about it. Then he was gone and so was the black boat. Next, she was on a deserted beach, alone, except that she was not alone. There were birds in the sky and someone was touching her arm, stroking her hair, caressing her shoulder. She couldn't see who it was, she wanted to, but she couldn't turn her head. It felt so good, so calming, so reassuring. It felt so right . . . so perfect. The slamming of a door shook her out of her reverie. She heard voices, loud excited voices. At first she didn't hear words, just noise. Then she began to hear words, not sentences but enough that she jumped out of bed and went toward the voices. Boat . . . Daniel . . . Black boat . . . Tell Max . . .

"Tell Max what?" she said as she came around the corner and saw Digit and Nancy standing by the front door.

At the sound of her voice, they both froze. Digit looked up and his eyes locked with Max's. Nancy turned and her eyes locked onto Max as well. She repeated the question. "Tell me what?"

Nancy spoke first, "Max, Daniel is gone. The boat is gone."

"What do you mean he's gone?"

"He's gone."

Digit interrupted, "This morning just before dawn I came into the fuel dock so I could get gas and some ice from the co-op as soon as they opened. I was planning a long fishing trip today out to the reef. As I tied up my boat, I saw that Daniel's boat was gone. I knew that you and he had had some problems and that was why I brought you here last night, but I didn't think that they were so bad that he would leave."

"When did he leave?" asked Max. Her heart was beginning to race.

"I don't know exactly, but it must have been shortly after midnight. I asked around, but no one had seen anything. The boat was just gone. Then while I was at the co-op, this old guy came up to me and said that he had seen the boat leave. He told me that he had been drinking all night in the bar and had gone outside looking for a cigarette when he decided to relieve himself behind a tree on the beach. While pissing, he saw the boat sail off and didn't think much of it. He went back into the bar and stayed until it closed then passed out on the beach. I thanked him, then while I was carrying a cooler of ice back to my boat, he came up to me again. This time he told me something else and that is why I came right over here."

"What did he say?" Max said with a noticeable quiver in her voice.

"He told me that just before sunrise, a black boat came up to the fuel dock. It had a really powerful engine that was loud and that it woke him up. He didn't recognize either the boat or the man at the helm and thought it strange that anyone would be out so early. Then a gringo showed up and went straight to the black boat. The men had words. The man from shore was obviously upset and finally he jumped into the black boat and they took off."

Max felt paralyzed. The pounding of her heartbeat echoing in her ears almost made her deaf to what Digit was saying. She stared at him with a crazy look on her face. He paused when he saw Max's reaction.

Nancy spoke next. "Go on, what happened next?"

"Nothing."

"What do you mean nothing?"

"Nothing. The old guy just saw the black boat leave in a real hurry, and he went back to sleep."

"Where did they go?"

Digit shrugged. "I don't know. I asked him, but he couldn't remember anything else."

"What did the man on the black boat look like?" asked Max.

"I'm sorry, I didn't ask," was his reply.

Max sat down in a chair, visibly shaken. Nancy moved to her side and as she reached down and touched her shoulder. Digit looked on feeling quite helpless as Nancy tried to calm her. Finally he said, "Listen, I'm going to go ask around some more and see if I can find out anything more."

He closed the door softly and Nancy knelt in front of Max, took her hands and looked into her tear-reddened eyes, "Everything will be all right. We'll find him. Here's a tissue, now dry your eyes, go in the bath and wash up while I make us some tea. We are going to have a busy day."

The two women were just finishing their tea when Digit returned. They looked up at him expectantly, but could see in his eyes that he hadn't found out anything new. "Anything?" asked Max hoping against hope that he had.

"No."

"Something has happened. We have to find him. Will you help me?" Max said to Digit.

"Of course I will," replied Digit. "The fish will still be there tomorrow. Why don't you get ready and I'll meet you at my boat in an hour?" Max agreed and Digit left. While Max got herself ready, Nancy busied herself with preparing lunch for Digit and Max. "Okay, Max. I've made some lunch for you two. I'll walk with you down to the boat and we'll stop at the store on the way to pick up some water and drinks. Today will be hot and out on the water you will really need the water. Do you have a hat and sun block?"

"I have sun block, but I don't have a hat."

"I have one you can borrow," and with that Nancy disappeared into her room, returning shortly, hat in hand. She handed the hat to Max and said, "Ready?"

"Ready." The two women left and headed first to the store and then to the dock. When they got there, Digit was already there and waiting. He had the boat nosed up to the beach. Max handed him the drinks and the lunch that Nancy had packed for them and he put them in the cooler he had in the boat. As Max climbed in, he started the engine.

CHAPTER 83

AS DIGIT PUT THE BOAT INTO REVERSE and pulled away from the beach, Max looked at Nancy and waved good-bye. It only took moments for Digit to turn the boat and they headed away from Placencia at full speed. Between the whine of the engine, the staccato thumping of the hull against the water and the rush of the wind past her ears, Max had to stand close to Digit to hear what he was shouting at her. "We'll start by going southeast toward Ranguana Caye. There is a break in the reef there and if he were trying to get far away in the middle of the night, that might be the clearest way possible. I know some fishermen who are out there right now and if he went that way they would probably have seen him."

"How far is it?" Max shouted.

"It's only fifteen miles or so. It will take us less than an hour."

Max nodded and little else was said as they settled in for the ride, Digit standing behind the console, steering, and Max sitting on the seat in front. As they flew across the water, Max kept thinking about the black boat that was seen going out to *d'Riddem*, and it scared her. What if it was the same boat they had seen earlier as they traveled south? What if . . .? She shook those thoughts out of her mind and just focused on the horizon ahead. Within the hour, she began to see the bar code signature of their destination. As they sped along under that blue sky dotted with cotton ball clouds, over a darker blue-green sea those lines turned into palm trees and then a ribbon of sand appeared between them and the sea. Max shielded her eyes from the sun, scanning ahead, hoping to see the mast of *d'Riddem* against the backdrop of the palms.

She saw nothing. Closer, and the water changed from the deep blue-greens to bright turquoise and they could see the bottom. Dark olive-brownish spots appeared that signaled patch reef. They zigged and zagged until they were as close as you could get to the island. Nothing. There was no sign of life, nothing to indicate that he might have been there.

As they slowly moved past the caye, Max suddenly pointed out toward the reef. "Look, there's a boat. Maybe they saw something."

"Those are some fishermen from Placencia, I know them." They were out by the reef so he began to work his way through the coral toward them. Their boat was anchored, its large sail tied up on the boom, some laundry hanging from the rigging like so many signal flags. There were four canoes tied behind the sloop, bobbing in the swell, their owners sitting on the deck of the larger boat eating lunch and resting before going back out for the rest of the afternoon. Two more canoes were being paddled toward the sloop from the reef. They had drifted downwind and now were paddling furiously against the wind to rejoin their compatriots on the larger boat. As he came along side, greetings were exchanged and Digit asked them if they had seen *d'Riddem.* They hadn't.

They knew the boat and had been in this area for two days and had not seen it. Digit could see that Max was visibly disappointed and so he asked again if anyone had seen any other boats. The men all looked back and forth at each other. There was some conversation in the local Creole dialect that Max could not understand.

"What is it?" she asked. "What are they talking about?"

Digit turned toward her and said, "Early this morning, there was another boat. It was a black speedboat and there were two men in it and it was going very fast. It came from over there." He pointed to the south. "They didn't pay much attention to it except that it was going very fast."

Max's heart went cold. The black boat again. She didn't want to think what that could mean, but she knew it couldn't be good. Digit thanked the fishermen and then he and Max left. As they began to slowly work their way back through the coral toward open water, Max's stomach grumbled. "Hungry?"

Digit nodded, so Max opened the cooler and took out some lunch and a couple of cold drinks. As she handed a drink to Digit, he said, "Max, you're beginning to look like a red snapper; you had better cover up."

She looked at her arms and legs and saw that he was right. "I guess I should."

She put on the long sleeved shirt she had brought along and they ate in silence. As soon as they had finished, he pressed the throttle forward and they sped south toward Nicholas Caye. It wasn't long before it came into sight. Once again they slowly weaved through the patch reef as they drew closer to Nicholas Caye. Her eyes continued to strain to see what wasn't there. She spotted another fishing boat, but Digit had seen it first and was already steering toward it.

"I know that boat," said Digit as they moved closer. The boat was anchored and appeared deserted, then they saw a solitary figure. He was cleaning fish in the shade of an old worn tarp that was draped over the boom. As they pulled alongside, he asked him about the sailboat and the black speedboat. Again, there had been no sighting of *d'Riddem*, but he, too, had seen the black speedboat. It had been shortly after dawn and it had come from the direction of the mainland, perhaps from Monkey River town. Digit offered him a cold drink and they chatted for a short while about fishing, families, and the weather. Digit could see that Max was getting anxious, so he finally said goodbye.

* * *

As Max and Digit headed for Monkey River Town, Jack's flight was beginning final descent into Belize International Airport. Jack stared out the plane's window, his mind drifting from memories of his first visit to

Belize so many years ago. He thought of Max and what he was going to do and say to her when he found her, if he found her. *What if she didn't want to be found? What if she was happy with Daniel? What if she didn't care that Daniel probably was a murderer? What if . . .?* His thoughts were interrupted when the plane thumped down onto the runway in what felt like a controlled crash. The engines roared while everything inside seemed to shake and rattle, he could feel the rapid deceleration as the pilot finally hit the brakes hard and then all was quiet. They had stopped, just short of the end of the runway and the plane turned to taxi back to the gate.

Jack gathered his bag and joined his fellow travelers as they shuffled their way down the aisle toward the door. When he reached the door, he paused for a moment to let his eyes adjust to the bright sun. A warm breeze hit him first, then the tropical heat enveloped him like a long lost lover. It had been too many years since he had last felt its caress. Memories came flooding back. Miami, Maria, sailing, and even a long forgotten promise to return to Belize.

A soft yet officious voice returned him to the present. "Welcome to Belize. Please keep moving, stay in line. After passing through immigration, you will claim your luggage before passing through customs."

The slow shuffle out of the plane and onto the tarmac had now turned into a brisk walk as everyone began hurrying to stop and stand in line. It was too hot to hurry, so Jack slowly fell to the back of the line as other passengers hurried past him. He was one of the last people to pass through immigration, and since his only bag was with him, he went straight to customs, where he passed in his declaration form and was waved through.

Tropic Air would take him to San Pedro and their counter was just inside the terminal. He stepped into line. Reservation confirmed, his bag checked, boarding pass in hand, he crossed the terminal and entered the departure lounge. He noted that as busy as the terminal was, there was an easy rhythm to the hustle and bustle that surrounded him. Unlike the institutional and impersonal feeling of airports at home, here he felt human.

Almost as soon as he was inside, he heard a voice calling for his flight to San Pedro to board. The gate was simply a door, one of several leading out to the tarmac. The planes were lined up, and as soon as everyone was gathered by the gate, they were walked out to the plane by a nice young man wearing a Tropic Air uniform. They crowded into the small plane and by the time Jack crouched his way in, the only seat remaining was a single seat just in front of the door.

The flight to San Pedro only took fifteen minutes or so and as he looked out the window memories of twenty-five years ago flooded back. The water was still that amazing green, he didn't see many boats out sailing, but as they approached San Pedro he realized just how much development had taken place. San Pedro was no longer a sleepy little fishing village. It was a thriving metropolis, not in a stateside way, but in a Belizean way. The plane rolled to a stop at the gate. Jack noted that it really was just that, a gate in a white picket fence. He finally squeezed out of the plane and took a deep breath. He had arrived. He was in Belize, on Ambergris Caye in San Pedro where his quest to find Max would begin.

Across the street was the Sun Breeze Hotel. Dodging golf carts and bicycles, he crossed the street and went inside. It was cool and calm inside, in stark contrast to the bustle outside on the street. Down the hall past the registration desk, he could see a courtyard dotted with palm trees and across the courtyard a pool, a bar, and beyond, the water and the reef. While checking in he asked the desk clerk about Max. She knew nothing since she had just returned from vacation. The check in complete, he was shown to his room. As he stood in his room, alone, the reality of what he was doing hit him full force for the first time. He had made a commitment. By coming to Belize, he had now made a commitment to Max. Of course she didn't know, she couldn't, and he hoped that it wasn't too late.

He changed into more comfortable clothes and headed for the bar. Max had been here not too long ago and bars were always good starting points when looking for information. He also needed a beer. Jack sat down at the bar and ordered a beer. An ice cold Belikin was placed in front of him and he took his first sip. *Not bad,* he thought. Looking around he saw that the bar was several steps up from the dining area, which was open on all sides. The restaurant was nearly empty now, but preparations were in full swing for this evening's meal.

Next door, the dive shop was busy, as dozens of wet-suited tourists returned to terra firma after a day spent playing Jacques Cousteau. They looked both tired and exhilarated as they left the boats and began trudging across the sand, lugging their duffles of gear. He noted that some were staying at the Sun Breeze and others began walking down the beach. The dive shop's employees were swarming all over the boats. Some were unloading empty tanks that clanged against each other as they were lined up for refilling. Others manned hoses and scrub brushes as they washed away the evidence of today's trip and prepared for tomorrow's. Water taxis cruised back and forth as the last para sail rides of the day were being pulled back to earth. Soon the sun would set and a whole new rhythm would take over. *Max was right,* he thought, *This place could be a lot of fun."* His thoughts were interrupted when the bartender asked him if he would like another beer. "Sure." The beer was placed in front of him with its neck wrapped tightly with a napkin. "Here you go."

"Thanks."

"Just arrive?" asked the bartender.

"Yes, this afternoon."

"First time to Belize?

"Yes and no," was Jack's reply. "I was here maybe twenty-five years ago. It was a little different then."

"San Pedro's a changing place. Every year, there are more tourists;

it's growing fast."

"I can see that, but it seems to still have its small town charm."

"True. Are you here by yourself?"

"Yes, I came alone, but I'm looking for someone."

"Sounds serious. Business or pleasure?"

Jack thought a moment before answering. "I'm not exactly sure. Maybe you can help me."

Before Jack could ask him anything, he had to leave to tend to a group that had just arrived at the bar. They were animated and must have been here for a few days since their gringo pink was beginning to turn to brown, although there were a few sore looking, peeling noses. From what Jack could overhear, it sounded like this wasn't their first time in San Pedro and by their accents, he guessed that they were from Texas. Eventually, the bartender returned and said, "Sorry about that. Oh, my name is Chris," and he stuck out his hand to Jack. Jack reached over the bar and shook it saying, "Jack."

"Nice to meet you, Jack. So what can I help you with?"

"I'm looking for an old friend named Max."

"What's he look like?"

"She," Jack corrected him.

"Oh," said Chris after an almost imperceptible pause.

"She was down here just a few weeks ago. I think she stayed here. Redhead, really good looking."

Before he could answer, Chris had to return to the group from Texas. They needed a second round and Jack was content to just sit there observing this little corner of the world. His back was turned to the bar when Chris returned. He had been watching a group of kids walking up the beach.

"Jack?"

He turned when he heard his name.

"I think I remember her. She was here with this guy named Charles, he has been down here before, always with some beautiful woman. It was weird though. He insisted that his name was Daniel, not Charles."

Before Chris could continue, Jack interrupted him, his heart pounding "That's her. Tell me everything you can remember," he said and wondered if it could really be this easy.

Chris was taken a little by surprise at the way Jack reacted. "There really isn't much to tell. I only saw them here at the bar a couple of times and they pretty much kept to themselves. They had that honeymoon look to them. You know, eyes only for you, that kind of stuff."

That hurt. Jack didn't want to hear those kind of details. "I see. How long were they here?"

"Only a couple of days."

"Any idea where they went after they left? Did they meet anyone else?" Jack was trying not to seem too eager even though he thought he might explode.

Chris paused a moment before continuing. "I'm not really sure. You might want to try next door at BC's Beach Bar. I know they spent some time there." Then he added, "You know, she seemed to be into him much more than he was into her. He almost seemed a little distracted, not in any obvious way. It was just a feeling I got. I don't think she noticed. I could be wrong, but I see so many people." As soon as he said this last part, he wished that he could take it back.

"Chris, you have been a huge help," said Jack, trying to remain calm.

"No problem, man. You mind if I ask you something."

"Shoot."

"Is she your wife or something?"

Jack paused a moment before answering. He had to think a moment before answering slowly, "No, she's just a friend."

Chris was called away before the conversation could go any further and Jack just sat there lost in his own thoughts. Another beer was placed in front of him. "On me," said Chris as he turned toward a new customer. By the time Jack finished this last beer, the restaurant was in full swing and it was obvious Chris would not be able to talk much more. It was reassuring to know that he remembered Max, and Jack planned to talk with him about her tomorrow when things were quieter at the bar.

Jack left some cash on the bar, waved goodbye and left. He needed to stretch his legs so he decided to walk down the beach before going to BC's. He needed some time to think. First he walked north, joining the steady stream of people walking up and down the beach. Bars, restaurants, hotels, and guesthouses dotted the beach. He went past what could be considered the city park where a basketball game was in full swing. He could hear the voices of an evening mass in the Catholic church. San Pedro was vibrant and Jack began to feel its rhythm and it felt right. He finally turned around and walked back toward his hotel. The restaurant was still busy so he walked on, continuing south. The corner of the hotel's kitchen jutted out onto the beach and there was a small path between the water and the building. As Jack rounded the corner, there was BC's, right next door. He hadn't realized that it was so close.

There was a good crowd of people around the bar. Some were obviously locals and others just as obviously tourists. Everyone seemed to be having a good time and as Jack climbed the steps, he felt right at home. BC's was his kind of place. A seat opened at the bar and he took it. The bartender came right over and Jack asked for a beer, which materialized just as fast. He looked around. It was a square bar in the center of a large thatched roof hut, known as a palapa, with tee shirts from around the world hanging from its rafters. There were seats all around the bar and along the railing. Most were full and there were many people standing as well. Three bartenders were busy keeping everyone supplied with fresh drinks. When he saw that they served nachos, he ordered a plate with his next beer.

Before his second beer arrived, he was feeling completely at home.

People in bars are the same everywhere. The power of beer was the same everywhere and soon he was immersed in several conversations. His nachos were placed in front of him and as he took his first chip, he felt a tug at his elbow. He turned and was facing a wizened old man in baggy shorts, a tattered shirt, baseball hat askew on his head, with a cane in hand. His hand was held out and he said something that Jack could not understand although the meaning was clear. Before he could react, he heard a strong voice with a Scottish brogue say, "Hey, Miguel, leave the man alone. Come over here and I'll buy you a beer."

Hearing the magic words, the man turned from Jack and shuffled off toward a large man just around the corner on the other side of the bar. The man handed Miguel a beer and glanced at Jack with a wink and a nod and tipped his beer toward him. Jack acknowledged the gesture and ate another nacho. It took him two more beers to finish his nachos since his gringo tongue was not yet prepared for the heat of Belizean salsa. As he pushed his plate away, a seat opened up next to him and the Scotsman came over and sat down. "Hi, my name's Rusty," and he extended his hand.

"Jack." They shook hands. "Thanks. I wasn't sure just what to make of him."

"Oh, he's harmless, and you'll get to like the little guy if you're around long enough. All he wants is either some money or a beer. If you give him money, he'll just buy a beer anyway."

"Well, thanks again."

"So Jack, did you just arrive?"

"Yeah, this afternoon."

"First time?"

"Haven't been here in a long time."

"Alone?"

"Yeah, I'm down here looking for someone," he felt that he should clarify why he was here just in case. "Her name is Max."

"Interesting name. Looking for?"

"Yeah. She doesn't know I'm here and I'm not even sure that she is here, although she was."

Rusty's eyebrows lifted at this last statement.

Normally Jack wouldn't have engaged in this conversation with a complete stranger, but he was on a mission and he was feeling the power of beer. "I guess that doesn't sound right does it?"

"Well, it's a little confusing."

"Okay, I'll start again. Max is a good friend from home."

"Where's home?"

"Rye, New Hampshire."

"Where's that?" asked Rusty.

A voice from the crowd said, "Rye! I used to live in Portsmouth until I moved down here." Jack looked up, but didn't see where the voice came from.

"About an hour north of Boston," replied Jack in answer to Rusty's question.

"Okay, go on," said Rusty.

"So, like I was saying, Max is an old friend whom I care about very much. She ran off with this guy who I'm sure is no good and I'm here to find her."

The voice from Portsmouth spoke up again, "Did you say Max? Isn't she the redheaded bartender at Ben's?"

This caught Jack's attention. "Yes, that's her."

"I knew it!" the voice shouted to his friend. "That was her. She was here a week or so ago."

Jack finally saw whom the voice belonged to and he asked, "You saw her?"

"Yeah, she was right here with some guy. I don't remember his name, but there was something familiar about him."

"Was she all right?"

"Oh yeah . . . she was just fine. They were all over each other. She was looking pretty hot."

That wasn't what Jack really wanted to hear and it was at this moment that Rusty rejoined the conversation, saving Jack from more lurid details about Max and Daniel.

Rusty just looked at Jack for a second before beginning to grin. "You're here to rescue her? It doesn't sound like she really needs rescuing."

Jack could see that he was on the verge of losing the story to the crowd, but since the power of beer had kicked in, he went on. "Look, this guy may be a murderer. At the very least he's dangerous, and I'm down here to find her and get her home."

That statement took the grin off of Rusty's face. "Okay, so who is this guy?"

"His name is Daniel or maybe it's Charles, that is not completely clear. He's involved in the music business, signing bands to contracts. A former client of his ended up dead this past summer. As a matter of fact I found the body."

"You found the body? Before you go any further, we need some more beers." Rusty flagged down the bartender and said, "Go on."

By now Portsmouth and some of the other people at the bar began to move closer and a small group began to form around Jack as he continued his tale. "Let me go back a bit. I work part time at the same restaurant where Max bartends and we've been friends for years. It's called Ben's Place and in the summer they have this reggae band that plays every Sunday and it's an incredible party.

"It is," interjected Portsmouth. "I've been there."

Jack continued, "Max and I got really close last winter. We'd been friends for years, but..." his voice trailed off

More beers were ordered and the crowd listening to the story continued to grow.

"So why exactly are you here?" asked Portsmouth.

"He's here to find Max," said Rusty. "Let him finish."

"So this summer I guess I wasn't paying enough attention to her and this other guy—this Daniel—started hanging around on Sundays when the band was playing. He was there to get the band to sign a contract, but he began to hit on Max. By the time I realized just what was going on, it was too late. He took her to some big charity ball in Boston that turned into a long weekend. I was a jerk and instead of dealing with this directly, I ran, or rather sailed off on my boat."

A voice in the crowd said, "Dumb ass."

"Shut up," hissed another.

Then amid groans and before anyone could say anything else, Jack held up his hand waving off any further commentary. He continued, "'Nuf said. I was having a Class A pity party. Anyway, I ended up in Newport, Rhode Island where I met up with some old friends, who it turned out knew about this guy because of some shady dealings he had had down there. Only thing was they knew him as Charles."

Jack paused and sipped his beer, then he continued as another was put in front of him. "To make a short story longer, it seems this guy may have been involved in the murder up in Rye, but by the time I was able to get home with what I had found out, he and Max had taken off for Belize. That's all I really knew until her friend Patti got a letter from her and she described being here in San Pedro and that they were getting ready to sail south. I guess that this Daniel or Charles has a sailboat and a guy named Alfonso takes care of it for him."

"Hey, I know that guy. Alfonso. He takes people out to Hol Chan and Shark/Ray Alley. I think he lives over on the south side somewhere," said Portsmouth.

Jack looked at him, "Do you know how I could find him?"

"Not really, but since he takes people out to Hol Chan, he shouldn't be too hard to find. Check with some of the dive companies. They must know everyone."

Jack thought about this for a minute. A few others in the crowd added their opinions, but nobody really knew him—of him, yes—just not directly. Rusty had been silent through this last exchange and he now looked at Jack and said, "Jack, I think you're crazy, but you have a good heart. If I can help you in any way, just let me know. Here's my number." And with that he wrote down his phone number on a scrap of paper. Beers and time were catching up with Jack and he was exhausted. The crowd was beginning to thin out and he needed sleep. Goodbyes were said, his tab settled, and he walked back to the Sun Breeze where he collapsed into bed.

CHAPTER 84

WHEN MAX AND DIGIT LEFT NICHOLAS CAYE, it was already mid-afternoon. He pointed his boat west and they sped off toward Monkey River Town and the mainland. Shielding her eyes from the lowering sun and its glare off the water, Max stared ahead. The drone of the boat's engine, its pitch unchanging, and the *slap slap slap* of the waves against the hull had an almost hypnotic effect. Her mind began to wander. She thought about these strangers who were now her lifelines. Digit should have been out fishing and yet he was driving her all around looking for a man she wasn't even sure she should find. Nancy had accepted her like a sister and had taken her in without hesitation. Alfonso. How had he known that she would need help? What did he know about Daniel that would cause him to offer help?

Daniel or Charles? The more she got to know him, the less she knew. She had been foolish and rash. She needed the truth and now he had disappeared. Why was all this happening? Home. She thought of home, and Patti and Courtney . . . and Jack. She had hurt him badly, and for what? Before she was able to dwell on this last thought, Digit tapped her on the shoulder, she turned toward him and he pointed ahead. They were almost there. As the water changed from the clear, blue-green of the ocean to the muddy brown where the Monkey River met the sea, he slowed and motored over the bar that crossed the mouth of the river.

The town was on the left. It was nothing more than a small cluster of buildings wedged between the ocean and the jungle. Several boats were pulled up on the shore in front of what Max took to be a store and she could see several men gathered there. Digit pointed out that the only way to get to Monkey River Town was by boat and he pointed across the river, to the north side where several well-worn trucks and cars were parked. "That's the end of the road." Nosing his boat against the shore next to the others, he called out to the men by the store. No one had seen any sign of Daniel or his boat. He thanked them and was about to back away from the shore, when he stopped and shouted back one more question. "Did anyone see a black boat around in the past few days?"

This prompted some discussion among the group, then one of the men walked over to Digit's boat and said that they had. "It came from the south along the shore." He then nodded toward the group. "Jose was out fishing, they came up to his boat and asked the same questions you did. He told them no, and they left."

"Which way did they go?"

"They headed north."

Just as Digit was about to thank them, Max shouted out, "Did you see who was in the boat? How many people were in it?"

The reply came back that there were two men in the boat, one black and one white. Max blanched, for a moment her head got light and she had to grab the rail of the boat. It felt like someone had punched her in the stomach. She finally squeaked out, "What did the white man look like?"

Digit looked at her and asked if she was all right. She nodded. The men on shore hadn't heard her second question so Digit shouted it out again, "What did the white man look like?"

"Thin, sunburned, dark hair, definitely a gringo," came the reply.

Max sat silent. Digit thanked them, shifted into reverse and backed away from the shore turning his boat toward the river's mouth. With the current pushing them, he idled toward the sand bar at the mouth of the river. Max didn't move and as her color returned, Digit asked, "You okay?"

In a slightly shaky voice replied, "I'm okay. Let's get going."

As soon as they crossed the bar and reached blue-green water, Digit pressed the throttle forward. He stayed close to the shore where the water was less choppy as they flew along. Darkness was coming fast, making it hard to see. As they skimmed past the mangroves, and Digit shouted to Max that tomorrow they would return here to search. Nothing else was said the rest of the way back. By the time they reached Placencia, it was dark. As Digit guided his boat toward the sand where their day had begun, Max began to realize just how drained she was.

She felt faint, her eyeballs ached and her face was burning from the combination of wind and sun. It had been a long day. The boat crunched onto the sand and Digit shut the engine off. She sat there. The exquisite silence and stillness almost hurt. Digit could see her exhaustion. "Here," he said, offering her a towel that he had just wetted by dipping it into the ice chest. She took the towel and touched it to her face. It felt so good that it almost crossed that fine line from pleasure to pain. She pressed it over her eyes and felt the icy darkness erase the dull ache that had been her eyes. Removing the cloth, she handed it back to Digit. "Thank you," was all she could say.

"No problem. You gonna be all right? Shall I walk you back to Nancy's?"

"No, Digit. I'm fine. Thank you again."

He helped her out of the boat and said, "I'll see you in the morning. Tomorrow we'll go search through the mangroves."

"Okay, what time?"

"I'll meet you here at 8:00."

"Eight o'clock. I'll see you then." She took his hand and held it as she thanked him again, turned, and walked away.

CHAPTER 85

JACK RUBBED HIS EYES. The air conditioner above his head was blowing a steady stream of cold air down on him making him shiver, so he pulled the blanket up around his neck. He just lay there, listening. Outside his room, he could hear the echoes of doors opening and closing. He thought he heard rain, then there were voices. He couldn't understand the words but he knew that they belonged to tourists beginning their day in paradise, deciding where to go and what to do. Other voices belonged to the hotel workers greeting each other, starting their daily chores. His thoughts drifted to Max and he smiled. She had been here. She had heard the same sounds. The bartender remembered her. They recognized her at BC's. There was even someone who recognized her from home. *How could that be? What were the odds?* His smile disappeared as he remembered why she was here and why he was here now.

The tile floor was cool as he stepped into the bathroom. He took a warm shower, drank some bottled water, dressed, and thought about how he was going to find Max. Coffee, breakfast, Alfonso, Max. That was the list.

He took his first sip of coffee and felt its warmth fill his belly. He sighed, took a deep breath and looked out over the water squinting from the glare of the new day's sun as it steadily rose in the sky while he replayed last night's events in his mind.

He had walked down the beach to Estelle's for breakfast on the recommendation of one of the hotel's gardeners. There were a half dozen tables outside, each with a thatch umbrella for shade on a raised patio of sand. The sand ran inside where there were a few more tables. Amid the eclectic collection of memorabilia, the menu was written on a huge chalkboard in tightly scribbled, colored chalk. He had ordered the Mayan eggs, a mélange of scrambled eggs, ham and salsa with beans and fry jacks, before sitting down outside with his coffee.

As he sat there, coffee in hand, the moment consumed him. He closed his eyes to the glare of the sun's early light as it shimmered off the surface of the water, and he felt its promise of another hot day. The breeze caressed his skin and his toes played in the sand while the smells and sounds of a new day worked their magic on him. There was something about this place. He had been in San Pedro for not quite twenty-four hours and already he felt as if he were home. He took another sip as he tried to understand this feeling, but he couldn't put it into words. So he just sat there enjoying the moment. His breakfast came and he ate.

Satisfied and energized, Jack left Estelle's and began his search for Alfonso. He began with the waterfront dive shops. Everyone seemed to know of him, but few people knew him, and no one knew just how to contact him. After the dive shops he walked through town, stopping whenever he saw a sign promoting snorkel tours of the reef with the same result. He found himself on the lagoon side of town, away from the tourist businesses and he still had no luck. It was nearly noon and he was hot, tired and thirsty. That's when his luck began to change.

A taxi was passing by and the driver slowed and asked Jack if he needed a ride. Jack's first reaction was to say no, but before he spoke he found himself climbing into the taxi. As the taxi started moving, the driver began with the usual questions: Where to? Did you just arrive? Are you having a good time? Where are you from?

Jack answered the questions politely, still lost in his own thoughts until the driver said, "New Hampshire? That's near Boston, right? I met someone from New Hampshire a couple of weeks ago. I see lots of people from Texas and Louisiana, but not many from New Hampshire and now I've met two."

It took a second for this information to fully register with Jack. Curious, he asked, "Did you get a name? Maybe I know him."

"No, man. I didn't get no name, and he was a she."

"A redhead?" asked Jack now alert. His pulse quickened.

"How did you know?"

"Was anyone with her?"

"Yeah, she was with this rich dude: Mr. Charles. My cousin takes care of his boat. They're gone now."

"Son of a bitch," Jack mumbled.

Jack's heart was pounding and he had to take a deep breath just so he could speak. "Your cousin takes care of his boat?"

"Yeah, a few years ago this guy saved my cousin's life and so now he takes care of his boat."

"May I ask your cousin's name?"

"Alfonso."

"Alfonso?!" Jack said the name so sharply that the driver nearly went off the road when he jerked around in Jack's direction.

"Yeah, Alfonso. Do you know him?"

"No, but I'm looking for him. I need his help."

"Who are you and what for?" There was a cautious edge to his voice now.

"Look, my name is Jack. The lady is a dear friend and she may be in trouble."

"She your woman?" he asked while trying to hide a grin.

"No," then he paused before continuing. "No, not really, well sort of, but it's not that simple. Listen, I really need to talk to Alfonso, can you take me to him?"

"No."

"Why not?"

"Because he's out on the reef right now on a snorkel trip."

"When will he be back?"

"Soon." It was at this moment that they pulled up in front of the Sun Breeze. "I'll tell you what. Why don't you wait here? I'll try to find out when he'll be back and then I'll come get you."

Jack didn't see that he had a lot of options, so he agreed.

Jack paid his fare and stepped out of the taxi. He then went across the street into the Tropic Air terminal and picked up a flight schedule before returning to the hotel.

There was a telephone on the bar by the pool. His cell was useless here. Jack eyed it as he sat there sipping a cold beer. The bartender he had met last night wasn't due in to work until late afternoon. He asked the bartender who brought him his beer if he remembered Max. He didn't. Jack was impatient. Sitting and waiting was making him crazy. He looked at the phone again and then said to the bartender, "Can I call out on that phone?"

"Local calls, no problem, mon. If you want to call out, first you have to call the desk and they will help you."

Jack motioned for him to pass the phone over. "Thanks."

The bartender nodded.

CHAPTER 86

MAX WALKED SLOWLY BACK TO NANCY'S. She was physically and emotionally spent. As she walked, random images popped in and out of her head: The empty beauty of the sea, those first days sailing with Daniel, and the quiet solitude of the cayes they had visited. She thought of home, Courtney, Patti, Jack, and finally Digit and Nancy, and how these two people who were complete strangers just a few days ago were now such an important part of her life. She was hot, tired, hungry and homesick. As she reached Nancy's, a sudden calmness overcame her. It was as if she knew, at that moment, on some elemental level, that today was the beginning of an ending and that balance was going to be restored.

Morning came all too soon. Max lay in bed trying to find the energy to get up. Sunlight streamed into her room, the sounds of a reawakening world reached her ears. It wasn't until she smelled the coffee brewing and heard Nancy in the kitchen that she was able to force herself out of bed.

"Good morning, Sunshine," said Nancy when she saw Max standing in the doorway.

Max hadn't heard that greeting since . . . since she had last been with Jack. Memories flooded back and a tear rolled down her cheek.

"Are you all right?" Nancy asked as she handed Max a cup of coffee. "Here, you look like you could really use this."

Turning her head slightly and wiping her cheek with her hand she said, "Uh, yeah, I'm okay, just not fully awake yet. Thanks." She took a sip, and then asked, "What time is it?"

"It's just after 7:00. Are you and Digit going out again today?"

"Yes, we're meeting at 8:00."

Over breakfast, the two women talked, or rather Max talked and Nancy listened, as she recounted the previous day's adventures.

"You're really worried, aren't you?" asked Nancy.

Max paused before answering and in a quiet far away voice she heard herself saying, "I am, but whether we find him or not, I know it is over. I don't really love him. I was blinded by his money and his looks. I need more. There are too many secrets, too many lies for it to ever work."

"I'm so sorry," said Nancy as she got up from the table, circled it and stood behind Max and stroked her hair. "It's almost 8:00. Digit will be waiting."

"I know." She got up, turned and gave Nancy a hug, which was returned. "Thank you for being my friend." She drew away and went to get ready while Nancy began to clean up from breakfast.

Digit was waiting by his boat, which he had nosed up onto the beach. "Good morning. Did you sleep well?"

"Good morning, Digit, and yes I did, thanks."

"Climb in and we'll get going."

She tossed her day bag into the boat and climbed in over the bow and settled herself on the seat in the center of the boat. As soon as she was settled, Digit pushed the boat out into the water, and then jumped in, climbing past her to the engine controls. The powerful outboard roared to life and the gears clicked as he shifted into reverse, pulling the boat away from the beach. As soon as they were far enough from the beach, Max heard two distinctive clicks as Digit shifted out of reverse and into neutral and then into forward. The boat changed direction and shot forward carving a long gradual turn to the southwest away from Placencia.

The sea was calm and the breeze still light as they skimmed across the water under blue skies dotted with puffy white clouds. The drone of the engine and the steady, rhythmic sounds of the hull against the water made conversation difficult so they rode in silence. While Digit headed the boat toward the green watery world of the mangroves, Max sat there staring straight ahead lost in her own thoughts. *Why did Daniel leave? Was it his choice or did the black boat have something to do with it? Had he just used her or did he really care?* She needed answers.

Her thoughts were interrupted by the realization that they were heading straight at a wall of green at breakneck speed and there was no sign of a break in that wall. Max turned and looked back at Digit. There must have been a look of panic in her eyes because he just smiled and motioned for her to turn around. As she turned back, the boat turned sharply to the right and they were inside the wall of green speeding along what seemed to be a canal.

Mangrove forests form a natural barrier between the sea and the land along coastlines throughout the Caribbean. Their ability to extract fresh water from salt allows them to thrive in such a seemingly harsh environment. When a seedling drops off of a parent tree, it will either set root there, increasing that stand or it will drift away, pushed by tide and wind until it finds another spot to take root and start its own stand. The roots become an exposed tangle in the water, a perfect breeding ground and home for many species of fish, crustaceans and shellfish. The branches become rookeries for pelicans, cranes, and other sea birds. Over time they grow and spread, creating nature's own labyrinth, a perfect place to hide or be hidden.

It was in one of these mangrove forests that Digit and Max now cruised searching for Daniel and *I Got d'Riddem*. Digit had slowed the boat considerably so conversation was again possible. Birds could even be heard squawking their warnings as they ventured into this strange watery forest. There were some areas where the mangroves were young and not very big and there were others, much older, where they were high enough to hide even the mast of a boat. They cruised for hours. All the while, Digit provided a running commentary about the mangroves. He pointed out birds. They saw a manatee and even a crocodile. Max hadn't known that Belize had saltwater crocodiles and the thought of those prehistoric creatures lurking in the water, hidden by the mangrove roots gave her the creeps. When Digit began telling stories of man versus crocodile, her vivid imagination went into overdrive. Digit grinned when she moved to the center of the boat and wouldn't even put her hand on its gunwales. By midday, they had not found any sign of Daniel or the missing boat.

"Time for lunch," Digit announced as he tied the boat to a small mangrove in the center of what almost felt like a small lake. He shut the engine off and the first thing Max noticed was the silence. Neither of them spoke. They just sat and absorbed the silence. It was the kind of silence that you feel when you stand in a church, all alone, and you are afraid to move for fear of disturbing something. Slowly the silence gave way to nature's sounds. Subtle sounds. Soft sounds. The splash of a small fish jumping, the gentle lapping of the water against the hull. A slight breeze ruffling the leaves. An occasional bird squawk. It could easily have been a hundred years ago, a thousand years ago.

Max didn't move.

Digit looked at her then said, "Max? Lunch?"

"Oh, I'm sorry."

As she handed him his lunch she asked, "How much more is there?"

"We've covered about half the area where a boat the size of his could go."

"Oh," the discouragement was evident in her voice.

"You better put some more sun block on," he said changing the subject.

Glancing down at her arms, she saw he was right. "I will before we leave." Then she took a bite of her sandwich and while chewing, stared off into the mangroves. There was no further conversation.

When they finished eating, Digit started the engine and they were back in the twenty first century again. Max untied the boat from the mangrove only after looking very carefully for any stray crocs.

It was late afternoon when Digit guided the boat out of the mangroves and back into the sea. He could see the disappointment on Max's face. "There is one more place we can look today."

"Where's that?

"We'll go up the ship channel. It's up Big Creek where ocean freighters load and unload cargo. Maybe someone there will remember seeing something."

CHAPTER 87

ABOUT HALF WAY TO PLACENCIA, the channel markers came into sight and Digit turned to follow the channel. Progress up the channel was slow and deliberate as they scanned both sides for any sign that Daniel or the boat had been there. It was different from the mangroves where they had spent the day. Instead of mangroves on either side of the channel, there was jungle. Dense, impenetrable vegetation stopped at the water's edge. Rounding the final bend, they saw a small coastal freighter tied up to the pier. There was no sign of activity. Max glanced back at Digit and he said to her, "We'll go closer and see if anyone is around."

The pier appeared new and was made of concrete. A large blue roofed warehouse could be seen back aways, leaving plenty of room between it and the pier for moving cargo to and from ships. From a distance, everything looked neat and tidy. As they got closer, the scale of the facility became more apparent. Everything was large and industrial. Stains and scars could be seen on the pavement in front of the warehouse. There were several tractors and mobile cranes parked near the warehouse.

As obvious as it was that this facility was heavily used, today it seemed abandoned. There was no sign of life. The equipment sat idle, the doors to the warehouse were closed, and the ship was silent. The only sounds were Digit's outboard, a random bird calling out from the surrounding jungle, and the sound of the breeze through the bush. There was an eerie unearthliness to it all. Digit nosed his boat up to the pier at the stern of the freighter and realized that it was too high to see over easily and there were no provisions at this end for climbing up onto the pier. "Let's try the other end," Digit said as he backed his boat away from the pier and back into the channel.

Even though the ship was a small one, Max had never seen a vessel so large. Slowly, they began moving along the ship's length. Streaks of rust ran down its steel sides like streaks of blood on a scarred and wounded beast. Max could see that once it must have been a beautiful ship, all white and gleaming, but now it was just old and tired. It wasn't long before the straight side of the ship began to curve back toward the pier. As they followed the curve of the bow around, suddenly they saw her. *D'Riddem* was tied up to the pier, tucked into that space between the pier and the bow.

Neither Max nor Digit said anything as they stared at the boat. The low hum of the outboard was the only sound as they moved closer. As on the pier and the ship, there were no signs of life. *D'Riddem* just sat there, placidly, next to the pier, looking as if she belonged there. Max broke the silence first, almost in a whisper, "Do you see anyone?"

Digit shook his head.

When they were only a few boat lengths away, Max shouted, her voice shattering the silence, "Daniel?" There was no reply. "Daniel, are you there?" Again, silence.

"I don't see anyone anywhere," said Digit as he maneuvered alongside. Max grabbed hold of *d'Riddem* while Digit tied the two boats together. Her heart was pounding and she felt as if her whole body was shaking as she stepped over the side of Digit's boat and onto the stern step of *d'Riddem* and slowly climbed up onto the deck. Her voice was shaking as she softly called out his name again. "Daniel?"

The only answer was the squawk of an unseen bird in the surrounding jungle and the soft rustling of palm fronds being tickled by the breeze. She held her breath, every nerve in her body feeling as if it were vibrating to some unseen force. Her eyes began tracing a path around the boat. Everything seemed to be in place. There was just no sign of life.

"Daniel?" she called out again. Her concentration was so focused as she listened for a response, any response, that she didn't hear or feel Digit climbing up the steps behind her.

"Any sign of him?"

At the sound of his voice, she jumped and spun around, nearly falling in the process. Digit caught her arm and steadied her.

"Digit!" she hissed.

"Sorry." Then he found himself trying to suppress a smile as he asked, "Are you all right?"

In the moment it took her to catch her breath, she stared at him with fire in her eyes. As her heart returned to her chest, she finally exhaled her answer. "You nearly gave me a heart attack," then she too began to feel a smile. That was all it took, the tension was broken and they both laughed out loud.

Max climbed into the cockpit while Digit walked forward. Nothing seemed out of place. She hardly dared to breathe as she tugged on the door to the salon. Expecting it to be locked, a quiver went through her when it moved. Slowly she slid it open as she croaked out Daniel's name. She could feel a rush of heat as she peered in. All the hatches were closed, as they should have been, and it was hot inside. This brought a moment of relief. She knew that he would not have left the boat without closing it up and locking it. That relief was short lived as she realized that her hand was still on the door and it had not been locked.

"Daniel!" She called out again. And, as before there was only silence. Her nerves were on edge. She jumped again as Digit came up behind her, only this time it wasn't funny. She stepped inside, Digit followed silently. At first, nothing looked out of place and then she began to notice little things that were not right. Cupboard doors were ajar, and books and magazines that should have been stowed were scattered. Something crunched under her foot. It was a broken glass. As she bent down to pick it up, she saw one of the pillows that was usually on the settee under the table and there was some white fluff around it. Reaching for it she could see that it was torn and the white fluff was some of its filling. As she stood with the pillow in hand she realized that it wasn't torn, it had been slashed and there was a dark stain on it. Turning toward Digit, she handed the pillow to him without saying a word.

He took the pillow from her and looked at it then he looked at her. No words were exchanged, but each knew what the other was thinking.

A calmness came over Max. The blind panic was gone. Perhaps it was shock or perhaps she finally realized the truth about Daniel. Whatever it was, she was no longer scared.

"We won't find him," she said to Digit in the flat voice of resignation. Then she moved toward the cabin that she and Daniel had shared and that still contained most of her belongings. Digit moved in the other direction and descended into the starboard hull.

The cabin had been torn apart; clothing, pillows, blankets, the mattress, all tossed in every which way. It was obvious that whoever did this was looking for something and from the damage that was evident probably hadn't found it. She turned back toward the head. It, too, had been ransacked. While Max was in the port hull, Digit found a similar scene on the starboard side. They both climbed back up into the salon at the same time and looked at each other.

"Nothing," said Max.

Digit indicated the same response.

So they stood there, in the torn up cabin, each lost in their own thoughts, neither wanting to say the words as if the words would make it so. Then Max spoke. In a small soft voice, she uttered what neither had wanted to say. "He's gone. It looks like they got him."

"Maybe. I'll go ashore and see if there is anyone around who might have seen anything."

"Okay."

Digit climbed up the ladder that extended down from the pier and Max sat down at the nav station. She was numb. She saw but didn't see. She felt but didn't feel. Her hands drifted over and touched things scattered about: a pencil, a book, a magazine. Only a few short days ago, she had been sitting here, happy and carefree, and now, it was as if a lifetime had passed. She lifted the cover to the nav station and tried to straighten out its contents. She couldn't tell if anything was missing.

She wanted to cry, she wanted to feel something, but she felt nothing except the hopeless despair of not knowing what had happened and only imagining what might have. So she went back down the stairs and turned back into the cabin she and Daniel had shared. "Daniel, you son of a bitch. Where are you? What happened?" she said as she lashed out at the mattress with her fist. It was a feeble gesture, but it was something.

Her fist hit something that was hidden in the folds of the blanket on the berth. She stopped then she groped through the folds until she found what she had struck. It was the pouch in which he had kept his travel documents. She lifted it and slowly opened it. Everything seemed to be there, his passport, their airline tickets and some cash. She removed the passport, opened it and looked at his picture. Daniel Cummings, issued in Boston it read. Her hands began to tremble. *He wouldn't have left on his own without this,* she thought.

She was angry. She was hurt. She hated him, and yet she had been searching for him for two days. Why? He was gone. He had abandoned her. He owed her an explanation and apology, she kept telling herself. Her thoughts were interrupted by the sound of Digit's voice. "Max? Are you down there?"

She shouted back, "Yes, I'm down here. Did you find out anything?" She put the passport back in the travel pouch and tossed it back onto the berth. As she began to turn to leave the cabin, reflexively she bent down to pick up some of the clothes off the floor and as she did so, she saw an envelope. It was sticking out of a canvas tote bag that they had used for shopping and to just carry stuff around. It looked like it had last been used as a hamper judging from the dirty clothes that were still in it. She took the envelope out of the bag. It had her name on it. Slowly, she turned it over in her hands, studying it, almost afraid to open it.

"Max?" she heard Digit's voice again. She looked up and saw him looking around the corner at her. "What's that?" he asked.

"It's an envelope with my name on it. I found it in this bag."

"Go on. Open it. See what it is."

Max sat down on the edge of the berth, slid her finger under the sealed flap of the envelope, and opened the letter. Inside was a folded, single sheet of paper. Under Digit's expectant gaze, she removed the paper and unfolded it and began to read.

Dear Max,

I can't tell you how sorry I am that I dragged you into my life. When I first saw you on that hot summer's day, something happened to me. I couldn't get you out of my mind. I knew that I had to have you. The time we have spent together has meant more to me than you could ever imagine. I've done some things in my life that I'm not proud of and when I met you, I knew that I wanted to change.

Max stopped reading and looked up from the piece of paper and said under her breath, "Daniel, you are so full of bullshit." Digit watched her and was about to say something when she looked back down and continued reading.

I have to explain somethings to you. My real name is Charles Daniel. In my line of work, I have found it necessary to use other names. The last time I was in Belize I used the name Charles Gowings. That's why everyone kept calling me Charles. When I met you I was using Daniel Cummings. Regardless of what name I used, I was the same person—the person who fell for you.

I'm sorry that I wasn't completely honest with you. Deep within, I knew that if we were to be together, there must be complete honesty and trust between us. I've never been ready to do that with anyone before you. At the same time, I wanted to insulate you from the dark side of my life and the only way I could do that was to tell you nothing and to hope that we could just disappear. Since you are reading this letter, my worst fears have been realized and we will never see each other again.

Max read on, a kind of paralyzing fear began to overtake her. A single tear fell from her eye onto the page. She wiped her eyes with her hand before continuing.

When we first met last summer in Rye, I was there to sign the band to a contract. You knew that. Everything was going fine until Python showed up. He was going to mess everything up and my employer told me to take care of it. That meant only one thing. I was to kill him or have him killed. You have to believe me when I tell you that I didn't do it. I don't know who did. I thought I was off the hook. My employer couldn't stand not knowing who had killed him and why. I don't even know who I work for, only that he is rich, powerful, and ruthless. Once I overheard reference made to The Raven *when someone else was talking to him on the phone. I have no idea what that means and I was smart enough not to let on that I had heard even that.*

He wanted to see me. I found this out when we were in Boston and I knew then that he was tying up loose ends, me being one and probably you, by association. I couldn't let that happen so that's why the quick trip to Belize. I didn't think he would be able to find us, or at least not right away, not until I was able to figure out a way to completely disappear. Then I would be able to find out what had really happened. When that black speedboat found us, I knew that my dream was over and it wouldn't be long. I had hoped to buy some time in Placencia to figure out my next step, both with you and with my problem. When you told me about the man in the bakery asking about the boat, I knew that I would have to leave. I had to abandon you. It was my only hope of saving you.

Max began to tremble. Digit saw this and moved toward her to offer comfort. She waved him away.

Max, I'm sorry. I truly do love you and I wish we could just sail off together. I know now that that won't happen. I have no one. I had only you. I want you to have d'Riddem. *She's yours. Take care of her and she will take care of you. I will never see you or her again. I have made arrangements to transfer access to a bank account in San Pedro to you for the upkeep of the boat or for whatever you wish. Alfonso will help you with that. Max, this is all I can do. They are coming now. Good bye. I love you.*

Daniel

CHAPTER 88

SHE LOWERED THE LETTER and sat there on the edge of the bed feeling nothing. She didn't believe it. This couldn't be happening. She read it again quickly and as she finished Digit stuck his head back into the cabin and said, "Max, I hear voices outside."

"Who is it?"

"I don't know. I didn't see anyone when I was up on the wharf."

"Go see who it is."

"Sure."

She could hear the voices more clearly as they talked down to Digit, but she couldn't make out all the words.

It was only a moment before she heard Digit's voice loud and clear, "Max, it's the port captain."

Those words brought her back to the present. As she fought off a feeling of panic, she looked down at the letter and around at the mess in the cabin. Right or wrong, she knew that, at this moment, it would be best to keep him off the boat. Stuffing the letter in her pocket she called out to Digit, "I'll be right up."

Digit must have reached the same conclusion as Max because as she stepped out on deck, she could hear Digit trying to convince the port captain that there was no reason for him to board the boat. As soon as Max appeared, all three men went silent. From the expressions of surprise on the faces of the port captain and the other man, Max could tell that they had not expected to see a red haired white lady on board the boat with the six-fingered fisherman in the well worn tee shirt.

"Hello," said Max. "Can I help you?"

The port captain had regained his voice. "Yes, miss. I would like to know who you are, why the two of you are on this boat, and why this boat is here." He flashed a glance at Digit for emphasis as he posed the questions.

Max took a breath and began speaking in the most authoritative voice she could muster she began. "My name is Max, and this boat belongs to my boyfriend who is back in town waiting for some parts to arrive from Belize City. I hope that it isn't a problem for us to be here. We had some problems with a pump and we had to tie up last night. It was late and we didn't see anyone around to ask if it was okay. Then, since we couldn't find the parts we needed in Placencia, we had to order them and they were due in today. My boyfriend went to the airport to pick them up. While he went to do that, Digit here . . ." she nodded her head in Digit's direction. ". . . brought me back in his boat so I could get some fresh clothes since we will be staying in town tonight before we come back tomorrow to fix the boat and head out again."

The men listened to Max's story. The captain motioned to Max to wait a moment and then the two men stepped back from the edge of the wharf and Max could hear the port captain dressing down the man who was with him. Max looked at Digit. Digit returned the look. Her story was a little thin, yet they seemed to be buying it. Several minutes passed before the port captain returned. "It will be fine for you to leave your boat here another night, but it must be removed first thing in the morning."

Max's stomach was doing back flips while she calmly replied, "Thank you. We'll return early and will be gone as soon as we make the repair. It shouldn't take long with the new part." The port captain wished them a goodnight and reminded them again that they must be gone in the morning. Without thinking, Max suddenly called up to them. "Excuse me, sir, I have one more thing to ask?"

The captain turned, and with a hint of impatience in his voice said, "What is it, Miss?"

"Early in the morning, before sunrise, I thought I heard some noises outside the boat, I got up and peeked and saw a black speed boat with two creepy looking men in it. It was as if they were checking us out. Will our boat be safe here? Do you know who they might be?"

"Miss, your boat should be perfectly safe here. I haven't seen such a boat around, they don't sound like locals. Don't worry."

"Thank you again."

The captain turned to leave when the man with him stopped him and said in a sheepish voice, "I think I saw that black boat."

"You what? When?"

"It was early this morning, just before I was leaving."

"Why didn't you tell me this?"

"It didn't seem important. You were away all day and I forgot."

"You forgot!" The captain was now more visibly upset and he continued, "First you forgot to tell me about this boat tied up here. Now I hear that another boat was nosing around. You forgot?"

"I'm sorry, sir. The sun was just coming up. I saw the top of this boat's mast and I was walking down to investigate. Before I was close enough to see over the edge of the wharf, I heard a large engine start up and I saw a black speed boat leaving in a real hurry. I was wrong to not report it, but, well, you were away and . . . I'm sorry, it just didn't seem important at the time."

The port captain was getting more visibly upset with these new revelations. He turned away from his compatriot and said to Max, "I'm sure that your boat will be fine tonight," and with that, he flashed a glance toward the watchman.

"How many men were in the black boat?" asked Max.

"I don't know. There were at least two but by the time I saw them they were getting pretty far away."

"Thank you again," said Max.

"No problem, Miss. Just get underway in the morning."

"We will."

The two officials turned and walked off and Max went inside the main salon where she slumped down on the seat. Digit watched her from the doorway. After a moment, she pulled the letter from her pocket, unfolded it and began to tremble as she stared at it. Before Digit could say anything, she began to cry uncontrollably.

"Are you all right?" Digit asked. He could see that she wasn't but didn't know what else to say or do.

Between sobs, nods and sniffles, Max managed to indicate that she was okay and just wanted to be alone.

Darkness was falling rapidly and they would have to leave soon. Not knowing what else to do or say at the moment, Digit busied himself in the cockpit and on deck making preparations to leave. By the time he finished, he could no longer hear Max crying. He stuck his head into the cabin and asked again, "Are you all right? What was in that letter?"

Max looked down. She still had the letter in her hand. She looked up at Digit and said in a soft voice, "Digit, I don't think we will find Daniel."

"What makes you say that?" said Digit trying to sound hopeful.

"This letter is his final good bye. He gave *d'Riddem* to me. He would only do that if he wasn't coming back."

Digit remained silent for a few moments then said, "Max, we should get going. It's getting dark, there is nothing we can do here tonight." He touched her shoulder gently as she looked up at him. "I know," was her soft reply.

The lights of the port disappeared behind them and as they left the channel, they could see the lights of Placencia ahead. They rode in silence over now inky water. The brilliant colors of the day had been replaced by darkness and reflections. The rising moon's light made the surface of the water look like scales on a huge black and silver fish. There was the one bright silver streak that radiated out from the rising moon and it followed them the same way the needle of a compass tracks to the north. The gentle scratching of sand against hull signaled the end of their day as Digit ran his boat up onto the shore so Max could get out. She turned toward him. “Thank you.” It was all she could say. He clambered past her, climbed out of the boat, tied it to the stump of an old palm tree. “Come on, Max. It’s time to go home and get some rest, I’ll walk you to Nancy’s.” She stood and had to catch herself as the boat shifted, then she took Digit’s outstretched hand, climbed over the bow and stepped onto the sand.

CHAPTER 89

JACK TOOK ANOTHER SIP of his beer and then picked up the phone and called the front desk. "I'd like to place a call to Rye, New Hampshire, USA," he said into the mouthpiece. After giving all of the appropriate information, he heard the phone ringing. It rang once, twice, then on the third ring, he heard Courtney's voice. "Hello." She sounded as if the previous night had been a long one. He paused for just a second before saying, "Hi, Court."

"Jack?" her voice began to loose its fogginess.

"Yeah, hi. Sounds like you had a late night."

She was fully charged now and started right in. "Jack, I'm so glad you called. Last night was a late night but not in the way you are thinking. Tom arrested Python's murderer."

"What?"

"Tom arrested Python's murderer."

"Who? What happened?" Jack was stunned.

"Apparently the day after you left, Tom went to ask the guys in the band some more questions about Python. Percy was the last guy he talked to and from what I hear he just confessed. I really don't know much more than that."

Jack was stunned, and before he could ask any more questions, Courtney began, "So how's Belize? Have you found Max yet?"

"Slow down. Percy? What happened?"

"We . . ."

"Who's we?"

"Patti, Dave and I. We had gone up to Dover to see the band again and that's when we found all of this out. Percy wasn't there, we thought that maybe he was sick or something. When they took a break, Joshua and Leslie came over and told us that he had been arrested."

"Son of a bitch," Jack said softly to himself, then to Courtney. "So when was he arrested? Have you talked to Tom? Why didn't anyone call me?"

"Slow down Jack. It just happened last night, and you just woke me up so I really haven't had time to call you." She paused for effect then added, "Yet!"

"Okay, Okay. Point taken. Will you call Tom for me and ask him to call me? Do you have a pencil? I'll give you the number."

"Just a minute, I have to go get one." The phone clunked as she put it on the table and Jack could hear her walking around looking for paper and pencil. He sat there, stunned at this news. "So if Daniel didn't do it, then, could it be . . .?" His thoughts were interrupted when Court picked up the phone and said, "Okay, give me the number."

Jack did.

"So Jack, have you found her yet? What's it like there?"

"Slow down, Courtney. No, I haven't found her yet, but she certainly did make an impression on everyone here. I've talked to a lot of people and they all remember her. Funny thing, they kept referring to Daniel as Charles."

"Charles?"

"Yeah, Charles. It's strange. Anyway, I'm meeting with a guy named Alfonso soon and he may be able to give me some leads. She's not here in San Pedro anymore."

"What's San Pedro like? Is it as wonderful as her letter made it seem?"

"Yes, it is. I think you guys would like it here."

"It sounds too good to be true. Jack, bring her home. We miss her."

Jack saw the taxi driver from earlier walking toward the bar. Jack waved at him and said to Courtney, "Listen, I've got to go. Remember, have Tom call me. Bye," and he hung up.

Jack put some money on the bar, got up and walked toward the taxi driver. “Hey, man,” he said.

“I talked to Alfonso’s wife and she said he should be home soon. We should be able to catch him between trips.”

“Great. Let’s go.”

CHAPTER 90

IT TOOK ABOUT TWENTY MINUTES to get to the south end of the island where Alfonso lived. Finally, they turned and with leaves slapping the sides of the taxi, they made their way slowly down the narrow driveway to his house. The house was small and simple, raised up on stilts with a red tin roof. It was painted white and had a porch overlooking the water. There was a dock with a turquoise boat tied to it and from the color of the water, Jack could see the channel that ran out to deeper water. The driver honked his horn as they came to a stop near the house and they got out of the car.

"Hey cuz. Que pasa?" said the man who came out to greet them, as he looked first at the driver and then at Jack.

The driver called back, "Hey, man. You remember a couple of weeks ago when Charles showed up with that redhead and you asked me to keep an eye out for anyone who didn't seem to belong on the island?"

"Yes."

"And I told you about that gringo I saw who didn't seem right."

"Yes," said Alfonso as he glanced over at Jack. "Who's this?"

"This guy is looking for them too, and I thought you should talk to him."

Jack stepped forward and extended his hand in greeting. "My name is Jack Beale, I'm a friend of Max's." Alfonso took his hand and shook it while staring into Jack's eyes as he spoke, then he responded. "Come on up and we'll talk." The three men walked up the stairs to the porch. Alfonso motioned for them to sit.

"Something to drink?" asked Alfonso.

"No thanks," was Jack's reply. Alfonso's cousin had walked to the other side of the porch since this was between Alfonso and Jack. "Do you know where I can find Max?" continued Jack.

"Tell me again why you want to find her?" he said with icy civility.

Once again Jack told his story. Alfonso listened politely, but as details about Daniel, his shadowy job, mysterious employer, and finally the murder and what he might know about it were told, Alfonso's interest was piqued. When Jack finally finished, he asked again, "Now you know why I must find her."

"Jack, that's quite a story. It explains a lot to me about my friend Charles and why he wanted everyone to call him Daniel. It also explains why he was concerned that others might be looking for him. The fact remains, I owe the man my life. He could never kill anyone, and he was crazy for Max. However, I always had the feeling that something else was going on. Just after they left, a large black sailing yacht showed up. It only stayed for a few days before leaving, but it was obvious that they were looking for something or someone. Now with what you have told me, I think that it may have been Charles. I'll tell you what I can. Maybe that will help Charles as well."

And so he told Jack about Charles' recent arrival, his departure, and about the letter he had given to Max to deliver to his sister in Placencia. "I have many cousins throughout the country. We are close even though we don't see each other often. I put the word out for all of them to watch for Charles and his boat. I heard this morning that Max is safe, staying with my sister, but Charles has disappeared and my cousin Digit is helping Max search for him."

Jack sat and listened without moving or saying anything. When Alfonso finished, Jack stood, walked to the railing and looked out over the water, the only sound was the rustling of palms in the wind. After what seemed like an eternity, he turned and faced Alfonso.

"Thank you for your kindnesses toward Max. Thank you for keeping her safe. Now I've got to get to Placencia. Hopefully I can convince her to come home with me."

"Good luck," said Alfonso as he offered his hand to Jack. As they shook hands he said, "Let me give you my sister's address and telephone number."

He went inside and returned with a piece of paper, which he handed to Jack. Jack thanked him again, turned and walked down the stairs to the taxi. The two cousins spoke quietly before parting. Just before the house slipped from view, Jack turned and looked back briefly. Alfonso was still on the porch, watching them drive off.

The ride back seemed to take longer than the ride out, probably because Jack was so eager to see Max. But it was already mid-afternoon and the rumble in his stomach reminded him that he hadn't eaten since breakfast. As they drove along, Jack quizzed his driver about Placencia. He told Jack that he had only been there once and that was many years ago. What he did remember was that it was small fishing village and it was pretty quiet there. When they arrived at the Sun Breeze, Jack thanked him for all of his help, paid his fare, added a generous tip, and went into the hotel.

He stopped at the front desk to tell them that he was going to Placencia and to see if they could recommend a place to stay while there. "Of course. We also have a message for you," and the clerk went into the back room returning with a sealed envelope and handed it to Jack.

He took it and said, "Thanks. I'll be at the bar having some lunch." As Jack walked toward the bar, he studied the envelope turning it over and over in his hand as if that simple act would give him a clue as to what was inside, but he didn't open it immediately. No one was at the bar and the bartender was looking out toward the reef. Jack chose a seat facing the water, tossed the envelope on the bar and the noise of his chair scraping across the floor alerted the bartender that he was there. It was Chris. He smiled when he saw Jack and came right over and asked, "Belikin?"

"Yes, thank you," was Jack's reply.

While Chris pulled the beer out of the cooler, opened it and wrapped a paper napkin tightly around its rim, Jack looked out over the water. The sun was behind him and getting lower in the sky so the brilliant greens and blues of the water were masked by a silvery sheen. Chris brought him his beer and as he placed it in front of Jack and asked, "Have you found your friend?"

"No, not yet, but I think I know where she is."

He could see that Jack was preoccupied so he didn't press the conversation. Jack picked the envelope up, slid his finger under the corner of the sealed flap and zipped it open. He took out the neatly folded piece of hotel stationery, opened it.

Call me. I'll be in my office at 5:00. Tom

Jack refolded the note and looked at his watch. It was only three o'clock and he would have to wait until four to call since Tom was an hour ahead. Another rumble of his stomach reminded him of why he was there so he asked for a menu. He ordered a burger and another beer and as he looked out over the water, the same scenario he had seen on the night he arrived in San Pedro began to repeat itself. The dive boats began to return, disgorging their cargoes of tired, bedraggled and yet happy black suited charges after a day under the sea. Empty air bottles clanged as they were unloaded and prepared for refilling. Boats were cleaned and soon all would be quiet as the action moved to the bars and restaurants along the beach. Jack wouldn't be alone for long.

His burger was placed in front of him with another beer and it wasn't until he took his first bite that he really realized just how hungry he was. He devoured it, all the while watching the transition slowly taking place as San Pedro prepared for the evening. He thought about all that he had learned and as anxious as he was to get to Placencia, he would wait until tomorrow. Besides, he had to talk to Tom.

Jack waited until ten past five before asking Chris for the phone. He dialed the front desk and was cheerfully connected to an outside line. It wasn't until he heard the first ring on the other end of the line that he began to get nervous. What more would Tom have to tell him? It rang a second time. Court had already told him about the arrest. A third ring. "Hello, Rye Police, Tom speaking."

"Tom. It's Jack. Sorry I wasn't around when you first called."

"Jack. Finally. How are things in Belize?"

"I talked to Courtney and she told me about the arrest. What happened?"

"It's really pretty simple. Just after you left, I went back to talk some more with the band and Percy confessed. I guess his conscience got the better of him and it had been eating him up inside. It appears that it was accidental, but he'll still be charged."

They continued to talk for another fifteen minutes or so. Before hanging up, they agreed on two things. There was something wrong about Daniel, and that Max could possibly be in trouble. Tom would continue his investigation of Daniel and Jack would find Max and bring her home. Goodbyes were said and once again Jack was left with more questions than he had answers for. He paid his tab and returned to the front desk. The desk clerk told him that a room was available at Miss Cecilia's Guest House in Placencia and if he wanted them to book it, they would do so immediately. While they did that, he went across the street to Tropic Air and booked a morning flight for Placencia.

As soon as the words "Your flight is confirmed for 9 AM, to International and then on to Placencia with one stop in Dangriga," were spoken, Jack felt as if a weight were lifted off of his shoulders. Once again, he had direction. He was one step closer to finding Max.

* * *

He returned to the bar which was now crowded and noisy. Those divers he had seen come ashore earlier in the evening were now revived and in full voice as they recounted their adventures. It didn't take long for Jack to find himself in an animated conversation with a large man from Texas and another from Tennessee. Fueled by beer and tall, cold tropical drinks and following the twists and turns of bar talk, their conversation was far ranging. When asked why he was in Belize, Jack told them about Max and Daniel and the story of Python's murder. "That's rough Podna', I hope you find your friend," said the Texan as he clapped Jack on his shoulder.

"Thanks," said Jack. "Now, what brought you down here?"

"This trip is both pleasure and business. We've been buddies for years and once a year we get together to go diving and deep-sea fishing. This year it worked out to do a little business as well."

"What business would that be?" asked Jack.

"I'm a talent scout and my friend here owns a record label in Nashville. There's this guy here we've heard about who has a good local following and does some original stuff. We want to check him out, you'll have to come with us." Through this entire conversation the man from Tennessee, who was much quieter than his gregarious friend from Texas, had said little and just sat listening intently and watching. Then he said, "Tell me a little more about this Daniel person and what happened."

Jack was taken aback. "Why?" he asked.

"Back a few years there was a guy down in my area running a similar scam and he screwed over quite a few guys I knew. I was about to sign one of them and suddenly he took this other deal. Within a year he was back page news and his career still hasn't recovered."

"Really," said Jack.

"Yeah, it was real unfortunate. Don't get me wrong. The business I'm in isn't the most honest that there ever was. There are lots of hucksters and guys preying on musicians. Makes it real tough for those of us who are trying to do it right."

"So why do you think that Daniel might be the same guy?"

"I didn't say that exactly. What I said was that this sounded like the same kind of scam. From your description, your guy, this Daniel, is not the same guy, but the scam was the same. There were some rumors floating around that he worked for someone well connected and that you didn't want to cross him. Only rumors, but they did make some sense."

The Texan rejoined the conversation, "I remember hearing that. Now that you have me thinking about it, something similar happened down my way as well. We always thought that it was just bad luck and bad judgment on the part of the band that got screwed." He paused and said more to himself than to Jack or his friend, "What was the name of that label?"

"Well, from everything you have told me and what I had learned before coming down here, it makes me glad that I'm not in the music business," said Jack.

"It's all about the money. There is so much to be made that it brings out the worst in folks. Don't get me wrong, there are lots of good honest people in the business, you just don't hear a lot about them. Face it. Dirt is a lot more interesting. Is anybody else getting hungry?" said Tennessee, changing the subject. That question elicited a positive response from the other two and the decision was made to go to Fido's for dinner since that is where the guy they wanted to see would be playing later.

The three men sampled the menu: The lime marinated chicken, shrimp creole, and grilled snapper with tomatoes, peppers, and onions were all pronounced delicious. By the time they had finished eating, Reef Wreck John was all set up and began his first set. He was a transplanted gringo from Alabama and performed mostly original songs that captured the laid back feeling of San Pedro. He was equally skilled on keyboard as he was on guitar and was a natural showman, and it wasn't long before the bar was packed with locals and vacationers alike, drinking, dancing and singing along.

During his first break, they invited him over to their table to talk. It was mostly small talk about San Pedro, how he ended up there and compliments about his music. Jack just watched, fascinated to see how the two men worked. He knew what the singer didn't and he could see how they were working him. It was like fishing. Tonight they were baiting the hook. They flattered him, they were on vacation and it was only in passing that anything was said about the business they were in. It was all so casual and low key, calculated. After he went back on stage, Jack said his goodnights. He was exhausted. Tomorrow would be a big day and he wanted to be ready. Besides, his new friends had work to do. As he walked towards the door, the Texan called out to him, "Raven Records." Jack turned and said, "What?"

"Raven Records was the name of the label I was trying to think of."

"Thanks. Goodnight." said Jack and he turned and walked back down to the beach for the walk back to the hotel. As he walked he thought about all that he had learned today and the name, Raven Records, kept echoing in the back of his mind.

CHAPTER 91

WHILE JACK WALKED THE BEACH pondering what he had learned, Digit was guiding Max back to Nancy's. As they walked along in silence, the sounds and smells of the village settling into its nightly rhythms were reminders that life went on. The gentle rustling of palms in the breeze and the soft *schwooshing* of the sea against the beach was interrupted by the sharp staccato of a barking dog. Muffled voices of villagers in their homes mixed with other muffled sounds from unseen televisions and radios. Aromas, rich and spicy from pots simmering on stoves, the smokey smells of fish grilling over hot coals mixed with the sweet fragrances of hibiscus and other tropical flowers, and even the occasional burp of a septic system.

She was numb. Daniel was gone. His letter explained everything and yet it explained nothing. *What happened to him? Was he safe? Who were those men in the black boat? How did his boat end up tied to that pier?* These questions and others flooded her mind as she walked silently toward Nancy's. Her world felt empty; she felt alone. When they reached their destination, Max climbed the stairs as if in a trance. Nancy came out onto the porch when she heard their footsteps and without a word, Max gave her a quick hug, then walked past her, into the house and closed herself in her room. Nancy looked at Digit, her eyes asking all the necessary questions. He looked at her and said, "We found the boat."

"Did you find Daniel?"

"No."

"Come in and tell me about it."

Digit followed her into the living room, they sat down, Digit in a chair and Nancy opposite him on a stool. She stared into his eyes, as if willing him to tell her. He stared back and then began to tell her the story. He told her how the last place they looked was up the shipping channel and how the boat was tied up to the pier. He told her about what they found or more importantly what they didn't find. He mentioned the letter, but felt that Max should tell her about that herself. Nancy sat transfixed as she listened to his tale.

Just as he finished the story, a door opened and they heard the sound of bare feet on wood. Digit stopped talking and looked up. Nancy turned around. Max was standing there, her eyes red from tears with a piece of paper in her hand. Nancy stood and went to her, extending her arms toward Max offering the solace of an embrace. Max took a small step forward and the two women came together, Max's body sagged against Nancy's, her head coming to rest on Nancy's shoulder and her arms remained limp at her sides. Nancy's arms enveloped Max and she held her tight, gently stroking her back and whispering in her ear, "It's all right, honey. Everything will be all right."

Max sobbed and Nancy could feel her body trembling as she cried. Digit went outside onto the porch. There wasn't much he could do at the moment. It was maybe fifteen minutes before the two women emerged from the house, holding hands. Digit looked from one to the other and then back at Nancy and asked, "Are you going to be all right?"

"Yes, she's going to be fine," Nancy answered. "Thank you, Digit, for all that you have done."

Max looked up at him with a tear-stained face, went over to him and gave him a small hug. "Thank you," was all she could say.

Digit took this as a good moment to say goodnight, promising to come back in the morning so they could go and retrieve the boat. After he left, Max sat down on one of the porch chairs, leaned back, closed her eyes and felt the night breeze gently caress her face. Nancy went back inside and returned in a few minutes with two Smilin' Wides.

"Here," she said as she handed one to Max. "I think you need this and we have more to talk about."

"Thanks," said Max and she took a sip. The ice-cold liquid felt good as she swallowed the first sip. Then she took another, she hadn't realized just how hot and thirsty she was. The sweet fruit taste was refreshing and the rum began to have the desired effect. "Nancy, what am I going to do? He lied to me. He left. I should be relieved it's over, and yet I'm worried about him. I keep wondering . . ." her voice drifted off.

"I don't have those answers for you, but you can stay here for as long as you need to."

"Thanks." Max handed the letter to Nancy. "Read this. Tell me what you think." Nancy took the letter and began reading as Max sipped her drink, the breeze rustled the palms, the surf continued it's gentle schwooshing and it was so peaceful. When Nancy finished, she put the letter down, took another sip of her drink, looked up at Max and said, "I think he's still alive."

"You do? Why?" said Max in a dry lifeless voice. She had not even considered this as an option. She thought about how the inside of the boat had been torn apart, and the blood on the pillow. She was so convinced that the worst had come to pass that she hadn't even considered that option.

Nancy hesitated before answering, "Digit told me about how you found the boat tied up so neatly at the pier, right?"

Max thought a moment then answered, "Yes."

Nancy trying to sound optimistic, continued, "The inside was a mess, but outside there was no sign that anything had happened. If there was blood on a pillow, wouldn't you think that there would have been some on the outside?"

"I suppose so."

"The letter does sound like a final goodbye, but it's too reasoned. It sounds planned. It doesn't sound desperate enough to have been written by someone contemplating his death. I agree that he doesn't intend to ever see you again and he is leaving you the boat. Maybe to ease his conscience, I really don't know, but it sounds that way to me." Nancy handed the letter back to Max. She took it and looked at it again, not saying anything.

"Nancy, you might be right, but I just don't get it. I was so sure that we had a real connection, at least at first."

The rum was kicking in and Nancy's tone began to change. "Max, he was using you. That much is plain to see. There may have been some real feelings there, but in the end, he was using you. I suggest you take the boat and enjoy it. Screw him. He gave it to you; you earned it."

Max looked up at her a little surprised. This was a new side of Nancy she had not seen before.

"Nancy, are you all right?"

"I'm sorry if I came on a little strong there."

Max took another sip of her drink and then raised her glass, "A toast. To men, the bastards."

"The bastards," said Nancy raising her glass in response.

CHAPTER 92

AS AFTER EVERY LATE NIGHT, morning comes much too quickly. Jack was up with the sun and needed coffee badly. He showered, dressed and then walked around to Front Street to Ruby's Cafe. He had heard that it was the best place for early morning coffee and breakfast. It was just a hole in the wall with a line of people moving in empty handed and coming out clutching a coffee in one hand and a small brown bag in the other. It was the same for Jack. His brown bag contained a johnny cake with ham and cheese and a slice of rum cake. The coffee was large and hot and he sipped it as he walked back.

He found a chair on the beach in front of the hotel and sat down. After nestling his coffee in the sand beside his chair, he opened the bag and took out the johnny cake. It was still warm and at that moment not even the fanciest of gourmet meals could have tasted so good. He sat there, feeling the heat of the sun on his face, enjoying his simple meal and thought about the day ahead. *Would he find Max? Was she safe? Would Daniel be there? Would she be glad to see him or would he return home looking foolish?* After his last sip of coffee, he took a deep breath, the kind you take moments before jumping off a cliff. He got up, went to his room, packed, checked out of the hotel and walked across the street to the airport and to the edge of his cliff.

The plane was the same kind of small plane in which he had flown to San Pedro, and as before, the plane was full. Sunburned and bleary eyed tourists, hung over after a last night on vacation, business men in neatly pressed suits and a woman's group from a local church wearing big hats and clutching large bags to their large bosoms filled the plane to capacity. Fifteen minutes later, he was back on the ground awaiting his next flight. He was anxious and a beer from Jet's Bar eased the wait.

He could feel the energy that was present in every airport, large or small throughout the world. Adventure. The hustle and bustle of arrivals and departures. Everyone feeling the same two conflicting emotions of looking forward to where they were going, and the sadness of departing from where they had been.

As he sat, sipping his beer, staring out over the tarmac he began to have second thoughts for the first time. *Now that Daniel had been cleared of the murder, was Max really in danger? True, Daniel was a skeevy character. After all, he did use several aliases. How much of his relationship with Max was based on deception? How much was real? Did Max know, and if she did, did she care? In his opinion she deserved better, but was he any better than Daniel? He had managed to ignore all of her signals. He had given Daniel the opportunity and instead of rising to the challenge, he had sailed off. And now, he was chasing after her. For what? To save her from a danger that only he imagined.* This line of thought and self-doubt was beginning to turn into a pity party when he heard the call for his flight. He finished his beer, took a deep breath and said to himself. "Too late to turn back. By the end of today, I will either be a fool or a hero. Time to suck it up."

By the time he reached the plane, it was nearly full and he was directed up front to the co-pilot's seat to the right of the pilot. As he fastened his seat belt, he looked around. He studied the mass of gauges and dials and realized that they really weren't all that mysterious: Airspeed, altitude, orientation to the horizon, fuel consumption, each one in duplicate. The plane felt small as it took off from the runway made for commercial jetliners. They turned south and began to follow the coast at only 2500 feet. From his seat, he watched the countryside pass underneath. Brilliant green jungle, brown snaking rivers and neat orchards dotted the landscape. Roads were few and far between with houses and settlements even scarcer. In just fifteen or twenty minutes, he could see ahead what he presumed to be Dangriga, their one stop.

His assumption was confirmed when the pilot began to descend toward the jungle. Jack strained to see an airport. He didn't see anything that looked even remotely like an airport. There was what looked like a small road cut into the jungle and he could see a speck of orange at the far end in contrast to the green of the brush.

Landing always made him nervous and it didn't matter whether the plane was large or small, but this was different. He was sitting next to the pilot and it offered a whole new perspective. As much as he didn't want to look, he was fascinated as he alternately glanced at the pilot and stared out the windshield.

A tiny gash in the jungle was the runway and it did not look like there was enough room for the wing tips to clear the brush until they were nearly on the ground and even then it looked too close. *Thump.* They were down and it wasn't until that thump that Jack realized he had been holding his breath. He exhaled and took a deep breath as the plane shook and shuddered over the rough surface as it slowed. As they slowed he noticed that everything was wet and there were puddles on the ground. *What would the pilot have done if they had arrived while it was raining?* he wondered. A vision of an intense tropical downpour, the kind where it rained so hard that it was impossible to even see flashed in his head. Before he could consider this possibility further, his thoughts were interrupted as two buildings came into view. One had a sign that read Tropic Air and the other Mayan Air. There was another plane on the ground in front of the Mayan Air terminal and Jack could see bags being loaded onto it.

The sun was hot and he could feel its heat through the windshield and he could almost see the puddles shrinking as he stared out his side window. As they came to a stop in front of the Tropic building, his plane pivoted to face the runway. The engine was shut down. The propeller stopped spinning and it was silent and still. The ground crew quickly opened the doors and the heat flooded in. He could smell the heat and dampness outside.

I guess we won't be here long, Jack thought when he noticed that the pilot didn't even unbuckle his seat belt as he talked to a man on the ground who held a clipboard in his hand. The combination of passengers squeezing off the plane and their luggage being removed caused the plane to shake and bounce and no one new climbed aboard. His conversation finished, the man on the ground pushed the pilot's door closed and the pilot latched the door, leaned back in his seat, and started the engine in preparation for take off.

As all this was happening, Jack sat watching the other plane. The luggage compartments were closed and the passengers began filing out of the terminal building. It was a mirror image of his flight: several businessmen, a family with two small children, several large women in their brightly colored dresses and hats, and Daniel. Then they disappeared behind the plane.

Daniel! His heart began to pound. He was no longer casually watching the other plane. He was straining to get another look at the man he swore was Daniel. Faces began to fill the plane's windows. A lady with a big hat, a child. He felt his heart race. All at once, a thousand thoughts and emotions rushed though his head. *Was it Daniel? If it was, then what was he doing here? Was he alone? Where was Max? Max, where was Max?* He hadn't seen her. He stared at the other plane as if more intensity would allow his eyes to penetrate its skin. *Maybe it wasn't him,* he told himself, trying to calm down. *There was no reason for him to be here. It couldn't have been him.*

After what felt like an eternity, Jack saw him through the last window on the side of the plane facing Jack. Jack's focus was so intense that the only sound he heard was his own heartbeat pounding in his ears. It was at that moment that the man he presumed to be Daniel looked out his window in Jack's direction. Their eyes locked. In that split second, Jack knew for certain that it was him. It was Daniel.

A tap on his shoulder caused him to turn away. "You must buckle your belt."

"Of course. Yes, I'm sorry," he began to fumble with the five-point buckle while still trying to look out his window. It took what seemed an eternity before he heard the last metallic click of the buckle locking. As it clicked, the other plane's engine roared and it began to move. Jack watched it as it moved onto the runway where he got his last look at Daniel who stared back at him. Then the plane accelerated down the runway, rose into the air and banking right, took Daniel away and left Jack behind.

In stunned disbelief, he watched as the plane disappeared from sight. Questions raced through his head. The sounds of the doors clicking shut and the whine of the engine brought him back to the present. He was dripping with sweat and his panic must have showed since the pilot asked him if he was okay. He nodded and mumbled yes. Slumping in his seat as the propeller spun into invisibility and drifting between thoughts of what he imagined and what he knew, Jack felt a great weight lifting as all of his self doubts evaporated in that moment. He knew he was right and that he had to find Max. He willed the plane off the ground. He couldn't get to Placencia fast enough.

CHAPTER 93

AFTER SEVERAL MORE SMILIN' WIDES and some serious man-bashing, Max slumped back in her chair and closed her eyes. Nancy, while just as tipsy as Max, was not as emotionally and physically spent as she was. So with much tugging, pushing, and prodding, she managed to get Max out of the chair and into bed. "Why do we let men do these things to us?" said Nancy quietly to Max before she left the room. Max didn't hear her; she was sound asleep.

Shortly after sunrise, Max opened her eyes. She squinted and closed her eyes again against the early morning light. She smelled coffee brewing, but didn't move. She was thirsty, her head was throbbing, and her body felt like lead. As consciousness returned, so did memories of the previous day flood back. *The boat. She and Digit had found the boat. It was torn up inside and she had found the letter. Where was the letter?*

She strained to remember last night.

All at once it came to her. *Nancy.* She remembered handing it to Nancy last night. She sat up too quickly and her head felt as if it would explode. She sat still until the flash of pain subsided, then she stood slowly and walked to the door. She had to see the letter again.

"Mornin,'" Max managed to croak as she leaned against the doorframe.

Nancy turned. "Oh baby, you need a big cup of coffee," she said with a chuckle.

Max managed a moan and Nancy poured her a cup of coffee and motioned for her to go and sit down. Max turned slowly and shuffled toward the couch. Nancy followed with the coffee and handed it to Max.

"Thanks," mumbled Max as she took a first tentative sip. The hot liquid burned her tongue and she made a face.

"You all right? You look awful."

"Yeah, I'll be okay. I just burned my tongue." Placing the cup on the table she asked, "Where's the letter?"

"Right there, on the table in front of you."

Max hadn't seen it. The letter was on the table, open, inviting her to pick it up. She stared at it, didn't move, took another sip of her coffee, put the cup on the table, then reached out slowly for the letter. She knew what it said, but she needed to read it again. She needed to understand what it said. She read in silence, Nancy watched her from across the room. When Max finished, she looked up, placed the letter back on the table and said in a distant voice, "I have to pee," and she left the room. It was several minutes before she returned. Her hair was brushed and its edges were damp from the water she had splashed on her face. Her eyes were clearer.

"He's gone and he gave me the boat," she said in a soft lifeless voice.

"I know, you let me read the letter," was Nancy's reply.

"Why would he do that?" Before Nancy could answer Max continued, "Last night, I remember you saying that you thought he might still be alive."

"I did. I'm not sure why, but it's just a feeling I have."

"I don't have that same feeling. Even if he's not dead, he's gone for good and he might as well be dead."

"Perhaps."

At this moment there was a knock on the door and Digit popped his head in. "Are you ready to go?"

"Ready to go?" Max responded, not quite sure what he was talking about.

"Yeah, we have to go get the boat before the port captain calls the police or something. Remember we told him that your boyfriend was waiting for some parts and that we'd be back in the morning to make the repairs and leave?"

"Give me a few minutes to get ready." With that, Max headed to her room.

"Is she all right?" asked Digit.

"She's fine. We just drank a little too much last night and I think she's still in shock over what has happened. She needs to be busy and an early morning boat ride may be just the thing," said Nancy as she disappeared into the kitchen.

Digit didn't follow, instead he talked louder. "One of my cousins is coming with us so that he can bring my boat back while I help her with the sailboat. I truly hope we don't have to deal with the police."

Nancy and Max rejoined Digit in the living room at the same time. Nancy was carrying a bag and handed it to Max. "Here's some food and water for you."

"Thanks."

Max took the bag that was offered, put her sunglasses on and moved toward the door.

As Digit turned to follow, Nancy touched his arm. "She's still in shock, take care of her."

"Don't worry." And he turned and walked out, hurrying to catch up with her.

"Drink plenty of water," said Nancy as they disappeared down the walk.

* * *

The boat ride to *d'Riddem* under any other circumstances would have been a delight. The sea was flat, the sun brilliant and the temperature comfortable. Digit and his cousin tried to make light conversation, but those efforts ended in failure so they rode in silence. They could see Max tense up as they began the ride up the shipping channel. The rusty, old ship was still there. There was still no sign of life on board.

D'Riddem bobbed quietly right where they had left her the night before. Digit nosed his boat up to the catamaran and his cousin took over the controls while he and Max climbed aboard. "You know how to run this?" asked Digit.

Max looked at him. "Now you ask?"

"I just assumed that you did?"

"I think I can. Daniel let me sail it and I'm pretty sure I remember everything."

"Then let's get out of here."

Max went below and found the engine keys, returned to the cockpit and started the engines. Digit busied himself with untying the boat and his cousin waited patiently in the channel. They were ready. Digit cast off and Max gingerly slipped the cat into gear and they slid away from the wharf. She made a sweeping turn around the ship and headed out the channel just as the port captain appeared on the edge of the wharf. Max waved and Digit breathed a sigh of relief.

As Max followed Digit's boat down the channel, he busied himself with coiling the dock lines, pulling in the fenders and throwing each in turn into the open anchor locker. Max could see him pulling the final fender up and just as it looked like he had it, he dropped it back over the side. Then he knelt down on the deck, his toes curled in the trampoline's netting and leaned out looking over the side. Max saw him do this and shouted to him, "Is everything all right?"

Any answer that he may have offered was unheard because he was still leaning over the side of the boat. Max craned her neck to see what he was doing but couldn't. Anxiety began to crawl over her.

"Digit! Talk to me," she shouted.

He waved his hand and continued leaning over the side. It seemed an eternity, but in reality it was less than a minute before he came walking back to the cockpit without having pulled up the last fender.

"What is it? What were you looking at?" asked Max.

He looked at her, reluctant to answer her questions, then he said, "It looks like there is blood on that last fender."

"Blood!" cried Max. Now her anxiety turned to panic. "Where?"

Before he could say anything else she left the wheel, pushed past him and rushed forward to the spot where he had been leaning over the side. All he could do was take the wheel, steer the boat and wait. She knelt down where he had been, leaned through the lifeline and stared over the side. The bow of the boat swooshed and gurgled as it sliced through the water and she could feel the vibration of the engine through the hull and deck. Mesmerized, she watched the fender as it kissed the water and slowly spun around suspended by the line that tied it to the boat. As it completed a rotation, she saw what Digit had seen and what she hoped she would not see. There, near the top, a bloody hand print appeared which then turned into an ugly smear as it slid down the fender, disappearing in the water as if someone had tried to hold onto it and couldn't. The fender continued its slow rotation as its end dragged through the water and with each spin and splash a little bit more of the ugly smear disappeared and the hand print seemed to wave at her each time it rotated by. She froze and for a moment the only sound she heard was her own breathing as she tried to comprehend what she saw.

She was numb, her mind a jumble of terrible thoughts. Silent and stunned she stood, looked back at Digit and then turned back and slowly untied the fender and lowered it into the water. It tugged and pulled as if it were a fish on a line. With each turn, more and more of that handprint disappeared until it was no longer waving at her.

That's when she pulled it up over the rail, untied it, then holding onto its line, she gingerly carried it to the open locker and without touching it, dropped it in with the other fenders and lines, closed the locker cover and slowly made her way back to Digit.

"Why did you do that?"

"Do what?'

"You know, clean it off. Are you all right?" he asked.

"Yes, I'm fine."

"We'll have to call the police."

"No, we won't."

Digit looked at her in astonishment. "Why not?" he asked.

"Because . . . because we just can't. I need some time to think. Maybe there is a simple explanation."

Digit looked at her incredulously, then he said, "Daniel is missing. Those men in the black boat caught up with him. Remember how torn up things are below?" Before he could continue, she cut him off. "Digit, I need some time. We are not going to the police right away. I'm not saying we won't, but we are not going to them now."

"All right," said Digit with resignation. A slight breeze had begun to blow, providing some relief to the already increasing heat of the day. Max looked at him then she reached out and touched his arm, "Digit, you have been so kind to me. I know it is a lot to ask. Please trust me."

He didn't reply. He just stared straight ahead, guiding the boat toward Placencia. Max went below, surveyed the mess and then sat down at the table. She was too numb to even clean up. She took out his letter and as soon as she did, she began to shake.

Memories filled her head, of last summer, how wickedly wonderful it felt when she gave in to him, the excitement and adventure that seemed to touch everything they did together. Then her thoughts began to darken the more she remembered. She never really knew all that much about him. When she would ask him questions, he would skillfully turn the conversation back to her. It was always about her, and she loved it. Had he ever loved her, or had he been using her all along she wondered. Other words leapt off the page at her . . . *I was to kill him . . . Since you are reading this letter, my worst fears have been realized and we will never see each other again.* As she reread the letter, she remembered little things that could have innocent explanations, but could also have been signs of the true darkness that surrounded him.

Why had he done this to her? Had she only been a convenience, to be used and discarded? Her sadness turned to frustration, then anger. She hated the lies and deception. She hated the black boat and what it stood for. She was glad that he was gone, and yet deep within a small part of her still cared and still felt a need to know what had happened. Had they, whoever they were, caught up with him? Did they take him away or did they kill him? Was it all an illusion to dupe her? Whatever the answer, her fairy tale world had come crashing down and now she was alone in a foreign country, dependent on the kindness of her new-found friends. He had given her the boat. What was she going to do with it? Sell it? Keep it? It was all so confusing. She needed answers. She needed help.

It was at this moment that Digit called down to her, telling her that they had arrived and he needed her help to anchor the boat. She put the letter back into her pocket and joined him in the cockpit. "Let me take the wheel while you go forward to drop the anchor," she said.

"Are you sure?"

"Yes. He taught me how to do this."

Digit went forward, and waited for Max to give him the signal. Finally, with the splash of the anchor hitting the water and the clattering of chain, *I Got d'Riddem* was back where she had started in what seemed several lifetimes ago. Max shut down the engines and took a moment to enjoy the silence before . . . before what? She didn't know.

CHAPTER 94

WHILE MAX WAS ANCHORING THE BOAT, Jack's flight was landing at the other end of town. His thoughts still on Daniel, Jack followed the other passengers as they exited the plane and walked around the Tropic Air terminal to wait for their luggage in front of the building. There was no wait since the luggage cart followed right behind them. As Jack took his bag off the cart, a voice from behind caught his attention. "Need a ride, skip?"

Jack turned, not fully cognizant that the voice was talking to him until he found himself facing a smiling face and was asked again, "Need a ride?"

"Uh, yes."

"Come with me. Here, let me take your bag."

Before Jack could react, his bag was taken from him and the man with the smile was walking towards an old, dusty, Toyota van. By the time Jack caught up to him, his bag had been put in the back and the man was opening the door for Jack.

"My name's Tommy. Ever been to Placencia before?"

"No, no I haven't."

"Well then, let me welcome you to our little village."

As Jack climbed into the van he paused, looked around, shrugged his shoulders and said, "Thanks, Tommy. My name's Jack."

As Tommy started the van he asked, "Where are you staying?"

"Miss Cecilia's Guest House."

"I know her. She's my wife's sister's second cousin."

He shifted into gear. The Toyota lurched forward and they were off in a cloud of red dust as Jack sat silently looking out the window.

The road was unpaved and pocked with potholes forcing Tommy to slalom slowly around them as he tried to not shake his van apart. Slowly they moved east along the north side of the runway, then just before the beach, the road took a sharp right turn across the end of the runway, then another sharp right back alongside the south side of the runway until they were at a point nearly opposite the terminals where it took a sharp left turn south toward Placencia.

Jack looked over at Tommy as the dirt road became paved and they began to accelerate, "That's a rough way to get across the runway."

"They say they ran out of money, but I think they stole it. It was supposed to get paved all the way to the next town."

"Just like home," mumbled Jack.

As they hurtled toward town, Tommy honked and waved at seemingly everyone they passed as he kept up a running commentary on life in Placencia.

Jack could tell that Tommy wanted to have a conversation, but he didn't, so he quietly stared out his side window, the warm breeze blowing in on him, providing some relief from the hot sun. As they neared town, Tommy's monologue turned to food, and when he said something about the best pies in the Caribbean being made by Nancy the pie maker, Jack turned toward him. "Did you say Nancy the pie maker?"

"Sure did, Skip. She makes the finest pies around. Have you heard of her?"

"I have. I met her cousin in San Pedro and I told him I'd look her up."

"That will be easy, her store is right near Cecilia's."

Jack drifted back into his own thoughts again and they rode in silence the rest of the way into town.

The settlement of Placencia was nothing like what Jack expected. The road split the town in half and businesses and residences were all mixed together.

"The original settlement is all along here," said Tommy as he pointed out his window toward the many colorful houses that were up on stilts amongst the tall palms. "They put them up high like that to catch the breeze from the water. The beach is not too far over and running down the center is the famous mile long sidewalk. On that side of the road," he said gesturing toward Jack's side of the car, "is the lagoon side and that's where I live."

Jack looked over toward where Tommy was pointing but remained silent, hearing most of Tommy's narrative, but not really listening. Suddenly Tommy jerked the wheel to the left and they stopped at what appeared to be a sandy path between some of the houses.

"We'll have to walk from here. Cecilia's is just down this path about halfway to the sidewalk," he said as he opened his door and got out.

While he retrieved Jack's bag from the back, Jack got out, stretched and joined Tommy at the back of the Toyota. He looked up and saw a small hand painted sign nailed to post that pointed down the path. Tommy had already started down the path and Jack followed. It wasn't a long walk, only a hundred yards or so to the sidewalk. Tommy turned right and two buildings down he stopped.

"Welcome to Cecilia's."

Jack looked up at a brightly painted building, raised up on stilts. He thanked Tommy, paid him and climbed the steps. Up on the porch, he saw a door with a sign that said office and he went in. A diminutive black woman greeted him with a big smile and twinkle in her eye. There was an energy about her that made it impossible for him to guess her age, she could have been sixty or she could have been eighty, Jack couldn't tell. "Welcome to Cecilia's. I'm Cecilia and you must be Mr. Beale," she said with a singsong voice that was a mixture of Creole and king's English. Jack was surprised by this greeting as he replied, "Yes, I am, but please call me Jack. How did you know?"

"The hotel in San Pedro called and told me you were on the way. I must say you are much better looking than their description." Jack blushed a little and managed a small thank you. "Let's get you signed in and I'll show you to your room." Jack had never met anyone quite like her. She maintained a nonstop monologue as he signed in and it continued as she walked him out onto the balcony and around to his room. She talked about Placencia, her cousins, the weather, things to do and places to see. Jack had reached the point where he was only hearing noise, the words having become nothing more than sound until she said, "You know, your redheaded lady friend is staying with Nancy." Jack stopped dead in his tracks. "What did you just say?"

Cecilia paused, confused for a moment. She had been talking so fast about so much she looked up at him with a bit of a question in her eye. "You mean the Lobster Festival in June? You really should come back here for that, it is quite the time."

Jack held up his hand, "No, before that, what did you say about a redheaded lady?"

"Oh, you mean Miss Max. She's staying with Nancy the Pie Maker. She arrived on a sailboat maybe a week ago and she had a big falling out with the guy she was with. There were some other men asking about him and then he disappeared, leaving her here alone so Nancy took her in. She and Digit . . ."

Jack interrupted, "Who's Digit?"

"Digit is Nancy's cousin and he's been helping Miss Max search for her missing friend."

"How did you know she is a friend of mine?"

"Carlita from the Sunbreeze Hotel told me when she called about renting you a room. She said that you were asking lots of questions and looking all over for this red haired lady. It's obvious that she must be special to you otherwise why would you be doing all of this?"

Again Jack held up his hand for her to stop. He needed a moment to let all of this sink in.

"You know, Mr. Jack, Belize is a small country and Placencia is even smaller. We all know each other's business. It's probably not my place to say, but that guy she was with was no good. I think she'll be happy to see you." This last statement was made with a wink and a nod.

"Where can I find Nancy?" asked Jack.

"Oh, that's easy, her shop is just around the corner. She's probably there although your lady friend and Digit left early this morning."

"Thank you."

"If you need anything, just ask," and with that she turned and shuffled off.

Jack was stunned. He went into the bathroom and splashed some cold water on his face, looked into the mirror and said, "Jack, you're doing the right thing. You should never have let Max get away. Don't blow it this time." He dried his face, left his room, and walked to Nancy's store.

* * *

The bell on the door tinkled as Jack opened it and stepped into Nancy's shop. He was greeted with the aroma of freshly baked pies and the smell made his stomach rumble. He was studying the pies in the display case when a voice from out back called out, "I'll be right out, I'm just pulling a pie from the oven."

He didn't answer, as he continued to look at the pies in the display case.

"Hello. May I help you?"

Jack looked up and said, "Yes, I'm looking for Nancy."

"I'm Nancy. How may I help you?"

Jack took a deep breath, "My name is Jack Beale and I'm looking for someone. Her name is Max and I was told that she was staying with you."

She said nothing. She just stood and stared at Jack, her eyes asking the questions.

"We're old friends and I think she may be in trouble."

"And?"

He stared back. Whether it was nerves or fatigue, he didn't know, but words began tumbling out of his mouth. "Last summer there was a murder back home. She became involved with the man who was suspected of being the murderer. I came down here to warn her and hopefully bring her home before it's too late." Then he stopped, embarrassed at this outburst of information.

Her expression hadn't changed. "Who is this man?"

Once again, Jack found himself rambling on. "He goes by several different names. When she met him he was Daniel Cummings. He's been known as Charles Gowings and I'm sure there are other names that he has used as well. Since coming down here, I have found out that he wasn't the murderer, but I'm still worried and I need to see her."

Nancy continued to stare at him.

He wasn't sure what was going on or why she was standing there just watching him. He had just told this woman way more information than perhaps was necessary and she just continued to stare at him. His frustration must have become apparent. "Look, can you help me or not?" he blurted out.

"Yes, I can," she said slowly.

"Will you?" asked Jack in a softer, more pleading voice.

"Yes. She's staying here with me. She's out right now, but she should be back soon."

"Where is she?"

"She went with my cousin Digit to bring back the boat."

"The boat?"

Now it was her turn to offer information. "Daniel's boat. He disappeared several says ago and they have been looking for him. Late yesterday they found the boat, but he is missing."

Nancy continued talking but Jack didn't hear her words. He was remembering back not too many hours ago when he had seen Daniel on the other plane.

"When will she be back?" he interrupted.

"Soon. They should be back soon."

* * *

Both Nancy's last words and Jack's thank you were swallowed up by the tinkling bell and slap of the door as he rushed out.

Jack was all but running as he hurried down the sidewalk and by the time he reached the end he was drenched in sweat. Only then did he slow and walk down onto the beach. The sun was blinding and sweat covered his face, stinging his eyes as he looked out over the water at the dozen or so boats anchored not too far from the shore. *Where is she?*

Shielding his eyes from the sun he moved into the shade of a large tree that offered some relief. He continued to scan the anchorage for any indication that Max was there. He saw no movement on any of the boats, several of which were catamarans, as they sat undisturbed out on their anchors. His heart began to slow, his breathing returned to normal and the sweat on his face was beginning to dry leaving the taste of salt on his lips. It was quiet and peaceful. The only sound other than the breeze rustling the leaves above him and the sound of tiny wavelets lazily sloshing against the shore, were the cries of the parrots in their cage.

It was then that he heard the sound of an outboard engine start up and a small boat darted out from behind the fuel dock and sped out toward the boats. It disappeared behind one of the catamarans. It felt like an eternity before it reappeared and when it did, there were two more people in it, another black man and a woman. Jack shielded his eyes from the sun and stared at the boat as it came closer, straining to see if the woman had red hair. Finally the boat was close enough. It was

Max. He had found her.

As the boat was driven up onto the sand next to the fuel dock, one of the men got out first and tied the boat to a nearby tree stump. Then the other man climbed out and standing in ankle deep water extended his hand to her and helped her out. She faced the man and they stood there talking and Jack watched, paralyzed with anxiety. With his heart pounding in his chest he wanted to call out to her, to run to her, but he didn't move, couldn't move.

Finally, she turned and began walking slowly in his direction. Her head was down, her feet sifting through the sand as she moved, and he could tell that her thoughts were elsewhere. Jack continued to watch her as she drew closer, unaware of his presence, and for a moment he questioned again whether he should be there.

She was nearly halfway to the tree when he stepped out from under its branches. He wanted to call her name, but his voice had abandoned him. At that moment, she looked up and stopped dead in her tracks. Their eyes met and Max said, "Jack?" Jack continued to stand there unable to move. "Jack!" This time Max shouted his name and began running toward him. He moved toward her and they came together. There on the sand, by the sea, thousands of miles from home they embraced, clinging to each other as tears of joy flowed freely. In that moment, months of hurt and heartache were vanquished. They were back together and it was right. They held each other while tears were gently wiped away with gentle touches and tender kisses.

"Jack, you're here. How? Why?"

"Max, are you all right?"

"Yes, I'm fine."

"I came because . . ." here he paused, then he blurted out, "I came because I love you and I couldn't stand by anymore and I was worried . . . all of us were worried about you."

With these words, Max buried her head into his shoulder and cried softly. He could feel her shaking. He could smell her hair, he felt her tears on his shoulder and it was all good. All of his doubts evaporated in that moment.

* * *

"Max?"

The moment was broken when another voice, a deeper voice called out her name. Jack looked up and saw one of the men walking toward them and Max pulled away from Jack slightly and turned her head in its direction. "Max, who are these guys?" asked Jack.

Wiping the tears from her face, she did a small pirouette out of Jack's arms, while still holding onto his hand and faced the men. "Digit, I'm sorry. This is Jack. He's my dearest friend in the whole world. Jack, this is Digit, he's a cousin of Alfonso's and he's been helping me search for Daniel."

Jack noticed that when she said his name, a sadness came over her. The two men shook hands and Jack thanked him for taking care of Max. After this greeting, Digit excused himself leaving Jack and Max standing on the sand still holding hands, each lost in their own private thoughts as they watched him go.

When Digit reached his boat, they both spoke at once, neither understanding what the other said.

Jack said, "You first."

"Jack, he's gone. Daniel disappeared several days ago and we just found his boat and brought it back, but he's gone. The boat was a mess, there was a letter to me and we found some blood on one of the fenders." This was said rapidly, and all in one breath.

"Slow down, Max."

She took a deep breath.

"Okay."

"Now, start over. Slowly."

"We, Digit and I, have been searching for days, and last night we found Daniel's boat tied up at the commercial wharf up Big Creek."

"Have you called the police?"

"No."

"Why not?"

"I just couldn't. I'm scared. So much has happened."

"You said that he's gone and there was blood on the boat. Was it his?"

"I don't know. Then I found a letter on the boat… I guess that is part of the reason I didn't call the police."

"What letter?" asked Jack.

Max started to get it out of her pocket then she pushed it back into her pocket as she said. "Let's go somewhere where we can sit and talk. I'm hot and I need something to drink."

"Okay. You lead the way."

She said, "Come on," and led him off toward the road. "We'll go to the Pickled Parrot. It's cool and shady and they have good drinks. Now, you said you had something to tell me?"

"It's a long story, let's wait until we get to . . . where are we going again?"

"The Pickled Parrot."

* * *

They walked the rest of the way engaging in the small talk of two old friends who hadn't seen each other for a long time. They were just enjoying the fact that they were together again, all the while avoiding the more serious questions and answers to come.

Several hours and several drinks later, Max and Jack were still talking. Each had told their stories. Jack read the letter then he told her that he had seen Daniel getting on a plane. The more they talked, the more the mystery of Daniel deepened and as the power of beer kicked in, theories were espoused, debated, and discarded. The bar had filled and emptied several times while they sat at their corner table lost in each other. Suddenly Jack looked up. "It's dark. What time is it?"

"I don't know, but I'm really hungry." answered Max. The kitchen was still open, so food was ordered and they ate, enjoying the fact that they were together. "It's not quite that little restaurant in Switzerland, but I think I like this more," said Jack. Max agreed.

Dinner finished and exhausted from the emotional roller coaster of the day, they finally left the Parrot and walked toward the sidewalk. The soft sand made an already unsteady gait even more wobbly causing them to hold onto each other for support as they giggled their way to the sidewalk. When they finally stood on its hard surface they stopped, turned and faced each other.

Their laughter stopped, neither dared breathe and for a moment time froze, neither ready to make the first move. Then ever so slowly, they came together and each held onto the other. Sometimes a simple hug is the most intimate form of expression between two people. The warm tropical breeze enveloped them in a sensuous blanket of sweet fragrances while the soft rustling of palms and swooshing surf provided a soothing refrain. They held onto each other for probably less than a minute, but it felt like an eternity. Max could feel Jack's heart pounding as she pressed her face against his chest and Jack could feel Max trembling in his arms. The moment over, they began the slow unsteady walk up the sidewalk toward Miss Cecilia's and Nancy's. They walked alternately hand in hand, then arm in arm like two lovers, although some of the bumping and nudging was surely the result of too many rum concoctions, but not all. Little was said until they reached Miss Cecilia's Guest House. "Here's where I'm staying," said Jack, trying not to sound hopeful.

"Well, I'm not. Walk me home," replied Max with a laugh.

As they continued on, still holding onto each other, the moon emerged from behind some clouds and bathed the world in its silvery light. As they got closer to Nancy's, a tension began to develop. The earlier high created by the alcohol and the joy of their reunion was beginning to fade. As much as they didn't want to part, they both knew that tonight was not the night. Daniel was still out there and maybe the people who had been after him as well. Too much was still unresolved, too many questions remained, although one had been answered. They both knew that they belonged together.

The silence was broken when Max said, "We're here."

Jack looked up at the house.

"Shall I walk you up to the door?"

"No. It's late and it would be best if I went up alone. When will I see you tomorrow?"

"How about I come by in the morning? What time?"

"Pick me up at 9:00, then we can go get some breakfast."

"9:00 it is." That settled, they stood facing each other in that awkward moment before the final goodnight. Jack extended his arms toward Max, she stepped forward and leaned into him, her arms wrapping around his waist and they embraced again. Jack softly kissed her hair and whispered, "Max, I'm so glad I found you. I was a fool and I'll never let you go again."

Max sighed and in a muffled whisper said, "Thank you for finding me."

Their embrace lasted a few more moments then they pulled apart and said goodnight. Max went up the stairs and Jack watched her before turning and heading back to Cecilia's.

* * *

The house was dark, but as soon as Max stepped on the porch, a voice came from out of the darkness. "I see that he found you."

"Nancy!" Max jumped. "You scared me."

"Sorry. It was such a nice night I just felt like sitting out here and enjoying the night air."

"Liar," said Max looking in the direction the voice had come from. "You were waiting up for me."

"Maybe. So what happened?"

Before Max could answer, Nancy said, "I'm going to get us some tea. I'll be right back." Max heard her get up and watched her shadow move into the house. A light went on in the kitchen and Max could hear the clanking of dishes as Nancy worked on the tea. While Nancy was busy in the kitchen, Max staggered her way inside to wash up. Max returned to the porch first, sat down in a chair and waited in the shadows. It wasn't long before Nancy returned, her way lit by the candle she had put on her tray with the cups of tea. Sitting within the flickering shadows from the candle, the two women sat without saying a word. Nancy broke the silence, "So are you going to tell me?"

Max remained silent.

"Digit stopped by."

Max didn't reply.

"He told me about the boat and what you found."

Max still didn't respond, undeterred she tried again to get some kind of a response from Max.

"I met Jack earlier. I told him where to find you."

Max still hadn't said anything and Nancy was beginning to wonder if she were still awake so she went in for the kill. "You know, he really loves you."

That got Max's attention. She stirred, looked over at Nancy and said, "What did you just say?"

"I said, he really loves you and, I might add, I think you feel the same, only you won't admit it."

"He does, doesn't he? I guess I've always known. It's just . . ." her voice got low and she started to drift off.

"No, you don't. You're not crapping out on me until you talk to me. You started to say something, it's just, what?"

"Nancy, I'm really tired. I just want to go to sleep."

She gave up. "Come on Max, Let's get you to bed." She took hold of Max's arms and pulled her up, then with her arm around Max's waist, she walked her to her room, aimed her at the bed and guided her into a controlled crash landing. Max was out. Nancy pulled the cover up over her, and softly said, "You've had quite a day. Two men, one has left you just as the other, who truly loves you, has found you. Sounds like a cheap trash novel. We'll talk in the morning." She turned and left the room. Max didn't hear what she said. She was already far away in the world of dreams.

* * *

Jack thought he was moving with the silence of a ghost as he climbed the stairs at Cecilia's. Suddenly a door opened and a shaft of light hit him and he froze like a deer in headlights. Blinded, he heard a voice demand, "Who's out there?"

It was Cecilia and he must not have been as silent as he thought he was. "I have a machete and you had better not be up to no good."

"It's me Miss Cecilia, Jack Beale. I'm sorry if I disturbed you."

"I thought the ghosts of the dead were coming for me with all the noise you were making."

"I'm sorry that I disturbed you." Jack's eyes were beginning to get used to the light now and he could clearly see Miss Cecilia and she did indeed have a machete in her hand.

"You found your girlfriend, didn't you?"

"Yes, I found her."

"So why aren't you with her?"

"Miss Cecilia, I'm sorry I disturbed you. I'm really tired and I'd just like to go to bed. Good night," said Jack, avoiding her question. He moved toward his room while she stood in her doorway, machete in hand, still talking. Jack closed his door and fell onto the bed. His eyes closed with Miss Cecilia's question still ringing in his ears, "So why aren't you with her?" He was asleep before he could think of an answer.

CHAPTER 95

AS JACK STOOD ON NANCY'S PORCH, his head still foggy from last night, the smell of fresh brewed coffee wafted out through an open window. He knocked. He could hear muffled footsteps moving toward the door, the pounding in his head became more intense as his heart raced. He took a deep breath as the door opened and there stood Max. For a moment neither said anything, they just stared at each other.

Max spoke first. "Jack." There was an unmistakable warmth in her voice.

"Good morning, Max," replied Jack.

"Come in."

"That coffee smells wonderful," said Jack woodenly. He felt tense and awkward.

"Nancy makes the best coffee. She started it and then left for the shop. I think it's ready."

He watched her move into the kitchen. She was wearing those same khaki shorts and bright colored top he remembered from when they played mini golf last summer and she looked even better now than she did then. *Grow up*, the little voice in his head said. Jack just grinned. Max returned carrying two cups of steaming coffee.

"What are you grinning at, Jack Beale?"

"Nothing. I just like looking at you," he replied. "That coffee really smells good."

She let his answer go. She knew what he was grinning at. It was no accident that she was wearing that particular outfit, but he didn't have to know that. "Here's your coffee. Let's go sit out on the porch."

They moved out and sat down.

"Thanks for the coffee. I needed this," said Jack.

The sun, while warm, only hinted at the heat to come. The breeze was light and just barely rustling the palms, an unseen bird squawked. They sat sipping the strong coffee in silence, each remembering fragments of the previous evenings conversation, not knowing exactly what to say to each other this morning. This awkward silence slowly gave way to the almost forgotten comfort that they felt with each other. They started to speak at the same time, then they stopped together and they laughed. The ice was broken.

"Okay. Did I ever thank you last night for being such a good friend?"

"Yes, you did."

"Tell me again. Why did you really come down here, especially after the way I left?"

He thought a minute before speaking. "Max, you have always been special to me. Last winter, after Switzerland, I guess I just thought that we were good, and we were, in a way, but I took you for granted. Somehow I just assumed too much. Then when Daniel began to pursue you, I froze and didn't know what to do, so I ran. While I was busy avoiding things, you left with him. Tom had asked me for some help finding out about Python and his death and it seemed that every time I found something out, Daniel was involved in some way. The more I learned, the more worried I became. It was almost as if there was some unseen force continually leading me back to you. I had to find you. In my mind, I had to save you from yourself as much as from Daniel." He paused. "I'm sorry. I'm babbling and not making much sense."

"Jack, don't apologize. You're not. I was wrong. I love what you are saying. I deserted my best friend and for that I am truly sorry but, I . . . we still have to deal with Daniel. I need to know what happened to that son of a bitch. He hurt me. Part of me wants to forget him, but another part can't. Until I know what happened, he'll always be there coming between us. I need answers. Will you help me?"

He answered, "Of course I will. I'm not going to let you get away again." That said, he thought *It's not as if I have much choice.*

"Thanks. More coffee?"

"Please, and do you have that letter he left for you? I'd like to read it again if you don't mind."

"Coffee and a letter coming right up." Max got up and went inside while Jack leaned back and closed his eyes and smiled.

"Hey, it's not time for a nap. Wake up." The sound of Max's voice made Jack open his eyes. She had returned with more coffee and after handing him his cup, she reached in her pocket and pulled out the letter and handed it to him.

"I wasn't sleeping, I was thinking."

"About what?"

"Things. Last night. What we talked about or at least what I can remember of what we talked about."

"So?" said Max drawing out the word into a question.

Jack waved his finger at her as if to say, wait a minute and he took the letter out of the envelope, unfolded it and read it. Max watched him. When he finished he sat back and stared absently at the ceiling.

"What?" asked Max.

"Max, he's not dead. He may want everyone to think he's dead."

"But what about the boat? What about the blood? What about those men in the black boat?"

"I don't know, but what I do know is that I saw him getting on that plane."

"How can you be so sure?"

"I just am."

"Why?"

"I don't have any answers Max, I just have a feeling and I'm getting really hungry."

"Jack, how can you think about food at a time like this?"

"Because I'm hungry. Listen, let's go get something to eat and then go out to the boat."

"I want to know why you think he's still alive."

"Let's go eat and then we'll talk some more out on the boat. I need to see what you have described and then maybe I'll be able to explain better."

Jack folded the letter and put it in his pocket and they got up to leave. Just then they heard footsteps coming up the stairs. Digit's head appeared and he said, "Good morning. How's everyone this fine morning?"

Then looking at Jack and trying to stifle a grin, he said, "I heard that Miss Cecilia nearly chopped you up last night."

Jack kind of blushed and grinned while Max turned to him sharply and said, "What? You didn't tell me about that. What is he talking about?"

"Max, it was nothing."

"Oh, Miss Max, It wasn't nothing. To hear Miss Cecilia tell the story this morning down at the market, it was nearly a life and death struggle."

Max shot another look at Jack that said, "Fess up . . . now!"

"I'll tell you on the way to get some breakfast."

"Okay. Digit will you join us?" asked Max.

"No thanks. I've already eaten."

"After we eat could you give us a ride out to the boat?" she continued.

"Sure."

The three of them walked together down the sidewalk to the end by the water. By the time they had gotten that far, Max and Digit were laughing hysterically at Jack's recounting of his adventure the night before with Miss Cecilia. The laughter was infectious and even Jack was beginning to see the humor in it by the time they stopped. Digit said, "I have to go into the cooperative. I'll meet you by my boat in an hour. It's over there pulled up on the sand."

"Thanks, Digit." said Max. "We'll see you in an hour. Come on, Indiana Jones, let's go eat."

CHAPTER 96

DIGIT WATCHED THEM WALK off toward Wendy's Island Café bumping, nudging, pushing, tugging, pulling and laughing, and otherwise acting like two people who were much more than just friends. He smiled.

They each had bacon, eggs with salsa, fry jacks and some more strong Belizean coffee. Breakfast finished, they walked down to the fuel dock and found Digit waiting for them. "You ready to go?" he asked.

"Yes, let's go," said Jack as he helped Max into the boat. He then helped push it free of the sand, jumping in just as Digit started the engine. It took less than a minute for them pull up next to *d'Riddem.* Jack was wide-eyed as he looked up at the boat. "Max . . ." He wanted to say more, but he was speechless. "Come on. Give me your hand," said Max steadying herself with his help as she climbed aboard. Jack followed Max onboard and Digit said good-bye.

They climbed up into the cockpit and just stood there. Jack looked around, with a look of wonderment on his face while Max watched him. "Max. This is amazing. I can't believe that this is yours."

"Jack, I'll consider her mine until we find Daniel, then she will be his again. I know he really loved this boat. Now, let me show you around."

Max opened the door to the salon and they stepped in. It was hot and the air inside was stale and it was still a mess. They opened hatches and port lights and the change in atmosphere was instantaneous. "Down there," Max pointed to the starboard stairs that led down into the hull, "There are two cabins, one forward and one aft." Then, she said, "Follow me," and led Jack down similar stairs on the port side. She showed him the head, which was aft, then led him forward into the cabin she had shared with Daniel. "This is where I found the letter."

Clothes were still all over the cabin and Max picked up Daniel's travel pouch and handed it to him saying, "This was still here, intact. Even the money is still there."

Jack took the pouch from Max, unzipped it and looked inside. "Whoever went through the cabin wasn't very thorough to have missed this."

"I know. Listen, I need to straighten up this mess," said Max as she absently folded some of the clothes that had been thrown about.

Jack was feeling a bit uneasy standing in the cabin that Max and Daniel had shared, since it was still filled with his clothes. "I'll tell you what. While you do that, I'm going to get out of your way and look around."

"Okay. I'll be up soon."

Jack took the travel pouch with him and went up into the salon, then pushing aside some of the mess, he sat down at the nav station. He opened the pouch, took out the contents, laying them out in front of him. There was nearly a thousand dollars in cash, some U.S. and some Belizean. There were two open return airline tickets to the States, assorted receipts, and a passport. The last thing he did was open the passport. Daniel's name and picture stared back at him. He remembered the man he saw getting on the plane in Dangriga. There was no doubt in Jack's mind that it had been Daniel getting on that plane.

After finishing with the pouch, he replaced the contents, set it aside and lifted the top of the nav station. Inside was exactly what he expected to find: pencils, dividers, manuals and all the requisite tools needed for navigation. Charts were on the counter next to the station. He closed the lid and slid out of the seat and began looking around the cabin. He opened cabinets and looked through lockers. There was nothing either present or missing that leapt out at him. All was as it should be. He went down into the starboard hull and did the same. By the time he returned to the salon, Max was there, tidying up more of the mess. He could see that she had been crying and he went to her. He took her in his arms and hugged her. "Jack, why?"

"I don't know. You'll have to ask him when we find him. Let's go outside, I want you tell me again about how you found things on the boat. They went out, sat down in the cockpit and Max went over the story again. When she got to the part about the fender with the blood on it, Jack stopped her.

He wanted to see it, to see where it had been. He wanted her to show him exactly what she'd done. They left the cockpit and went forward and she showed him. Lastly, she opened the locker and pointed at the fender, described the blood that had been on it and how she had rinsed it off. When she finished, they went back to the cockpit and sat down in the shade.

It was just after midday and the sun was merciless. Even with the breeze and the shade, sweat glistened on their faces and began to stain their shirts. Jack had found some bottles of water in the fridge that were still cool and he gave her one. She opened it, took a sip then poured a little into the palm of her hand and wiped it on her brow and then did the same to the back of her neck. Jack tried not to stare, but the way her eyes closed, the look of relief on her face when the cool water touched her neck and the way her now sweat soaked shirt clung and stretched as she moved, made him regret even more that he had taken her for granted and had nearly lost her.

"Thanks for the water," she said.

"You're welcome."

"You really believe he's alive?"

"I do, more than ever."

"But the boat, it was torn apart and his passport, money, and tickets were still on the boat. He wouldn't have left them behind."

"You wouldn't think so, but it makes sense. He staged it. If I hadn't seen him on that plane in Dangriga, given what he left behind, I'd think he was dead too.

"Couldn't you be mistaken?"

"No."

"You're that sure?"

"I am. The boat had been carefully tied up at the port, not exactly a place to leave it if you didn't want it to be found, but it would have been a convenient place for Daniel to leave from. If his pursuers had found it, and by all accounts they did, a quick look around would have easily convinced them that he had left in a hurry. Remember you told me the night guard said he saw them leaving in a hurry? It seems to me that two things were going on here. On the one hand, he wanted them to think he had fled so they would leave and continue their search elsewhere, and would hopefully leave you alone."

"And the other?"

"He wanted you to think he was dead, thereby freeing you from him."

"Jack, that's a little far fetched don't you think?"

"I don't think so, not really. It seems to have worked so far. He knew you'd find his passport and money, and draw the conclusion that he wouldn't have left without them. Then there was the letter that implied that he was done for. He knew that you would retrieve the boat after reading the letter."

"No one can be that calculating."

"I think he is."

"But what about the blood on the fender?"

"That was a beautiful touch. If all that other stuff didn't work, he left the bloody fender."

"He left it?"

"Of course. He left it for you to find so that you would think he had been taken or killed. Think about it. Blood was on only that one fender, not the lifelines, not the hull, only on that one fender and the way the boat was tied up it was not visible unless the boat were moved. Those guys who were apparently after him wouldn't move the boat. They only wanted him. You, on the other hand, would move it, especially after reading the letter. And that's exactly what you did. He knew that's what you would do."

"What do you mean he knew that's what I would do?

"Max, the guy was a professional con man. His job was to sell an idea to unsuspecting victims, to manipulate them. He was good and that's why he was so successful. Most of his 'clients' never knew they had been taken.

"I suppose."

"Trust me. That's what he did. He's good." There was almost a hint of admiration in Jack's voice as he finished his explanation.

Max sat silent for a few moments digesting all that Jack had surmised then she looked at him and in a weary voice said, "Okay. I'll agree that what you have said makes some sense."

So they sat. Sweating in silence, sipping on their water when Max turned and looked at Jack and said, "So what are we going to do now?"

"What do you want to do?" returned Jack.

"I want to go home. I want to know what happened. I want to find Daniel so I can tell him what a cold-hearted bastard he is. I want all of this to be over."

"Fair enough. Will you let me help you?"

"Jack, I've been a complete shit to you. I realize now just what you mean to me and I wouldn't . . . no, I don't want to do any of this without you. Can you ever forgive me?"

"There's nothing to forgive. We both are responsible. How about we start over together?"

"Deal." And with that Max, leaned toward Jack and kissed him.

The kiss was gentle and heartfelt, but not lustful. It said all that needed to be said at that moment.

CHAPTER 97

THE REST OF THE AFTERNOON WAS spent making plans for getting home. The refrigeration was charged, charts reviewed and Max showed Jack as much as she could remember about the boat. A lowering sun and pangs of hunger signaled that it was time to go ashore. The day had been a reaffirmation of all that had been said the previous night, even the parts that they couldn't remember. They were together again and that was enough for now. The dinghy was lowered and they motored in, tying it up at the dive shop near the fuel dock. Permission was granted for them to leave it overnight and they began the walk home, back to Nancy's.

Nancy greeted them at the door with a big smile and lots of good smells coming from her kitchen.

"I was wondering if you two were ever going to return."

"I'm sorry. It was rude of us."

"It was all my fault," said Jack. "We went out to the boat and we got distracted."

Nancy's eyebrows went up and she paused slightly before saying, "I see."

Max realized what she was thinking and blushed and quickly replied, "It wasn't like that. We cleaned up the boat. We talked. Jack is going to help me find Daniel. We both agree that he must still be alive."

"I told you that when I first read his letter."

"Yes, you did. And now I'm convinced of it." Then Max's stomach rumbled loud enough for all of them to hear, effectively changing the subject.

"What smells so good?" said Jack, rejoining the conversation.

"I'm making a fish stew; I knew you two would eventually show up and that you'd probably be hungry." She got that same sly little look on her face again. Jack didn't notice, but Max did and she telegraphed a return look that said, *No. We didn't.* Max was the first to speak up. "I'm going to wash up," and she excused herself.

Jack asked if there was anything he could do to help.

"Come with me. You can help me set the table while I make some drinks." Jack followed her and went to work on the table while ice clinked in glasses and Nancy made Smilin' Wides. "She's been through a lot, you know."

"Yes, I do," said Jack.

"You're going to help her?"

"Yes. If she doesn't resolve the mystery of Daniel, he'll always be there. I want her all to myself, I don't want to share her."

"She loves you. You know that, don't you?"

"I guess I do." The conversation was beginning to make Jack uncomfortable and he was relieved when Max reappeared.

Nancy turned when she heard Max come into the room. "Oh Max, there you are, just in time," she picked up two drinks and first handed one to Max and then one to Jack while saying, "Jack and I were just talking about what your plans were."

Jack needed to wash up, so he excused himself saying that he'd be right back. When he returned, dinner was on the table and the two women were sitting there laughing and talking. He sat and Nancy began serving the fish stew along with a loaf of warm bread. As soon as the first bites were taken, there was no more conversation. It was delicious and Jack and Max were starved. It didn't take long before their appetites were sated and conversation began again.

"Nancy, that stew was incredible. Can I have the recipe so I can give it to the chef at Ben's when we get home?" asked Jack.

"Of course, but it's not all that special."

"Oh, yes it is. Don't you agree, Max?"

"Yes. I can just imagine it out on the deck. It would feel just like we were back here."

"The recipe is yours. I need another drink. Anyone else?"

Jack and Max said "yes," in unison. Nancy stood and picked up their glasses and headed to the kitchen. Jack and Max followed with armfuls of dirty dishes. While Nancy mixed, they washed and in very short order all three were back at the table. The rum was beginning to take effect and Nancy asked, "Now, tell me. What are your plans? What about the boat? What about the two of you?"

Max spoke first. "We are going to take the boat back to San Pedro and leave it with Alfonso, just like Daniel had. Then, we'll head home and begin the search for Daniel."

"I see," she replied and then sat silent, obviously thinking about something.

"What? You have a look on your face," said Jack.

"I wasn't going to say anything …

"What?" They both said at the same time as they stared at Nancy, each wondering what she was thinking. "While you two have been busy with the boat and each other, I've had time to think about all of this and, well . . ." she paused.

"Nancy, come on, spill it," prodded Max.

"It's the black speed boat. Ever since you first told me about it, something has been bothering me and today I finally figured it out."

"What are you talking about?"

"You said you first saw it in Porto Stuck and that Daniel began acting strangely. Then when it reappeared in Bluefield . . . well, you know what happened there. Then it was here and always just ahead of you and Digit as you searched for Daniel, then you were told that it sped off after they found the boat just before you did."

Max stopped her at this point and said, "We know all that. I'm not sure I see where you are going with this."

She held up her hand then continued. "Remember in his letter Daniel said that he overheard a mention of the word raven, and that he didn't know what it meant."

"Yes."

"Well, I think I do, or at least I have an idea."

"So what is it?" said Max as she looked intently at Nancy then she glanced over at Jack to see his reaction.

He, too, was staring at her, but there was a strange far away look on his face. "Jack?"

He just stared.

She nudged him. "Yes. Yes I'm fine." Then he said to Nancy, still obviously distracted, "Go on. What about it?"

Max looked back at Nancy. "Come on. Tell us."

Silence continued around the table for another moment before she continued. "I think that I met Jack when I was a girl."

"What!" Max all but shouted.

"Max, do you remember when I told you how I got into baking? How my father and I sold some lobsters to a man on a big black sailboat, and how he really liked the bread I had baked?"

"Yes, but what does that have to do with anything?"

"The boat was named *The Raven.* In Daniel's letter, the one you found on the boat, he mentioned the word 'raven.' I bet they are one and the same. If that were so, it would explain how that black speedboat managed to follow you. I've thought about it over last few days more memories came to me. There was a young man on the boat who brought us some cold drinks. I remember that the boat's owner called him Jack and the next day he came ashore to buy some more bread. I was just a little girl and it was a long time ago, but I know I'm right." She paused and looked at Jack.

He returned her look without saying a word, his mind racing, trying to remember a time so very long ago.

She continued before he could say anything. "That was what made me want to become a baker and eventually I did manage to go to the United States to learn how to be a baker."

She stopped and looked over at Jack again. A strange look came over his face. He slowly put his drink down and stared at her. Only the sounds of the wind in the palms filled the room as all three sat in momentary silence, then in not much more than a whisper, he said, "Oh my God. It's you. I remember."

Max looked first at Nancy then at Jack. "Will someone explain to me what is going on? Jack?"

He didn't answer and Nancy looked into Jack's eyes. Saying nothing he returned her gaze.

"You're the girl." He grinned in disbelief and sat back in his chair staring at the ceiling. "It's you," he said, only this time a little louder. "Son of a bitch."

"You remember now? I'm not crazy?" asked Nancy.

"Yes, yes I do."

"Jack, what's going on?" demanded Max.

"Max, so much makes sense now. *The Raven*, yes," and with that, Jack sat back and to himself said softly, "Damn."

Jack stared straight at Max while he spoke. "This explains a lot. I was on was a large black sloop and it was named *The Raven.* Remember, I told you the story."

"I kind of remember."

"It was when I was just out of college and living and bartending in Miami. That's when I met Tom and we became friends. The owner of *The Raven* was a very rich customer and he hired me as a member of his crew. I was young and looking for adventure so I took the job. As it turned out, he was the subject of one of Tom's investigations and Tom convinced me to become his eyes and ears while we were at sea. The trip was completely uneventful until we got to Belize and I saw something I shouldn't have seen. A man who had joined us was executed. Fortunately no one knew that I had seen it or I probably would have been killed as well."

"But what does that have to do with Daniel's disappearance?"

"Max, I didn't make the connection until now. Remember in Daniel's letter, he said that he overheard a conversation he shouldn't have and that he heard the word 'raven' mentioned? Now this is a stretch, but bear with me. It's been a long time, but what if the raven in Daniel's letter is the same *Raven* I had sailed on, and that his mysterious employer is the same man I saw carry out that execution? That would certainly explain Daniel's fear."

"That's a little far fetched, don't you think?"

"Maybe, but there are too many coincidences not to consider the possibilities. As soon as we get home I'll talk to Tom to see what ever became of Mr. Raven . . . Raven … What the hell was his name? I remember we referred to him as Mr. Poe because he liked Edgar Allen Poe and was always quoting from his stories, *The Raven* being a particular favorite."

Nancy who had been quiet through all this suddenly spoke up. "If it is any help, I think I still have an old picture of my father and me on the boat when we sold them the lobsters. There are some men in the background. Maybe one of them is Mr. Poe."

"What?" said Jack.

Nancy repeated what she had just said, this time adding that the picture had been sent to her sometime after the boat had departed. She never knew who had sent it.

Jack sat back in his chair, his mind moving at warp speed. "Marcus Ravenski or Ravenowicz."

"What?" Both women said at the same time.

"His name. It was Marcus Ravenski or Ravenowicz, something like that." Now he was anxious to get back to Rye. He had to talk to Tom. "Nancy, can I see that picture?"

"Of course. It's in my room. I pulled it out earlier today while you to were out on the boat."

Returning with it, she handed it to Jack. It was an old, grainy, black and white photo, perhaps only four inches square. A little girl and an older man were standing on the deck of a large boat and he was holding a lobster that looked almost as big as the girl. There were some men in the background, but they were so blurred it was really hard to make out their faces. He studied it, trying to remember who those faces belonged to. He thought that one was the owner, but he couldn't be certain "Can I borrow this?" asked Jack. "I'd like to show it to Tom at home and maybe it can be worked on so we can see those men more clearly."

Before answering she looked deep into Jack's eyes then said, "Sure."

"I'll take good care of it and I'll get it back to you."

The rest of the evening was spent talking about the trip back to San Pedro, and promises to return.

CHAPTER 98

AS JACK WALKED ALONE BACK TO Cecilia's, he felt charged. Lying in bed, he couldn't sleep. Scattered memories kept coming back to him. Tom had been the one to encourage him to take the job on *The Raven.* As it turned out the owner had been under investigation by Tom and when Jack had taken the job on the boat, Tom had asked him just to observe whatever he could and to report back whatever he saw with no other explanation. For Jack, it had been just a sailing adventure until the execution he'd witnessed. That was when he realized how dangerous his situation was and as soon as the boat returned to the States, Jack left *The Raven.* He remembered how pissed he was at Tom for not telling him more about Rav... whatever his name was. By the time he found Tom, he had cooled off some and Jack allowed Tom to explain why he did what he did. Jack listened and reluctantly understood. Those days were never spoken of again and as far as Jack knew, nothing ever came of Tom's investigation. Now, Jack was eager to get home to talk to Tom.

The next several days were spent preparing for the trip north. Between the many tasks to get the boat ready, Max and Jack began to relax and reconnect. They swam, they sat on the beach, and they talked, and even though they wanted to, neither one would make the first move toward bed. It was a time of anticipation and the tension made it all the more intense. On their last day, they went fishing with Digit out on the reef and returned to a party that Nancy had organized. The last thing Jack did was contact the Sunbreeze Hotel and book two adjoining rooms. The morning after the party, they departed with promises to stay in touch.

CHAPTER 99

THE FLIGHT ATTENDANT'S VOICE woke Jack up. "Ladies and gentlemen, we will be landing shortly. Please place all personal items either back into the overhead bins or under the seat in front of you. Return your seats to the upright position. Make sure your seat belts are fastened and tray tables put away. The current time in Boston is 10:45 PM and the temperature is 39 degrees under cloudy skies."

He didn't hear the last of her speech as he gently shook Max awake. As he did, he noticed that his shoulder was damp. She had drooled on it. He didn't say anything, but she noticed it and said, "Oh Jack, I'm so sorry," and then she giggled.

Jack feigned dismay and then he laughed also. The plane thumped down onto the runway. "Well, we're home," said Jack.

At this hour, except for the passengers off their flight, the terminal was deserted. Jack and Max walked slowly down the length of the terminal while other passengers rushed by. They were the last to arrive at the baggage carousel on the lower level just as the first bags appeared. Jack called the offsite parking service to tell them that they had arrived while Max retrieved their bags. Complete, they went back up the escalator and stepped outside to wait for the shuttle bus. "Damn. It's cold." said Jack as he zipped his jacket up. "Are you all right?"

Max shivered a "Ye . . . yesss," and he pulled her close for warmth. Within five minutes, the shuttle bus pulled up and they climbed aboard. They were the only passengers. "D'ja have a nice flight?" asked the driver. "Yes, we did. It's nice to be home," said Jack.

"Where did you fly in from?"

"We've been in Belize and returned through Miami."

"Warm down there?" Jack could tell that the driver had no idea where Belize was and that he was just making conversation.

"Yes, a lot warmer than it is here."

"I figured, you've got pretty good tans."

"Thanks." Max had snuggled back up to Jack's shoulder for warmth and he had his arm around her holding her close.

"Honeymoon?"

"What?" Jack asked and the corners of Max's mouth began to lift into a grin.

"Were you on your honeymoon?" the driver repeated.

"No. We're just old friends." As soon as Jack had said that he regretted it. Max bumped him. She would have hit him except her arms were pulled in tight trying to stay warm. The driver went silent and Jack braced himself for what he knew was next. "Old friends?" she said under her breath.

"What else was I to say?" he replied in a hoarse whisper that requested penance. She didn't answer and little else was said while they retrieved Jack's truck and headed for home. It wasn't until they were on Rt. 95 north that words were spoken again.

"I'm sorry, Max. You know I . . ."

She cut him off, "Don't be. We are old friends. The best."

"Thanks." It was one of those times when they each wanted to say more, but neither could get the words out so they continued riding in silence until just after the Hampton toll booths. "Jack, are you going to see Tom tomorrow?" Max asked.

"Yes, first thing. Do you want to come along?"

"You know I do."

"I'll come by. How about 9:00?"

There was just the hint of a pause before she said, "That'll be fine." It wasn't fine. She wanted him to stay with her, but she wanted him to ask to stay so she could say yes. As independent as Max was, as much as she could easily control her life, there were times when she wanted to be wanted, times when she wanted to be the object. Daniel had understood that and that was why she had succumbed to his charms the way she had and why she had given him so much. All she wanted was a little of that from Jack. She knew he was capable, so she resolved to just be patient.

The front light was on when they got to Max's. Jack walked her to the door and took the keys from her. As he pushed the key into the lock, he could feel his heart begin to pound in his chest and suddenly every nerve in his body seemed awake with anticipation. The lock clicked as he took a deep breath and pushed the door open. Warm air rushed out and for a split second he imagined that they were back in Belize. Still not moving he reached inside and felt for the light switch, found it and flipped it up and the room came to life.

"Come on, Jack. I'm freezing," said Max as she gave him a gentle push. He blinked from the bright light and stepped inside with Max right behind. Everything was as it should be, warm, cozy, and inviting. The smell of the fresh flowers that were on the table flashed another tropical memory. He saw that next to the flowers was a plate of cookies and an envelope that had "Welcome Home" written on it. He pushed the door shut then followed Max over to the table. While she read the note, he helped himself to a cookie and continued looking around the room. "Oh, Patti is so sweet," said Max as she handed the note to Jack. Then she smelled the flowers, picked up a cookie and began nibbling on it while watching Jack read.

He looked up and caught her watching him. "What?"

"Nothing, I just like watching you."

"Mmmph," he grunted. They were both feeling the awkwardness of the moment. Until this point there had always been something else to do, something else to say, always something else. Now, it was just the two of them, alone, at the end of an adventure. Max turned toward Jack. He looked at her and she him, then slowly, they moved toward each other. Max leaned against him, her face buried in his chest, arms around him, and she could feel his heartbeat as it quickened again. He held her tight, closed his eyes, inhaled her scent, felt her body melt into his and tried to breathe. She felt so good. They stood there, just holding onto each other, exhausted and relieved. They were home and safe.

* * *

"Good morning!" Courtney's voice rang out as Jack walked out to his truck in the morning.

"Morning, Courtney," he replied.

"When did you get home? Where's Max?"

"We got home around midnight and she's at her place."

"I was up then. I didn't see or hear you come in."

"I stayed at Max's for a while. It had been a long day and we just needed some time to decompress."

"Decompress? Okay. Whatever you say," said Courtney with a sly grin.

Jack did his best to ignore her tease and said, "Listen, will you be around later? I have to go pick up Max right now. We need to talk to Tom."

"I'll be at Ben's most of the day. Stop by. We have a lot to talk about."

* * *

Jack found Tom's office door open enough to stick his head in. Tom was studying a file and he didn't look up. "Knock, knock." said Jack. Tom looked up and when he saw Jack peering from behind the now partially open door, his look of surprise quickly turned to welcome. He put the file down and stood and came out from behind the desk toward Jack saying, "Jack, when did you get back?" As the door swung more fully open, he saw Max standing behind him so he went right past Jack, straight to Max and gave her a big hug. "Max. It's good to have you home," he said.

"So what am I, chopped liver?" said Jack, feigning hurt feelings.

Tom turned and said, "Not at all, she's just a whole lot prettier." Then he clasped Jack's hand and pulled him in for a man hug with back slaps. "It's good to have you back, too."

"Thanks. Listen, Tom. Do you have a few minutes?"

"Of course, come in, sit. Can I get you some coffee? Soda?"

They both declined the refreshments. Those few minutes turned into the rest of the day, as there was much to talk about. After the initial pleasantries, Jack asked about Percy's arrest.

"Before I tell you how that all went down, let me thank you for the heads up on Percy. Your hunch was spot on," began Tom. Then he proceeded to tell them that the day after Jack had left, he had gone to see Percy to ask him some more questions. Percy had seemed nervous and as the questioning became more specific about Daniel, his nervousness increased until he finally sat down, put his face in his hands and confessed. "I had never had a confession like that before. He was so racked with guilt that you could see the relief come over him as he told me what happened," said Tom.

"So what did actually happen?"

"Well, it seems that Python had been trying to convince the band that they should not sign any contract with Daniel. He told them how he had been screwed and that it was all a scam. Percy didn't want to hear that. He needed the money and his ego probably affected his judgment. On that Sunday, after they had finished playing, Daniel was hanging around talking to Joshua and the others while they broke down their equipment. Eventually Daniel left. The band continued to hang out in the parking lot talking and Python joined them. He was a little drunk and he really began ranting about how they should stay away from

Daniel, how he was evil, how he had screwed him. Percy walked off and Joshua and Leslie were left to deal with Python. It was getting late and as soon as they were able to get him to calm down, they left, leaving Python sitting in the parking lot and Percy out walking around somewhere. By the time Ben's closed down, Python had sobered up some and when Percy returned, he tried to talk to him. It wasn't long before they were at it; punches were thrown, Percy knocked Python down and as he fell, he hit his head and was knocked unconscious. Percy, thinking that he had killed him, panicked and threw the body into the marsh where he did, in fact, drown. He thought the tide would take it out to sea, but it got caught on the dock."

"That's it?" said Jack, a little disappointment creeping into his voice.

"That's it," said Tom.

"So Daniel didn't kill him?" said Max after listening in silence to Tom's narrative.

"No, he didn't," replied Tom.

Silence returned to the room while Jack and Max absorbed all that Tom had just told them.

Tom finally broke the silence, "Now, how about you fill me in on what you two have been up to?"

"We need your help," said Jack as he motioned for Max to begin the story, which she did.

She had reached the point in her narrative where Daniel had disappeared and had paused to get her emotions in check, when Tom's stomach rumbled loud enough for all to hear. Max tried to ignore the interruption by looking over at Jack, but that just made her start to giggle.

"Sorry about that," said Tom blushing in embarrassment, then he added, "Is anyone else hungry?"

Until the question was asked, neither Max nor Jack had realized just how hungry they were.

"Food sounds like a good idea," said Jack.

"Then let's take a short break and get something to eat." Subs were ordered and eaten while Max continued her story. ". . . and that's when Jack showed up."

She paused and Tom, who had mostly just listened up to this point said, "Max, you are very lucky. I don't think he would have ever hurt you, but you were put into a potentially dangerous situation." And then looking at Jack he said, "So you arrive?" posing the statement as a question.

Now it was Jack's turn. He told how he found Max in Placencia and of the things he learned about Daniel during his search for her. By mid-afternoon, most of the story had been told and that's when Jack asked Tom the question that would change everything. Looking into Tom's eyes, he leaned forward and with great intensity asked, "Do you remember when we were in Miami and I took a job tending bar on a yacht? The yacht that belonged to someone you were investigating. A Mr. Ravenowicz or Ravenski, something like that. Was that case ever closed?"

Tom was taken by surprise by not only the question, but by the intensity with which Jack posed it. He sat back, his hands locked behind his head and closed his eyes in thought and then slowly he replied, "Yes. I remember." He paused again. "I don't know. I left Miami shortly after your return and moved up here. I have no idea. Why?"

Jack didn't answer that question but instead posed his own. "Do you remember why I got off the boat?"

"Yeah, I do. You saw him execute someone, but you didn't know who it was or why . . . where did it happen? I don't remember."

"It happened in Belize."

"Interesting coincidence."

"Let me tell you about some other interesting coincidences. When I was on that yacht, before the execution, we were anchored in Placencia."

Tom interrupted, "Where you found Max?"

"Yes. We had anchored in Placencia and bought some lobsters from a local fisherman. His young daughter had baked some bread and we bought that as well. That young girl as it turns out is still there in Placencia. Her name is Nancy."

"You're not going to tell me that she is the Nancy who took care of Max, are you?"

"I am. She was the young girl I met all those years ago."

"That's fascinating, but what's the relevance to today other than it being a great small world story."

"I'll tell you. That yacht I was on was black. The owner, Mr. Rav..., whatever his name was, was a very secretive man. The boat's name was *The Raven.* The speedboat that was chasing Max and Daniel around was black. In Daniel's letter to Max, he said that he had once heard the word raven mentioned in a conversation he should not have heard. I'm thinking that it may have been the name of his boat, the same boat I had been on. If that were so, and the same man, the man I had seen execute someone, the man you were after when we were in Miami, was Daniel's employer. That would explain a lot, like why he would want Daniel dead, and why Daniel would want to disappear."

Tom didn't move. He just sat there silently looking at Jack. Finally, he said, "Jack, that is quite a story, a little thin, but interesting."

"I know, but what if it's true? What if he's behind the music scam that led to Python's death? What else might he be involved in? I'm sure Daniel is alive and I want to find him if for no other reason than for the way he used Max." Looking over at Max he said, "Sorry."

"You're forgiven," said Max.

"He used Max in staging his disappearance."

"I'll make some calls in the morning," and he looked down at his desk and scribbled some notes on a piece of paper.

"Tom, there's one more thing."

He looked up when Jack said, "I might have a picture of him."

"A picture?"

"Nancy had an old photo that was taken on that boat. It's of her and her father holding a large lobster. The crew is in the background but it's hard to see their faces clearly. I thought you might be able to work on it and maybe identify some of them."

"Do you have it with you?"

Jack pulled an envelope out of his pocket and passed it to Tom. He opened it and took out the old black and white photo and studied it. "I see what you mean. Are you in this picture?"

"I think so, but I can't be sure."

Tom stared at it again. "Let me see what can be done with this. It may be useful."

"Thanks, Tom."

Tom looked at his watch. "I didn't realize how late it was. I'm late for an appointment in town. I'll make those calls in the morning and get back to you, but don't get your hopes up too much."

"We won't. Thanks."

Goodbyes were said and Jack and Max left the station. It was already dark and the wind was cold and raw. They clung to each other for warmth as they scurried to Jack's truck. Inside the cab, Jack said "Damn, it's cold," as he blew on his hands for warmth. Max shivered her agreement. "Wwhy ddin't I wwear mmy ggloves?"

"It's not too late to go back to Belize," suggested Jack.

"I know, but we can't. At least not right now."

"You're right, but . . ."

"Is there heat yet?" asked Max.

Jack turned the blower on high and put his hand over the vent. "Almost."

Then he looked over at her and asked, "You okay?"

"Yeah. Do you think Tom will be able to help us find Daniel?"

"I hope so. Tomorrow, we'll know more after he makes those calls." Jack felt for the heat again and announced, "We have heat. Are you ready for some food?"

"Yes, let's go to Ben's and have Smilin' Wides. It's not Belize, but at least we can dream."

"Perfect." Jack shifted into gear and they drove to Ben's. The cab was toasty warm by the time they pulled into the parking lot at Ben's. The only place to park was in the corner farthest from the door so it would be a long cold dash from the warmth of the truck to the building. Jack turned off the lights, but left the engine running, making no move to get out. Max looked over at him also not making any move toward getting out. Neither said a thing. The heater fan was still set on high, filling the cab with ever increasing warmth.

It was like one of those cozy, intimate childhood moments when you and your best friend would drape a blanket over some chairs to make a cave and then you would climb in together feeling like you were completely alone and safe, hidden from the world. Jack looked over at Max and she back. The noise from the heater's fan smothered the silence from their held breaths as their eyes fixed on each other. Then slowly, without thought they moved toward each other. Ever closer, until the silence was overcome by their shallow breathing and pounding heartbeats. Their lips touched, softly and gently, every nerve tingling from lips to finger tips. This moment was long overdue. The past year of pretending that they were just friends was ending, each finally beginning to admit that they belonged together. Whatever questions may have lingered about their true feelings toward each other disappeared with that first tentative kiss. There was nothing tentative about the second kiss. There was an urgency to it. It was hot. It was wet. It was passionate. It had been a long year since Switzerland, a year too long, a year of distractions, a year of hurt and neglect, a year of distance, and now it was over. They were together, and together they would find the answers they needed. Before a third kiss consumed them, the lights from another car, either arriving or departing washed over them tearing down their invisible tent, exposing them and the moment was over.

They pulled back from each other, hearts still racing and each a little embarrassed. Max spoke first, "We should go in."

"Yes, we should," then just before reaching for the door handle, Jack turned toward Max and said, "Max . . . "

She cut him off, "I know. You don't have to say anything."

The walk from the far corner of the parking lot didn't seem as cold or long now as they walked with arms around each other. As they entered the building, they released each other and walked down the hall toward the bar. Voices could be heard; it sounded like the bar was busy and when they turned the corner collective cries of "Surprise! Welcome Home! Happy Birthday!" greeted them. Jack had completely forgotten that it was his birthday. The surprise was total. They stood there with dumb grins on their faces as they looked around the room. Jack looked at Max and asked, "Did you do this?"

"No. It must be Courtney's doing. I haven't even talked to her since we got back."

Courtney rushed over and gave them each a big hug. Patti was next, followed by Dave, and then Max and Jack were swallowed up by the crowd, drinks were handed to them and a very long evening began.

Stories were told and retold, the Smilin' Wide was introduced and Jack and Max didn't see each other until the end of the evening. By the time the bell was rung announcing that it was time to close, only a few revelers remained and the guests of honor reunited. Final thank yous and good-byes were said and they walked out into the cold that now didn't seem quite so cold. Jack began to walk toward his truck while searching for his keys.

* * *

"Are you looking for these?" asked Max as she held up his keys and jingled them.

He turned and looked back. "How did you get those?"